or: the tale of signs and cities

BOOKS BY SAMUEL R. DELANY

BABEL – 17
THE BALLAD OF BETA 2
DHALGREN
DISTANT STARS
THE EINSTEIN INTERSECTION
EMPIRE STAR
THE FALL OF THE TOWERS TRILOGY
    OUT OF THE DEAD CITY
    CITY OF A THOUSAND SUNS
    THE TOWERS OF TORON
THE JEWELS OF APTOR
NEVERYÓNA
NOVA
TALES OF NEVÈRŸON
TRITON

Samuel R. Delany

or: the tale of signs and cities

Some Informal Remarks Toward the Modular Calculus, Part Four

BANTAM BOOKS
TORONTO · NEW YORK · LONDON · SYDNEY

NEVERYÓNA
A Bantam Book
April 1983
FIRST EDITION

ISBN 0-553-01434-X
Library of Congress Catalog Card No.: 82-90321

Published simultaneously in the United States and
Canada

Bantam Books are published by Bantam Books, Inc. Its
trademark, consisting of the words "Bantam Books" and
the portrayal of a rooster is Registered in U.S. Patent and
Trademark Office and in other countries. Marca Registrada.
Bantam Books, Inc., 666 Fifth Avenue, New York, New York
10103.

—for
Frank Romeo

CONTENTS

This nostalgia for a past often so eclectic as to be unlocatable historically is a facet of the modernist sensibility which has seemed increasingly suspect in recent decades. It is an ultimate refinement of the colonialist outlook: an imaginative exploitation of nonwhite cultures, whose moral life it drastically oversimplifies, whose wisdom it plunders and parodies. To that criticism there is no convincing reply. But to the criticism that the quest for "another form of civilization" refuses to submit to the disillusionment of accurate historical knowledge, one can make an answer. It never sought such knowledge. The other civilizations are being used as models because they are available as stimulants to the imagination precisely because they are not accessible. They are both models and mysteries. Nor can this quest be dismissed as fraudulent on the grounds that it is insensitive to the political forces that cause human suffering....

—Susan Sontag/*Approaching Artaud*

or: the tale of signs and cities

I

Of Dragons, Mountains, Transhumance, Sequence, and Sunken Cities, *or*: The Violence of the Letter

... the modality of novelistic enunciation is *inferential*: it is a process within which the subject of the novelistic utterance affirms a sequence, as *conclusion to the inference*, based on other sequences (referential—hence narrative, or textual—hence citational), which are the *premises of the inference* and, as such, considered to be true.

—Julia Kristeva/*Desire in Language*

She was fifteen and she flew.

Her name was pryn—because she knew something of writing but not of capital letters.

She shrieked at clouds, knees clutching scaly flanks, head flung forward. Another peak floated back under veined wings around whose flexing joints her knees bent.

The dragon turned a beaked head in air, jerking reins—vines pryn had twisted in a brown cord before making a bridle to string on the dragon's clay-colored muzzle. (Several times *un*twisted vines had broken—fortunately before take-off.) Shrieking and joyful, pryn looked up at clouds and down on streams, off toward returning lines of geese, at sheep crowding through a rocky rift between one green level and another. The dragon jerked her head, which meant the beast was reaching for her glide's height ...

On the ground a bitter, old, energetic woman sat in her shack and mumbled over pondered insults and recalled slights, scratching in ash that had spilled from her fireplace with a stick. That bitter woman, pryn's great-aunt, had never flown a dragon, nor did she know her great-niece flew one now. What she had done, many years before, was to take into her home an itinerant, drunken barbarian, who'd come wandering through the town market. For nearly five months the soused old reprobate had slept on the young woman's hearth. When he was not sleeping or incoherent with drink, the two of them had talked; and talked; and talked; and taken long walks together, still talking; then gone back to the

3

shack and talked more. Those talks, the older woman would have assured her great-niece, were as wonderful as any flight.

One of the things the barbarian had done was help her build a wooden rack on which stretched fibers might be woven together. She'd hoped to make some kind of useful covering. But the talk, the funny and fanciful notions, the tales and terrifying insights, the world lighted and shadowed by the analytic and synthetic richness the two of them could generate between them—that was the thing!

One evening the barbarian had up and wandered off again to another mountain hold—for no particular reason; nor was the aunt worried. They were the kind of friends who frequently went separate ways—for days, even weeks. But after a month rumor came back that, while out staggering about one winter's night, he'd fallen down a cliff, broken both legs, and died some time over the next three days from injury and exposure.

The rack had not worked right away.

The marshpool fluff that pryn's great-aunt had tried to stretch out was too weak to make real fabric, and the sheared fleece from the winter coats of mountain nannies and billies made a fuzzy stuff that was certainly warm but that tore with any violent body movement. Still, the aunt believed in the 'loom' (her word for it in that long-ago distant language) and in the barbarian, whose memory she defended against all vilification. For hadn't he also designed and supervised the construction of the fountains in the Vanar Hold, one of the three great houses around which fabled Ellamon had grown up? And hadn't the Suzerain of Vanar himself used to nod to him on the street when they'd passed, and hadn't the Suzerain even taken him into his house—for a while—as had she? While her friends in other shacks and huts and cottages felt sorry for the young woman so alone now with her memories, it occurred to the aunt, as she sat before her fireplace on a dim winter's afternoon, watching smoke spiral from the embers: Why not *twist* the fibers first before stringing them on the rack? The (also her word) 'thread' she twisted made a far smoother, stronger, and—finally! —functional fabric. And the loom, which had been a tolerated embarrassment among those friends to whom she was always showing it, was suddenly being rebuilt all over Ellamon. Women twisted. Women wove. Many women did nothing *but* twist thread for the weavers, who soon included men. That summer the aunt chipped two holes in a flat stone, wrapped the first few inches of twisted fibers through them, then set the stone to spin, helped on by a foot or a hand, thus using the torque to twist thread ten to twenty times as fast as you could with just your fingers. But with the invention of the spindle (not the aunt's word, but an amused

4

neighbor's term for it), a strange thing happened. People began to suggest that neither she nor the long-dead barbarian were really the loom's inventors; and certainly she could not have thought up thread twisting by herself. And when it became known that there were other towns and other counties throughout Nevèrÿon where weaving and spinning had been going on for years—as it had, by now, been going on for years at fabled Ellamon—then all the aunt's claims to authorship became a kind of local joke. Even her invention of the spindle was suddenly suspect. And though he never claimed it for himself, the neighbor who'd named it was often credited with at least as much input into *that* discovery as the barbarian about whom the aunt was always going on must have had into the loom. For the barbarian turned out to have been quite a famous and fabled person all along, at least outside of Ellamon. And the spindle? Surely it was something she had seen somewhere. It was too useful, too simple, and just not the kind of thing you 'thought up' by yourself. The aunt spun. The aunt wove. The aunt took in abandoned children, now of a younger cousin, now of a wayward niece, and, several years later, the grandson of a nephew. For wasn't her shack the warmest in the village? When she had made it, she had filled every chink of it with a mixture of oil and mud, into which she had blown hundreds and hundreds of small air bubbles through a hollow reed; it would hold both warm air and cool air for more than twenty-four hours. (She had told the barbarian—whose name had been Belham—about her insulation method that first day in the market; and wasn't that *why* he had consented to stay with her when the Suzerain of Vanar had put him out?) From all the looms of fabled Ellamon bolts of goats' wool and dogs' hair cloth and sheep wool rolled out, slower than smoke spiraling over winter embers. The great-aunt spoke little with her neighbors, loved her little cousins and great-nieces (and her great-nephew—seven years older than pryn—who had recently become a baker), and grew more bitter. What mountain pasturage there was about the High Hold was slowly given over to sheep, already prized for their thin but nourishing milk. (Sheep wool clearly made the strongest, warmest cloth. But that, alas, was not among the aunt's particular discoveries.) And more and more milkless, fleeceless dragons leapt from the pastures' ledges and cliffs, with their creaking honks, to tear their wings on treetops and brambles decently out of sight.

Because the slopes around Ellamon sported more rockweed than grass, the local shepherds never could raise the best sheep: Ellamon's fabrics were never particularly fabled.

Today pryn's great-aunt was over eighty.

The barbarian had slipped drunkenly down the cliff more than fifty years ago.

Bound to the sky by vines twisted the same way her great-aunt still twisted goats' fleece and marshpool fluff and dogs' hair into thread that bound that bitter, old, energetic woman to the earth, pryn flew!

Flying, she saw the crazily tilting mountains rise by her, the turning clouds above her, the rocking green, the green-licked rock. Somewhere below, sheep, bleating, wandered over another rise. Wind rushed pryn's ears to catch in the cartilages and turn around in them, cackling like a maiden turning from her shuttle to laugh at a companion's scabrous joke. Air battered her eye sockets, as a wild girl pounds the wall of the room where she has been shut in by a mother terrified her child might, in her wildness, run loose and be taken by slavers. Air rushed pryn's toes; her toes flexed up, then curled in the joy, in the terror of flight. Wind looped coolly about pryn's arms, pushed cold palms against her kneecaps.

They glided.

And much of the space between pryn and the ground had gone.

She had launched from a ledge and, through common sense, had expected to land on one. How else to take off once more? Somehow, though, she'd assumed the dragon knew this too.

Trees a-slant the slope rose.

She pulled on the reins, hard. Wings flopped, fluttered, flapped behind her knees; pryn leaned back in wind, searching for ledges in the mountains that were now all around.

She glanced down to see the clearing—without a ledge any side! Treetops veered, neared.

That was where they were going to land . . . ? Leaves a-top a tall tree slapped her toes, stinging. She yanked vines. Dragon wings rose, which meant those green membranes between the long bones would not tear on the branches. But they were falling—no, still gliding. She swallowed air. The dragon tilted, beating back against her own flight—pryn rocked against the bony neck. Reins tight, she knuckled scales. Dragon muscle moved under her legs. A moment's floating, when she managed to push back and blink. And blinked again—

—because they jarred, stopping, on pebbles and scrub.

A lurch: the dragon stepped forward.

Another lurch: another step.

She pulled on the reins again. The slow creature lurched another step and . . . halted.

She craned to see the trees behind her. Above them, rock—

"Hello!"

6

The dragon took another step; pryn swung forward.

The woman, cross-legged across the clearing by the fireplace, uncrossed and pushed to one knee. "Hello, there!" She stood, putting a hand on the provision cart's rail. "That your dragon?" The ox bent to tear up ragged rockweed; the cart rumbled for inches. The rail slipped under the woman's palm.

Swinging her leg over the dragon's neck, pryn slid down scales, feeling her leather skirt roll up the backs of her thighs. On rough ground she landed on two feet and a fist—"Yes . . . !"—and came erect in time to duck the wing that opened, beat once, then folded. "I mean—I *rode* it . . ."

The woman was middle-aged, some red left in her hair. Her face was sunburned and freckled.

With suspicion and curiosity, pryn blinked. Then, because she had flown, pryn laughed. It was the full, foaming laugh of a loud brown fifteen-year-old with bushy hair. It broke up fear, exploded curiosity, and seemed—to the woman, at any rate—to make the heavy, short girl one with the pine needles and shale chips and long, long clouds pulled sheer enough to see blue through.

That was why the woman laughed too.

The dragon swung her head, opened her beak, and hissed over stained, near-useless teeth, tiny in mottled gum.

The girl stepped up on a mossy rock. "Who are you?"

"Norema the tale-teller," the woman said. She put both hands in the pockets of her leggings and took a long step across the burnt-out fireplace. "Who are you?"

"I am pryn, the . . . adventurer, pryn the warrior, pryn the thief!" said pryn, who had never stolen anything in her life other than a ground oaten cake from the lip of her cousin's baking oven three weeks before—she'd felt guilty for days!

"You're going to have trouble getting that dragon to take off again."

The girl's face moved from left-over laugh to scowl. "Don't I know it!"

The ox took another step. The cart's plank wheels made brief noises among themselves and on small stones. The ox blinked at the dragon, which stood now, one foreclaw raised.

Dragons sometimes stood like that a long time.

"You're not one of the regular dragon grooms—the little girls they keep in the corrals above Ellamon . . . ?"

The ox tore up more rockweed.

The girl shook her head. "But I live in Ellamon—just outside Ellamon, actually. With my great-aunt. I've seen them, though, flying their dragons with their trainers and guards for the tourists

7

who go out to the hill to watch. They're all bad girls, you know. Girls who've struck their mothers or disobeyed their fathers, stolen things, sometimes even killed people. They've been brought from all over Nevèrÿon—"

"... adventurers, warriors," Norema suggested, "thieves?"

The girl looked at the ground, turning her bare foot on sand. "You're a foreigner. You probably don't know much about dragons, or the bad girls who ride them."

"Oh," Norema said, "one hears fables. Also, I've been through this strange and ... well, this strange land before. What were you doing on that dragon?"

"Flying," pryn answered, then wondered if that sounded disingenuous. She bent to brush a dusty hand against a dusty knee. "It's something I've always wanted to do. And I'm growing—everyone always tells me how much I'm growing. So I thought: soon I shall be too tall or too fat. I'd better do it now. The girls they use for riders up in the dragon corrals are all half-starved anyway, till they're thin as twigs. They're all twelve and thirteen years old— forever, it seems like." She smoothed her overblouse down her waistless stomach. "I'm short. But I'm not thin."

"True," Norema said, "you're not. But you look strong. And I like your laugh."

"I don't know how strong I am either," pryn said, "but I caught a wild dragon, bridled her, and led her to a ledge."

"That seems strong enough."

"You've been here before ...?" It sounded more suspicious than pryn meant. But suspicion was a habit of tongue picked up from her aunt more than a habit of mind; and, anyway, her laugh belied it. "What are you doing here now?"

"Looking for a friend," Norema said. "A friend of mine. Years ago she used to be a guard at the dragon corrals and told me all about those ... bad girls. My friend wore blue stone beads in her hair and a black rag mask across her eyes; and she killed with a double-bladed sword. We were companions and traveled together several years."

"What happened to her?" pryn asked.

"Oh," Norema said. "I told her tales—long, marvelous, fascinating tales. Sometimes I wasn't sure if they were tales told to me when I was a child, or tales I'd made up. I told her tales, and after a while my masked friend grew more interested in the tales than she was in me. One night, sitting on her side of the campfire, cleaning her double blade, she told me she was going off next morning to see if one particular tale were true. The next day when I woke, she and her bedroll were gone—along with her double-bladed sword.

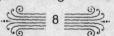

8

Nor was I worried. We were the kind of friends who frequently went separate ways—for days, even weeks. But weeks became months; and I did not run across my friend's campfire on the rim of the Menyat canyon, nor did I hear any word of her tramping along the northernmost Faltha escarpments, nor did I meet her taking shade in one of the Makalata caves at the rim of the western desert, nor did I hear rumor of her lean-to set up a mile further down the beach at Carness."

Squatting, pryn picked up a stick. "So what did you do?" She scratched at spilled ash.

"I decided to take my cart and go look for her. I've looked many places, and no doubt I'll look many more. But I've come to Ellamon because my friend once worked here and was happy."

"Mmm," pryn said, suspiciously.

The woman looked down to see what pryn had been scratching. " 'Pyre,' " she read. " 'Ynn.' Pyre-ynn?"

" '. . . pryn'," pryn said. "That's my name. In writing."

The woman stepped around the figures and squatted too. "Here." She took the stick and added a line above the two syllabics the girl had etched in ash. "You, 'pryn'. *That's* your name. In writing. That line there means you squish the two sounds together into one. Otherwise you'll have people mispronouncing it every which way."

In late sunlight pryn squinted at the woman. "How do *you* know?"

"Actually—" the woman looked back at pryn with a moment's uncertainty—"because I invented it."

The girl frowned. "Invented what?"

"Writing. A long time ago. I must have been about your age— now I don't mean I invented *every* kind of writing. I just added the idea of making written signs stand for particular words, so you could *say* them. Till then, you know, written signs stood for animals, foods, amounts, tasks, instructions, ideas, even people, even *kinds* of people—whole complexes of notions. But written *words*— that's *my* innovation."

"You did that?" The girl blinked.

The woman nodded. "When I was a girl. I lived on an island— that's where I invented my system. I taught it to my island friends, many of whom were fishers and sailors. Years later, when I came to Nevèrÿon, I found my writing system had preceded me. With changes, of course. But most of the signs were quite recognizably the ones I had made up when I was a child."

"Everyone says this kind of writing came across the sea from the Ulvayns." Looking at the tall, middle-aged woman, pryn thought of her own, short, bitter aunt. "You invented . . . my name?"

"Only the way to write it. Believe me, it comes in very handy if you're a tale-teller. But you know—" The woman was apparently not as comfortable squatting as pryn, so she put one leather legging's knee on the ground. She scratched the name again, this time above what pryn had written. "—I've made some changes in my system. About names, for instance. Today I always write a name with a slightly larger version of the initial sign; and I put a little squiggle down under it, like that—" She added another scratch. "That way, if I'm reading it aloud, I can always glance ahead and see a name coming. You speak names differently from the way you speak other words. You mean them differently, too. The size of the initial sign stands for the way you speak it. The squiggle stands for what names mean that's different. So everything is indicated. These days, you have to indicate *every*thing, or nobody understands."

The girl looked down at her name's new version, below and above the old one she herself had glyphed.

"Really, it's quite useful," Norema went on. "My friend, for example, was called Raven. Now there are ravens that caw and fly—much more efficiently than dragons. And there's my friend, Raven. Since she left, I find that now, more and more, both will enter my stories. The distinction marks a certain convenience, a sort of stability. Besides, I like distinguishing people from things in and of the land. It makes tale-telling make a lot more sense."

The girl grinned at the woman. "I like that!" She took the stick and traced the syllabics, first the larger with the mark beneath, then the smaller, and last the eliding diacritic.

She read it.

Then Pryn laughed again.

It was much the same laugh she had laughed when she'd dismounted; but it sounded richer—to Pryn, at any rate. Indeed, it sounded almost as rich and wild to Pryn as it had before to Norema—almost as though the mountain, with its foaming falls and piled needles and scattered shalechips (all named 'Pryn' by the signs now inscribed thrice on its ashy surface, twice with capitals, enclosing the minuscule version), had itself laughed.

And that *is* my name, Pryn thought. "What tales did you tell?"

"Would you like to hear one?"

"Yes," Pryn said.

"Well, then sit here. Oh, don't worry. It won't be that long."

Pryn, feeling very differently about herself, sat.

Norema, who had taken the stick, stood, stepped from the fireplace, turned her back, and lowered her head, as though listening to leaves and dragon's breath and her ox's chewing and some

stream's plashing just beyond the brush, as though they all were whispering to the tale-teller the story she was about to tell. Pryn listened too. Then Norema turned and announced, "Once upon a time ..." or its equivalent in that long-ago distant language. And Pryn jumped: the words interrupted that unheard flow of natural speech as sharply as a written sign found on a stretch of dust till then marred only by wind and rolling pebbles.

"Once upon a time there was a beautiful young queen—just about your age. Your height, too. And your size."

"People say I'm clever, that I'm young, and that I'm growing," Pryn said. "They *don't* say I'm beautiful."

"At this particular time," Norema explained, "young queens who looked like you were all thought to be ravishing. Standards of beauty change. And this happened many years back. Once upon—"

"Was your friend my age?"

Norema chuckled. "No. She was closer to *my* age. But it's part of the story, you see, to say the queen was the age of the hearer. Believe me, I told it the same way to my friend."

"Oh."

"Once upon a time there was a beautiful queen, about your age and your size. Her name was Olin, and she was queen of all Nevèrÿon—at least she was supposed to be. Her empire extended from the desert to the mountains, from the jungles to the sea. Unfortunately, however, she had an unhappy childhood. Some evil priests shut Olin, her family, and her twenty-three servants in an old monastery on the Garth peninsula, practically from the time she was born until she was, well ..." The woman questioned Pryn with narrowed eyes. "Fifteen?"

Pryn nodded.

"When she was fifteen years old, for arcane political reasons, the evil priests decided to kill her outright. But they were afraid to do it themselves—for more political reasons, equally arcane. They couldn't get any of her family to do it, so they tried to hire her own servants, one after the other, all twenty-three. But the first servant was the queen's nurse, an old woman who loved the girl and came to her young mistress and told her what the priests intended.

" 'What shall I do?' the queen cried.

" 'You can be afraid,' said the old servant. 'But don't be terrified. That's first. You see, I have a plan, although it's a sad and sorrowful one. I've made a bargain with the priests, which they'll respect because they think me a great magician. I've told them I will betray you *if* they will pay me one gold piece. And I have also made them promise that if I fail, they will hire the next servant to do the same deed for *two* gold pieces—twice what they have paid me. And if

11

that servant fails, they will hire the next one to do the deed for four gold pieces, twice again the amount paid the former. And if he fails, the next will be hired for twice the amount paid to the previous one. And so on.' The old woman produced from the folds of her gown a single gold coin—and a knife. 'Take my pay and hide it. Then take this knife—and strike me in the heart! For only my death will corroborate my failure.'

" '*Kill* you?' demanded the queen.

" 'It's the only way.'

"The queen wept and cried and protested. 'You are my beloved friend, my faithful bondswoman, and my dear nurse as well. You are closer to me than my own mother!' But the old woman put her arms around the girl and stroked her hair. 'Let me explain some of the more arcane politics behind this whole nasty business. These are brutal and barbaric times, and it is either you or I—for even if I *do* kill you, the wicked priests plan to dispense with me as soon as I stab you. They cannot suffer the murderer of a queen to live, even the murderer of a queen they hate as much as they hate you. If you do what I say, you will have the gold coin as well as your life, whereas I shall lose *my* life in any case.'

"And so, after more along the same line, the queen took the coin, and the knife—which she thrust into her old nurse's heart.

"Not so many days later, a second servant came to Queen Olin. 'Here are two gold coins and a rope with which I am to garrote you. Take the coins and hide them; then take the rope and strangle me—if you yourself would live. For *my* life is over in any case.' Again the queen protested, but again the servant prevailed. So the young queen took the rope and strangled him. A few days later a third servant came with four gold pieces and a great rock to smash in the queen's head. After that a fourth came with eight gold pieces and a draught of corrosive poison. The fifth had sixteen gold pieces. The sixth had thirty-two coins. The next—"

Pryn suddenly laughed. "But I've heard this story before! Or one just like it—only it was about grains of sand piled on the squares of a gaming board. I don't remember how many squares there were, but by the end, I remember, all the sand in the world was used up. Am I right about the ending? At the end of the twenty-three servants, she had all the money in the world . . . ?"

Norema smiled. "She certainly had all the money in the monastery. And at that particular time, all the money in the monastery was pretty much all the money in Nevèrÿon."

"That *is* an old story. I know, because I've heard it before. The version about the sand grains, that is."

"That part of the story is old. But there are some new parts too.

For example, after she had killed all her servants, the beautiful young queen felt very differently about herself."

Pryn frowned. "How do you mean?"

"Well," Norema said, "for one thing, in less than a year she had stabbed, strangled, bashed out the brains, poisoned, beheaded, and done even worse to twenty-two of her most faithful bondsmen and bondswomen, who were also the closest things she'd had to friends. After that she began to act very strangely and behave quite oddly. On and off, she behaved oddly the rest of her life—even for a queen. And in those days queens were expected to be eccentric. Often, after that, she was known as Mad Olin."

"I thought you said there were twenty-*three* servants."

"There were. But the last survived. He was not only a servant, but also her maternal uncle—though, alas, I can't remember his family name. And there're reasons to remember it, too, but for the life of me I can't recall what they are. Anyway. Years before, he had fallen on bad times and had indentured himself to the queen's mother, which was why he was with Olin in the first place. But he had always set himself apart. Along about the queen's murderings of the nineteenth, twentieth, and twenty-first servants—all particularly gruesome—the evil priests were, financially speaking, in rather bad shape. Olin was by then quite well off—though mentally she was a bit shaky. Her maternal uncle, who, like the first servant, was also something of a magician, had, with the help of the rest of the family, managed to engineer an escape for the queen. It took a good deal of the money; and Olin took the rest—to hide lest the wicked priests manage to trick it back, even as her first wise and faithful servant had tricked it from the priests." Norema sighed. "Raven and I once visited that monastery—it's still there today. And there are still priests—at least there were when we went. Now, I'm not sure. Anyway, you could certainly tell that the place had seen better times. Clearly they hadn't gotten their money back."

"Are the priests still wicked?"

Reddish brows lowered. "Well, I doubt if either my friend or I would ever stop there again—unless we absolutely had to."

"What about Olin's escape?"

"Ah, the exciting part!" Norema said. "Her uncle spirited her away from the monastery in the middle of the night, with the money in a caravan of six great wagons, each pulled by six horses. It was a lot of money, you see, and took more than one wagon to carry. Also, there was a lot more than gold coins in it by now—jewels and iron trinkets and all sorts of precious and semi-precious stones. The uncle took her to his family home, there in the south, and that evening he went with her up into a tall tower—at least that's how

13

one version of the story goes. In another version, he took her up on a high rocky slope—"

"Shouldn't you choose one or the other for the sake of the telling?" Pryn asked.

"For the sake of the story," Norema answered, "I tell both and let my hearer make her choices."

"Oh," Pryn said.

"In the stone chamber at the tower top—or in the rocky cell at the top of the rocky slope—the uncle began to read her the sequence by which the gold coins had come to her: one, two, four, eight, sixteen, thirty-two, sixty-four, one hundred twenty-eight, two hundred fifty-six, five hundred twelve, one thousand twenty-four, two thousand forty-eight, four thousand ninety-six—"

"I *see* how fast it goes up!" Pryn exclaimed. "That's just halfway through them, and it's already almost five thousand gold pieces. Two more, and it'll be over twenty thousand. Twenty thousand gold pieces must be close to all the money in the world!"

"That's what *you* see." Norema smiled. "What the young queen saw, however, was a city."

Pryn blinked.

Norema said: "The queen blinked."

"What city?" Pryn asked. "Where did she see it?"

"Precisely what the queen wondered too—for she blinked again ... It was gone! Through the stone columns at the stone rail, the queen looked down from the tower—or down to the foot of the slope—and saw only some marshy water, an open inlet, rippling out between the hills to the sea. But the queen *had* seen a city, there among the ripples, as clearly as she now saw the hills on either side of the inlet, or, indeed, as clearly as she saw the swampy growths that splotched the waters where they came in to the land. When she told her uncle what she had seen, immediately he stopped reading the numbers and showed her all sorts of magic wonders, including a circle full of different stars, which he gave her to keep. Then he took her down from the tower—or down from the rocks—to a great dinner that had been prepared for her, where they talked of more magic things. Then he did something terrible."

"What?" Pryn asked. "So far, this story sounds more confusing than exciting."

"To the proper hearer," Norema said, "precisely what seems confusing will *be* the exciting part. When the queen came back from a stroll in the garden between courses, the uncle gave her a goblet of poison, which she, unknowing, drank."

Norema was silent a long time.

Finally Pryn asked: "Was that the end of the queen? I'm sure her

uncle probably wanted the money for himself. This doesn't sound like a real story to me. What about the 'circle of different stars'? I don't even know what that is! I mean, it doesn't *seem* like a story, because it ... doesn't really end."

"It certainly doesn't end there," Norema said. "It goes on for quite a while, yet. But that always seemed to me an exciting place for a pause."

"What *did* happen, then?"

"See, you *are* caught up in the excitement, the action, the suspense! You want to know the outcome—I think it's very important to alert your listeners to the progress of their own reactions. I can foresee a time, after lots more tales have been told, when that won't be necessary. But for now it's a must. Well, the poison *didn't* kill the queen. It put her in a trance—and when she woke, if indeed she wasn't dreaming, she was on a rocky ledge. It was night, and as she pushed herself up on her hands and looked around, she saw she was lying between two white stones, one taller than the other— now here, again, there's another version that says the queen woke up in a boat which sailed in to a strange shore that morning, and on the shore she found the white stones—one higher than the other; at noon on the longest day of summer, this version says, one stone casts a shadow three times as long as—"

"But in *this* version—" Pryn tried to blot the image of sun and glaring sand that had itself blotted her image of darkness, full moon, and cool air—"it was night?"

"Yes," Norema said. "And the full moon was up."

Pryn started to ask, *But how did you know?*, then decided that if she were going to hear the end, she'd best stop interrupting. Besides, it was the teller's tale; the teller ought to know what happened in it, for all her multiple versions.

"The remaining money was in huge piles beside the queen, in heaps and bags and bundles, and the circle of different stars lay on the rock near her knee. Down the ledge from her, the water was covered with fog. The moon looked ghastly, a yellow disk hanging over a fuming inlet. Water flickered beneath mists. Olin sat on the rock, hugging her knees in the chill light, biting her inner lip, her chin on her kneecaps. A bird woke up and screeched! The queen looked to see green wings starting from the branches of a pecan tree. She got to her feet unsteadily, still groggy from the poison. She stood on the ledge and cried out across the waters, just as if someone had told her what to say (though none of the versions I know says who): 'I am Olin, and I have come to warn the Worm of the Sea of the Northern Eagle's evil gaze!' Then she took a step back and put her wrist up to her mouth as if she were afraid she

15

had said something blasphemous. She stepped to the ledge's edge again and looked down toward the foggy water. The mists were a-broil, and now and again splashes geysered up hot silver.

"There was a rumbling, as of some vast engine, not only from the water, but from the ground. Trees trembled; small stones shook loose to roll down into fog. Below slowly swirling fumes waves swirled even faster.

"Water surged, now into the land, now away. At each surge away, water lowered; and lowered.

"Olin saw the first broken building tops cleave mist and waves— three towers and a bridge between, dripping. Waves broke higher than fog; foam fell back, roaring, to the sea. More buildings emerged. Water poured from their roofs. Through fog, water erupted from stone windows. Fog rolled and roiled off. Green and white water lapped away through mud and weeds and clotted alleys. Water rushed from a street where pillars still stood. Water carried weed and mud from patterned blue flags; other pillars were broken. One lay across its square pediment. At the same time she saw the cleared street, she saw other avenues still silted, dark, and wet. Shapes that might have been buildings were mounded over with mud, glistening, black, and green. To the earth's rumblings and the water's ragings, the city rose.

"The young queen, half running, half falling down the slope, only just managed to get her feet under her—when she plunged shin deep in muck. She staggered on, arms flailing, till she reached the first cracked paving—nowhere near as clean as it had looked from the ledge. Mud clung to the walls beside her. Weeds in windows hung down dripping stones. Fallen masonry, scattered shells, and soaked branches made her progress by the carved pillars almost as slow as it had been in the mud. Dirty-footed, wet-handed, scratches on her shoulders and legs, the young queen pushed between stones and driftwood, making her way by broken walls, their carvings veiled in sea moss.

"What movement down what alley made her stop, the queen was never sure. Off in the wet green filling another street, something dark as excrement flexed, shifted, slid. The building beside her was heaped over with runnelled mud. That moved too, quivered, rose— not mud at all, but some immense tarpaulin. The sheet shook itself loose.

"Olin looked up.

"The moon lit yellow fogs which shifted over roofs. Through them, over them, the wing rose—not a soft, feathered, birdlike wing, but a taut, spined, reptilian wing, sheer enough to let moonlight through its skin, here and there darkened by spine or vein.

16

"That wing blotted a fifth the sky!

"Wind touched the queen's cheek, her wrist. A second wing, as huge, rose from where it had lain over buildings at the street's far side. Ahead, beyond the pillars, something slid forward, pulled back.

"To the extent she had seen it at all, she'd thought it was a toppled carving, a sculpted demon's head, big as a house and fallen on its chin. A gold and black eye opened; and opened; and opened, wider than the wide moon. Then, perhaps fifteen feet away, from under a rising lid, the other eye appeared. A lip lifted from teeth longer and thicker than the queen's legs. The head, still wet, rose on its thick neck, clearing the near roofs, rising over the towers, spiring between the wings.

"The dragon—a giant dragon, a sea dragon many times the size of her mountain cousins—was coiled through the streets. She'd slept with the city beneath the water. But now as the city rose, the dragon rose above it, to stare down at the young queen with black and gold eyes.

"Again Olin cried out, loud enough to hurt her throat: 'Oh great Gauine—' for that was the dragon's name, though I don't know where she learned it—'I have come to hide my treasure with you and warn you of the Eagle's antics—' "

Squinting silvery eyes in the sun, the ordinary mountain dragon just then put her foot down and hissed at the ox; the ox shied, backing up five steps. The cart trundled and creaked. Norema turned to grab it.

Pryn pushed up to her feet and snatched at the dragon's swinging reins. Green wings flapped futilely.

Norema calmed her ox. Pryn led her dragon to a tree and lashed it. Norema came over to give her a hand, then walked with Pryn back to the fireplace. Pryn rubbed her hands together. Her palms were sore where the reins, first in landing, then in tethering, had jerked through. "The story you were telling?" Pryn asked. "What happened next?"

"Not much," Norema said. "Using the magic circle of different stars as a guide, Olin and Gauine hid the money in the city. Then Gauine settled down on top of it to guard it—just in time, too. For water began to roll back through the streets. Once more the city began to sink. The queen clambered up the slope to the ledge, barely managing to escape drowning. And the moon was down."

Pryn frowned.

"Oh, Gauine was a very exceptional dragon," Norema explained. They stopped by the cart; the ox nipped more weed.

"But then, if she hadn't been," Norema went on, "I doubt the queen would have entrusted the treasure into her keeping. The next day, wandering half-dazed along the beach, Olin was found by traveling mummers. Fortunately, over the night she'd been gone, the rest of her relatives had managed to defeat the evil priests. The young queen was taken to Kolhari, capital of all Nevèrÿon, where she was crowned queen for real. From all reports, she was never popular and led a horrid life. She went through several kings and a number of children, most of whom ended up frightfully. But she managed to make several arcane political decisions which have always been considered praiseworthy, at least by people who count such things important."

"Queen Olin," Pryn mused. "I've heard other stories about her, here in Ellamon. She was the queen who set up the dragon corrals and decided that bad little girls would be condemned to work there."

"One of the more interesting fables," Norema said. "Well, she was always fond of the animal, since it was a giant sea dragon that guarded the sunken treasure on which her power rested."

"That was the story your friend set out to find was true or not?"

Norema nodded.

"She wanted to find Mad Queen Olin's treasure in the sunken city guarded by the dragon Gauine?"

"That's what she said."

Suddenly Pryn turned around and looked off at her own winged mount swaying at its tree. "Brainless, stupid beast! I thought I'd fly you away from home to excitement and adventure—or at least to a ledge from which I could return. But here—" she turned back to Norema—"she has landed in this silly clearing and can't take off again!"

"You want to leave home for good," Norema said seriously.

"Yes," Pryn said. "And *don't* tell me not to!"

"You aren't afraid of slavers?"

Pryn shook her head. "You're traveling alone, and *you're* still a free woman."

"True," Norema said. "And I intend to stay one." She considered a moment. "Let me give you two more gifts—besides my tale."

Pryn looked perplexed. She hadn't thought much of the story. It had stopped and started, leaving her anxious and expectant precisely where she wanted answers and explanations.

"You can be frightened," Norema said. "But don't be terrified. That's first."

"I'm *not* terrified," Pryn said.

"I know," Norema said. "But that's the way with advice. The part you can accept you always already know."

"I'm not afraid either," Pryn said. Then she frowned again. "No, I

am afraid. But it doesn't matter, because I made my mind up to it a long time ago."

"Good." Norema smiled. "I wasn't going to argue. One of my gifts, then, is a packet of food, that I'll give you out of my provisions cart. The other is some geographical information about the real world over which you've just so cavalierly flown—both are things one cannot trust tales to provide. Oh, yes, and another piece of advice: Untie your dragon and let her wander into the mountains where she belongs. Left to herself, she'll find the ledges she needs, as you must, too—but you can't be tied down with dragons that won't fly where you want to go, no matter how much fun the notion of flight. Through those trees, maybe a hundred yards on, you'll find the junction of two roads, giving you a choice of four directions. The one going—" Norema glanced at the sun—"towards the sunset will take you, with three days' walk, to a white desert with dangerous tribes who sew copper wire up the rims of their ears. Take the road leading in the opposite direction, down between the mountain hills, and with four days' walk you'll reach the coast and a brave village of rough-handed men and women who live from the sea. Take the road running to your right as you approach the crossroads, and you'll be back at the High Hold of fabled Ellamon in no more than three hours. Take the path that runs away from the junction to your left, and seven days' hike will finally bring you to the grand port of Kolhari, capital city of all Nevèrÿon—like in my story." Norema smiled. (That so famous city had not played much of a part in the tale, Pryn thought; though certainly she knew enough of Kolhari by other report.) "Along with my tale, I think my gifts should stand a young woman like you, off to see the world, in good stead."

"Thank you," Pryn said, because her aunt, for all her bitterness, had taught her to be polite.

Some hours later, when Pryn was several miles along her chosen route, she stopped a minute. Of all the day's marvels it was neither her own flight, nor the tale of the dragon and the sunken city, nor the food pack tied on her back—with twisted vines—which held her thoughts. She picked up a stick from the highway's shoulder and scratched her name in its dust, new capital and eliding mark. She put the stick down. Again she read over her name, which seemed so new and wondrous and right.

Then she walked on.

An hour later a dead branch, blown out on the road by a mountain gust, obscured it beyond reading.

 19

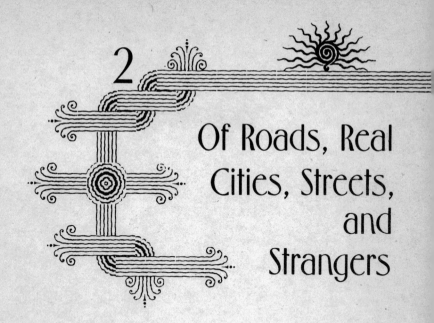

2

Of Roads, Real Cities, Streets, and Strangers

A city sidewalk by itself is nothing. It is an abstraction. It means something only in conjunction with the buildings and other uses that border it, or border other sidewalks very near it ... if a city's streets are safe from barbarism and fear, the city is thereby tolerably safe from barbarism and fear.... But sidewalks and those who use them are not passive beneficiaries of safety or helpless victims of danger. Sidewalks, their bordering uses, and their users, are active participants in the drama of civilization versus barbarism in cities. To keep the city safe is a fundamental task of a city's streets and sidewalks.

This task is totally unlike any service that sidewalks and streets in little towns are called upon to do. Great cities are not like towns, only larger. They are not like suburbs, only denser. They differ from towns and suburbs in basic ways, and one of these is that cities, by definition, are full of strangers.
—Jane Jacobs/*The Death and Life of Great American Cities*

This is how, after seven nights' unchanging stars, eclipsed only by passing clouds or moon glare, Pryn came to be standing on a roadway atop a hill one dark dawn, looking down at port Kolhari.

Fog lay on the city, obscuring detail. But that hulking edifice to the west had to be the High Court of Eagles. East, regular roofs suggested some wide street between—Black Avenue, perhaps, or even New Pavē. She'd heard travelers in the Ellamon market talk of those wonder-ways—

The sea!

Pryn had been looking at the city itself at least that long before the foggy vastness beyond it closed with its right name. It *had* to be the sea! A mountain girl, she'd never seen so much water—indeed, so much of *any*thing before! Mists lay here and there on gray-flecked black. Obscuring much of the watery horizon, mists became one with gray sky. Well, it was quite as impressive as she'd heard it was. At the shore, like pine needles sticking up through the fog, she saw what must be ships' masts along the famous Kolhari water-

front. Nearer, roofs of sizable houses lay apart from one another—perhaps wealthy merchants' homes in the suburb of Sallese or maybe mansions of hereditary nobles in Neveryóna. My fortune, Pryn thought, may hide down there. A memory of her great-aunt returned, in which the old woman wrung her hands. "If your father could only see you . . ."

When Pryn was a baby, her father had died in the army somewhere to the south—of a sudden peacetime fever outbreak rather than wartime wounds. Her mother, when she visited from where she now lived, several towns away, had several times told Pryn the story of the black soldier who had come through Ellamon with the news, much as Pryn's aunt told the story of the long-dead barbarian. Still, as a child, Pryn had kept some faint fancy of finding that vanished phantom parent.

Down there?

She answered her own dark morning question, as she had answered it many times before, now on a solitary dawn walk through sunny mountain pines, now standing at evening on some shaly scarp, now at a bright trout pool spilling through noon between high, hot rocks: No. (One thing about riding dragons, Pryn reflected; such childish expectations could be, in the momentary wonder of flight, forgotten—not just put aside by active effort.) Her father was dead.

Pryn? That was her own name; and her mother's—not her father's gift. Her mother and father had not been overly married before her mother had become pregnant and her father, upon finding out, had gone off to fight for the Empress. 'Not overly married' meant that certain bonding rituals had been publicly observed between them, but certain others that would make those early ones permanent had not. Her mother's abandonment had occurred within a margin of respectability—inconvenient as it was. But then, the army had not been that convenient for her father, either; its stringencies had apparently given him enough appreciation of the domestic life he'd left so that on his death pallet he'd asked a dusky friend to return his sword, shield, and sundry effects to Ellamon—which Pryn's mother had immediately sold, giving the money to the aunt to maintain her baby while she went to seek work in another town. Growing up with that wise woman and her other cousins had not been bad.

Pryn was a girl who knew who she was and could now write her name correctly.

Somehow she'd already connected that, as indeed she connected almost all about her she felt to be mature, with accepting that parental death and suppressing those childish fancies that perhaps the black soldier had been mistaken (had found the wrong woman, the wrong city . . .), or had been part of some trick by a father even more scoundrelly than her mother, when in her cups, sometimes claimed that brave soldier to have been, or had simply lied from caprice. No, she thought again. He is dead. I am alive.

And my fortune?

Her memory turned to the tale teller's city, risen in mist from the waters, its grand dragon guarding the queen's treasure in those flooded streets.

Sunlight had begun to break through the overcast. Clouds pulled from swatches of blue.

The real city below, under real fog and real sun, the one now giving way to the other, was ominous. She wondered if the tale teller's friend—was it Raven?—with her blue beads and her mask and her double blade had ever stood like this, on this rise, this road, looking down on this city as the earth heaved from dark dawn to morning . . .

Pryn did not hear the hoofbeats till they were almost on her. (Three times over the week she'd hidden in the bushes while mounted men in leather aprons herded dusty men and women, chained collar to collar, along the road ruts. She'd seen slaves chained to planks outside the walls of Ellamon, six or ten together, waiting to be fed. She'd seen slaves, two or three, chained in the sunny corner of the Ellamon market, under the eyes of an overseer, waiting to be bought.) She whirled about, then dashed for the road's edge. But she had seen the three riders—which meant the riders had seen her.

The three horses hammered abreast of her, halted.

The tallest and, from his reddish beard and open face, the youngest grinned. "What are you looking at, girl?" Some teeth were missing.

Pryn recovered from her crouch, thigh deep in scratchy brush. "Are you slavers?"—though in asking, she'd realized they were not.

Another rider, a weathered man, squat, muscular, and hairy-shouldered, threw back his head and laughed. His teeth, the ones visible, were large, yellow, and sound.

The third was naked, save a cloth tied about his forehead and hanging to his shoulders. "Do we look like slavers?" His voice was rough enough to suggest a throat injury. On the right side of his body, Pryn saw, as his horse wheeled and wheeled back over the road, long scars roped him, chest, flank, and thigh, as though someone had flung blacksnakes at him that had stuck. "Do you think we look like slavers, girl?"

Pryn shook her head.

"Slavers!" The youngster laughed. Despite his height, Pryn was sure he was not a year older than she. "Us, slavers? Do you know Gorgik the Liberator? *We're* going to join him and his men at—" He stopped, because the other two grimaced. The squat one made half a motion for silence. The youngster leaned forward, more soberly. "You want to know if we're slavers? Well, we have a question for you: Are you one of the Child Empress's spies, in the pay of the High Court of Eagles?"

Once more Pryn shook her head.

"That's what *you* say." The youngster lowered his voice. "But how do *we* know?" His gappy grin remained. "The Liberator isn't the most popular man in Nevèrÿon. The Empress's spies are cunning and conniving."

Pryn stepped onto the road. "*You* know I'm not a spy the same way *I* know you're not slavers." What she thought was that they might be bandits; she did not want to act afraid. "You don't look like slavers. I don't look like a spy."

The youngster leaned even lower, till he looked at her right between his mount's red ears. "While you and I both may very well have seen slavers, and so know what slavers look like, what if we here have never *seen* a spy . . . ?"

Pryn frowned. She had never seen a spy either.

The squat one said: "Spies often look like other than spies. It's one sign by which you know them." He moved thick fingers in the graphite-gray mane.

The naked one with the headrag and the scars said: "This road runs from the Faltha mountains to port Kolhari. Which way do you go?"

"There." Pryn pointed toward the city.

"Good. Come up on my horse. We'll take you into town."

Again Pryn shook her head. "I can get there by myself."

The scarred rider pulled a four-foot lance from a holder on his horse's flank. "If you don't come with us," he said evenly, "we'll kill you. Make your choice, spy."

Pryn thought of bolting from them, thought of running between them, and stood.

The rider held his lance with his elbow against his scarred side so that his forearm was at a right angle to his body. The metal point showed the hammer marks of its forging. "Our friend here—" he jerked his chin toward the bearded boy—"has said more than he should have. You're going into the city anyway. Ride with us. You *may* be a spy. We can't take chances."

Pryn walked across the road toward his horse. "You don't give me much of a choice."

The scarred man said: "Sit in front of me."

Angry and frightened, Pryn reached up to grapple the horse's hard neck. The naked man bent. He shoved his lance back into its holder and slid his hand under Pryn's raised thigh to tug her up, while she got one leg awkwardly before his belly. (I've climbed on a dragon without help!) As she slid back against him, one of his hands came around her stomach. The mare stamped dirt. The rider behind her, stomach against her, flapped reins before her. She felt him kick the horse—not to a gallop but a leisurely trot. The others, trotting, cantering, trotting again, came abreast. Pryn's capitulation made her anger more acute. "Since I'm being punished for what your young friend knows and almost said, at least let me know what it is. Who is this Liberator—and take your hand off my breast!" She pushed the rider's hand from where the dark fingers had moved.

The squat rider laughed. "You want to know about Gorgik? Once he was a slave; now he's vowed to end all slavery throughout Nevèrÿon. Some say that someday, if not soon, he may be emperor! Myself, I knew him years ago when he was an officer in the Child Empress's army. One of the best, too." The squat man rubbed a wide, studded belt bound high on hairy ribs. "I fought under him—but only for a month. Then they broke up our division and sent me off with another captain. But we're going to fight under him again—if he'll have us. Hey, boys?"

"Aye!" came from the one boy beside her.

The naked man put his hand lightly back on Pryn's stomach.

"Only with him a month, yes." The squat rider grew pensive. "He won't remember me. But we loved that man, we did—every one of us under him. And slavery is an evil at least two of us know first hand." He laughed again and guided his horse around a branch fallen on the road. Other hooves smashed leaves. "That's why we three go to—"

"Move your hand!" Pryn shoved the naked rider's arm from where it had again risen. Hoisting herself forward, she glared over her shoulder. "I didn't want this ride! I'm not here to play your dumb games! Cut it out!"

"Look, girl," the rider said from the rags about his dark face. "You sit behind me. That way, you can—"

"—she can put *her* hands where she wants!" cried the bearded youth. His face and the squat one's held the wide grins of stupid boys.

Pryn decided that, of the three, the bearded youngster *was* the

fool. Till then she'd vaguely thought that, since his age was closest to hers, he might be the easiest to enlist for help. But he talked foolishly and was probably too intimidated by the older two anyway.

Her rider reined. She swung her legs over the horse's neck and slid down to the road. The squat one back-stepped his horse to give her another unwanted hand. (Remember, Pryn thought, as she came up behind one smooth and one scarred shoulder, within the week you have ridden a dragon ...) Filthy and frayed, vine cord knotted the rag to her rider's head. Those scars? A mountain girl living in harsh times, Pryn had seen women and men with wounds from injury and accident. What was before her, though, suggested greater violence than the mishandling of plowhead or hunting knife. She put her hands on the rider's flanks. His flesh was hard and hot. She could feel one scar, knobby and ropy, under her hand's heel.

Slavery?

The horse trotted.

The flapping headdress smelled of oil and animals. Pryn leaned to the side to see ahead—mostly trees now, with the road's ruts descending into them. Gripping the horse's sides with her knees and the rider's with her hands, she settled into the motion.

Once she thought: A beautiful young queen, abducted on the road by fearful, romantic bandits ... But they were not romantic. She was not beautiful. No, this was not the time for tale-teller's stuff. It was a bit scary. But as yet, she reflected, she was not yet *full* of fear. From the threat of death to the straying hands, it all had too much the air of half-hearted obligation.

Once more she moved her head from behind the flapping cloth and called to the bearded boy who had been riding beside her almost ten minutes, "Where is this Gorgik the Liberator? Go on, tell me."

Clearly, from boyish excitement, he wanted to. But he glanced at his companions. As clearly, she had been right about his intimidation. "You'll see soon enough," he called back across the little abyss of hooves, dust, and wind.

The shift from country to city Pryn never quite caught. Now there was a river by the road. The horses' hoofbeats changed timbre. She looked down—yes, the road itself along which they trotted was, now, paved with flat stones set in hard mud. She looked up to see green-tiled decorations interspersed with terra-cotta castings on an upper cornice of a wealthy home beyond a stone wall lapped with vines. On the other side of the road she saw an even higher roof, over a higher wall, moving up toward them as the other fell behind.

And the river was gone.

"You wanted to know where Gorgik the Liberator is?" her rider called back. "Look there!"

They wheeled off the main highway.

Ahead, armed men stood before a gate in another wall. Above, Pryn saw the top story of another great house. Much of the decorative tiling had fallen away. Behind the crenellations a dozen men ambled about the roof, some with spears, some with bows. At the corner one sat on a cracked carving—dragon or eagle she couldn't tell—looking down into the yard.

The younger and older either side, Pryn's rider reined at the wooden door in the stone wall, which was half as high as the youngster on his horse.

The squat one bawled out in a voice much too loud simply to be speaking to the men in leather helmets either side of the gate, with their broad knives hanging at their hips: "Go in and tell your master, Gorgik the Liberator, that three brave fellows have come to pledge hands and hearts to whatever end he would put them!"

With the blue eyes and frizzy blond beard of a barbarian—rare enough in northern Ellamon to cause comment when you saw one in the market—a guard stepped toward them, pushed up his helmet, and bawled back: "What names might he know you by?"

"Tell your great and gracious master, Gorgik, that the Southern Fox—" he gestured toward Pryn's rider—"and the Red Badger—" which was, apparently, the bearded boy—"and myself, the Western Wolf—" the thick hand fell against his own black rug of a chest— "have come to serve him! Ask him what he knows of us, and whether the tales of our exploits that have preceded us are sufficiently impressive to allow us to join his company! Let him consider! We shall return in a few hours to seek admittance!"

The barbarian guard nodded toward Pryn, then said in a perfectly ordinary voice: "There're four of you . . . ?"

In an equally ordinary voice the Western Wolf said: "Oh. I forgot the kid." He turned back to the gate, took a breath, and bawled: "Tell him that the Blue Heron is also among our number and to consider her for his cause!"

Then Wolf, Badger, and Fox, with the Heron behind (thinking of Raven and capital letters), wheeled from the gate. Dust struck up from the road high as the horses' haunches.

As the great houses drifted by her behind high walls and palm clusters, what Pryn thought was: Here, I am suddenly in this world of men, made to ride when I want to walk, touched when I want to be left alone, and given a new name when I've just learned to write my old one, all under some fanciful threat of death because I *might*

be a spy. (Just what tales, she wondered, had *they* been listening to?) I don't like it at all, she thought. I don't like it.

As unclear as the shift between country and city had been, Pryn was equally uncertain—as she was thinking all this—where the change had come between suburb and center. But when the horses clattered across a paved and populous avenue to splash into a muddy alley of stone houses with thatched shacks between, she realized it had.

They crossed another street.

Down another alley water flashed between masts.

They turned onto another avenue. Noise and confusion dazzled her. Living on the edge of a mountain town, without ever really considering herself part of them, Pryn had known the gossipings, prejudices, and rigidities of town life that had played through Ellamon's quiet streets. But here, the hustle and hallooing made her wonder: How, here, could anyone *know* anyone?

Twice in one block the Fox's horse danced aside to avoid someone, first a woman who dashed from the crowds at one side of the street, a four-foot basket strapped to her back, to plunge among people on the other side; second, three youngsters chasing after a black ball. Pryn clung to the Fox's twisting back. (The little girl, naked as Pryn's rider and muddy to the knees, grabbed up the black pellet, which had ceased bouncing to roll a ragged course between cobbles. With a barbarian boy in a torn smock tripping behind, the children fled off down another side street.) The horses began to trot once more beside the hurrying men and women; one man hailed a friend across the road; another ran after someone just departed—to tell her one last thing.

When the white-haired woman left the corner, she was deep in conversation with a younger, who wore a red scarf for a sash. A man and a woman servant behind held decorated parasols over them—or tried to. The sunlit edge kept slipping back and forth across the older woman's elaborate coif and silver combs. Now she pushed bracelets and blue sleeves up her arms and turned to another woman in her party with short hair pale as goat's cream. This one—not much more than a girl, really—wore leather straps across bare shoulders; a strap ran down between abrupt, small breasts. She carried several knives at her belt and walked the hot stones barefoot. Pryn saw beyond the scarred shoulder she clung to that another woman servant had despaired of shading this sunken-eyed, cream-haired creature. (Was she yet eighteen? Certainly she was no more than twenty.) She stepped away here, then off there, now looking into a basket of nuts some porter carried by her, now turning to answer the older woman with the combs. A

woman at least forty, the servant frowned at her and finally let the parasol shaft fall back on her own shoulder.

Pryn had assumed Fox, Badger, and Wolf had seen them too—but the horses, grown skittish at the traffic, must have distracted them. And the women's course veered closer than even Pryn had expected—

One of the servants gave a small shriek.

The horses reared.

The white-haired woman turned in startled anger. She stepped back, hands down in blowing blue. The woman with the red scarf at her waist took the older woman's shoulder and gave a wordless shout of her own. Servants scrambled. One dropped a parasol. The woman with the scarf turned from the older to grab it up.

The horses reared again.

Pryn clutched the Fox and clamped her knees to keep astride. Forehooves clattered to the street. The man-servant shouted: "Country ruffians! What's wrong with you! Out of the street, now! Out of the street! Don't you know enough to let a woman of Madame Keyne's standing in this city have the right of way? Rein your horses back! Rein them, I say—!" The Fox's horse started to rear again, but jarred, stopping.

Pryn felt it ankle to jaw. It was as if a dragon in airborne career had suddenly smashed rock. What had happened was that the small, cream-haired woman had grasped the horse's bridle and, with a jerk, brought the beast up short.

The little woman's gray eyes were sudden centers where lines of effort and anger met. The horse jerked against her grip three times, then stilled. "*Stupid*—!" the woman got out between tight teeth. The angry eyes swept up by the Fox to meet Pryn's. The horse quivered between Pryn's legs. Under Pryn's hands, the Fox's scarred shoulder flexed and flexed as he tried to rein his animal from her.

Suddenly the little woman released the bridle and stalked off after the others, who had collected themselves to hurry on, again deep in their conversation. Servants hurried behind them, parasols waving.

The horses moved about one another. Fox, Badger, and Wolf were all cursing: the women, the city, the sun above them, the people around them. Swaying at the Fox's back, Pryn tried to look after the vanishing group. Now and again, across the crowd, she thought she caught sight of the cream-haired woman behind the party, off in some alley with sea at its end.

"Get down!"

Pryn looked back at the dirty headdress, scarred shoulder right, unscarred left.

"Go on, girl!" the Fox demanded; the horse stilled. "We brought you to the city, where you wanted to go. Get down now! Be on your way!"

Confused, Pryn slid her foot back, up, and over, then dropped to the cobbles, with the sore knees and tingling buttocks of a novice rider—dragons notwithstanding. She stepped back from the moving legs, looking up.

The three above her, on their stepping horses, looked down.

The Badger, with his red beard, seemed about to ask something, and Pryn found her own lips halting on a question: What of the Blue Heron and Liberator? Despite her anger, her impressment had at least provided a form for her arrival. Aside from roving hands, she'd believed their high-sounding purpose. But as she ducked back (someone else was shouting for them to move), she realized they were, the three of them, country men, as confused and discommoded by this urban hubbub as she was.

"Are you going to kill her now?" The Badger blurted, looking upset.

"She's no spy!" The Western Wolf leaned forward disgustedly to pat his horse's neck. "She's no different from you, boy—a stupid mountain kid run off from home to the city. I've a mind to turn you both loose and send you on your ways—"

Pryn had a momentary image of herself stuck in this confusion with the young dolt.

But the Fox said, "Come on, the two of you and stop this!" He turned his horse up the street; the two turned after him.

Pryn watched them trot off—to be stopped another half-block on by more people crossing. People closed around Pryn. After she had been bumped three times, cursed twice, and ignored by what must have been fifty passers-by in the space of half a minute, she began to walk.

Everyone else was walking.

To stay still in such a rush was madness.

Pryn walked—for hours. From time to time she sat: once on the steps in a doorway, once on a carved log bench beside a building. The tale-teller's food had been finished the previous night and the package discarded; so far she'd only thought about food (and home!) when she'd passed the back door of a bread shop whose aromatic ovens flooded the alley with the odor of toasted grain.

Walking, turning, walking, she wondered many times if she were on a street she'd walked before. Occasionally she *knew* she was, but at least five times, now, when she'd set out to rediscover a particular place she'd passed minutes or hours back, it became as

impossible to find as if the remembered landmarks had sunk beneath some sea.

Several workmen with dusty rags around their heads had opened up the street to uncover a great clay trough with planking laid across it, which ran out from under a building where half a dozen women were repairing a wall by daubing mud and straw on the stones with wooden paddles. (Now, she *had* passed them before ...) A naked boy dragged along a wooden sledge heaped with laundry. A girl, easily the boy's young sister and not wearing much more than he, now and again stooped behind to catch up a shirt or shift that flopped over the edge, or to push the wet clothes back in a pile when a rut shook them awry.

Pryn found herself behind three women with the light hair of southern barbarians, their long dresses shrugged off their shoulders and bunched down at their waists, each with one hand up to steady a dripping water jar. Two carried them on their heads; one held hers on a shoulder.

They turned in front of her, into a street that sloped down from the avenue, and, as the shadow from the building moved a-slant terra-cotta jugs, thonged-up hair, and sunburned backs, Pryn followed. (No, she had *never* been on this street ...) There were many less people walking these dark cobbles.

"... *vevish nivu hrem'm har memish* ..." Pryn heard one woman say—or something like it.

"... *nivu homyr avra'nos? Cevet aveset* ..." the second quipped. Two of the barbarians laughed.

Pryn had heard the barbarian language before, in the Ellamon market, but knew little of its meaning. Whenever she heard it, she always wondered if she might get one of them to talk slowly enough to write it down, so that she could study it and learn of its barbaric intent.

"... *hav nivu akra mik har'vor remvush* ..." retorted the second to a line Pryn had lost.

All three laughed again.

Two turned down an alley that, Pryn saw as she reached it, was only a shoulder-wide space between red mud walls. With the sun ahead of them, the two swaying silhouettes grew smaller and smaller.

Ahead, the remaining woman took her jar from her shoulder and pushed through the hanging hide that served for a door in a wood-walled building.

Pryn walked down the hill. Here, many cobbles were missing; some substance, dark and hard, with small stones stuck all over it, paved a dozen or so feet. A woman overtook her. Pryn turned to

watch. The woman wore a dirty skirt, elaborately coiffed hair, and dark paint in two wing shapes around her eyes. It was very striking, the more so because Pryn—looking after her narrow back—had only glimpsed her face. Two boys hurried by on the other side, arms around each other's shoulders. One had shaved his head completely. Both, Pryn saw, wore the same dark eye-paint—before they, too, became just backs ahead of her.

Sitting on steps leading up to another street, beggars argued loudly. One was missing an arm and an ear; among them a woman, with a crutch under one shoulder, its splintered end protruding over the stone step's edge, complained about a jar of wine she had stolen from the dried-up earthworm of an innkeeper. It had been bad, but she had drunk it anyway and gotten sick and lain—sick—in the street three days. The stump of her missing leg was crusted with scab.

Pryn hurried by.

On Pryn's right lay a littered yard between three cracked and yellow buildings. In the middle was a circular stone wall, waist high, long boards over its top. It was about three meters across. Pryn walked up to the enclosure and looked down through the strip of black between the weathered planks. Below, a dark head moved to blot a strip of reflected sky.

Again she turned down the street.

Buildings ended; Pryn looked across to an embankment. The bridge entrance had waist-high stone walls either side. A tall woman at the corner newel was fastening a white damasked collar, sewn with metallic threads and set with jewels. It was one of the decorative collar-covers house-slaves in wealthier families sometimes used to hide the ugly iron band all slaves wore by law. Having trouble with the clasp, however, the woman removed the cloth to shake it out. Her long neck was bare. She raised the collar-cover again.

The clasp caught—as halfway over the bridge someone hailed her. Along the bridge's walkway, in colorful robes and veils (many with painted eyes), young women and men stood, leaned, talked, stared, or ambled slowly.

The woman with the collar-cover ran to grab the arm of the heavy, hairy man who'd called. He wore a helmet like the ones Pryn had seen outside the Liberator's headquarters.

Watching them stroll away, Pryn crossed to the bridge. She reached the post where the woman had stood, put her hand on it, and looked over the stone rail.

Green water glimmered around moss-blotched rocks, clotted with wood, fruit rinds, broken pottery. Some barbarian children climbed out by the carved stanchion stones. Behind her she heard:

"Twenty!"

"Five—"

"Nineteen!"

"Five!"

"Eighteen?"

"*Five*, I say!"

"Seventeen!"

"All right, eight!"

Pryn looked up. Coming forward through the loiterers was a portly, middle-aged man in a smart toga with red ribbon woven about the white sleeves, neck, and hem. His hand held the shoulder of a naked, green-eyed, barbarian boy, a year or so younger than Pryn. The boy was arguing in his odd southern accent and gesticulating with one closed fist and one open hand: "You give me sixteen? I go with you and do it for sixteen! All right? You give me sixteen, then!"

"Ten!"

"Sixteen!"

"Ten!"

"Sixteen!"

"Oh, eleven!"

"No, *six*teen!"

"*Six*teen for a dirty little weasel like you?" returned the man with a grin. "For sixteen, I should have you *and* your three brothers. I'll give you twelve!"

"You give me *fifteen!*" the barbarian said. "You want my brother? Maybe we go find him and he come too. But he don't do anything, you know? He just watch. For fifteen I go get my brother and—"

"Now what would I want with two of you!" The man laughed. "One of you is bad enough. I'll take you by yourself, and *maybe* I'll give you twelve . . ."

A black man in a long skirt led a camel up over the bridge. The high humps, rocking gait, and clopping hooves made the loiterers smile. The creature had just soiled herself and suddenly decided to switch her tail—

Pryn herself flinched, though no drop struck.

But the man snatched his hand from the boy's shoulder and rubbed the flat of his palm, now against his gray beard, now against his splattered shoulder, sucking his teeth and shaking his head.

The young barbarian cackled. "Now who's dirty, old turd-nose! You smell like camel pee!" With a disgusted wave he stalked off over the walkway.

The portly gentleman looked up from his scrubbing, saw the boy

leaving, and hurried after. "Thirteen! I'll give you thirteen, but no more!"

Which halted the boy at the stone rail. "Will you give me *four-teen*? You give me fourteen, and I'll ..."

Pryn looked over at the water below. Two women, a soldier between, made their way over the rocks. Just before they went under the bridge, the heftier woman, red wooden beads chained through her brown braids, began to pull away; the soldier kept pulling her back. Pryn tried to hear their altercation, but though their heads were only fifteen feet below, from the angle and the children's shoutings echoing beneath, she could not make it out. She leaned, she listened, wondering what she might do if one of them looked up to see their incomprehensible quarrel observed—

"What—!" came an agitated voice behind her. "You again ..."

Pryn stood and turned, slowly so as not to look particularly interested in what might be going on—

A huge man stood directly behind her, heavily veined arms folded high on his stomach. He wore bronze gauntlets, dark with verdigris and busy with relief. On his chest hung a copper chain.

"I saw her first—not you!" the voice came on—not the giant's. "Get away and leave her, now. She's not to your taste anyway! Don't you think all of us around here have seen you enough to know what *you're* after?"

The giant had a scar down one cheek. Rough hair, some salted white, made a thick, clublike braid over one ear—only, half of it had come half undone. Rough hair shook in the breeze.

Arms still folded, the giant turned his head a little—

"Now go on! Go on, I say! She's no good to you! The young ones *need* my guidance if they're to make a living here." The man talking so excitedly stood a few steps off, shaking a finger at the giant. "Go on, now! Why do you stay? *Go!*"

And Pryn thought: How handsome he is!

The young man's eyes, blinking between blond lashes, looked startlingly blue in his sunburned face. He wore only a loincloth, with the thinnest blade at his chain belt. His arms were brown and lithe. "You don't need her!" he continued his complaint. "I do! Come on, now. Give her to me!" On his extended hand he wore many, many rings, two, three, or more on a finger—even two on his thumb. (The fist by his hip was bare.) Stones and metal flashed in the sun, so that it took Pryn moments to register the hands themselves: the skin was gritty and gray. Below the jeweled freight, his nails, over-long at the ends of long, long fingers, were fouled spikes, as if he'd been down playing like a child in the clotted river's sludge.

Arms still folded, the giant turned his head a little more—

The handsome young man with the beautiful rings and filthy fingers actually jumped. Then he scowled, spat on the flags, turned, and stalked off along the bridge, where a number of loungers and loiterers were still laughing over the camel.

Pryn looked up as the giant turned back to her. In surprise, she swallowed.

Around the giant's tree-trunk of a neck was a hinged iron collar.

Pryn had always regarded slavers with fear. Perhaps that fear had spread to the notion of slaves themselves. She knew great families sometimes had them. She had seen slaves in the Ellamon market and more recently on the road. But she had never talked to one, nor had she ever heard of anyone who had. To be standing in a strange city, facing one directly—and such a big one! It was quite as frightening as if *she* were being appraised by a slaver herself!

"What are you doing here, mountain girl?" the great man asked in a voice that, for all its roughness, bore a city accent.

"Looking ... for someone—" Pryn stammered. It seemed she *must* answer something. "A friend of mine. A woman." Later she would think that it was only after she'd started to speak that the image of the tale-teller's Raven, with her mask and her double blade, leapt into her mind like a protective demon. "But she's not here, and I ..." She looked at the people about the bridge. "I was with some men, before; they were looking for someone called the Liberator ... a man named Gorgik."

The big man leaned his head to the side. "Were they, now?" Shaggy brows drew down.

"They were going to keep me with them at first, because they thought I was a spy. For the Empress. Then they realized how silly that was, and how difficult it would be trying to keep track of me in the city. So they turned me loose." She took a breath. "But now I don't know *where* to go!" The next thought struck the same way the memory of Raven had a moment back. "But I've ridden on a dragon! My name is Pryn—I can write it, too. I read, and I've flown on a dragon's back above the Faltha mountains!"

The giant grinned. A third of one front tooth had broken off, but the rest were whole enough. "You've flown on a dragon above the Falthas, over the narrow-minded, provincial Hold of fabled Ellamon ...?" He unfolded gauntleted arms.

Each callused finger, Pryn saw, was thicker than three of hers bunched together. She nodded, more because of his grin and his recognition of her home than for his judgment of it.

"And did you bring dried mountain cactus fruits to the market and try to sell them there to unwary tourists as eggs of the fabled

beasts themselves, you dragon-riding scamp?" The grin softened to a smile. "You see, I *have* been through your town."

"Oh, no!" Pryn exclaimed. "I'd never do that!" Though she knew of girls and boys who had, she also knew it was precisely these—at least the girls—who ended up imprisoned as grooms in Ellamon's fabled corrals. "If my aunt ever heard I'd done a thing like that, she'd beat me!"

The man laughed. "Come with me, mountain girl."

"What are *you* doing here?" Pryn blurted. Talking had turned out to be easy enough; but the notion of going with the slave frightened her all over again.

The shaggy eyebrows raised. "I, too, was looking for ... a friend."

Pryn found herself staring at the collar. Did slaves, she wondered, *have* friends? Did this slave want to make friends with her?

The man said: "But since I've found you instead, I'll put such friendships off for a while."

"Are you going to take me to your master?" Pryn asked.

The giant looked a little surprised. "No." Then surprise dissolved back into the scarred smile. "No, I wasn't going to do that. I thought we might walk to the other end of the bridge. Then, if there were someplace you wanted to go, I'd take you there. After that, I'll leave."

Pryn looked down at the slave's feet: horny, dirty, cracked at the edge, barred with ligaments under tangled veins, the ankle's hock blocky beneath the bronze greave. Above bronze, calf hair curled over the chased rim. That's not a foot, Pryn thought. That's a ham someone's flung down on the street! She looked at his chest. On the copper chain hung a bronze disk the size of her palm—really it was several disks, bolted one on top of the other, with much cut away from the forward one, so that there were little shapes all over it with holes at their points; and some kind of etching on the disk beneath... Around the rim were markings in some abstract design. She looked at his belly. It was muscular, hairy, with a lot behind it pushing muscle and hair forward. He wore five or six loose belts, a thick one and a thin one of leather, one of braided rope, one of flattened silver links, and one of ordinary chain. They slanted his hips at different angles. From one hung a wide, shaggy sheath; from another, some kind of purse; attached to another was a net of mail that went between his legs (a few links had broken) to pouch the rougher hair and darker genital flesh. She looked again at his face.

He had raised his hand to gnaw a thumbnail.

Pryn thought: Is this how people have looked at him when they

purchased him at some auction ...? Her cheeks and her knees suddenly heated.

The scarred face moved toward some question, but he dropped his hand and smiled. "Come. Let's walk."

And somehow she *was* walking with him along the bridge.

"How long have you been here?" he asked.

"In the city?" She looked up. "Since this morning."

"I thought it couldn't be longer." He chuckled. "Do you know where you are?"

"You mean in Kolhari?"

"Do you know *where* in Kolhari you are?"

Pryn looked at the men and women loafing and leaning on the bridge's low wall. She shook her head.

He pointed with a thick thumb over the side. "That muddy ditch there is the Khora Spur. Three quarters of a mile up, it runs off the Big Khora. Both go down to the sea, to make this neighborhood in front of us into an island in the middle of town. It's also called the Spur—the oldest, poorest section of the city. Right now it's mostly inhabited by barbarians, recently from the south. But it tends to house whoever is poor, new, or down on luck."

"Do you and ... and your master live there?"

The big man considered a moment. "You *might* say I do," which struck Pryn as a complex answer for a simple question. "This street here, running across the bridge, is the upper end of New Pavē. It runs back up into the commercial part of the city, crosses Black Avenue, and finally turns along the sea to become part of the Kolhari waterfront. Here, at this end, it's called Old Pavē. The bridge itself? We call it the Bridge of Lost Desire, though it had another name, officially, thirty years ago, when all of Kolhari was known as Neveryóna; but I don't remember what it was. The Bridge of Lost Desire is the older name. On it, you'll find working most of the city's—"

Ahead, a man shrieked.

Pryn looked at her companion—who hadn't looked at all.

When she looked back, though most people had only moved a step or turned by no more than a small angle, the shriek had created a center:

At it, the handsome young man buried his bare fingers in brown braids to shake the heavy young woman's head—a red wooden bead broke from its chain, fell to the flags, and rolled.

"What do you *mean* ...!" the young man shouted, shaking his jeweled fist about his shoulder. "I don't want to hear that from you! He didn't give you *enough*? No, not from *you*! What do you mean! Tell me! No, I don't want to hear it ...!" As he shook, the woman

seemed intent on keeping her face blank, her arms limp, and her large feet under her.

Suddenly the young man threw her head away, stepping back. "You don't think I'll *do* anything to you? You don't?" He struck his dirty, ringed fist back against his own chest, grinding. "Look—" He shoved his hand on past his shoulder; the beautiful features grimaced—"if I do that to myself—" Points and edges had caught the smooth skin as though it were rough fabric, to tear a two-inch cut, from which blood ran, turning aside at his nipple to dribble down his flank—"what do you think I'll do to *you*? Look—" Suddenly turning, he struck his ringed fist on the arm of the nearest bystander, a boy whose made-up eyes widened as he backed away, blood welling through his fingers where he clutched his arm (someone grabbed the boy and called, "Hey, now! What are you doing, now—! Come on . . . !)—"if I do that to *him*—and I don't even know the little faggot—what do you think I'll do to you!" Working himself up, dancing about, the handsome young man suddenly lunged, ringed hand open and falling toward her face—

The woman flinched.

Then something very complicated happened.

The hand stopped.

One thing making it complicated was that, unlike you and me, Pryn had been watching the woman (who was about Pryn's age and Pryn's size). What had first seemed a kind of apathetic paralysis in her, Pryn saw, was actually an intense concentration— and Pryn remembered a moment when, bridling her dragon, the wings had suddenly flapped among the bushes, and for a moment she'd thought she would completely lose control of it; and all she could do was hang on as hard as possible and look as calm as possible, trying to keep her feet from being jerked off the mossy rocks; for Pryn it had worked . . .

Another thing making it complicated was that Pryn had *not* been watching the man she was with.

And he had not been watching the encounter.

We've spoken of a center the encounter had created. The big man's course took them within a meter of it. He had not stopped walking; and because Pryn had not been watching him, she had not stopped walking either.

As they came within the handsome young man's ken, his hand had halted.

His head jerked about, his face for a moment truly, excitingly ugly. "All right!" he demanded. (Now they did stop.) "What is it, then? You want to be the Liberator of every piece of camel dung on this overground sewer?"

The woman with the beaded hair did not look at Pryn's companion, but suddenly stalked off, arms folded across her breasts in what might have been anger, might have been embarrassment. Five other women, waiting outside the circles within circles, closed about her, one holding her shoulder, one leaping to see over the others' if she were all right—as though they had not seen them either.

The handsome young man took a step after them, then glanced at the giant, as if unsure whether he had permission to follow. Apparently he didn't, for he spat again and, making a bright fist by one hip and a soiled one by the other, turned his bleeding breast away and walked off in the other direction.

People looked away, turned away, walked away; and there were three, half a dozen, a dozen, and then no centers to the crowd. Pryn looked at her companion.

Examining his knuckles, the giant moved his gnawing on to another nail. Once more they began to walk.

As they passed more on-lookers, Pryn demanded, "Who *was* he . . ."

"Nynx . . ." the giant said pensively. "I *think* someone told me that was his name." He put his hand to his belly, scratching the hair there with broad nubs. "He manages—or, better, terrorizes—some of the younger women too frightened to work here by themselves."

"You must have beaten him up in a fight, once!" Pryn declared; she had heard of such encounters between men in her town. "You beat him up, and now he's afraid you might beat him up again . . . ?"

"No." The giant sighed. "I've never touched him. Oh, I suppose if it came to a fight, though he's less than half my age, I'd probably kill him. But I think he's been able to figure that out too." He gave a snort that ended in the scarred, broken-toothed smile. "Myself, I go my way and do what I want. Nynx—if that *is* his name—reads my passings as he will. But from the way he reads them, I suspect I will not *have* to kill him. Someone else will do it for me, and within the year I'll wager. I've seen too many of him." He gave another snort. "Such readings are among the finer things civilized life teaches. You say you can read and write. You'll learn such readings soon enough if you stay around here."

"What did he want with me, before?" Pryn asked.

"Probably the same thing he wanted from the girl. There used to be a prostitutes' guild when I was a youngster—lasted up until a few years ago, in fact. It retained its own physicians, set prices, kept a few strong-armed fellows under employment for instant arbitration. They rented out rooms in half a dozen inns around here at cheap, hourly rates—today they charge double for an afternoon's

41

hour what they charge you to spend the night alone. With all the new young folk in from the country, you see, the old guild has moved out to Neveryóna, and its established members have all become successful hetaeras and courtesans. The new lot struggle for themselves, now, here on the bridge with no protection at all." The giant went on rubbing his stomach. "Beer," he remarked pensively after a moment. "I hear it was invented not more than seventy-five years back by barbarians in the south. Whoever brought its fermentation up to the cities has doomed us to a thousand years of such bellies as mine—" He glanced at Pryn—"and yours!" He laughed.

Pryn looked down at herself. She didn't know the word 'beer' and wondered if it could be responsible, whatever it was, for her plumpness.

As they neared the bridge's end, the giant said: "Here, why don't I show you through the—"

The naked boy who ran around the newel to stop just before them, if he were not the barbarian she'd seen before with the portly man in the toga, could well have been one of his fabled brothers. Green eyes blinked, questioning, at the giant, at Pryn, and back.

The giant said: "Not now, little friend. Perhaps later on—I'll come meet you this evening, if I remember. But not now."

The boy held his stance a moment, then ran off.

"Come," the slave said, before Pryn could question the encounter. "Let me show you around the Spur's most interesting square—the Old Kolhari Market."

For beyond the bridge stretched rows of vending stalls, colorful booths with green and gray awnings, and single- or double-walled thatched-over sheds. Porters pushed between them with baskets of fruit, tools, grain, pots, fabric, fish—some were even filled with smaller baskets. Women wheeled loud barrows over red brick paving. Here and there, brick had worn down till you could see ancient green stone beneath. As they walked into the square—five times the size of the market in Ellamon, at least—the tall slave, whom, till now, Pryn had thought of as friendly but somehow reticent, began to talk, softly, insistently, and with an excitement Pryn found stranger and stranger.

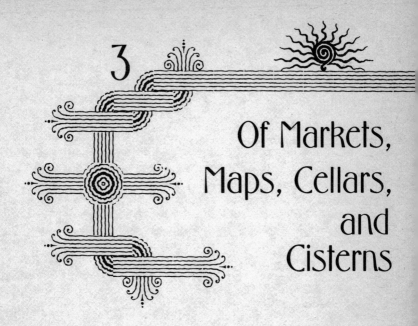

3

Of Markets, Maps, Cellars, and Cisterns

Let us bear in mind, however, that a long oral recital made by
the central figure of a novel to a willing, silent listener is, after
all, a literary device: that the hero should tell his story with
such precision of detail and such discursive logic is possible,
say, in *The Kreutzer Sonata* or *The Immoralist*, but not in real
life. . . . Nevertheless, this literary convention once conceded,
it depends upon the author of such a *récit* to put into it the
whole of a being, with all his qualities and defects as revealed
in his own peculiarities of expression, with his judgments sound
or false, his prejudices unknown to him, his lies, his reticences,
and even his lapses of memory.

—Marguerite Yourcenar/*Coup de Grâce*

"The city fascinates—as all who come to it expect it to. Do certain
country markets necessarily secrete cities about themselves? Must
a nation raise markets, and cities around them?" The giant slowed
as they entered between two rows of stalls. Those left held wooden
rakes and brass-headed mallets. Those right were filled with leafy
green, knobbly yellow, and smooth red vegetables. "The city sits in
the midst of empire, a miniature of all that surrounds it: a map on
which—true—you cannot read distances and directions, but on
which you can mark qualities of material existence as well as the
structure of certain spiritual interactions. People come from the
country to the city with country wares, country skills; you need only
look at who walks in its streets, who lives in its hovels and High
Courts to know what is abroad in the land. I told you, over there live
the barbarians most recently up from the south? A bit west, above
the Khora, is a neighborhood of northern valley folk who still wear
pastel robes, loose hoods pulled up about the old women's faces
and thrown back from the corn-rowed heads of the men, their
hems stained to the knees with brackish street-muds that would
never soil them in their own green-walled land. Two streets below is
an enclave of desert families, the men with copper wires sewn
about their ears, the women with tell-tale dots of purple dabbed on

their chins. If you walk the unpaved alleys between, you will see desert boys, in moody clusters stalking close to the mud walls, suddenly spot a lone valley dweller in pale, ragged orange crossing at the corner; and you will hear the desert youths call the same taunts that, as grown warriors in the land of their parents, they would cry from their camels as they rode to meet the long-robed invaders.

"But look!

"The Old Market here is only a particularly recomplicated inscription of the nation around it. The woman there, out in the sun, turning her dripping pig on its spit above that pan of coals, where folks gather to buy her good slice on a piece of bread for a coin—her mothers cooked such pigs for holy festivals in a province ninety stades to the west, where, in the proper week of spring, you can still ride by to the smell of hot crackling. Across the crowd from her, you see that bearded man forking baked yams into the trays strapped to the necks of the waiting boys? Those boys will run with them back across the bridge and up through the cobbled streets, by shops and inns and merchants' offices, selling them for iron coins—just as boys sell them from door to door in the province of Varhesh, where the bearded man hails from. And the yellowing chunks of sugar beet those children coming toward us are munching? The youngsters buy them from a vendor just down the way, who cuts them with a curved copper knife. Once a month, he makes the journey to his home province in Strethi, where he loads his cart full. The knife he uses here in the market is the same sort as the women of the Avila plains use at the beets' harvesting. What is sold him there, what makes its way here, is part of the harvest that does not go into the great stills of that region in which are fermented its various poisonous rums—which, indeed, one can buy only three stalls away out of the sealed clay jars that stand under the dark red awning. But all those foods so quickly obtained here, those foods one can munch or sip as one wanders from stall to stall, looking for staple purchase, are signs of the great distilleries, piggeries, religious festivals, and diligently hoed fields about the nation, the ease of consumption here murmuring of the vast labors occurring a province, or three provinces, or ten provinces away.

"But see that woman, with the dark rags around her head: on the rug before her are ranged some three-legged cooking pots—she's from a good family, though she's fallen on hard times. Many of her pots are chipped. Most of them are second-hand. Such domestic tools tell much of the organization of our nation's industry, if not its economy.

"Glance at the stand beside hers. When I passed this morning, a man was observing those sharpened sticks which the women in the most uncivil parts of our nation use to break up the soil in their turnip fields—and which the wealthy matrons in the suburbs of Sallese and Neveryóna use in their gardens when a passion for a single bloom compels them to tend a foot of soil with their own hands, draping protective gauzes over it against marauding insects, wrapping the stem in wet fabric, mixing chopped meat and grain with the broken earth, and chanting certain spells to encourage one rare pink and gold orchid to bloom—while acres are left to the gardener. Do you see: the same man is back, trying to sell the vendor his bundle of raking sticks, each of which has a head carved into *three* prongs. From what we can see of the interchange, it looks as if the vendor will actually take them.

"But come around here, and see the stall that sits just behind them. What a great stack of four-legged cooking pots! Even as we stand here, the barbarian women passing by have bought two; now three more—now another man is running up; and the helper has just sold another at the stall's far side.

"These challenges of commerce sign the endlessly extended and attenuated conflict of local custom against local custom, national tool against national tool, that progression of making about the land so slow only the oldest can see it, and then usually only to lament the passing of the good old days, the good old ways, the way things used to be, and be done.

"Three-legged pots? Four-legged pots? Single-pronged yam sticks? Three-pronged yam sticks? We observe here stages in a battle that, in one case, may have been going on for decades and, in another, may only be beginning. Only after another decade or three or seven will wanderers in this market, ignorant of its beginnings, be able to see its outcome. But come down this way.

"That's right, along here. Next to the domestic and agricultural tools, this is my favorite stall. Do you see what's spread out over this counter before us? This pair of calipers here is locked to a single measure and thus cannot really measure anything. Observe these mirrors, thonged at the four corners so they may be tied to various parts of the body. Those little disks of wood, you'll see if you pick them up, mimic coins, though no weight or denomination is marked on center or exergue. Unfurl that parchment there; that's right—the surprise on your face is a double sign, reminding me that you know how to read and at the same time announcing that you cannot read what is inked on that skin. (Yes, put it back, before the old man with the tattooed cheeks sees us—he is one of the touchiest vendors in the market.) The northern sage who went to the cave of Yobikon and sat with his ink block, brush, and vellum in

the fumes issuing from the crevices in the cave floor to take the dictation of the goddess of the earth could not read those marks either, be assured. Still, he bears the honor of having been amanuensis to deity. These scripts are its trace. Those wooden carvings, with thongs on them like the mirrors, are tied about the bellies of male children in the tribes of the inner mountains of the outer Ulvayns. They assure prowess, courage, and insight in all dealings with goats and wild turtles. These metal bars? From the markings on them, clearly they are some sort of rule. But like the calipers, the graduations on them are irregular and do not come all the way down to the edge, so that it would be hard, if not impossible, to measure anything with them. But you have guessed by now, if you do not already know such trinkets from your own town market: each of these is magic. The one-eyed woman, the tattooed man's assistant, back in the corner pretending to sort those bunches of herbs but really watching us, will, if she takes a liking to you, explain in detail the magical tasks each one of these tools is to perform. You would be astonished at the complexities such tasks can encompass or the skill needed to accomplish them—tasks and skills at least as complex as any of the material ones employing the tools we have already seen a single aisle away. But can you follow how such tools map and mirror the material tasks and skills we have left behind? How many of these are concerned with measurement! (Doubtless the scroll is an inventory of spiritual artifacts and astral essences.) Each is the sign of the thirst and thrust to know; each attempts to describe knowledge in a different form, each form characteristic of some place in the national mind: once again, this map does not indicate origins, only existences. But the one-eyed woman has signaled to the tattooed man, who is coming over. We'd best pass on. From fear of contagion, if not true sympathy for the heightened consciousness these tools presuppose and require, he is perhaps the most insistent among these vendors that whoever handles his wares should purchase.

"But you have noticed those barrels there. Have such casks come as far north as Ellamon? They contain the southern beer that so puzzled you a moment back, though in Kolhari it has become the passion of nearly every free laborer. The thirsts it satisfies, you might well mark, not only mirror but mock those spiritual thirsts we've been talking of. Certainly the children lugging up their double-handled beer pots, ready to carry them here and there for a working aunt, or father, or uncle, or the houseboys and market maids there with their waxed leather bags, the insides still moist with yesterday's draught, attest to the materiality of such thirsts, however much our poets try to spiritualize them. Note that young

woman, with her pitcher, hesitating behind the crowd lined up at the syphon.

"I shall talk more of *her* in a moment.

"But have you marked the smaller barrels further down, attended by that wizened little woman with country labor stamped all over the flesh of her hands and in the muscles that band her wrinkled cheeks? Notice how she holds her bristly chin high, which means her neck once wore the iron collar—wore it many years. The casks she oversees contain a delicate cider from the family estate, high in the northern hills, of the late Baron Inige. Its taste pleased his family and his family's guests for generations; and in his own lifetime, thanks to his interest in horticulture, that taste reached a piquancy unsurpassed in the nation—at least that's the claim of those who can afford to pursue such investigations. One or two of our more prosperous waterfront taverns managed to import it only a handful of years ago, making the journey up to the hills and bringing it back in their own carts. In the last year, the estate itself, fallen on hard times since the baron's death, has let that freed retainer there bring in a few barrels from time to time to sell in the market here.

"But I was speaking of the young woman who hesitates with her pitcher between the two. For, though I have never been inside her home, simply from passing her in the market, seeing her on the street with her mother, watching her run across Black Avenue to greet her father, I have learned a great deal about her—and her situation. Her father is a workman, who loves his beer with the best, but who, some years back, had the notion and the money to hire several of his fellows, specializing in the laying of underground clay pipes; his skill and the skill of the artisans he employs has improved his condition in every way. The girl's mother was once a washer woman who laundered fine fabrics for the families of Sallese; but when she and her husband built their new home in the prospering tradespeople's district on the west side of the city, a sense of decorum made her sacrifice her laundering to the very real duties of her newer, larger home. The girl's brother, as a boy, was apprenticed to a successful pot spinner down in Potters' Lane to replace an erring youth who disappeared from the same position into the barbaric south with money and franchise orders some years back. The girl is terribly proud of her younger brother, for you know that the very gods of our country are represented as patient, meticulous craftsfolk, who labor at the construction of the world and who may never be named till it is completed.

"The girl plays beautifully on several of the stringed instruments they carve so well in the east. When she was a baby, a wise woman, begging from door to door in the city, saw the child, cast bones

and wooden coins on the pavement, and read in the array of a great and profitable musical talent asleep in the infant's fingers. The parents accordingly set the child to study with one of the eastern music masters who had recently located here, as soon as she was old enough. The prophecy seems to be fulfilling itself, and her talent has awakened. Already she has composed several sacred litanies, and several times, now, her mother, presuming upon that old acquaintance with the mistresses for whom she once did washing, has taken the girl to wealthy homes in the suburbs to play. Several times, now, the girl has been requested to entertain at gatherings of the lords in Neveryóna, for which she and her family have been handsomely compensated. Only last week, in fact, she was playing some of her compositions for the discerning and glamorous lunching about a flowered and be-statued pool, when an elderly baronine, moved deeply by the young woman's song, suggested, so rumor has it, that if the artist would compose something in praise of the Child Empress, an audience might be arranged at the High Court itself. Yes, that is the very girl we are observing now, her pitcher on her thumb, hesitating between sophisticated cider and common beer.

"Certainly, by now, you have your own notions about which direction she will finally turn. Will contagion or sympathy govern her choice? How many of the factors I have outlined will go into the final overbalancing we call decision? All, I suspect—if only because she *is* a particularly sensitive person. (Some say her voice and her fingers were fashioned by our gods for some celestial craft-fair competition!) In her own songs she has praised both the delicacy of the one drink *and* the heartiness of the other.

"Come, let's leave her to choose, appreciative of the complexities that play now so silently on her spirit. Only be certain that whichever way she turns, it will be to assuage thirsts far more intricate than those the tongue alone can know. Now take your place in line with me, to drink the water from this gushing, public stone. The underground stream that feeds the fountain here, before brick and pavement encircled it, closed over its tributary, and civilized it, is what first made this a trading spot back when all around was merely a brambly field, with the wide, rocky brook of the Khora running by it to the sea. But remember, as you touch your lips to the water breaking and flashing on your palm, your own movement here will sign, as much as anyone else's in the market—to the proper reader—aspirations, ideals, and nostalgias that pervade an empire.

"Have you drunk your fill?

"Good.

 50

"Let's wander on.

"Do you see those yellow and blue birds twittering in their reed cages—loosely woven baskets is what they really are. The mottled objects piled on the counter across from them are the eggs of the same caged creatures, collected in the wild and pickled in vinegar till their shells soften and their insides congeal as though steeped in boiling water. Right above and to the left, on the shelves at the stall's back, are still the same birds, this time carved in wood or molded of clay, but painted far more gaudily than the colors their live models ever wear, even when they flash in the sun-dapplings between frond and vine in the southern jungle. Note that short, grave man with the shaved head who stops to make a purchase, now at one counter, now at the next. The white collar-cover he wears hides the same iron I carry on my neck. Owned by a wealthy family visiting the city, he is making purchases his master and mistress decided on during a trip here yesterday afternoon. That someone could want all three—live bird, pickled egg, and carved bird—seems to sign a voraciousness in our attitude toward that odd construct of civilization, nature, a voraciousness abroad wherever the conceiving engine that builds villages, towns, and cities is at work, almost as if the central process of civilization itself were to take a 'natural' object and possess its every aspect: the thing itself, its material productions, its very image.

"Look down that aisle, and you will see a fragment of the same process without the mediation of middleman and purchase order.

"Those good folk are running with their baskets and bags toward that vendor wheeling his barrow up from the waterfront. A mountain dweller, you have probably never heard of the fare he vends, for until a month ago no one would have considered it fare—except perhaps some of the more primitive shore tribes along those bournes where civilization has not yet inserted its illusory separation of humans from the world which holds them. Till then, what this man now sells at exorbitant prices was part of the slough and garbage that tangled a fisherman's net: lobster, crab, oyster, shrimp ... About a month back, down where the waterfront gives way to the beach, some of our city's more fashionable young folk were taking an evening stroll, when they saw a madman on the shore devouring the soft, inner flesh of these repulsive, armored sea beasts. Nearly all of the company were properly appalled; but one, however, thought she caught a glint of some mysterious and unnameable pleasure in that madman's eye. Later, with a hammer and a wooden blade, she contrived to get hold of one of these creatures for herself and taste of its protected innards. Now it has been known for years among primitive fishers that a clam eaten at

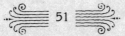
51

the wrong time of year can kill; or, indeed, that these beasts fall into noxious decay even faster than fish in general. Yet such is civilization's appetitive passion that it cannot allow the madman lone access to his skewed, mystical, minuscule pleasure, rare enough in the circling contradictions of his unreason. I say this incident took place a month ago; but really—it has hardly been a full three weeks.

"Look at them!

"Have you seen a more animated and enthusiastic group about any vendor here? Already woodcarvers and metalworkers have begun to fashion special mallets, picks, pliers, and prongs to assist in extracting the delicate, sweet flesh. No doubt the jeweler will shortly cast the same implements in gold, set about with agates and tourmalines—for these new flavors will reach the imperial palate before the songs of our young musician reach the imperial ear, despite the baronine's entreaty. News of these flavors, these pleasures will penetrate the walls of the palace; news of this fashion in food will work its way throughout the land. And I tell you this: if one could map the progress of this news—fascinating, outrageous, appalling, marvelous—moving north, south, east, west of us, one would have a guide to the most trustworthy communications net-work we possess, putting to shame the Empress's highways and winded couriers, jogging along with messages from merchant, bandit, politician, and pleasure-seeking prattler alike in their hide sacks.

"But I see you staring down that aisle there, at the end of which the people gather. Above them, the old woman in the young boy's mask is helping to set up the platform for the performance. Those mummers cast another sort of reflection of our country; as you can see, it's one that many are anxious to watch. The actor there in the mask of a girl, with bits of glass in his hair, supposed to be diamonds, and the white dress down to the ground, no doubt represents our beloved Child Empress Ynelgo, whose reign is personable and practical. It is an image our nation holds of her from her ascension—back, indeed, when I was about your age now. The other one there, in the mask of a man with a scar down his cheek and who wears a wooden version of the iron collar, would seem to be the Liberator, Gorgik, of whom you spoke. So, we are to have a political satire. The populace will see an amusing distortion of its own preconceptions of these figures; as the audi-ence recognizes the skewly familiar, it will laugh. Had the Liberator or the Empress the patience, no doubt each might learn some-thing of the way he or she is publicly perceived. But *I* certainly do not. And the Empress is not the sort to come wandering, veiled and obscured by time and inaccessibility, into the publicity of her realm. But from the props and painted pieces coming out of the wagon, I suspect the scene is to be Kolhari. The young actor there, dressed as an old woman vendor? The little girl playing a potato-selling boy? I wouldn't be surprised if they had chosen to lay their fictional encounter here in the Old Market itself, just where we have been walking. Come away, girl. The truth is that both our Empress's conservative supporters and our Liberator's radical adherents will soon lose patience with the liberal distortions the mummers will impose upon the real that, finally, both agonists share. Which side, given its head, would shut them down the faster is as moot as the decision between cider and beer. Both parties I know would rather opt for a more realistic portrayal of, say, a simple encounter, in a market place such as this, between a real young girl who might, indeed, have really dreamed of being a queen and a real slave who might well have had some real thoughts on the desirability of freedom: what these two saw, what they said, their points of human contact, their inevitable moments of distrust and hostility—that, certainly, is the performance the radicals would applaud. Of course an equally realistic encounter, say, between an aging woman who must bear not only the idiotic title Child but also the real weight and responsibilities of state with, say, a real slave who, indeed, had really dreamed of becoming a political leader and a savior of his class, an encounter in which we might observe the real ignorances of such a slave and the queen's real sympathy and wisdom about the very real political matters the slave would correct by overweening will and inefficient magic—that is the performance the conservatives would applaud. Either would be preferable to the shenanigans shortly to be abroad. But as we make our demands in the name of that meeting point between ethics and art, we overlook that both radical and conservative versions are no less concoctions than the concoction we would have them replace: one has a real queen and an unreal liberator, the other has a real slave and an unreal queen. And it is the notions of reality and unreality themselves which finally become suspect when either one is mirrored in art, much less when both are mirrored together. The liberal audience, claiming to be equally tolerant, or intolerant, of both sides (and one suspects, alas, they really comprehend neither), no doubt reads, as we have been reading, for the final sign of the mummers' value: they may be equally offensive to *both* sides. And it is only some perception of that reading—and not the fact or referent of the performance which is read—that allows the agonists to suffer their antics. I can only *Humph* and walk off in silence, because I am the man I am ... a slave to all the forces whose flow and form we have been

trying here to mark. You are a free woman, which, from my position, means you are probably ignorant of what forces compel you.

"I would not be one of them.

"Stay here, if you like, chained by their lies and illusions no less magical than the coins and calipers on the counter behind. But, I see, you *are* following me ... Is it inertia, fear, or merely politeness that makes you abandon their enthralling spectacle of variety and unity, singly expressed by the best intentioned misdirection, for my monotone drone, picking at awkward distinctions?

"Myself, I *can* find the toys for sale at this counter amusing, at least for a while. Those clay dolls for young boys and girls; these rubber balls for older children; the gaming boards for young men and women—like material tools, each seems to proclaim its intelligible task: how to erase boredom, in some useful way, from the leisure civilization imposes. The answers these toys suggest at first seem innocent enough: 'We shall initiate amusing rehearsals of future tasks without the goad of responsibility,' they declare. 'We shall exercise the body, while it is free of the paralyzing knowledge of real dangers that hang on the outcome of necessary action. We shall stimulate the mind without the mind-numbing political constraints a truly meaningful decision imposes.' Considered not in terms of their ends but of their origins, however, they become more ominous.

"The doll? Who decided that the young should rehearse the physical care of infants, so that they know them as objects to be bounced, cuddled, or abandoned when boring before they know their own, real infants as living beings full of the responsiveness anterior to language that is the basis of all expressed reason?

"The ball? Who decided that youths should develop speed, agility, and rhythm before they have become comfortable with the physical realities of endurance, perseverance, and steadfastness that alone can make any play, political or artistic, yield true satisfaction?

"The game board? Who decided that the women and men of our nation must stimulate the faculties of strategy and count before they have learned to note, analyze, and synthesize—the knowledge that alone can direct such skill toward responsible employment?

"And here we have become entrapped in our own gaming, faced with the unpredicated and unpredicted consequences of our lightest notion. Such oppressive threats are precisely what we fall to the moment we try to free ourselves from the oppressions of the game of art. But where have we wandered to?

"I do not recognize these aisles and counters. Do they sell the

newest wares that I have not the experience to read? Do they sell the oldest, whose secrets I have never before been able to penetrate? Lost in unfamiliar lands, we are merely creatures uninformed, foundering, asking, and finding. Lost in the map of those lands that is the city among them and the market within it, we become one with the map, cartographer and cartograph, reader and read; the separating line can only be scribed with a magic rule and measured with magic calipers, its position and direction only obtainable with an astrolabe set to unknown constellations in an imaginary sky, the distinction in the value of the respective sides calculable only in unmarked coins—a division which vanishes as we stare at it, which, as it vanishes, erases with it all freedom, all power and possibility of choice.

"Thus lost, the only image we are left is that of ourselves as one of those great, nameless craftsfolk, intently playing at a game equally nameless, whose end is the creation of precisely that reality—and unreality—so obviously bogus when it is politically decreed or imaginatively modeled: that image, I fear, is the final concoction, worshiped as freedom, by the totally enslaved. But—be thankful, girl!—we have reached the market's edge and are almost loose from this insidious commercial pollution!"

Pryn had listened to much of this, but from time to time she had let her mind, if not her feet, wander down alleys entirely different from the ones down which her companion would have led her. She forced open the ripe fig a woman a stall behind had handed her and bit the sweet purple, flecked with white seeds, turning her own thoughts, which had gone their own ways as she had strolled between awning and awning.

Occasionally the huge slave's monologue had seemed to coincide with the real market they walked through; more times than not, however, it seemed to exist on quite another level. One man with a green-painted tray, for example, had grinned at Pryn and handed her a succulent peach, which Pryn had eaten to its red, runnelled pit—then thrown that pit down onto the brick. It had all occurred without a mention from the giant extemporizing beside her. Another example? The musician whom the slave had *described* was certainly as sweet and attractive and docile a creature as might have existed. The young woman Pryn had actually *seen*, however, hesitating between the beer barrel and cider keg, was rather shabbily dressed in what may once have been an elegant bit of fabric; now it was quite frayed and stained and bunched about her, every which way. Her hair was wild, her hips were wide, her shoulders narrow, and she blinked and turned, from booth to booth, one finger hooked through her jug handle, swinging it as if to some clanging inner rhythm. The moment the slave had turned toward the fountain, Pryn had seen the young woman suddenly fling the jar down—so that red clay shattered on red brick! Then she'd stalked off between the stalls. Four or five times more Pryn saw her, now at the end of this aisle, now crossing another, arms folded, staring ahead, making her headlong way around this stall or that. Was she thinking of some great musical composition, Pryn had wondered; or perhaps she was contemplating her own explanation for the array of tools and produce about them. Once, coming around a stand of flowers, the musician actually brushed against the slave (it was between mummers and toys); she stepped back, unfolded her arms, and blinked up at him with baffled but distinctly approving surprise that clearly held recognition. Then she folded her arms once more and marched off. But as she had already had her place in the narration, none of this registered on the low voice winding on and on among the vendors and porters. Seconds later another vendor had suddenly held out two blood-black plums. Pryn had taken one and sunk her teeth in it, nodding her gratitude. The giant, however, had not even noticed—nor had he halted his per-oration. The vendor, smiling and shaking his head, had put the other plum back. This slave and I? thought Pryn. It is as if we are walking through different markets, in different cities. But the fig, offered her by a woman behind a counter piled high with them, had brought Pryn's thinking to its turn. Vendors were not handing free fruit to everyone among these stalls and aisles, she realized.

It is something about me?

But the only thing about me, she went on to herself logically, is that I'm walking with him. Could it be that she was walking through his city, his market, in some way she did not yet know?

The giant, who had been quiet a while, spoke again: "You said your companions were looking for Gorgik the Liberator?" For the first time since they had left the bridge, he looked at Pryn directly. "Would you like me to take you to him?" He smiled for the first time since they had left the Bridge of Lost Desire.

"Is the Liberator your master?" Pryn asked.

Again his scarred face became grave. "You ask very simple questions that are almost impossible to answer."

Pryn started to speak, but a notion overtook her that no doubt overtook you several pages ago—indeed, if it took Pryn longer to realize than it took you, it was not because Pryn was the stupider; it was simply because for her this was life, not a tale; and it was all a very long time ago, so that the many tales that have nudged you to such a reading had not yet been written.

"Come," the giant repeated. He started to leave the market by a narrow street.

"Shouldn't we go back across the bridge and up into the city?" Pryn asked. "The men who brought me into town stopped at a great house out in the suburbs, where the Liberator stays—"

The man half snorted, half laughed. "If you want the Liberator, come with me!"

Tossing away the fig stem, Pryn hurried up to reach the giant's side. "He . . . isn't *in* the house in the suburbs?"

The giant looked at her, considering. "It's a trick I learned when I worked as a messenger for a great southern ruler, the Dragon Lord Aldamir. Many people are curious as to the whereabouts of the Liberator. I make sure there are endless loud voices answering that curiosity. There have been no open conflicts as of yet directly traceable to the High Court—but there *have* been spies." He narrowed his eyes. "It's a good idea, when people are curious, to give them something to sustain that curiosity—and direct it."

"You're not really a slave," and it was much easier to say than Pryn had thought it would be, "are you?"

"I've sworn that while a man or woman wears the iron collar in Nevèrÿon, I shall not take the one I wear from my neck."

They turned a corner.

"The opposition says that the only reason I exist is because the reign of the Child Empress is itself lenient and liberating," he went on. "But though the slave population in urban centers has always been low—and is getting lower—there are still road-, mine-, and agricultural slaves by the gangload, as well as a whole host of house workers and estate slaves, owned largely by hereditary royalty. Do you see that old tavern building three streets down?" He stopped to point. "In the basement of that inn are the real headquarters of Gorgik the Liberator."

When Pryn glanced up, the giant again wore his scarred smile. "But, like all things concerning the Liberator, one approaches it by a somewhat devious route. Come along here."

The alley he led her down certainly didn't go toward the indicated inn but in a completely oblique direction. The sense of adventure that had dissolved into a kind of quivering anomie when the riders had left her on the street was now rewritten across the field of its own dissolution without really reforming it. She felt excitement; she also felt discomfort. Earlier, she definitely *hadn't* wanted an adventure—but would have accepted it. Now, dragons notwithstanding, she was unsure if she wanted an adventure at all and was equally unsure what accepting one might mean.

"This way, girl."

Off the alley was another yard. In it stood another cistern. The stone wall came up to Pryn's waist. The man walked to it, grabbed

one of the split birch logs lying across it, and swung it back. Frayed bits of rope were tied to it, as though a canvas had once been lashed there.

The man picked up a bit of white mortar from the wall's top and tossed it in.

Moments later, its clatter on the rock floor echoed up. "You see?" He grinned. "No water." Turning to sit his naked buttock on the wall, he swung one leg over, then the other. "Follow me down." He grasped some handhold within, moved to stand on it, and dropped, by stages. His head vanished; his hand disappeared from the ledge.

Had Pryn read, or even heard of, those tales we have mentioned, she would doubtless have used this opportunity to flee—as indeed I would advise any of my readers to do who might find themselves in a similar situation. But this *was* a long time ago. She could not have heard such stories. More to the point, the great slave who was not a slave could not have heard them either. And bridling, positioning, and urging her dragon from its ledge had been unpleasant, angering, and frustrating.

Feeling unpleasant, angry, and frustrated, Pryn climbed over the wall at the same spot as the man, to find, inside, immense, rusty staples set in the inner stone, making a kind of ladder. As she climbed down by lichen-flecked rock, as shadow slid up over her eyes like water, Pryn wondered briefly, as well might you, what if this man were not who he implied he was, but rather some strange and distressing creature who would hack her to pieces once she set foot on the bottom. (Though most of those tales had not been told, a few, of course, had.) She stumbled—the last rung was missing—to be grasped at her shoulder by his great hand. "Watch yourself. This way."

If the water was gone from the cistern, the bottom was still pitted and puddled. In sunlit bands falling between the overhead logs, she saw half a dozen broken pots on the wet flooring, a few pieces of wood, some bricks, and a number of small, round things too smooth to be stones. At one place the wall had fallen away to form a . . . cave?

"In here." He had to bend nearly double to enter it—head and knees first, huge hand lingering in a slant of sunlight on the stone jamb, an elbow jutting in shadow. Then elbow and buttocks were gone; then the hand. Pryn followed them into the dark, feeling the moist walls beside her with her palms, vaguely able to see him ahead; feeling along beside herself; then unable to see at all. (Well, she thought, if he *does* turn around and try to cut me to pieces, I'll be able to get out faster than he will.) She could hear her own

breath; she could hear his breath too; a pebble clicked against a pebble on the ground. After a long while she heard him stumble, grunt, and call back: "Step down."

Five steps later, Pryn stumbled. And stepped down. She moved her toes to the next ledge, and down, still going along the wall with her fingers. Exactly when she noticed the orange flicker on the damp wall, she wasn't sure. But soon she was walking on level dirt and blinking a lot—and she *could* make out his dark shape, walking upright.

Here the ceiling was very high between the close-set stones. At first Pryn thought the great pile of darkness before them was dirt; but when she stepped around it, it turned out to be sacks with rope-lashed corners. The wall to the left had, by now, fallen back.

The man paused below a torch burning in a niche high in the rock. Pryn came up beside him. The flickering banked at his scar, pulsing and falling and threatening to overspill onto his cheek. He smiled at her—turning his face, with its broken tooth, into a mask a mummer might wreak terror with. There was a flat glow on his shoulder. Despite the demon look, Pryn breathed easier for the first time since they'd entered the alley.

He started ahead through a vaulted arch into a room with half a dozen torches about, shadowing and brightening the dirty mosaic floor. As she followed him in, a man and a woman carrying a split-log bench between them came in by another wide entrance, glanced at them (the woman smiled), set the bench on a pile of benches by the wall, and nodded to Pryn's companion. The smile and the nod, if not simply the couple's presence, somehow abolished the momentary demonic image and moved friendship from a possibility to be gambled on to a probable fact. Then they went.

Pryn followed the giant into the next room with even more torches on the walls—these in iron cages. Perhaps twenty-five men were there; and half a dozen women. Some who had been sitting on benches now stood. All looked. Most standing stepped back. One man called: "So, our Liberator has returned from his survey of the city! How did you find it, Gorgik?"

The big man did not answer, but only raised a hand, smiling.

One woman turned to another near her and said something like: "... *vabemesh har'norko nivu shar* ..."

Gorgik's response was an outright laugh. "Ah—! Which reminds me," he called to her. "I've been meaning to ask you something for a while now—"

Another man interrupted: "The others are waiting for you, down in the receiving hall, Gorgik."

"Yes, of course." Gorgik nodded and walked.

As the others moved after him, Pryn wondered if she should fall back among them; but one man stood aside to let her go forward just as, a few feet ahead, Gorgik looked at her and beckoned her to him.

She hurried up. This time his hand fell on her shoulder, reminding her for all the world of the portly gentleman in the toga and the naked barbarian boy she'd seen on the bridge—quite ludicrously, though she could not have written why unless she invented new signs.

This archway was hung with heavy drapes. A man before them pushed the hangings aside, and she and Gorgik went through, to start down wide steps.

Pryn blinked.

So many more flares and torches along the walls of this hall, yet it seemed so much darker—it was dozens of times as big! Distantly she heard free water. Because she associated the sound with outside vastness, this inside seemed even larger.

At the hall's center, a metal brazier, wider across than Gorgik was tall, flickered over its coals with low flame. As they descended, Pryn looked up to see half a dozen balconies at different heights about the walls. One corner of the hall looked as if it were still being dug out. Earth and large stones were still heaped there. On another wall she saw a carved dragon, three times a man's height—though from the rubble piled low against it, it, too, had only recently been dug free. Overhead, large beams jutted beneath the ceiling, from which, here and there, hung tangles of rope.

As they came down the steps, someone called: "The Liberator!"

A roar rose from the fifty, seventy-five, possibly hundred fifty people about the hall. (Pryn, unused to crowds, had little experience by which to judge such numbers.) It quieted, but did not die. The whispers and comments of so many, echoing under the high roof, joined with the sound of falling waters.

Pryn looked aside as she reached the bottom step.

Water poured between squat columns beside one of the balconies, the falls spewing fog that wet the rock behind it, to rush, foaming and glimmering, along a two-meter-wide ditch. The conduit ran between carved balustrades; after going beneath one bridge of stone and one of wood that looked as if it had been recently built between the remains of a stone one which had fallen in, it ran off through an arched culvert in the dragon-carved wall.

Some of the floor was tiled, but most was dirt, scattered with loose stones. As they walked, Gorgik bent to whisper, "Yes, that stream is part of the system that feeds the public fountain ..."

"Oh," Pryn said, "yes," as if she had been pondering precisely

the question he had answered. Was that the way one began to think like a Liberator? she wondered. It's as though *all* of Nevèrÿon makes sense to him! At least all of this city.

They crossed the wooden bridge and passed near enough to the brazier to feel heat from its beaten, black walls. Ahead were more steps, five or six. They led up to a large seat, half covered with skins. A stone wing rose at one side from under a tiger's pelt. From the other, a sculpted bird's head, beak wide in a silent screech, stuck from black fur.

The others halted. Hand still on Pryn's shoulder, Gorgik went to the steps. At the first one, he bent again. "Sit at the foot here."

The third step from the bottom was covered with white hide. Pryn turned and sat on it, running her hand over it. She felt grit. White cow? Horse? (Who, she wondered, had charge of cleaning them?) She put her heels on the edge of the step below, while Gorgik mounted to the seat.

Pryn looked out at the people waiting about the hall. She looked up at Gorgik—his horny toes with their cracked edges and thickened nails pressed the black and white hair of a zebra skin four steps up and level with her nose.

"My friends—!" The Liberator's voice echoed under high vaults. (Pryn glanced at the ceiling and thought of the tavern above. Had it been anywhere near the size of this subterranean vastness?) "It's good to see so many familiar faces—and good to see so many new ones!" The foot moved a little. Firelight shifted on tarnished bronze: Gorgik sat on the hide covering the seat. (Was it as dusty as the one under her own heel?) "Still, it reassures me that our number is small enough that I can address you informally, that I can gather you together so that my voice reaches all of you at once, that I can walk among you and recognize which of you has been with us awhile and which of you is new. Soon, our growing numbers may abolish that informality."

Pryn again looked over the faces that had, at least a moment back, seemed numberless.

She started!

Beyond those standing nearest, she saw, in his ragged headdress, the scarred Fox turn to whisper to the bearded Badger, while just behind him the squat, Western Wolf frowned—at her!

"That so many of my friends *are* here in the city warms me. That so many of you have come here to the city to offer me your support speaks to me of the unrest throughout Nevèrÿon because of the injustices marring our nation. The difference between the number of you here yesterday and the number of you here today tells me of the growing power that informs our cause. Yesterday, I

left you with a question: Would I be able to get a hearing at the High Court to present my case? Today, I bring you a gratifying answer: Yes." A murmur rose over the water's rush, then fell. "I received the news earlier this afternoon—and went to walk in the city, while it rang in my head, while it afflicted my eyes, till the city itself seemed wondrous and new, and the market, where I so frequently go to hear the harmonies of labor and commerce, seemed a new market, ringing with new music, a market in which I had never walked before." Again Pryn turned to look up. Mostly what she could see was a large knee obscuring the face and a rough elbow that moved behind its gesturing hand. "The High Court has agreed to give me an audience with one of its most powerful ministers, Lord Krodar!"

Amidst the approbations, one woman called, "Why won't they let you speak to the Child Empress herself?"

"—whose reign is monstrous and monotonous!" called a man.

Coming from a place where such things just weren't said, Pryn was as startled as she had been by the sight of the Fox and the Wolf. But others laughed. Hearing that laughter, she decided she liked the feeling of freedom it gave—and remembered flying.

"My plans are prudent and practical," Gorgik countered, which brought more laughter with it, "monstrosity notwithstanding. I am satisfied with this as a beginning. You come from all over Nevèrÿon," Gorgik's voice echoed on. "You come with your different reasons, your different gifts. This young woman at my feet comes with no more than curiosity." Pryn looked up again. The face—what she could see of it beyond the knee—smiled before it looked back up. "I accept that; and I am as happy to have her with us as I am anyone here. You there—" Over Pryn's head the great hand went out. "You hail from the foothills of the Argina, am I right? I can tell by the leather braiding about your arm. Once, when I passed through your province, I saw a low stone building with seven sharply pointed triangular doors, the stone head of a different animal at each apex. When I asked what the building was, I was told a phrase in your language . . . ?"

" '*Ya'Kik ya Kra Kyk*!' " a heavy man with close-cropped hair called out.

"Yes," answered Gorgik. "That's it! And can you tell me what it means?"

"It means the House of the Goddess who Weaves Baskets to Carry Grain to Women, Children, and Animals."

"And is she a goddess of freedom or slavery?"

The man frowned. "She's a goddess of prosperity . . ." He raised a hand to tug self-consciously at the leather braids looped on his

fleshy biceps. "She's a goddess of labor. So I *guess* she's a goddess of freedom ..."

"Good!" called Gorgik. "Then she might smile on us and our cause, here, even though there are few women among us and, today at any rate, only one child ..."

The laughter, friendly enough, made Pryn look up. Beyond his blocky knee, the Liberator looked down at her, while Pryn wondered at her demotion from young woman to child. She looked out again at the Red Badger, who, with his big mouth, missing teeth, and new beard, had gotten her into the first trouble of her journey.

"It is important for all of us to learn about, and learn to respect, the customs over all our land. You there—" This time he pointed toward the barbarian woman who, again, had leaned to whisper to a neighbor.

She looked up.

"When I was a youngster, running in the streets of this city, I used to hear the women from the south talking the southern language together. The word that again and again fell out of those lingering, liquid sentences was *nivu*. When I first began to learn a few words of the tongue from your men, it never came from their mouths. Yet even today, walking in our streets, one hears you southern women talking of *nivu* this and *nivu* that. Tell me; what does it mean? I know enough of your language to ask for food and lodging and to tell when a man is saying he's full-fed and content or when he's saying he's sick and hungry. But I still don't know the significance of this word."

The woman's rough yellow hair, tied behind her neck, clearly bespoke barbaric origins. "My Liberator," she called out in a friendly enough voice, but with the thickest barbarian accent Pryn had ever heard, "if you knew anything of our life and language, you would know that *nivu* is not a man's word."

Gorgik laughed. "So I was told once before. But we are all friends here, men and women, with a common cause that will benefit us both. We work for justice; and justice should have no secrets. Tell me the meaning of the word."

"Very well, my Liberator. *Nivu* is an old barbarian term that means—"

"FOOLS—!"

Later Pryn realized she had seen the man—squatting on the rough stone balcony by the falling water—some minutes before he stood up, arms out from his sides, belly jerking visibly with the breath he heaved into each word:

"YOU FOOLS—the *lot* of you!"

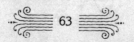

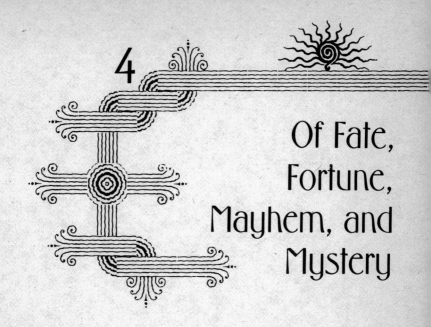

4

Of Fate,
Fortune,
Mayhem, and
Mystery

... the psychoanalytic notion of sexuality, says Freud, comprises both *more* and *less* than the literal sex act. But how are we to understand an extension of meaning which includes not only *more* but also *less* than the literal meaning? This apparent paradox, indeed, points to the specific complication which, in Freud's view, is inherent in human sexuality as such. The question here is less that of the meaning *of* sexuality than that of a complex *relationship between sexuality and meaning*; a relationship which is not a simple *deviation* from literal meaning, but rather, a *problematization of literality as such*.

—Shoshana Felman/*Turning the Screw of Interpretation*

"**E**very one of you—duped *fools!*"

Pryn heard the barbarian accent across the echoing hall, saw his yellow hair, his close-set eyes. He grasped the rope then ran toward the ceiling beam, jerked it loose from where it was tied to the balcony's rim, and went on shouting:

"You think you have a Liberator before you? Can't you hear the voice of a tyrant in the making? Before you sits a man whose every word and act is impelled by lusts as depraved as any in the nation, who would make a slave of all and anyone to satisfy them, calling such satisfaction freedom! If you can't see what's in front of you, then look behind you! Look at Small Sarg—Sarg the barbarian! A prince in my land, I came to yours a slave! The man you call 'Liberator' bought me as a slave—and, true, he told me I was free; and, true, for three yars we fought together against slavery throughout Nevèrÿon. But when he was finished with me, he *sold* me! Sold me as a slave! To traders on their way to the western desert—thinking that he would never see me again! But I have escaped! I have returned from slavery! And as I love my freedom, so I have sworn his death!" Gripping the rope, wrapping it about one forearm and again about one leg, the barbarian was over the rail, in the air, swinging down. As he passed above the brazier, his sword, high in his free hand, flared with light.

Above Pryn, on the fur-covered seat, Gorgik pushed himself up, flung out a hand. Pryn saw the big foot slide on fur and threw herself to the hide as the barbarian on the rope hurtled—so slowly, it seemed. Was it the size of the hall . . . ?

Then, so quickly, a man leapt from the gathering—most of whom, Pryn saw with her cheek pressed to the rug, were either crouching or staggering back.

Bound at the instep with leather bands, a bony foot struck the hide before Pryn's face. She twisted her head to look up at a very thin blade coming out of a rough-out leather sheath, rising in a leather-bound fist.

The barbarian was suddenly in front of her, only this stranger in the way. Pryn heard body and body smack. Bodies grappled, falling at, or more likely on, the Liberator's feet as Gorgik, grunting, tried to scramble aside.

The released rope dragged away across dirt.

The struggling men thumped, thrashing, down the steps. A foot hit Pryn's hip, which was when she looked again; so she didn't see whose. The men rolled out on the dirty tiles.

Gorgik stood, his own blade finally drawn. Pryn scrambled up the furs to crouch by him.

At the steps' foot, grunts and gasps and snarls: the barbarian and the man with the leather-bound hands and feet pummeled and bit and gouged at each other.

There was blood on the white hide.

Those who had rushed away rushed back.

Up from the grappling men, blood spurted—a crimson arch, half a meter high. Blood puddled the tile. The spurt fell. At the puddle's edge, red wormed along a grouted crevice.

The barbarian was still, curled on his side like someone suddenly gone to sleep.

The other pushed himself up on all fours, head hanging. He went back to one knee. His shoulders were thin and sun-burned. As well as his hands and feet, his knees and elbows were wrapped with leather. His black hair was long and in one place matted together—but by old dirt, Pryn realized, not blood. Breathing hard, he turned to grin at the throne.

And Pryn saw he had just one eye.

The pupil was black, wet; the white was deeply bloodshot. The eye looked ready to weep.

Momentarily Pryn thought he must have just lost the other; but the way the whole eyeless side of his face was sunken, with only the thin slash of a permanently sealed lid—the loss must have occurred years ago.

"You're safe, master!" The little man laughed. The gaps and rots rimming his gum would have made the Badger's mouth seem sound. He took big, gasping breaths. The muscles over his narrow chest looked strained to the tearing with them. "See, master? You're safe!" He grinned; he panted. The eye still seemed near tears. Looking about, he pointed at the barbarian's sword, some feet away. "No harm from that now!"

The hilt of his own thin knife jutted awkwardly in the barbarian's chest.

Somewhere off in firelight, the rope still swung, slowly.

"Say—do you know me, master?"

Others moved up to crowd behind those already crowding.

"Do you remember little Noyeed, from among the slaves at the obsidian mines . . . ?"

The Liberator frowned.

"No, you don't remember me, master! I was an ugly, awkward, dirty boy. You were the foreman of our work gang, a slave like the rest of us—oh, yes!" The little man looked about at the gawkers. "He *was* a slave, you know—my master. In the obsidian mines at the foot of the Faltha Mountains. I was a slave with him!" The little man threw up his chin, grabbed the flesh of his neck with bloody, bound hands and pulled the skin taut. "See! I am free! I am free! I escaped the mines! My neck is bare! And *he* still wears his collar, in our name! Wears it for us all! But when he was a slave, when *I* was a slave—" Noyeed turned back, his wet eye blinking over his atrocious grin—"he saved my life! You saved my life, master! And I have saved yours! I'd save yours a hundred times and give mine in the bargain; I've never forgotten you, master! Never!"

Gorgik still frowned. "I . . . remember you, Noyeed. And I—" Gorgik stepped down a step. "I saved your life? . . ."

"Aye, you saved me—so that I could go on to become Noyeed the runaway, Noyeed the scavenger, Noyeed the bandit—" He grimaced—"Noyeed the murderer!" With a shrill laugh, he shook his head. "No, master, I'm *not* a good man!" He got to his feet. "But you saved me—so that twenty-odd years later I could meet this barbarian dog, himself only just escaped from slavers in the west, hiding out in the caves of Makalata at the edge of the desert, skulking there among beggars, bones, and ashes, with his tales of treachery and betrayal, his plots for revenge and assassination! A madman, I tell you! A madman! He was going to assassinate my Gorgik, my master, the great and famous Gorgik, the Gorgik men and women speak of as the Liberator over all Nevèrÿon—the

69

Gorgik without whom I never would have lived to make what little I have of my poor life!" Noyeed turned to the throne. "I followed him, master! I followed him all the way across Nevèryon. I followed him here to the capital and finally to this subterranean hall! I tell you, half the time I couldn't even *believe* his madness—that he would try to kill you! But when he made his move—" The little man scurried to the corpse, one hand touching the ground three times in the journey (Pryn thought of dismounting from a dragon), grasped his hilt, and tugged the blade free to raise it in torchlight—"I was here to make mine!" He looked at Gorgik with his wet, black eye. "I was here for you, master, as you were for me—when I was a boy and we were both slaves in those cursed mines. Remember it?"

"From what *I* remember," Gorgik said, "you might have more reason to hate me than to love me, Noyeed."

"Hate my master? Hate the man who saved me?" Noyeed laughed again. "You are a great man now, master. Myself, I'm only a breath of freedom better than a slave. But I do not pretend to understand the jokes and jests of the great." He turned to the others. "My master jokes! But isn't he a great man, my Liberator, my master, my Gorgik?"

The mumbling through the gathered men and women seemed more confusion than agreement. But it also seemed to serve the little man for corroboration. He grinned again, poking his blade-tip about for its sheath.

Men had crowded onto the steps, trying to see. One brushed Pryn's arm. She glanced up to see the Western Wolf, at this point oblivious to her.

"Shall I tell you how he saved my life?" Noyeed looked back at Gorgik. "Shall I tell them, master?"

Gorgik came down another step, his frown—because of the scar, Pryn decided—particularly fierce. "Yes. You may tell them. Tell us all."

The little man turned back to the others and drew another gulping breath. "I was not much below fourteen when I and some friends, playing near our village in the east, were taken by slavers. We fought, my friends and I—and I watched my nearest friend torn in three by two slavers who would slake their lusts on her body there. I saw my brother's legs broken and his ribs cracked so that two stuck from the skin of his side—a day later they threw him, still breathing, down a cliff—I heard that. Him breathing. I didn't see it. One of them had hit me in the face with the blunt end of a stick so hard the eyeball burst in my head—" He jabbed a thumb at his sunken socket. "I walked with them three days completely blind. Only after that did the first shadows of sight return in my remaining eye. Somewhere in it a birthday passed that I did not speak of and neither did they. A week later, they sold me among an even dozen to the obsidian mines, where I was given over to one of the barracks where Gorgik here—" the thumb jabbed toward the Liberator—"was the slave foreman. Oh, he was a slave, yes! But he was a powerful one! Had we been working on the grounds of some great lord's estate, and not in that stinking Imperial pit, he would have worn the white collar-cover of the highest ranking slave —everyone said so! And he deserved it! But no such honors were given in that deadly hole. You see that scar on his face?" Again the little man pointed; and Pryn wondered if this were a tale he'd told frequently at taverns and campfires across Nevèrÿon, or if it were a secret story, rehearsed silently and continually for one glorious recitation. "You see it? Didn't he have it the first time I blinked my good eye clear of what stuck my lashes together, half out of my head with fever and weak from thirst, and saw him for the first time, standing above me, looking down at me where I lay on my foul straw? They told me later he had gotten it in a brawl with another slave who went after him with a pickax because Gorgik had protected the other boy from the torments of the first—it was legend in the camp. All talked of it. Am I right, master?"

"Was it, now?" Gorgik snorted. "And I cannot even remember the other boy's name. Go on, Noyeed."

"He was kind to me, my master was. I was just a child, smaller than that girl—" which was a thumb at Pryn—"half blind, almost too sick to walk—though that didn't stop them from working me. They sent me down in the hole anyway, to carry out scraps of rock through the mud and dark. A slave who did not go down into the mines received neither food—which perhaps I could have done without a day or two—nor water—which I needed to guzzle, constantly and continuously, for I always felt my skin was on fire over my bones. My master there, often he held my head while I drank— or while I threw up when I drank too much; or he would let me rest against the mine wall, looking stern at any man about to protest my indolence. And when, in the evening, back in the barracks, I would fall on my straw, too weak to fight for my supper and water, he would bring me food and a full gourd to drink from and sometimes would even sit and talk with me, joking to cheer me up, staying with me long enough so that no one came to steal my supper—making a little easier my steady slide towards a death that, even then, I only saw as an inevitable relief from the terror. I thought I would die. So did they. One night a bunch of miners in the dark came to my corner, held me down, and used my boy's body like a woman's, one after the other, now grunting, now biting

71

my shoulder, now hissing threats of death should I cry out." (Leaning against the fur-covered arm of the throne, Pryn shifted her hip and wondered just how this little man thought a woman's body was to be used.) "The next day, even the guards declared I was too far gone to go down into the pit. A day without food and water would probably have allowed me to put the second foot over the threshold of death where, clearly, I had already put the first. But Gorgik joked with the guard: 'Oh, I think I can get another day or two of work from him. Give him an hour or so, and he'll perk up.' Then he carried me into the hole himself, and throughout the day brought me water to drink, and for the rest left me alone. As for the others, well ... clearly there was no reason to keep it from me. Now and then I would hear one of them talking within my hearing. Some that had abused me the night before, since I was not expected to last much longer, whispered to each other how they would be back that night to get what use they could of me—I tell you, if at the height of their lusts I had gone from live meat to dead, it wouldn't have bothered them, till my actual corpse had got too cold to heat their night-labors. I knew that if what had been done to me the previous night were done to me again, by dawn I *would* be dead. But that evening, after supper, Gorgik brought a big-hipped man with a large nose, who wore clean blue wool, to my pallet—a eunuch of some noblewoman whose caravan had stopped for the night at the foot of the Falthas. She wanted a slave—for what reason I never knew. But Gorgik, as a foreman, had been asked to pick one out; and chose me—seeing clearly that any such change would have had to be for the better. The eunuch took me back to the lady's tents and camels and provision wagons. It began to rain, I remember, while we walked. Twice, between the barracks and the caravan, I fell, and the eunuch, with many grunts of disgust, helped me to my feet. I remember standing alone among the tents, my eye closed, my head up, tasting the drops, feverish, more asleep than awake, and knowing—" the bright eye blinked—"as I knew *you* knew, master, that those who came to abuse me *that* night would find only my soiled straw, stained with the blood that had run between my legs from the night before and stinking of the urine I had spilled there because I was too frightened to crawl to the pee-trough." The little man, standing by the fallen barbarian, joggled the shoulder with his foot. "The noblewoman didn't buy me. Why anyone might want such a sick and half-blind puppy as I was—why I should *think* anyone might, or why Gorgik there should think so ..." The little man blinked his eye. "Such is not really thinking; only the desire from desperation! Eventually the eunuch took me back to the mine. By now I was stopping every five or ten

72

meters, my body blasted and shaken by a rasping cough, the snot flying, the mucus stringing my chin—I think I remember the eunuch, out of something between disgust and compassion, taking out his key and unlocking the hinge of my collar so I might breathe easier, though he left it around my neck. It was still dark and raining when I was brought back to the barracks. Nobody noticed that my collar was open. And the eunuch was quickly off to find a replacement. But I had been given one more night of life—for it was too late, now, for men who had to work the hours we worked to indulge such sport as had been planned. One more night of life—with death waiting ahead of it just as surely as it had been before. But something had happened. Sick as I was, I had walked through damp fields, had passed by trees and looked at starlit mountains almost as a free man might look. Frequently the barracks were not secured on rainy nights—where might a slave go in his iron collar? But my collar was loose! I was exhausted, yet also feverishly awake. The guard was gone in the rain with the eunuch. I pushed to my knees and made my way to the door, refusing by main force to cough again, keeping my mouth wide or clenching my teeth by turns, gasping through my nose to suppress any sound that might give me away. The other slaves slept. I was outside the door—and fell in the mud. And crawled in the mud, I tell you now, with the pebbles cutting my knees and my hands. I know how weak I was; that night I crawled no more than a thousand feet from the mine encampment; and lay the day in the woods. Why they didn't come looking for me, I don't know. Perhaps they thought I *was* dead—perhaps the guards, hearing of the plan to abuse me as I had heard it myself, simply assumed I had died in the assault and my body been summarily disposed of. Such disposals were common in that place. Given my obvious destiny—death—perhaps they thought it better not to pursue me. Perhaps it was simply because I was no man and not much of a boy; or perhaps they were discouraged by a word from my master." Noyeed flashed another lopsided grin at Gorgik. "I know that toward evening I began to drag myself along again, starvation now joining my other ills. Still crawling, I finally reached a clearing, which, from the worn footpaths and the pattern of tent-post holes across the ground, I realized was the camp the caravan I had been to the previous night had, earlier that day moved on from. Such a wealthy caravan as that leaves a wealth of garbage. That night I ate their garbage, slept in it, and woke to find myself rained on as I lay in it and slept again without moving; and, no doubt, ate more of it when I awoke. I left my collar in it. Somehow, even open, its stiff hinge had made it cling about my neck till I pulled it apart with my own hands. No doubt it's still there,

73

where I buried it, in that muddy refuse pit beside the caravan site at the base of the ragged Falthas. What I ate or where I slept over the next three nights, I don't remember. The next I recall I was crouching in the dark outside a circle of firelight, blinking with my one eye at the conviviality of the travelers sitting about the flames, smelling the food they passed among them till I was sick with it. I did not dare enter. I was too frightened. On another night, I watched a band of slavers with their sorry wares make camp near a stream; and I asked myself if I were any better off than those chained and collared folk, who at least were being fed a double handful of oaten mush, spooned on the board laid down between their double line, their hands roped behind them, their chains clicking and clicking the plank as their heads bobbed, eating. And somehow my fever passed. I chewed my roots, and when one root made me sick, chewed no more like it. Somehow I sensed the ones that gave me nourishment and dug up more of the same. I ate beetles that scurried over logs before my dirty fingers. And when, on still another night, I walked into the firelit circle about still another gathering, whose camp and food preparations I had watched for hours till the sun had pulled all darkness down between the trees, I did not care if they were slavers or worse, so long as they would speak to me, look at me, beat me—even kill me." An incantatory delight had informed the little man's tale till now. But here he drew his shoulders in, looked about nervously, as if he were suddenly struck with the amount of time he'd talked before this audience who'd just watched him kill. "The like of you fine folk *would* consider them worse. They would, master! They fed me. They beat me. They washed me. They made fun of me. They gave me a place to sleep. They joked with me, and they cursed me, and they set me hard—and, later, even dangerous—tasks. And though I ran away from them almost as long ago as I crawled away from the mine, they were the closest thing I ever had to a family, once I was snatched from my own. I follow their profession to this day—they were bandits!

"I admit it!

"I'm proud of it!

"To be a bandit is better than to be a slave!

"Ah, master, my memory muddies much of this. But what I recall clearly through it all is *you*! You, master! You were the one who carried me up and down from the pit when I was too sick to walk. You were the one who sent me out of the slave pen with the noblewoman's eunuch the night the others would have set upon me and killed me with their lusts." The little man looked down at the corpse; Pryn could see a sheepish grin pulling through the hard muscles of his face. "Treachery? Betrayal? The things this dog accused you of, even if you *had* done them, are nothing so special. Believe me, I've done my share of both! If all of us who'd done so had to die for it this day, there'd be few left in Nevèrÿon, either in the High Court or the pits."

One woman and several of the men chose to laugh at that, which made the little man look up, grinning.

"I remember you in the mines, Noyeed," Gorgik said. "I remember holding your head while you drank, and carrying your small, hot body against me down into the hole. No doubt I shooed a few miners away who thought to put the rations of a dying boy to better use than you might. Such was my nature then; it's much the same now. Tell me, Noyeed, do you remember the seven men who came to your straw that night and covered your body with theirs; and who—yes—whispered of coming to you again? There *were* seven—four common pit-slaves, a foreman, and two guards among them. Do you recall?"

The little man's face twisted; he shook his head. "I've cursed my memory a thousand times—remember them? Remember their faces? Oh, no, it was too dark! Their voices? It was all grunts and whispers, while my ears rang with fever. If you could name me one, I'd kill him as quickly as I killed this dog!"

Gorgik snorted. "To be sure."

Noyeed laughed again. "Master, *you* gave me life! *You* sent me from the mines to have that taste of freedom that returned to me the possibility of life in the midst of death! That's why you must live!" Turning, he spat on the corpse. "That's why this barbarian dog had to die!"

"Don't dishonor his body." Gorgik came down the last step and put his hand on Noyeed's shoulder, much as he had done with Pryn when they'd first entered the hall. "I remember you, Noyeed; and I remember all you tell of. Perhaps I remember it better than you. You've proved yourself a friend. But that man, dead on the tile, was also a friend—once. Had his friendship not been so great, his hatred might have been less."

From the back of the crowd a man cried: "What's up there? What's that up there on the—"

People about Pryn turned.

On another balcony, a man stood with a short spear in his hand. His spear arm drew back—

Noyeed grabbed the Liberator's wrist. "Master, it's the dead dog's allies! He *told* me he might have more with him! But I didn't believe him, especially once he attacked you without any—"

The spear sailed through the air.

Again Pryn flung herself away, rolled over down shallow steps, came up on her knees, and pushed to her feet amidst confusion. Weapons were out all about her. She looked up to see a dozen strangers running down the far steps, weapons waving, on the other side of the water—to meet another dozen, from among those gathered in the hall, who were running up.

Someone staggered against her; Pryn looked to see the Red Badger. He was opening and closing his mouth, reaching behind his back for—she saw it as he turned—a spear haft that jutted off center between his shoulders. He staggered three steps forward and fell across the dead barbarian, new beard striking the tile, to twist his head at a preposterous angle while blood rolled out over his lower lip.

Pryn ran past.

Two men struggling at the culvert edge fell in and splattered her—though she was not near them. Three others swung down on ropes, two on one, one on another. Some of the invaders, surging up on the lower balconies, just jumped. Pryn saw one near her grab a fleeing woman, who turned, shrieking in his arms, to beat against his face, still shrieking, and, while she was beating, did something with her knee, hard, between his legs, so that he gasped, let her go, and, doubled forward, staggered backwards—till he hit the brazier! He stood up, screaming. It cut through the shouts and calls. He toppled forward, shoulder and buttock raw. The flesh still seared to the metal smoked and bubbled and blackened.

Gorgik, with his wide knife in one hand and a sword in the other, turned to hack before him, hacked again behind.

Pryn dashed across the wooden bridge as another man swung down on a rope. As he came off, she nearly collided with the Wolf, who, with his sword, was fighting off an assailant who kept making feints with a vicious-bladed pike.

Was it because she saw the third man coming? She grabbed the pike's end and yanked. (The man wielding it had not even seen her.) The Western Wolf leaped forward and thrust. The pike came loose in Pryn's hands. She turned with it to see fragments: a raging face shouting at her, a raised sword falling toward her, a sandaled foot stamping dirt below her, a fire-lit buckle holding a scabbard to a hairy thigh. Hard as she could, Pryn thrust the pike's blunt end low into the belly she thought, rather than saw, was someplace among them all. Jarred to the shoulders, she watched the details become a single man, gasping, reeling along the water's edge, dropping his sword, falling back—she heard the man's head crack rock. (One man? She'd been sure it was at least five!) He rolled over the edge. Water sheeted away on both sides, then clapped over him.

The Wolf still stood, blinking in surprise.

Pryn turned to strike another intruder, who staggered up, unseeing. She hit hard, and then was off the bridge and bringing the pike down on the head of a man who had another man down, while another tried to tug him off—

Something smacked Pryn's flank. Burning, stinging, it sent her falling, made her lose vision—though she didn't drop the pike. When she could see, what she saw was a man, blind with blood from a gash across the eyes, swinging his wide blade, now left, now right, with shoulder-wrenching fury. She was on the ground, trying to get up on one knee. For a moment she wondered if the man had simply severed her—but she felt her side (while the knuckles of her fist, still grasping the pike, rubbed rock); there was no blood, no cut. The raging man swung above her, stepped over her leg— which she jerked back. He was holding the sword so that the blade had connected with the flat, rather than the edge. Until it had struck her nearly senseless, she hadn't even *seen* him ... Pryn was up again, running. She dodged one man who hadn't seen her, then another who had. As she neared the wall, she saw, on the balcony, practically above her, two men climbing to leap—now they were falling with drawn swords.

It wasn't fear that made her do it. Rather it was a vague, glittering anger. It all happened with astonishing clarity and rapidity, within the generalized pain that she felt not as a sensation in her side, but rather as a prickling enclosing her entire body. She swung her pike up against the short sword of the falling man so that it swung back into his face—not flat-sided, either.

As he landed, she brought the pike up over his head and down against the back of his neck. He pitched forward onto the blade that had already gotten caught under his chin. (The other shouted as he landed, because he'd twisted his ankle.) The first man bubbled red from ear and nose, the blade tip up under his jaw, somewhere in his brain. With the pike ahead of her, Pryn rushed up the stairs and pushed through the hangings. Only when she was in the anteroom with the benches did she realize she had been holding the pike with its metal point towards her own stomach. At any stumble or fall she could have gutted herself as surely as she had ... *murdered* the invader at the stairs' foot with the sword in his head.

Slowing only to right the pike, she dashed into the dark. Clambering around the piled sacks, she hurried into the high-roofed tunnel. Had there been this many turnings? The pike's point scraped the corridor's wet walls. Three times the pole jammed at a too-narrow bend. She tripped on rising steps. With darkness and the word "murder" filling her mind, anger threatened to spill over into terror.

Then, between one breath and the next—pain!

For a moment she thought it was new. But it was the one in her side. It had been there, yes. But now it was *not* all about her. It was in one place the size of a hand and clutched her flank incredibly. The end of each breath was a dull horror to get through. She lay the awkward pole down and stumbled through darkness, hurting too much really to fear. Had a rib cracked? One hand on wet stone, with the other she felt her side—too sore, really, to touch. Suppose, she thought, there are branches and turn-offs here in which I shall be lost forever? Mercifully the pain made it impossible for her to dwell on labyrinthine possibilities. She walked, wondering if she might have to lie down. I have ridden a dragon, she thought. She whispered, "I have murdered a man ..." She corrected herself: "Maybe murdered several." Distressingly little to it when you were on the murdering side—though this pain was mortal reminder how chancy it was, in such business, that one didn't end up on the other.

The pain passed some rib-crunching peak and at last began to subside. Once she leaned against the wall, taking very small breaths. Murder and labyrinthine possibilities became confused in her thought. What was it the tale-teller had said about the girl who'd killed so many people she'd begun to act oddly? Once more Pryn walked, thinking: I'm *looking* for something in all this darkness. *What* am I looking for? Again an image came: The tale-teller's masked friend with her twin blades. Am I *this* frightened? she wondered. Why am I telling such tales? Well, perhaps tales were better than the hacked, drowned, and skewered carnage behind her—which is when Pryn was suddenly seized with the conviction she was being followed.

Her own breath roared in the darkness—she couldn't hold it more than three steps before it came squeaking and wheezing out. Her feet sent loose stones clicking, and in the echo she was sure she heard steps behind her, stumbling as she stumbled, stepping as she stepped. On the rock there was a beating—one of her pursuers pounded his sword hilt against the wall as he came on ...

Staggering from the low entrance onto the cistern's floor, she nearly fell. Gray light dropped between the overhead logs.

My heart! she thought as she turned to grasp the iron staple. It's my own heart! And the pursuers were *only* her echo ... She climbed—and wouldn't think about the dullness pulsing in her side. When she was half a dozen rungs up, she paused. The pound-

ing continued. But she could feel, in the flesh between her thumb and forefinger gripping the tarry bar—she *could* feel her heart; and it was beating far faster than the pounding, which she realized now was a real noise, echoing.

Someone was chanting, too, only she couldn't make out the words. She climbed again. Her head came up between birch logs. She took another painful breath and turned to look about.

Across the cistern, just beyond the wall, Pryn saw a barbarian girl bouncing a ball; other children watched. Now that Pryn's head was above the wall, the sound was stripped of echo. The pounding was the ball's rhythmic *thack, thack, thack* . . . and the chant, the girl's shrill rhyme:

> ". . . . *and all the soldiers fought a bit*
> *and neither general cared a whit*
> *if any man of his was hit*
> *and blood filled up the cavern's pit*
> *and every firebrand was lit;*
> *the hound took flight, the horse took bit,*
> *the child took blood at mother's tit* . . ."

Another girl—maybe nine, maybe ten—glanced at Pryn, but seemed to find nothing special in a plump, bushy headed young-ster climbing out of a cistern. She turned back:

> ". . . *and the eagle sighed and the serpent cried,*
> *for all my Lady's warning!*"

On *warning* the ball slammed into the corner of the cistern wall to go soaring. Children went prancing and jumping below it, strain-ing to catch. One small boy kept calling, "It's my turn now! *My* turn! No, it's my turn!"

Sun down, summer evening lingered in the tangled streets. Stopping now and again to flex her arm or touch her ribs, Pryn wandered through one, then another alley; minutes later she walked out onto the empty, red-brick square. In the center was a human-high stone, from which a water jet fell to a natural basin.

She'd almost reached the fountain when she realized this was the Old Market. Stalls and awnings had come down for the day; the vendors had carried off their trays, rolled away their barrows. Portable counters had been moved out, the refuse swept up, and the square cleared for night. The sky above the western roofs, coppery pink, was streaked with silver clouds. Some became near-black when they reached the eastern blue. Pryn stopped at the rock. Bending

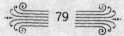

over the foaming basin, she had to hold the edge, realizing how sore her ribs still were. So were her shoulders—the strength to batter about her with the pike was more than you used to rein a lizard. As her face fell to the water, the sky's reflection broke up and darkened with her own.

Where am I going? she thought. What am I looking for?

She splashed her cheeks, drank from her cupped palms, rubbed wet thumbs on her eyes, then walked on across the square toward the bridge.

There, at any rate, activity seemed almost as great as it had earlier. The loiterers' faces were mostly new, but their colorful, ragged clothes, their curious painted eyes were the same. Walking, she tried not to show nervousness or hurt, to find the effort moved her along more quickly when she wanted to look leisurely, made her look away when a painted eye glanced.

When the ringed hand grabbed her shoulder, Pryn caught her breath, turning, tried to push away—

"Well, you're back!" With their bright freight, the dirty fingers held. The other hand—as dirty, but ringless—grappled Pryn's hair. "So you found he didn't want you after all. Anyone here could have told you that! Don't fight me, girl, or I'll break your teeth with one smack and your eardrum with another—and *still* make you work the bridge for me!" Over his naked chest, she saw for the first time many little cuts, small scars, scratches . . .

She hit at him, because she was angry again—and did not hit as hard as she might, because she was surprised and sore and, yes, exhausted. He jerked her hair. Handsome features slid about on one another with the effort. She blinked to see his hand falling to slap her. Over his shoulder, onlookers moved away as others stepped up.

Then something happened.

Sliding features locked.

The hand halted, inches from Pryn's flinching jaw.

A muscle quivered in his cheek. An eyelid twitched, lowered . . . His mouth, half open, began a creaking noise like an old hinge, or maybe someone trying to suck air through a constricted throat.

Fingers in her hair loosened.

Pryn jerked her head away.

Nynx began to sag; and Pryn saw, behind him, gray eyes below a thatch of cream-yellow.

Nynx fell, his hand pulling from Pryn's other shoulder, where it had momentarily and limply caught, to flop on the bridge, gray fingers opening as if stone and metal were too heavy to hold in a fist.

80

Pryn looked at the blade the pale-haired woman gripped.

"Stupid ..." the young woman said, a little hoarsely.

Pryn blinked.

"... dead," the woman added. "Yes." She grimaced. "All right. Come with me."

Pryn was about to protest. But the woman barked at the on-lookers, "Why are you gawking? It's only a corpse! There're six more like it, rotting in the river. Just throw this one on top!" She gave a high, breathy laugh and took Pryn's upper arm in her very strong fingers. "Let's go, I said." Pryn went, because—well, she was frightened and also because she had gone rather numb. If my rescuer had been a black-haired woman with a rag mask and a double-bladed sword, Pryn thought as they left the bridge and crossed to an alley's narrow entrance, I *wouldn't* protest ... The gaunt, pale-haired murderess—but hadn't Pryn also murdered less than an hour back?—was not more than three years older than Pryn, for all her sunken eyes and tightly muscled frame. As one murderess led the other around another cistern, Pryn managed to ask, "What ... what do you want?"

"To take you to my mistress." The fingers stayed painfully tight. "I waited for you three hours—though I thought I'd get to you before you got yourself in trouble with someone like that!"

"Waiting for me ...?" Pryn tried to work her arm free; the grip hurt, and her side was still sore. "There? But why there ...?"

"Same reason as that bridge louse." The high, hoarse laugh. "I knew you'd be along the same way he did. You're an ignorant mountain girl in this strange and terrible city—where else could you have come?"

Pryn started to say that she *did* know writing—a good bit of it, too. But the blond-white murderess released her arm and gave her a little push ahead to hurry her. "Please," Pryn said. "Please, can't you tell me where you're taking me?"

"I told you. To my mistress. She has taken an interest in you. She wants to further your career."

The little woman was ahead of Pryn again, loping off down a even darker alley. There was nothing for Pryn to do but follow. "Who *is* your mistress?" Pryn asked. "What does she do? What does she want me for?" She tried to remember the people who had been with this strange creature when the Fox's horse had almost run into them on the street that morning.

"My mistress is a merchant woman—very clever. Very powerful. She likes to amass wealth and influence events—does a lot of both." The young woman put the point of her knife, which she had not re-sheathed, into her mouth to pick at something between her

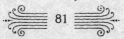

teeth. That she had not wiped the blade since the stabbing was, suddenly for Pryn amidst all the day's violences, the *most* coldly perverse thing she'd seen.

"And you . . . ?" Pryn asked. Chills cascaded her back, made the skin of her thighs pull in. If it was fear, she'd never felt this particular sort before. She had no idea what to do with it; so she tried to go on as though she weren't feeling anything. "Who are *you*? What do *you* do . . .?"

The alley opened out. A covered cart with a single horse stood in the shadow of an arch.

"Me?" The woman took down the horse's reins. "My mistress calls me the Wild Ini. Her secretary calls me the Silver Viper. (*Her* name is Radiant Jade, but that's because she's a barbarian!) You'll probably find your own name for me—if we know each other long enough. What do I do?" The breathy laugh. "I do what I like. And I like to kill people. A lot!" Then she pushed Pryn up the short ladder at the cart's side, while Pryn, with aching flank and bruised arm, reached for balance into the darkness among the cart's maroon hangings.

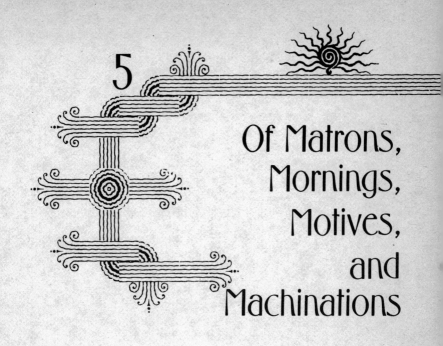

5

Of Matrons, Mornings, Motives, and Machinations

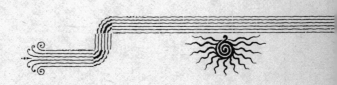

Psychoanalysis tells us that fantasy is a fiction, and that consciousness itself is a fantasy-effect. In the same way, literature tells us that authority is a *language effect*, the product of the creation of its own *rhetorical* power: that authority is the *power of fiction*; that authority, therefore, is likewise a fiction.

—Shoshana Felman/*To Open the Question*

"**D**awn is the loveliest time in this garden," Madame Keyne said. "One would think that these blue dahlias, that those black tulips had been set in the shadow of this high rock or banked beside that grotesque stone beast to catch the precise subtlety of this light and no other. Will you walk with me up this path?"

"I'm very confused, Madame Keyne," Pryn said. "Why have you brought me here?"

"No doubt you are also frightened. The Wild Ini can be very frightening if seen in the proper light. But she is useful. She tells me she pulled you from the arms of a street pander—put a knife in him, too! You do not look like a woman used to such violences. Certainly you must have been terrified!"

Pryn thought of her dragon, of her own killings, of the carnage in the cellar. The pale-haired woman's blade (whose thrust into Nynx Pryn had not even seen) had, if anything, brought the mayhem to a close; and because Pryn had not seen the thrust, it had also seemed a closing that was, somehow, external to the mayhem rather than of it. "Madame, I was—and am—more confused than frightened."

"Ah?" Madame Keyne's blue skirts floated back in the light breeze from more sheer blue. (Pryn remembered the thick cloth from her aunt's loom.) "Well, I understand. Such violence engulfs the person caught up in it the way air supports a bird or water suspends a fish: one moves through it; it contours one's every move. Yet one hardly realizes it's there. I understand your state, believe me. A young woman of your sensibilities, brought to a strange house in a strange, if beautiful, suburb of the city, minis-

tered to by unknown servants, made to sleep in a strange bed, unsure of who might enter during the long night, while the violences of the day vanish simply through incomprehension—surely this calm and alien domesticity has produced in you the real terror?"

"Was that big woman who took my clothes and gave me my bath last night a servant?" Pryn asked. "I've heard of servants, but I've never really seen one—up close." Pryn looked down at the new dress she had been given. Her side was much less sore this morning, but she knew that beneath the green material was a wide, purplish bruise. "Before she turned down my bed and told me to sleep, she said I had nothing to be afraid of." Recalling the nights she had slept beside the road in the forests and the fields, Pryn wondered how to explain the half-sleep that had become natural to her. "It was easier to believe her—and sleep—than to doubt and lie awake till morning. Again, Madame, I was not so much frightened as confused."

Madame Keyne sighed. "My entire life I have found things seldom to be as most people expect them, and I have grown wealthy catering to people's expectations by my manipulations of the real. Yet my own expectations are as hard for me to let go as the superstitions of some barbarian living in ignorance and squalor in the Spur. I expect you to be terrified, and, quite mechanically, against all your protests I have done everything to alleviate that terror. Even accepting your protest is, for me, a matter of assuming my efforts have been successful—rather than admitting there was no need for my concern." She smiled at Pryn with an almost elderly irony. "So. You are no *longer* terrified. Very good. Perhaps we both can accept that. Such a marvelous morning!" Madame Keyne's white hair was coiled about her head on silver combs. Her deeply tanned skin, here smooth at cheek and forearm, there wrinkled at wrist and neck, glowed like noon. "Acceptance is *so* simple! I walk in my garden, here, at dawn, to find simplicity. Look around you—at the rising paths, the falling waters, the protective walls ranged about us, the tiled mosaics decorating my home, the large statues there, the little ones over here. For me, that *is* simplicity. And for you, it's confusion."

They were walking up a path paved with red brick—the same brick, Pryn saw, that had covered the market place. Here, however, moss reached across it from the path's edge or lapped out from carefully tended flower banks and sapling groves.

They gained a rise.

Beyond the garden wall, Pryn could make out another house, a house about whose upper stories much tiling had fallen away. A

dozen men, some with spears, all with leather helmets, ambled the roof behind cracked crenellations.

"Really, you know, I am the despair of my gardeners." Madame Keyne pushed her bracelets up her wrist—most of which fell jangling again. "One would think, by custom, this is the time they would be up, preparing the grounds for the later risers. But I have demanded Clyton keep the place free for this first hour after sunrise so that I might come and walk. But I notice your gaze has strayed to my neighbor's lawns—if one can call them that. The garden there is no longer tended at all. His soldiers stamp along the balustrades. Now and again someone rides up to shout an incomprehensible message, and someone rides away . . ."

"Do you know," Pryn began, "your . . . your neighbor?"

"*Know* him? He's no acquaintance of mine! That isn't even Sallese—over the wall is Neveryóna, the old neighborhood of Kolhari. Look how it's falling to pieces! That's what inherited wealth leads to, I tell you. Though he certainly didn't inherit *his*! Well, it's not surprising he would take over some ramshackle mansion *there*! Know him? Know this Liberator all the city talks of? I'm terrified of him! He rented that old run-down shell of a house six weeks ago. Everyone who borders on it thought he would soon have workers and artisans repairing, refacing, bringing that once-beautiful property back to a state we could all admire. But as you can see, he keeps his headquarters no better than a barracks. And within those littered halls and peeling chambers sits our Liberator—planning and plotting liberation, no doubt. It's quite unsettling. You spoke of servants? Six weeks ago, there were three times as many of them working here as there are today—*he's* scared them off! Myself, I think they've gone to join him, those that haven't simply fled. And you can be sure it's not *my* liberation he's planning! Terrifying, yes. If that's the way he treats his own house, what may he eventually do to mine?" Madame Keyne shook her head and took Pryn's arm—very gently—to lead her around a stone hut that had broken from the bushes at the top of the rise. Had Pryn been more used to gardens of such extent, she would have assumed it a storage shack for tools. As she wasn't, however, she wondered who might live in the little enclosure, for it had no windows—only some grilles set high in the walls. The recessed door was hewn of thick plank. The hedges and trees around it were arranged to hide it from you completely while you were not actually on its circling path. The stone bench at the hut's back, however, offered an extraordinary view. "Come, sit with me." The bench itself was a sculpted replica of one of the split log seats Pryn had seen in the inner city. Madame Keyne sat, patting the stone beside her. "That's right.

Right here. From where we are, the Liberator and his ugly home are comfortably out of sight—though, like so many such phenomena, once they have been put behind, they tend to pervade all that lies before. You can see almost the entire city from here. I had this bench set so one could sit and contemplate Kolhari, for there is no prospect opening upon it quite so impressive, at least from within city limits. There, of course, is the High Court of Eagles. That break among the buildings is the Old Market, just across the Bridge of Lost Desire, where you were last night. The trees there mark the Empress's newly designated public park; only a street away, in that open space between the buildings lies the New Market—the Old Market in the Spur, I fear, has become merely a quaint and archaic metaphor for commerce, whereas really to know the life and pulse of this city, one must lose and make a fortune or two in the New Market—don't you think?"

"I don't know," Pryn said. "How could I? Madame, why have you brought me here?" Pryn was, indeed, thinking of the ruined house behind her. Perhaps because Madame Keyne had suggested it, or perhaps because the suggestion was simply true, the notion of the Liberator had begun to extend for Pryn over the whole of the city, so that, though she was not really sure he was still alive, much less in the dilapidated mansion, he had become a figure of such invasive power that her next question, a moment before she asked it at any rate, seemed logical enough: "Does my being here have anything to do with the Liberator?"

Madame Keyne looked surprised. "Only insofar as many of the residents of both Sallese and Neveryóna have felt more confined to our own little worlds since he has been about in the great one. You might say one reason you are here is that I am attempting to live my own life more intensely."

"I don't understand."

"Yet there is nothing so strange about it, really. I have frequently taken an interest in the careers of exceptional young women. When I first saw you in the street, riding behind that scarred country gentleman, you struck me immediately as someone who ... well, had seen the stars, descried cities in the clouds, ridden dragons, gazed into the ocean and seen through to secrets the tides obscure!"

"I did?" asked Pryn.

"Oh, yes! Such characteristics always show on a woman's face—if another woman has eyes to read them." Madame Keyne sat back and regarded Pryn. "You are clearly a young woman who knows her own name."

"I am?" asked Pryn. "I mean—oh, I *am*!"

"I thought so." Madame Keyne folded her hands on her lap's blue. "Perhaps, then, you might tell me what it is . . . ?"

"Oh! Of course." Pryn looked around by the bench leg for a twig. She found one and bent down to scratch in the dirt. "It's Pryn." She glanced up at Madame Keyne, then turned back (her side *was* still sore) to glyph the syllabics, majuscule and minuscule, and add, finally, the diacritical elision. " 'Pryn,' " she repeated, sitting up and taking a breath. "There."

"Well!" Madame Keyne bent forward. "Not only do you know your own name, you know how to write it." She sat back amid tinkling bracelets. "That *does* make you exceptional!"

Pryn was surprised; she'd thought that was what the woman had been speaking of all along. But the pleasure of the compliment lingered despite her misreading—as did Madame Keyne's smile.

"My aunt taught me," Pryn explained. "Whenever anything new came to our town, like reading, or figuring, or writing, or a new kind of building, or a new medicine, my aunt was always there to see what it was and how it worked—at least she used to be. But she's very old, much too old to take care of me now. She's even older than you."

"To be sure," Madame Keyne said. "You ask why you're here? Well, shortly after we had our first surprising encounter on Black Avenue, one of my servants, on an errand back in that direction, reported seeing you put down on the street by the men you rode with. Clearly you were a mountain girl, unused to the city. My servant's account of your indecisions and hesitations over which way to go were sure signs you were on your own. I sent our little Ini to look for you in the three places an unaccompanied woman might end up in Kolhari. She found you, I might add, in the most predictable. Now you are here."

Pryn looked out at the city. There was no fog this morning—or rather, since they were within the city, the fog was only a general haze about them, and no longer a visible object with location and limit. "But certainly, Madame Keyne, many young women must come to Kolhari—many every day; from the mountains, from the deserts, from the islands, from the jungles. You can't possibly take an interest in the careers of them all . . ."

"But my dear, the thought of a poor child, a stranger in our town, without prospects or friends . . . ? It would not have let me sleep for a week! What do you suppose might have happened if our little Ini had *not* been there with her quick blade?"

To Pryn, Madame Keyne's words seemed more like ones that should have come before her question than after it. Indeed, trying to locate an answer in this woman's so sensible protestations was

like trying to see the fog that, from here, was only the faintest of dispersions. "Madame, my gratitude is real. But so is my confusion. Gratitude doesn't end it."

"But I don't know if I *can* speak of the reasons you want to hear." Madame Keyne suddenly turned to touch Pryn's shoulder. "Say that when your companions nearly ran us down in the street—say that when the horse on which you rode first reared to avoid us, say that when the morning sun caught so in your unkempt hair ... when the hooves stamped on the pavement, when you drew a breath so that your eyes widened in a particular way—well, there was a smudge of dirt on your calf, I recall, that I could not shake loose from my memory the whole day. It's gone, now, brushed from you in your bath last night by one of those marvelous new sponges, only recently imported from the Ulvayns. But it is fair to say that if the smudge, or the angle of your arm about the sweating chest of your rider, or the particular width of your astonished eyes had been other than what, in that instant, they were, you would not be here. There are, alas, no better reasons I can give. Girl—" The hand on her shoulder had grown heavier. "You are not traditionally beautiful; and you know it. We women do. But what most people mean by beauty is really a kind of aesthetic acceptability, not so much character as a lack of it, a set of features and lineaments that hide their history, that suggest history itself does not exist. But the template by which we recognize the features and forms in the human body that cause the heart to halt, threatening to spill us over into the silence of death—that is drawn on another part of the soul entirely. Such features are different for each of us. For one, it is the toes of the feet turned in rather than out; for another it is the fingers of the hand thick rather than thin; for still another it is the eyes set wide rather than close together. But all sing, chant, hymn the history of the body, if only because we all know how people regard bodies that deviate from the lauded and totally abnormal norm named beauty. Most of us would rather not recognize such desires in ourselves and thus avoid all contemplation of what the possession of such features means about the lives, the bodies, the histories of others, preferring instead to go on merely accepting the acceptable. But that is not who I am. That is not who I have struggled to be. Have I been struggling just the slightest bit harder since the Liberator has confined me, as it were, to my own garden? Perhaps." Madame Keyne lifted her hand. Bracelets clinked toward her elbow. "Say that you are simply here by magic. Do you know what magic is? It is power. But power only functions in the context of other powers—which is the secret of magic. The strongest man in the world—even the Liberator, who they say is a giant of a

man—may only 'liberate' as the play of power about him allows. Set him raging alone in a desert, and he will be as ineffectual as any other isolate, angry child—while the proper word spoken to the proper official of the Empress, whose reign is numinous though knowable, may result in the erection of a granite and basalt temple to the greater glory of our nameless, artisanal gods.

"Why are you here?

"The truth is simply that you are a young mountain woman who has come to the city. That is to undertake a kind of education. I, my secretary, the servants of this house, our little Wild Ini, are merely some among the instruments through which part of that education will occur. The city is very different from the country, girl. It is a kind of shared consciousness that begins its work on you as soon as you enter it, if not well before, a consciousness that begins to separate you from the country possibly even before you decide to journey toward it. It encircles you with forces much greater than the walls and gates which imitate tinier villages or towns. People who come to it come seeking the future, not realizing all that will finally affect them in it is their own, only more or less aware, involvement with the past. The way we do things here—really, that's all there is to be learned in our precincts. But in the paving of every wide, clear avenue, in the turnings of every dark, overhung alley, in the ornaments on every cornice, in the salt-stained stones of each neighborhood cistern, there are traces of the way things *once* were done—which is the key to why they are done as they are today. And you—you wish to know why a woman, knowledgeable in her city's history of infamies and generosities, would snatch an untutored country girl (of exceptional tutoring, as it now turns out) from the very arms of pain, abuse, and dishonor?

"Be content with this: It has been done before. No doubt it will be done again.

"And iteration abolishes the strangeness of any human action, making it merely repetition, while it reveals the purely human—desire—impelling it. Have I done what I was going to do? My girl, leave me a while and walk about the garden on your own. Yes!"

"Madame Keyne . . . ?"

For the woman, suddenly, lightly, closed her eyes and sat as though she were a moment away from major distress, hands surrounded by bracelets loose in her lap. "I have done it!" Moment followed moment.

"Madame Keyne, are you all right?"

"Leave me," Madame Keyne repeated, calm enough but with eyes still closed. "Enjoy the garden, the flowers, the falls, the fountains, the views of the city in all directions. And remember,

there is nothing here to hurt you. I would die first before I would let anyone hurt you. I would die. Now go."

Pryn started to touch the woman's arm. But Madame Keyne, whether she sensed it or saw it from beneath lids only half-closed, leaned away.

Pryn withdrew her hand.

What had begun as confusion had become by now a mental turbulence, like fog a-broil over waters through which she could make out no single wave. Pryn rose, began to walk away, glanced at the woman sitting on the bench, back against the hut's stone, eyes still closed before the city's panorama. Pryn, walking, glanced again—till the path's turning hid the woman, then the hut, with shrubbery, trees, flowers ...

A faint frown on her round, brown face, Pryn, in her new green shift, descended to the lower garden. She wandered about the grounds a while without seeing anyone else. Once she heard voices—more servants? She thought to push through the hedge to see. Then, with decision, she turned in another direction.

What is this garden other than a miniature forest? she thought. The number of trees, blossoms, and bushes whose names she knew from the mountains was overshadowed by the number whose names were unknown. The main point of it, she decided, was that one would never find such variety in the wild—at least not over such a limited space and laid out in such carefully edged sections. It's like a map of *all* the forests, she decided, a map on which you can't read distance or direction ... A feeling of distress interrupted the thought, but she could not find the source of it till she remembered who'd first given her those words.

This garden, this house, are all a part of the city, Pryn reflected. *What* is it here to teach me? It seemed a question she had been asking of the world from well before she'd mounted the winged beast. The real question, she decided, is not why this woman has brought me here. That, I suspect, is finally her affair. The question is what am I *doing* here? And I seem to have been doing a great deal lately. She stopped to look at a flower she had never seen before—a yellow and orange cornucopia smudged with black stripes. For a while she watched a stream break into three across a broad stone clearly carved for the purpose of diverting the water to three new paths, each winding off in its respective direction. For a while she walked beside a wall twice as high as she was, marveling at its permanence, its ponderousness, an image of all beyond it playing through her mind—an image which, as she examined it, was not much more than a vague castle in which dwelt a vague Empress (whose reign was vague and voluptuous), a market which was

neither old nor new, and a strange house with missing tiles whose roof was patrolled by strolling soldiers. The rest of the city was a blur—oh, not a meaningless blur by any means, but the blur that marks a first encounter with the truly new which has no history to clarify it, to highlight it, to give it context, to keep it from being wholly a presence, instead of a play of more and more greatly deferred origins.

When she reached the house, Pryn turned to walk along the wall, scuffing her feet in the earth where the grass no longer grew, next to where the wall went into the ground. She passed behind bushes. The building's front was all large pink and gray stones in gray mortar; but when she turned the corner, she found one section of smaller stones set in flaking yellow mud; then another of a single cement-like substance (with some large cracks in it); and another of irregular black brick, as though this side wall had been built (or repaired) at different times. Perhaps the builder, in the course of constructing it, had experimented with different materials . . . ? Her great-aunt would have found all that interesting in a house; and though, when rebelling against her aunt's tutelage, Pryn had claimed to be absolutely uninterested in the many such distinctions pointed out to her by the venerable woman in the various houses, streets, and official buildings in their walks around Ellamon, to read them, here, was nevertheless to engage in what was at least a familiar process; and thus, to feel more at home.

She passed one window with heavy cloth hangings blocking any view within; the next was boarded over, suggesting some window in the Liberator's headquarters. She turned another corner. Ahead was a wall of wattle; in it was a window whose bottom sill was level with Pryn's knee.

The opening was hung with a yellow cloth sheer as the gauze of Madame Keyne's skirts.

Light seemed to pour from it.

Pryn walked up and, moving to the edge, peered through.

Reddled and waxed, the room's stone floor was set perhaps two feet below the outside ground. Like some ancient great hall, it was without roof—though it was only of moderate size. The same sun that shadowed Pryn where the wall joined with the main house also fell out through the window over the grass and leaves.

Several counters inside were piled with square slabs, knives, reeds, splints, brushes, vella, and parchments. The only thing that moved in the room was the tiniest blue flame beneath a small tripod sitting by a few cups. The little fire wavered in the shadow of the long-handled pot above it.

Three stools stood about the sunken, sunlit chamber.

Then hinges creaked.

A shadow fell on maroon stone.

Someone walked in—

The woman—no, not last night's servant—lugged in a cloth sack; wet, it dribbled down her tanned back. She set it on a counter, grunting, and stood.

Whatever was in it went very flat along its bottom, like grain. Only it seemed heavier than grain. The woman had strong, distinctly muscled arms. There was a bluish scar on her shoulder—but it was too regular for a scar: some sort of tattoo.

As Pryn watched, the woman stepped back, reached down, and shrugged up her dress (the same green as Pryn's) over one wet arm. The red scarf was still tied at her waist. She left the other shoulder bare; one breast remained free. Her brown hair was pinned up; something about her carriage—it was the woman whom Pryn had last seen talking in the street with Madame Keyne when the horses had nearly run into them.

She turned to a curved ceramic mold that looked like a third of a large cylinder lying on the counter and, with her fingertips, lifted out first one, then another curved clay tablet and set it on a curved stand. Then she opened her bag, reached in, gouged, twisted, pulled something inside, took it out: wet clay.

She slapped the hunk, hard, on the counter; scraped it loose, slapped it down again; then again; and again. When the woman's arm came up, Pryn could see her breast shake. Finally she broke the clay apart and examined the inner surfaces. (For bubbles ...?) She smacked down each hunk separately a few more times, then went to put them in the mold. First with the heel of her hand, then with her fingertips, she pressed these new tablets into the corners.

At the side of the counter, under the metal tripod on top of which sat the long-handled pot, the flame flicked and fluttered.

The pot began to boil.

Bubbles climbed to the bronze rim and broke; a whiff of white whipped above.

Now the woman took the pot's handle in clay-grayed fingers and poured amber into one of the ceramic cups sitting near.

She put the pot down. Holding the little cup just under her chin in both hands, she blew on it, sipped, smiled—Pryn drew back beyond the edge of the window as the woman turned slightly.

The woman blew again; sipped again. With one hand, she picked up a wooden paddle and smoothed the surface of the clay on the tablet mold. Whatever was in the infusion the woman drank while

she worked finally reached through the sunny gauze. It suggested both spices and fruits, but in some odd refinement.

The woman put down both her cup and her paddle, bent below the counter, and lifted a small jar from a pile of jars. She stood, holding it up to look at the marks scratched in its surface.

Pryn saw two things about it: First, the jar had no opening. Second, the scratches read:

> se•ven•great
> jars•of oat
> en•flo•ur•of
> la•bor•er qua
> li•ty

Above the *flo* and the *ur* was the eliding mark Pryn now knew to be part of her own name.

A shelf on the wall with many compartments held a number of such jars—all too small to be "great jars of oaten flour." The woman reached out to file hers in one compartment—then paused, looking to the side.

Pryn pulled back.

Someone must have been passing beyond the door Pryn couldn't see.

The woman called, "Oh. Thank you, Gya, for preparing my morning drink." Her voice was feathered with the faintest barbarian accent—as startling to Pryn as her speaking at all.

A voice returned from someone obviously on her way somewhere else. "It wasn't me, Madame Jade. Madame Keyne was in there the moment she got up, to fix it for you herself." Yes, that voiced belonged to the servant who had bathed her last night. Pryn was sure.

"Oh, she *was* ...!" Jade called back, surprised and smiling. "How nice of Rylla."

Clay had dried here and there on her hands in lighter patches. She picked up the cup again, regarded the steaming amber, smiled again, drank again. "All her silly talk about that street girl *was* nonsense, then! I knew it when she left me working late in town at the warehouse yesterday afternoon. I knew it!" She laughed, secretly, throatily.

A sound—surely just wind in leaves, Pryn decided as she stepped away—made Pryn think she'd better wander on. If, after all, some passing servant were to see her, it would never do to be caught spying through the curtains. As Pryn glanced back, the woman—surely this was the Radiant Jade whom Ini had spoken of last

night—was checking over a handful of writing sticks, setting aside the dull ones for sharpening.

It was a task Pryn had done many mornings for her aunt.

She walked out into the garden and looked at more flowers.

Had anyone seen her, she wondered.

She walked back around the house.

Stepping through the arched corner entrance into the open, inner court, she saw the cushions, low stools, and benches on the raked white sand, the blue and green tiles, the fur throws kept marvelously clean. (Pryn recalled the gritty hides in the subterranean hall.) Diagonally across from her, the Ini appeared to have been asleep on a pile of cushions, for she was just sitting up. She punched first one fist overhead, then the other, her mouth twisting in a huge yawn as theatrical in its exaggeration as some mummer miming awakening on a performance wagon in a market skit. Ini's short, yellow-white hair was every which way, like a heap of feathery down. Her deep-set eyes, tightly closed, looked like bruises on her face.

Smiling, Pryn prepared to say good morning as soon as the yawn reached the open-eyed point.

Then two other figures appeared. In her blue gauzes and tinkling bracelets, Madame Keyne stepped through the doorway just down from Pryn and paused, one hand on the jamb. And from the stairs leading to the lower level rooms, the barbarian woman Pryn had just seen in the writing chamber came spiritedly up. She was tall—taller than Pryn expected barbarians to be. And for all her great-aunt's tales of Belham's brilliance, Pryn found herself thinking that it was unusual to see barbarians so well attired or even so clean. Jade's dress was now up on both shoulders, the red scarf neatly round her waist. Only some clay remained about her nails. The four of them, each near her respective corner of the courtyard— Ini on her cushions, Jade at the head of her steps, Madame in her doorway, and Pryn in hers—struck Pryn as an eminently pleasing pattern. She felt her 'Good morning' open up to include them all and was even contemplating something such as, 'Well, here we all are!' when the sunken-eyed Ini, recovered from her sky-shoving yawn, looked about and let her hoarsest, most hysterical laugh.

The laugh twisted up Ini's face into a howl. She rocked forward to punch the cushions before her, then leaned back as if she would cackle the decorative tiles from the balcony rail.

Pryn's own greeting was stifled. The smile on her face suddenly felt awkward. On the steps the secretary had pulled her clay-grayed fist up before her breast, her own look as distressed as Pryn's, behind her smile, felt.

Radiant Jade stared at Pryn. Her gaze went to Madame Keyne, to Ini, came back to Pryn, returned to Madame Keyne—as though judging some fine imbalance. "You *couldn't* have! You wouldn't have! Rylla, you didn't *really* ...?" Suddenly she drew a breath audible through the Ini's diminishing laughter, grasped the newel, and fled around into some door behind that led to other ground-floor chambers.

Pryn looked at Madame Keyne—as did Ini, chuckling now. Unlike Pryn's smile, the Ini's seemed full of happy expectation. It reminded Pryn of the grin of a child who had just built some towering construction of sticks, pots, and stones, the moment before pulling away the lowest support to bring it all toppling.

Madame Keyne's hand lowered from the jamb to her side. The faintest shiver crossed her face. She looked after the secretary—Pryn thought for a moment she might even follow.

Ini's laugh had become a smile of simple curiosity.

Madame Keyne sighed. What had begun as a shiver became a small head shake. "Pathetic ..." she whispered, then realized Pryn and Ini were watching. "... she and I? And the two of you ... so ignorant!" She turned in a swirl of blue to reënter the garden.

Pryn was surprised to be included in such an epithet, however restrained; the beginnings of anger snarled with the beginnings of embarrassment. Her cheeks heated.

Another laugh from Ini brought Pryn's eyes back from the empty doorway. She blinked.

Ini rolled off the cushions and stood, adjusting straps and buckles on her complex body harness. "I like you, little girl," she said suddenly, without looking at Pryn.

Pryn blinked again.

Ini pulled one strap down over her shoulder and let the buckle tongue slip into a hole two notches further on. "That's lucky for you—because if I didn't ..." She made a terrible face.

Pryn actually took a step back—

—And realized Ini's grimace was at the strap's tightness.

"I don't like killing women as a rule." Another tongue slid into another hole. "I much prefer men. I don't understand men. And I don't like them. They're much more complacent about misunderstandings. And that's why." She looked up again, deep-socketed eyes showing white above and below the gray irises. "There, is that what you wanted to know? Everybody else does—you too."

"I *don't* want to know such things!" Pryn declared. On top of the moment with Madame Keyne and her secretary, such a statement seemed the purest and most unrelated madness; and she *was* a bit frightened by this creature. "No, I don't—"

"Now there," Ini said. "Even though I know you're lying, I understand everything going on inside you: the fear, the curiosity, the fact that the fear happens, right now, to be greater. If a man were standing where you happen to be—just as afraid as you—he would say, 'How interesting!' Or perhaps he would smile and try to agree with me as far as he could, or maybe he would try to change my mind—explain to me that I was illogical, or ill, or evil. *Those* kinds of lies I don't understand at all. That's why I don't *want* a man standing where you are." Her eyes had gone back to the buckles; she finished the last strap and looked up with a faintly puzzled frown. "That's why I stay here. That's why I'd kill him."

Had she been threatened herself, Pryn would probably not have felt nearly as agitated. This odd safety she had been granted, however, was absolutely uncomfortable. Logic and reason were what were needed, and logic and reason seemed precisely what was here being attacked in favor of a kind of honesty that, at this moment, Pryn did not understand in the least. What calm there had been to the morning had, in these last minutes, vanished.

Just beside the doorway through which the secretary had gone were the stairs that led up to the room Pryn had slept in last night and had woken in that morning. She hurried across to them and started up.

"At least in this house—"

Pryn glanced back down. The Ini had fallen to readjusting all the straps and buckles to entirely different tensions.

"—there's less chance that a man *would* be standing where you are." Then she called: "You and I, we're in the same position here, now!"

Pryn hurried on. She had no notion what the Ini might mean, but the thought of any similarity, known or unknown, with the little murderess made Pryn as frightened as she ever wanted to be. Terror was only a step away.

A balcony, its heavy newels carved into lions, snakes, bulls, and birds, ran along two walls of the court. Off this balcony were the rooms.

Pryn had left the plank door to her own wide open when, that morning, she'd gone down to wander in the garden.

It still stood gaping.

She rushed inside and closed it loudly.

In the midst of her remarkable adventures, Pryn had woken here not an hour ago and seen nothing remarkable about it. Returning now, however, she saw the entire chamber—its plaster walls, fallen away from the stone in one corner, its rough wooden bed, heaped at the foot with an embroidered quilt worked with golds, reds, and blues, its intricate washstand holding an unglazed bowl with a cracked side—as marked with contradictions, contradictions within which she could read of all that was ominous without, as clearly as if warnings had been scratched across the pale designs on the painted plaster between the ceiling beams or inked over the waxed red floor tiles.

Some chairs stood along one wall, a few piled one on another. Was this some kind of balcony storeroom in which she'd been housed? Well, it wasn't a dungeon. All the dungeons Pryn had ever heard of were in basements, not on balconies.

How to get out? Simply walking through the door again seemed impossible, and the window, from which she could see the garden, was too high to jump.

There was a knock.

Startled, Pryn looked around.

The door pulled slowly open; Radiant Jade, holding a tray, edged in. She stood there for seconds with a very uncertain smile. "I'm sorry," she said at last, "but almost all the servants except cook, gardener, and a few of the kitchen help have gone. Really, it's some very nice fruit, though." The barbarian accent was so light Pryn kept losing it—and listening the harder for its faint feathering on the s's and r's. "Rylla said to stop my nonsense and bring you some fruit ... and some honey with it. But myself, I never take honey with my fruit in the morning—still, if you want, I'll go back ... ?"

"Oh, thank you," Pryn said. "No, I don't need any," and thought how nice it might have been to have had some.

"You're not used to servants, are you?" The secretary crossed the room and put the tray down on the window ledge. "Well, neither was Ini when she first came. But she got used to them fast enough. Just in time for them all to leave, too. So this morning everyone must double as house *and* grounds staff—nor are they happy about it, either. I won't be surprised if we lose another today. But not cook, though. Not gardener." While she'd been speaking, she'd been looking out the window. Here she leaned out further. "Gya and gardener are faithful."

"Why ... have they left?" Pryn ventured. She was not really being disingenuous but simply felt that in uncertain situations it was better to explore the already familiar. "What do *you* think the reason is?"

"You can't see it from here as well as you can from my room." (Pryn was not sure if that were part of an answer—or even if her questions had been heard.) "But it's there, nevertheless."

Pryn rose and went to the window. "What are you looking at?"

"There." Radiant Jade pointed. "The Liberator's headquarters."

Leaning over the wide ledge, Pryn could see, across the wall at the end of the garden, somewhere off in the next yard, the cracked balustrade with its ambling soldiers.

"I despair of having to replace cook. Training a new housekeeper will be bad enough—though heaven knows I've done it before. Still, cook is a position you don't want to keep reëstablishing in a house like this. But gardener is faithful—Gya, gardener, and me!" She pulled her head back in. "Isn't it interesting: it takes much less to liberate servants than it does for slaves. For servants, it seems, all you have to do is move in next door." Jade turned her back to the sill.

Pryn took up a yellow peach from the blue bowl on the tray and turned too, biting.

"Do you think he's going to liberate us here?" The secretary folded her arms and stepped away, looking quite on edge. "I wonder if he thinks that simply by moving in next door, he can loosen *her* grip on the subjects she rules?"

"The Empress . . . ?" Pryn took another bite.

Radiant Jade glanced back with a kind of bafflement that made the girl simply feel stupid. ". . . rules *us*? Here? In *this* house?"

". . . Madame Keyne?" Pryn offered.

The secretary shook her head with a tragic little grimace. "You think *she* is ruler here . . . ?" Suddenly another thought seized her, and she dropped her arms and straightened her back.

Pryn thought she was about to leave and said: "You're a barbarian, aren't you?" She took a third bite of the peach, which, for all its size and color, was completely unripe. The flesh was as hard—and as tasteless—as raw potato.

"Yes." Apparently Jade was not leaving but only waiting to change the subject.

"Do you speak the barbarian language?"

"Till I was seven years old, I spoke nothing else." She walked around the bed once and then sat on the foot, her hands on the knees of her green skirt.

Half-sitting on the sill, Pryn asked, "Do you . . . know what *nivu* means?"

Amusement joined the conflicting emotions already on Jade's face. "Where did you hear a word like that? Did you hear some barbarian call our home here a *chatja nivu*?"

"I don't . . . remember if that was the phrase," Pryn said, quite sure it wasn't. "And I don't think they were talking about Madame Keyne. What would it mean if I had?"

"*Chatja nivu* means a house where the women refuse to cook

for men. But *that* doesn't tell you much, does it!" Radiant Jade laughed. "In many barbarian villages, ones that still have very little contact with Nevèrÿon, there're lots of customs that more civilized folk are likely to think of as magic. In most tribes, for example, work is very strictly divided between the sexes. Only men can kill certain animals. Only women can kill certain others. Lashing together the thatch for the roof of a new hut is work only men may do. Cooking food—and no one may eat uncooked food in the south—is work only done by women. But sometimes when a husband sufficiently angers his wife, by refusing to do his own work, or by making love to another woman, the wife may refuse to cook for him. Then the man must wander about the village, begging other women to cook. And if no woman will—and they usually won't if his wife has real reason and simply isn't sick or busy—he will finally starve to death and die."

Pryn's eyes widened; she took another bite of hard peach.

"When a woman refuses to cook for a man, that, in my language, is *nivu*."

"But I've heard the word on the street," Pryn said. "I mean, here in the city. The barbarian women talk of *nivu* this and *nivu* that. *All* the barbarian women in Kolhari can't be starving their husbands . . . ?"

Jade laughed again. "Customs change when people come to the city—in most barbarian tribes customs have changed well before people leave. Here, today, on the streets of Kolhari, *nivu* may mean any lack of support a woman may show a man. Even the silliest disagreement may be spoken of with the word—in the city, I think there are always such disagreements. But you see, it also has the other meaning that is older and more powerful." Jade turned her hands back and forth on her knees. "In our own land, it is one of the most powerful of women's words—and here in yours, it has become one of the most trivial. Well, it is still a good word for you to know, even if you are not a barbarian—since you have found refuge in a *chatja nivu*."

"Doesn't the cook in this house cook food for the gardener?"

"Yes."

"And still this would be called a . . . a *chatja nivu*?"

"Your accent is very good." Radiant Jade moved her head a bit to the side. "But as I said, *nivu* does not *have* to refer to cooking."

Pryn was about to let herself smile, when Radiant Jade said:

"You know I'm not happy you're here. I think it was dreadful, dragging you off like that. But Rylla is impulsive."

"I might not be alive if she weren't!"

"So I've heard."

Despite the fruit's hardness, Pryn's teeth, in the next bite, touched pit. "I suppose I'm not that happy to be here either. I don't understand *why* I'm here. I know Madame Keyne likes to influence people and events. But if you're going to influence people, don't you think you should do it with their consent?"

The secretary pursed her lips. "You're better off here than you would be running loose in the streets."

"Maybe," Pryn said. "Probably, even. But still, nobody seems to want to tell me *why* I'm here."

"Rylla—Madame Keyne—has simply ... taken an interest in you."

"But her interest is so confusing," Pryn persisted. "Why me in particular? And why does she keep that frightening creature downstairs in her employ? Why are *you* here ...?"

Toying with the scarf at her waist, Radiant Jade suddenly stood and began to pace the room, as though she were the one trapped—though the door still stood wide. "Me? Why am *I* here? But I *shouldn't* be!" As she paced, she twisted the cloth harder. "I should be *any*where else! I should be in the forests, spearing hyenas. I should be in the mountains, hurtling onto the backs of winged worms to soar above the peaks. I should be on the sea, in a skiff, reaching to grasp the flying fish in my naked fingers. I should be—" She stopped suddenly and looked down—"in some little barbarian village, like the one where I was born, ignorant, dirty, illiterate ... not in this great, confining city, in this great, confining house."

Pryn wondered if she should mention her own dragon riding, or the part it had played in bringing her here. What she finally said was: "Why don't you leave?"

Jade looked up.

"You say the other servants have gone."

"With me—" the secretary blinked—"it's different. Rylla needs me." The scarf-wringing ceased. "She can't get along without me. Sometimes I *want* to leave ..."

Pryn felt a kind of sympathy with the distress of this woman whom she had watched earlier work and smile. But she also felt an equal frustration before that distress's indecipherable motive, a motive that insisted on remaining as hidden as the one behind Pryn's own presence. "How long have you been here?" Pryn asked.

"Oh, forever ... Many years—three years." Jade sighed. "But it seems like forever."

"Did Madame Keyne ... take an interest in you?"

Jade looked surprised. "I never thought of it in those terms

102

before. But you might say she did. Yes, you might very well say just that."

"Did she take an interest in the Wild Ini too?" Pryn asked eagerly, for she thought she detected the beginnings of a pattern.

"An interest?" From surprise, the secretary's face moved to total astonishment. "In the little Viper? I think she rather hates her and would like to see her dead!"

"But hasn't Madame Keyne hired her?"

Jade narrowed her eyes. "Yes." She looked down at her lap. "At last. Or at any rate, she has promised to—today. But it's only because you're here that she's consented." Jade blinked at her hands.

While she was waiting, Pryn put the last of the hard peach back on the tray, picked up a pear, and bit it. It was even harder.

Pryn put the pear down, moved the tray of fruit to the window's side, turned, and sat on the sill. "How did you meet Madame Keyne? I mean, how did she first . . . take an interest?"

At the edge of the secretary's lowered face, Pryn saw the expression change. When the face came up, it was smiling—which was not what Pryn had expected. "How did we meet?" The fingers left the knees to mesh between them. Radiant Jade had very strong, reassuring hands, for all their current nervousness. "It wasn't very complicated. When I left my little village, way in the south, I thought to come north to the city, because I had heard there was less chance for a lone woman to be taken slave here than in the smaller towns and holds."

"Did you ever *see* any slavers when you were traveling?" Pryn asked. "I did. Three times."

"Yes—I saw slavers. And I hid by the side of the road till they passed."

"Me too!" Outside, some cloud had pulled from the sun. Pryn felt her back warm; on the floor, both sides of her shadow, tiles reddened. "But how did you come here—I mean to this house?"

"When I came to the city, the first job I took—" the secretary glanced behind her at the door, then looked back to Pryn—"was with a desert man who lived in the Spur and who brought in laundry from the rest of the city—and I and a dozen other barbarian women washed it. I hated the job and would take every opportunity to sneak off to the cedar groves—the place the Empress designated a public park two years ago. Once, when I was sitting on one of the benches, a woman—our cook here, Gya—came to talk to me and told me her mistress, who had occasionally seen me there, wished to make my acquaintance. I went with her—and met Madame Keyne. She took me to a tavern, I remember, on the

103

waterfront; and in the curtained alcove for women at the back she bought me many mugs of cider. I thought it all terribly elegant at the time. Then she invited me to dine with her, here at her home, the same evening. When she first learned I was a laundress, she promised to give me all her laundry to do—then she found out I could read and write." Radiant Jade sat back and laughed. "So she made me her secretary—and for the next six months sent her laundry to the man in the Spur. She said she felt guilty for taking me away, though few of his girls ever worked for him more than two months anyway."

Pryn laughed too. "Madame Keyne sounds like a very kind woman."

"Oh, she is!" exclaimed Jade. "She is! Rylla is kindness itself! That's why I feel so awful, so guilty! It isn't fair—I tell myself that all the time. And yet there's nothing to be done. There are some situations in which we are not our own masters. I think she knows that—I know she does. How could she not know it if she brought me here? If she brought you?"

These questions seemed to take things back into the discomfort and confusion from which, a moment ago, Pryn had thought they'd emerged. To insert a clear and comfortable fact, Pryn said "I write—and read—too." She'd thought the statement a pleasantry, a sign of shared experience far less spectacular than their mutual experience of slavers, an emblem about which civility might flourish, if not friendship grow. From Jade's expression, however, Pryn realized that discomfort had intensified, if not purified.

"You . . . !"

Fear joined the emotions struggling on Jade's face, a fear Pryn herself had been fending off and which seemed equally divided between them.

"You—?"

Pryn stood up from the sill, then sat again when the secretary stood up from the bed.

Jade's fingers jerked about, now toward her face (without touching it), now toward her hips (without touching there either). "*You!*" She stepped unsteadily forward. "I should have known—the traitorous vixen! You can read—and *write!*" She turned and fled the room.

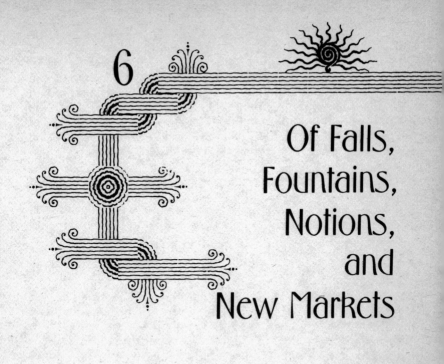

6

Of Falls, Fountains, Notions, and New Markets

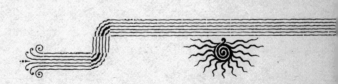

To use one of Kula's metaphors, one must keep looking down into the well, into the deepest water, down into material life, which is related to market prices but is not always affected or changed by them. So, any economic history that is not written on two levels—that of the well's rim and that of the depths—runs the risk of being appallingly incomplete.... English historians have shown that as of the fifteenth century the traditional public market was accompanied by what they have called the private market (I would prefer to stress the difference and call it the *countermarket*). For indeed, did it not try to free itself from the rules imposed upon the traditional market, rules that were often paralyzing in their excessiveness?
—Fernand Braudel/*Afterthoughts on Material
Civilization and Capitalism*

The alternation between ease and unease in Pryn's recent life had become so frequent she no longer felt the need to name it. She wandered around the room a while longer, now looking out the window at the garden, now looking through the door along the courtyard balcony. She examined corners, looked under chair bottoms. On one circuit she decided *not* to eat the grapes—the only untasted fruit remaining on the tray. A circuit later, she picked one, bit it: juice and sweetness exploded over her tongue. She devoured the bunch, one after one, till the little stems, their maroon crowns surrounding yellow nubs where the fruit had pulled free, prickled above the blue glaze between the brown pear with its white wound and the red pit with its remaining bite of pith.

Licking sticky fingers, Pryn thought she heard sounds in another part of the house. She stepped out the door. Yes, somewhere on another floor, someone was shouting at someone who was trying to quiet her. She looked over the rail at the inner court. Statuary, plants, benches were arranged, she saw now, in separate groupings, a low, inlaid table at the center of each.

She went to the stairway and started down.

 107

The muffled yelling stopped.

There were not even wrinkles in the cushions where the Ini had lain.

Pryn crossed toward the door—the one Madame Keyne had stood in. A metal gate, it stood ajar. At its sides heavy drapes were tied back, no doubt to be closed in breezier weather.

Pryn pushed through as the heavy-set woman, with a scarf around her head, came along by the house, three young women and a young man behind her. Pryn recognized the cook. She had lugged in the bathtub last night, but Pryn had not seen the others before.

As they walked, the red-scarfed woman instructed: ". . . and, of course, lateness will not be tolerated. Your duties among the chickens and pigeons are not arduous, Althia, but they are exacting; and you will be expected to take care of the swans and peafowl as well. Samo, you will learn most of your gardening duties from Clyton, who has been here for many years now; but you will also be expected to precede Madame to the country home in Ka'hesh by at least a week to help with the heavy cleaning there—the place is always a shambles at the end of winter, because she *will* rent it out to the local young nabobs when she is not using it; and they are none too careful, though it's a finer home than any of their own draughty piles . . ."

As they drew abreast of her, among the house girls Pryn saw the new gardener's assistant, a dark-haired youth, rather too thin, a bit round shouldered; still, he glanced at her with heavily lashed, very black eyes. I wonder, thought Pryn moving the waist about on her new shift, does he think *I'm* a woman of the house? which made her smile at herself. (And perhaps my father is alive . . . ?) No, I am not traditionally beautiful. Still . . .

She'd been trying to remember details of her distress at the Ini and her confusion over Radiant Jade. But when behavior seemed so completely without reason, especially when all around was new as well, it was hard even to think about it, much less hold on to the feelings it evoked—unless that behavior was directly before you. What *was* directly before her now? More trees, more rocks, more flowers . . .

She frowned over her memories of the morning.

The interests of these women, Pryn realized, were far stronger than she'd thought. But what, exactly, did they *do*? Since Pryn had done it with boys on several occasions (and rather enjoyed it), she fancied that she should know most of what there was to know, at least about that part of it. Certainly it couldn't be much different, she reflected, from what, only a year or so back, she'd come upon her girl friends Janina and Fetija doing behind the storage shed at the back of her cousin's bakery. She'd teased them about it for three days, till Fetija had cried and Jenina had punched her. And what Fetija and Jenina had done was finally not much different from what she herself had done once when she was nine with an older girl cousin—at the older girl's behest, of course.

Or was it different?

What she and her cousin had done had been interesting enough. But there had been a side to it that had bothered her—though whether that bother had been physical, emotional, or social, at nine she'd been unable to tease out. Irked by the knottiness of it all, she had, at nine, put those odd, if in themselves oddly pleasant, acts out of memory—though precisely that distress, she could now admit, had made her, as it lingered, tease Fetija so unmercifully till Janina's punch in the shoulder stopped it.

Well, Pryn thought, she was fifteen now and too old to be a tease; besides, she was too curious about what was happening in this strange garden—though once more she found her thoughts drifting toward the notion of putting the obstreperous physicality of it all out of current thought. It made it easier, somehow, to deal with.

While she frowned and wandered beneath shadowy trees, it suddenly struck her that—Jade, Madame Keyne, Ini, and her sore side notwithstanding—she actually *felt* about as fine as clear air and carefully tended gardens could make one.

She stepped across the red brick path, between dark pines, by clustered palms with shaggy scales, beside bushes of red lillies with yellow hearts. She passed a fanged and winged monster, carved in obsidian, dangling a dozen breasts like some aged bitch: for all her fierce face, she looked quite benign. The flowers carpeting about her claws made her the more motherly while her glistening blackness made their violet the more intense.

Pryn walked onto a stone-sided bridge crossing the stream below a waterfall.

Four fountains, one at each corner of the bridge, sprayed out into the stream.

As she reached the bridge's middle, Pryn looked up at the cascades. Jutting from the water's streaming face, rocks dangled foamy beards. Some were tipped with moss. Others dripped with grasses. Some of the rocks, she realized, were not natural but carved: the head and tail of a stone fish curved from the water, three feet of falls between them; a stone dolphin arched out near the top. Toward the bottom a great cuttlefish flung stone tentacles from the spume, the whole a living moment rigid in the midst of the unstoppable, inanimate rush.

Then one fountain's spray faltered, weakened, became a dribble

over its stone lip. Pryn was about to walk over and examine it when she heard, then saw, coming around the curving path ahead, an elderly man with curly white hair thick over chest and belly.

His brown head was bald.

Trundling a barrow filled with rakes, hoes, and shovels, he wore around his neck a scarf the same red as the one the cook had worn around her head, or Jade had worn at her waist. He wheeled his barrow straight up to the malfunctioning fountain, set it down, grasped the fountain head—a carved stone shell—and twisted, left, then right. With a great crunch, it came off.

What had been a defective spray became a defective spill.

The man put the fountain head on the bridge's planks. Rummaging in his barrow, he pulled out a stick with a hook at one end. He shoved the hook into the hole from which the water wobbled, prodding about to dislodge any obstruction.

Pryn stepped nearer to see.

The man glanced at her. "Morning." He prodded and turned.

Pryn smiled. "If this Liberator is making your helpers leave," she commented, "it doesn't seem to be stopping new helpers from applying for their jobs."

The man grunted. "A different breed."

"You don't think the new people will be as good as the ones who left?"

"Better or worse, I can't say." He pulled the stick free and examined the end. "Just different."

There was nothing on the hook.

Nor was the water flow any stronger.

He thrust the stick back in the spigot and poked some more, both arms wet to hairy shoulders.

Pryn walked on over the bridge.

The path took her up—but on a rise different from the one she'd climbed that morning with Madame Keyne. She climbed by hanging banks of fuschia and honeysuckle; the path moved away from the falls, then back, became a flight of red brick steps between wooden rails beside the splashing water, then became a path again. At last Pryn came to a level stretch, to look across the fall's rock-punctuated rim. The stream that fed it rushed beside the continuation of the brick. On the other side of the water were high, dank shrubs. Ahead, on her own side of the stream, Pryn saw four brick-edged tributaries leading away into four brick-ringed pools, each pool about five feet in diameter, one set just beyond the other.

By the far pool, the Wild Ini squatted. With a length of branch, she jammed and prodded something in the pool's bottom.

Pryn walked up.

Ini had taken a wooden grate out of the water. It lay by her knee in the wet grass.

As Pryn's skirt brushed a bush, Ini looked up, startled. "She wanted me to wear her scarf!" the pale-haired girl hissed. "Imagine! She said because I could be one of her employees now, that I should wear her damned red scarf!" Ini jammed the branch in again. She picked up a handful of leaves and pebbles she had gathered in a pile beside her, pulled the branch out of the water with one hand, thrust the leaves and pebbles in with the other, then fell again to packing and prodding them down into whatever conduit the grate had covered. "Me? Ha! *That's* where her scarf is now!"

Pryn had flinched at Ini's first look; surprise had left her heart pounding. As her heart stilled, it occurred to her that somehow, among all the last days' frightening experiences, fear itself had somehow become ... less fearful. She stood by the pool, watching, not unafraid, but not bothered so much by it.

The muscles in the Ini's shoulders knotted and flexed. Her breath came in small gasps. Suddenly she stood and flung the dripping branch down on top of the grate. Somewhere the gardener's barrow was crunching up a brick slope. Ini blinked at Pryn, then put her wet, dirty hands on Pryn's arms. "We better get out of here before Clyton sees us!" Her whisper was absolutely frantic.

Pryn followed Ini off around the pool and behind the trees, brushing leaf-bits, dirt, and droplets from her arms where Ini had touched her and marveling that the little murderess had not bothered to return the grate to the bottom of the pool or to scatter her pile of leaves and pebbles, or even to dispose of her branch—yet at the same time seemed so frightened of discovery.

Pryn walked beside striding Ini.

As they came around another bank of flowers, Ini suddenly asked: "Do you like this garden?"

"Yes. Very much." Pryn's curiosity at why Ini had asked raised the inflection on her final word.

Ini snatched a blue blossom from a bush. "So do I. It's beautiful, wild, surprising at all turns. I think that's why I like to walk around in it. It reminds me of a forest, but with even more color and confusion crammed in." Ini did not look at the flower she'd picked. As she walked, she mashed it in her fingers, so that bits of blue petal fell to the brick.

"Have you ever thought," Pryn offered, as they turned down another path that took them toward the rock wall, "how a garden is like a map of the forests outside it? You can't read distances and directions on it of course. But the various flowers and trees, arranged so carefully here, are, each of them, like samples of what you can find out in the wild—"

Ini's sharp, high laugh cut Pryn off. "*This* garden? A map? What nonsense! This wall, with which that silly old woman, who wants me to wear her silly red scarf, tries to separate her garden from the wildness outside, so that she can pretend there's order here—do you think it works? Do the people and passions you see inside these walls speak of an ordered household?" Ini laughed again and flung down the mashed bud. "No, it's all wild! *Her* mistake is to think that by something as simple as a wall—" Still walking, she struck the stone beside her with the flat of her hand, hard enough to make Pryn wince—"she can keep the wildness out!" Ini grinned. "But the very fact that the trees and shrubs and rocks and water and air and the people breathing it are here *means* that the wildness is in already. And the wall is not all solid, either. There's an arch built over the place where the stream comes in for the waterfall. There're bars along the arch through which the water flows. The bars go down into the water—to keep people out. But I dove down there once. Just below the surface, two of them have rusted away, and anyone could swim through. And down at the other end, at the corner, where the gardener almost never goes because it's grown up too thick to wheel a barrow, five or six stones have come loose to make a hole that anyone could crawl, from the Liberator's garden right into ours—though over there at the Liberator's house nobody ever goes *into* the garden. I know, because I've gone exploring in there, *lots* of times!"

"You have?" Pryn asked, impressed. She thought to recount her own adventures with the Liberator. But a second thought decided her to remain as ordinary seeming as possible in the eyes of this most extraordinary young woman. "You're very brave," Pryn said, recalling how quickly they'd fled the gardener.

"Yes," Ini said. "I'm not afraid of anything. Especially the Liberator. Or whatever's over there. In his garden. I just go over there and walk around in it! All the time. Just like I lived there! And nobody does a thing to me—they wouldn't *dare!*"

Which was when Pryn realized the little murderess's face practically glittered with fear—and that she was obviously and luminously lying!

"Where are you from?" Pryn asked.

"What do you want to know for?"

Pryn shrugged. "Because you're interesting. And I like you."

"You do?" Ini grinned at her. (Pryn immediately wondered if, indeed, she did. But she smiled back.) "I came from a little farming

province. But I got taken by slavers and sold in the desert—do you know what they do with slaves in the desert?"

"No," Pryn said to Ini's eager grin. "What?"

Pryn thought Ini was about to tell her.

But something happened in the Ini's face—as though the mind behind it had moved on to some memory that turned the features bitter, then angry. "What a stupid question!" Ini looked away. "I don't want to talk about it."

Pryn thought for a moment. "Did you escape?"

"Yes."

"Did you kill a lot of people when you escaped?"

Ini looked at her feet as they walked. "No. Not when I escaped."

"*After* you escaped?"

"No." Ini still looked down. "Before."

"You killed people when you were still a slave?" Pryn was confused. "Who did you kill?"

"Other slaves." Ini looked up at Pryn with the same startled expression as when she'd first looked up from the pool. "It was my job! That's why I did it! Otherwise they would have killed me—why did you *think* I did it!" She turned away sharply and stepped ahead of Pryn. Once she glanced back. "You think this garden is like the forest? It is no more like the forests outside it than that—" She stopped, suddenly, to point to a green leaf caught on the rough bark of a tree trunk beside the path—"is like that!" Her finger moved to indicate another green leaf, among a cluster of leaves, at the tip of a low twig.

"But ..." Stepping up to the trunk, Pryn frowned. "But those two leaves are as alike as leaves can be, aren't they?"

"You think so?" Ini grinned, suddenly and hugely.

Pryn bent closer, wondering if this were a joke, or perhaps more of the strange perception that allowed someone to *be* an Ini. The single leaf stuck to the trunk and the riot of leaves on the branches about them seemed, in themselves, a fine map of the relation between garden and the greater wilderness around.

Then, though there was no breeze, the leaf on the bark fluttered. It split down its central vein, revealing an insect body.

Beating green wings, the moth fluttered from the trunk a few inches, then landed again to compose itself once more into a 'leaf.'

Pryn looked at Ini, who now seemed again as angry as she'd ever been.

"You see? They're not the same at all! And I thought you said they were! The similarity is all illusion, a bit of chance—oh, yes, all very well for the moth. But all the illusion does is distract *us* from the difference! And once you *see* the differences between them ...?"

113

Ini's hand, still wet from the pool and dirty, smacked the trunk over the moth as hard as she had struck the wall. "Then you can control them—" She ground her palm, first one way, then back, while, with her other hand, she plucked the leaf from the twig, crushing it—"both."

Her hands fell from the tree.

The twig was bare.

On the trunk were a few green bits over a spot slightly darker than the bark around it.

Ini turned away, grinning again, and started down the red brick steps.

Pryn hurried behind her.

The path took them around and down, till they came out between high hedges. Ahead was the little bridge with the four fountains at its corners.

Madame Keyne walked across it toward them.

Ini slowed. Pryn caught up with her, slowing too. She wondered what she or Ini would say. Madame Keyne smiled.

Then they heard the trundling barrow.

The gardener rolled his tools from another small path. "Morning, ma'am." He nodded toward Madame Keyne, set his barrow down, and stood.

"Good morning, Clyton," Madame Keyne said. "You've done a fine job with the irises, I see. Such things don't go unnoticed. Gya has a new assistant waiting for you down at the kitchen. His name is Samo. Things should be back to normal for you—*and* the rest of us!—once he learns his chores."

"Yes, ma'am." Bending to rummage through his tools, Clyton pulled loose some piece of wet, wadded, and torn material and turned to the Ini. "Is this yours?"

"That?" asked the pale-haired young woman.

Pryn looked from Ini to Clyton to Madame Keyne. The older woman's brows were raised in the shadow of a question, with, about them as well, the shadow of amusement.

The gardener held out the ruined, red scarf.

Ini's pale eyes were wide, her lips tight. Suddenly she announced: "Yes! I think it *is* mine!" She stepped forward and took the dripping cloth from the hairy fingers. "It must have fallen off into the water when I was exploring the upper stream this morning!"

The waterfall plashed and cascaded over the stone beasts.

At either side the bridge, the four fountains sprayed their even and orderly waters.

Ini took the ends of the scarf and stretched it out. Wrinkled and ripped, it was still spotted with bits of gravel and leaf from where it

had been wadded into the conduit. She raised it, put it behind her neck, brought the ends before her, and knotted it about her throat—as Clyton wore his.

Then she let her unsettling laugh.

"Well," said Madame Keyne. "A bit the worse for wear. Still, I'm glad to see you've decided to join us. But Pryn—" (Pryn wondered if Ini were what Clyton had meant by a new breed of servant.) "—I was actually looking for you. I'm going into town, down to the New Market. I'd like you to accompany me, if you would . . . ?"

"Yes, Madame." Pryn glanced at Ini, who simply stood, watching Clyton pick up the handles of his barrow, to trundle off on another path.

Madame Keyne turned back across the bridge. Pryn left Ini to hurry after; she caught up with her at the bridge's far end.

As they walked along the shrub- and flower-banked path, Pryn imagined Ini following, no more than six steps back—possibly with knife out . . .

Pryn looked sharply around.

The path behind was empty.

Sighing, Pryn turned back—to see that Madame Keyne was watching her with that same expression of curiosity and amusement. Pryn felt her own face move toward an uncomfortable frown. "Madame Keyne, don't you think that young woman is . . . strange?"

"Strange?" Madame Keyne answered. "I think she's quite mad."

"And do you believe she just . . . dropped her scarf? In the water, I mean. By accident?"

"Of course she didn't!" Madame Keyne chuckled. "But then, I wouldn't want to wear it either." She chuckled again, more softly. "When I was a girl, a young noblewoman came to stay with my family, here at the house—this was before the Child Empress began her joyous and generous reign, so you know how long ago *that* must have been. The High Court was still under the rule of the Dragon, and the Child Empress herself was still incarcerated somewhere off in the south; and all Kolhari was supposed to be called Neveryóna—though no one ever did. The young noblewoman was ever so much more highly born than we were—once or twice removed, she was a second or third cousin to the Empress herself. She had suffered some terrible ordeal in the south that I didn't understand and nobody was supposed to mention, and she was being returned to her uncle in the east. While she was passing through Kolhari, we were honored with her presence—because whatever had happened to her meant she couldn't stay with her relatives over *there,* on the other side of the wall. At any rate, all her servants—and she came with ever so many—wore red scarfs. I thought it was very elegant, and I resolved that when I grew up and had servants of my own, I would have them wear the same." A third time she chuckled, though now there was no voice to it at all. "And I have!" Madame Keyne took Pryn's arm. "The young noblewoman later became the Empress's vizerine. And of course, at this point she is no more a young woman than I—though when she was our houseguest, the six or seven years that she had on me seemed like all the time in the world. Still, can you imagine a spirited child like our Ini submitting to such a silly, jealousy-founded, and capricious whim from someone like me? Really, I'd think much less of her if she *didn't* balk a bit. She has spirit. And I like that."

"You're not afraid of her?"

"Afraid?" Madame Keyne frowned. "Of Ini? No, I'm not afraid of her. Part of me is rather fond of her. Part of me is rather sorry for her. But you see, the Ini is fascinated by power. She wants to see how it works, wants to stand as close as she can to it, to stare down into it and watch it moving, pulsing, actually becoming—right before her! Currently, I have more of it than anyone else she knows. If she hurt me, or even displeased me in any way too severe, she knows she would be denied her favorite pastime: observing me. I don't believe she's ready to risk that." (Pryn recalled the little murderess's own assertion of her favorite pastime, and marveled at the woman's self-confidence—which seemed, somehow, quite as out of touch, in its way, as the behavior of Ini herself lurking somewhere behind them in the garden.) "Now if she ever met anyone with more power than I," Madame Keyne went on, "then I might have reason to fear. Blessedly rare as her sort is, she's not the first I've met. Reading such signs is among the things civilized life teaches. But until she meets such a person—or should I say, 'personage'—I feel rather secure." Madame Keyne pressed Pryn's arm. "Now if I were Radiant Jade, indeed I *would* fear her. But then, I suppose, precisely *that* danger is half the fascination, don't you think?"

"Radiant Jade is fascinated by her?"

"Well—" Madame Keyne mused—"one might say that my secretary . . ."

"—has taken an interest in her?" Pryn suggested.

Madame Keyne laughed again. "You might say that. Yes, that's a very good way to put it."

Pryn said: "Your secretary told me that you hated her."

"That I hated my secretary?" Madame Keyne frowned. "Or that I hated the Ini?"

"Ini."

Again Madame Keyne sighed. "The truth is, girl, I love Jade; and

116

for her sake I put up with the little monster—of whom, finally, I do think I have the greater understanding. Though I like to fancy I'm not as mad as Ini, in many ways we're astonishingly, if not distressingly, alike. If we weren't, I tell myself, why would Jade be able to move her own—" Madame Keyne glanced at Pryn—"interests from one of us to the other so easily?"

The path, taking them toward the great house, now swung them away toward an outbuilding, in front of which, among some fruit trees, stood a cart—the one Pryn had arrived in last night. It was hitched to the same horse. The hangings, however, had been roped back to the frame so that the inner space, save for the overhead awning, was free.

Madame Keyne walked up to it. "There's room for two on the driver's seat. Sit here—" She patted the board—"and we can talk." She helped Pryn up. Then, pulling in skirts and pushing up bangles, she climbed to the seat, as the black-eyed young man whom Pryn had seen earlier among the new servants came running out of the shed.

"Madame, if you would *like* me to drive, I'd be happy to—" He wore a red scarf around his waist.

"Samo," Madame Keyne said, "I told you before, *I* am going to drive. If we are all to be happy here, you must learn that this is not like the other houses you have worked in. I *shall* drive today. Now you run ahead and open the gate. That, today, is *your* job." Madame Keyne picked up the reins and flicked them.

Nodding, bowing, Samo dashed off down the driveway.

As Pryn settled on the seat beside Madame Keyne, the horse's haunches began to move; the cart lurched beneath them. They rolled forward. The trees scattered handfuls of light and shadow in their faces, over their laps.

Ahead, Samo tugged at the heavy planks in the high wall's entrance. Pryn felt a surge of comfort to be riding with, and indeed to be sitting so near, Madame Keyne, who, for all her dubiously placed certainty, seemed the most normal person in the household. Summer warmth had worked its way into the morning chill. Pryn looked about at the lawns, the outbuildings, the hedges, now at where some statues poked above a grove of shrubs, now back to the main house—where she saw Radiant Jade.

The secretary stood just at the house's corner, one clay-stained hand raised—to wave? No, she had simply raised it to touch the wall. Jade watched them.

Pryn turned back.

Samo's face passed by the cart's edge as he lugged the metal-studded planks a final foot; and they were out on the road.

As the cart rolled down the avenue, the widely spaced estates drew closer together, till at last the walls between them vanished and there were only unwalled houses, sitting one by the other, less and less land between. The cart turned. Beside larger buildings stood smaller, shabbier structures. Other carts joined them in the street—which had broken from its straight, tree-lined directness, to bend and branch as if it had become a tree itself.

Alleys siphoned carts and wagons away from them. Alleys poured porters and pedestrians and more wagons and carts in among them. Merchants, laborers, children—and more carts—filled the streets with noise.

Once Pryn touched Madame Keyne's arm. "You said we were going to the *New* Market? I only saw the old one yesterday ..."

Madame Keyne reined the horse again to angle left of another cart piled with sacks. "If you think you saw marvels in the Old Market, believe me, girl, in the New Market you will see wonders beyond imagining! Both locations have their advantages and disadvantages, of course—the Old Market is at the upper end of New Pavē and has the wares that can be purchased on the Bridge of Lost Desire as one of its added attractions. But the New Market is only a street away from the Empress's public park, which seems to be well on the way to fulfilling the same function—and on a somewhat less vulgar level of commerce. Though I swear—" Madame Keyne wheeled the cart away from some youngsters who ran out into the street—"if need be, I'll have that bridge transported to the New Market stone by stone!"

Pryn laughed at the notion, though she was as unsure just why Madame Keyne had suggested it as she was of any motivation within the Sallese gardens.

Jouncing along in the sun over a route she'd last traveled draped about in the dark, Pryn felt a reckless pleasure that was, after all, the legacy dragon riding ought to leave one with. "Madame Keyne, why did your secretary get so upset when she learned I could write and read?"

"Did she now? Hi, there! *Hi!*" which last, with much tugging and pulling, was to get around another cart, piled with bricks of a dirty yellow.

The brick cart was parked before some thatched awning, and the small, ragged woman who was its driver had climbed down, calling and calling for the shop proprietor to come out and look at the shipment—to no avail.

"She probably thought I wanted you to replace her in her job—as indeed I should!" Reins flicked again as they rumbled along the boisterous avenue. "Toss the two of them out, the ungrateful minx *and* her odious kitten! That's what I should do—what I would do if I were some uncivil aristocrat with a host of red-scarfed servants. But I am a poor, hard-working merchant, like my brother and father before me. My red scarves are all, as it were, borrowed from a tradition not mine. And for arcane reasons, which, no doubt, I shall never truly understand, that just doesn't seem to be the way we do things here. I can't bring myself to such behavior, nor would I respect anyone who could. So I am used and abused for my sympathies within the walls of my own home, the most helpless victim before the crazed and childish connivances of my inferiors." She laughed again, in a way that, for the first time, reminded Pryn of Ini. "Has it struck you that way before, girl? I confess, till this minute, it never seemed so to me. Well! Radiant Jade became upset when she learned you could read and write? Imagine! I've *never* heard anything more ridiculous!" She pulled the horses to the right, the smile still on her face as she strained. "But I refuse to discuss it further. After all, didn't I leave the house this morning to get away from such pettiness? We are going to market—to the *New* Market, the wonder of Kolhari! And what is the wonder of Kolhari today will be the wonder of the world tomorrow! Mark it on vellum, my girl. For I am not a woman to speak lightly when ..." Madame Keyne had been pulling the horse this way and that, but here traffic suddenly increased. A bare-breasted barbarian, one water-pitcher balanced on her head and another held on her shoulder, passed practically in front of the horse's nose—indeed, if the animal hadn't jerked up its muzzle it would have knocked at least one of the pitchers to the asphalt. The cart jarred in its traces. Madame Keyne half rose and hauled back on the reins.

From the side of the crowded street, a man rushed forward. He had a short red beard and astonishingly dark eyes, between coppery lashes. He grabbed the horse's bridle and, with a wild little cry, was lifted from the ground, bare feet waving—on his ankles he wore as many clattering and clinking circlets of silver, ivory, and wood as Madame Keyne wore on her arms.

The horse lowered him, pulling and prancing; the little man finally got the animal calmed, now clucking, now cooing, now patting the great red cheek.

"Well," Madame Keyne said, the reins again tight, looking unperturbed, "you're here, exactly where you said you'd be!"

"And I see you've kept our appointed meeting, just as you said you would!" The horse, stepping about, quieted. The little man, with his beard and jangling anklets, grinned up at Madame Keyne from sunburned wrinkles fanning about light lashes. "Have you

119

considered my plan for liquidating this Liberator, who plagues our city, our nation, our world with his schemes and plots and treasons?"

"Yes. I've reviewed your plan, carefully and in detail. I've been impressed by your thoroughness, not to mention the sincerity of your motivation." Madame Keyne switched the reins to one hand. With the other, she pulled up a blue bag of more solid cloth from among diaphanous folds and pleats. "You outlined the fine points of your expenses, and I completely agree with the rigor of your research and the exactitude of your estimations. You've told me—you've *convinced* me your plan will require twelve gold coins and five iron ones to purchase the weapons and hire the men that will insure its success." She reached into the purse and drew out some money. "Here." She thrust coins into the man's hands—he had to release the bridle to take them. "I give you *six* gold coins and *two* iron ones—and we shall see what comes to pass." She snapped the reins. The horse started.

"But Madame—" Clutching the coins, the man danced back with jangling ankles to avoid the cart corner.

"That is my decision," Madame Keyne called back. "I can do no more for you at this moment." They moved out into the traffic. Traffic moved between them and the confused, would-be assassin.

Astonished at the exchange, Pryn looked at Madame Keyne, who guided their cart through the morning crush. A memory of the cellars under the Spur; an image of that accusing barbarian—what was his name ... Sarg?—dead on the underground tiles. Who, Pryn wondered, had financed *that* attack?

When they had driven a few more minutes, Pryn asked tentatively, "You really want to ... liquidate the Liberator?"

Madame Keyne shrugged—or possibly it was just some motion in her driving.

"I mean ... do you think the Liberator's plan to abolish slavery plagues all Nevèrÿon?"

"All Nevèrÿon? How can I say? But I would be a very foolish woman if I thought it was going to help *me*." Madame Keyne urged the horse through a place where traffic had slowed for street construction. It might have been the place Pryn had been put down yesterday; she couldn't be sure.

The cart pushed on.

"But if you really wanted to have the Liberator killed, why did you give that man only half of what he needed—*less* than half! Did you think he was asking for too much?"

With lightly closed lids, Madame Keyne raised her eyes a moment to the sky. "By no means!" She blinked at the avenue again.

"That man is very good at planning the kind of thing he plans. And he was very anxious that I not think him excessive in his demands. Truly, he has whittled his budget down to the bare minimum for success. We spent several hours at an inn in the Spur, while he drew maps of underground passages leading from cisterns to cellars. But you see, I'm afraid that if I gave him his full twelve and five, our Liberator *would* be dead—it really *was* a fine plan. But I have not yet decided whether that's what I want. The little fellow's terribly well motivated, in that way which only conservative fanatics can be. With six and two, I have no doubt that in desperation he will mount his plan anyway—under-equipped, under-manned. Which means there's a good chance he will fail. But it will give the Liberator some trouble, which, at this point, is all I am prepared to do. Indeed, if he is any sort of Liberator at all, he should be used to such encounters! But as of now that's all I'm interested in—at least until I learn more about this Gorgik."

"But what do you want to know?" Though Pryn was not about to admit she had fought through such an encounter herself, she would have admitted to anything else she knew about the Liberator. And Madame Keyne's equanimity over the probable death of the man with the anklets and the possible death of Gorgik made the self-comparison with Ini no longer seem so fanciful.

Madame Keyne's attention was ahead of her on the crowds. "Girl, this isn't a pleasant subject. I didn't intend to bore a new arrival to our city with such tediousness. Besides, did you see that cart full of yellow brick? Myself, I've never seen bricks like that before. Very interesting to me, those bricks—"

"But Madame Keyne—"

"Enough, girl. We're almost at the New Market. What you must do now is prepare your mind for true wonders!"

The street here was clogged with humanity—most of it male. The cart's movement among them was quite slow. Many men were ragged. A good number were naked. Curly light hair; narrow shoulders; close-set eyes—the overwhelming majority were barbarians. As the cart rolled among the ambling, occasionally boisterous men, Pryn sensed a quality which she wondered how she might notate in written signs. She had seen poor people before—indeed, she'd never had any reason to think her own aunt anything more than on the upper end of poor. Still, poor for her had always meant a ragged woman or three with two to ten dirty children in a littered yard before a ramshackle hovel on the outskirts of Ellamon. This was the first time she had ever seen so *many* poor people, and men at that, amassed at a single center.

Poor men filled the street, building to building; with it and because

121

of it the street seemed filled with poverty itself. (That, Pryn decided, was how she would have written it down.) Holding the cart bench beside her, Pryn leaned toward Madame Keyne. "Who *are* these people . . . ?"

"These—" Madame Keyne pulled up on the reins again, for they had gone beyond the last building, to approach a sort of railing—"are the men who do *not* work in the New Market." Madame Keyne halted the horse.

The cart had come to the fence—a single rail supported just above waist-level by pairs of posts driven into the ground in narrow X's.

On this side barbarians milled.

On the other—a stretch of bare earth—a few people walked.

"And over there—"

"Madame Keyne!" The man who sprinted up across the clearing was not a barbarian. "There you are!" He wore a red scarf around his sweat-beaded forehead. "We never know which direction you're going to be coming from, or who's going to be driving!" He laughed. "I had my men stationed down at the Old Pavē, waiting for you—"

"—over there." Madame Keyne finished, "are the men who do." She wrapped the reins about the small post at the side of the driver's seat. "I hope you'll never find me *that* predictable." She stood up as the man ducked under the rail.

He was a tall man, a young man, and very strong. The wide leathers he wore around his wrists were dark at the edges with perspiration. "Here, Madame, let me help you down!"

Barbarians moved back from the cart.

Three other men ran up across the field, two of whom also wore scarves. They ducked under the fence. One took Pryn's hand—his own hot and callused—as she climbed out. Another told the other where to lead the horse.

Madame Keyne swept blowing blue skirts over jangling wrists and, with some jovial remark, ducked under the rail.

Pryn went to the rail, ducked, stood—

The clearing was huge!

From within the crowd, it had looked practically empty. But now, strolling across it, Pryn could see there were as many as thirty or forty men walking or standing about in it. Glancing at the rail, she looked back at the crowd they'd come through. Big as the clearing was, the herds of men on the other side of the railing went almost all the way around it.

Ahead of Pryn, Madame Keyne stopped a moment by another group of three, standing together on the bare dirt and looking over

parchment plans one held for the others to see. Now and again a man wheeled a barrow past, filled with stones and earth. Over there a foreman was pointing something out to a worker. Over there another, walking alone, stopped to squint up at the sun. Many, Pryn saw, wore the red scarf at head or waist—one man had it tied around his leg.

As Pryn walked by, Madame Keyne fell into step beside her. "Look at it!" She put her hand on Pryn's shoulder. "Isn't it *wonderful!*"

"But what *is* it?"

"The New Market, of course!"

"But ..." Pryn looked about, searching for stalls, porters, counters, vendors displaying the marvels she'd been promised. Suddenly she turned back to Madame Keyne. "But you're still *building* it!"

7

Of Commerce, Capital, Myths, and Missions

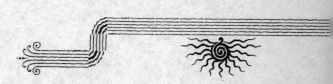

By contrast, the market economy is a constant subject of conversation. It fills page after page in urban archives, private archives of merchant families, judicial and administrative archives, debates of chambers of commerce, and notarial records. So, how can one avoid noticing it? It is continually on stage.

—Fernand Braudel/*Afterthoughts on Material Civilization and Capitalism*

"**W**ell, just look around you! You say you've seen the Old Market. This one is going to be six *times* the size of that spread of junk and garbage over in the Spur!" Madame Keyne's voice was triumphant. "Here there will be air, light, room for commercial growth, the encouragement of true diversity among products, marketing methods, competition and profits!"

"But *you're* laying the whole thing out!" Pryn exclaimed. "Does that mean the whole New Market will belong to you?"

"Nonsense! I'm merely financing its construction. You can see, we had to pull down practically a whole neighborhood. It wasn't easy. The demolition has only been completed for a week or so—"

"But *you're* going to lease space in your New Market," Pryn insisted, "so that you'll get something from everyone who uses it . . . ?"

"Only the *smallest* rent!" Madame Keyne leaned her head confidentially. "I am an ambitious woman. But I am neither stupid nor selfish. That lack is one of the traits that distinguishes me and my class from the aristocrats, who have laid so much misery on this nation—the Child Empress (whose reign is politic and permissive) excepted. No, I intend to take only enough to compensate me for my troubles in the building. I think of this market as a gift to the great city of Kolhari, a gesture that will make us worthy of world regard. That is the spirit in which the project was proposed to the Empress's ministers. That is the spirit in which we are carrying it out. Now—if you want to see what *is* mine here, you must come this way." Madame Keyne started along beside the fence.

Having momentarily slowed to watch the activities about her, Pryn hurried to catch up.

Coming by them now was a rather thick-set man. His red scarf was partly braided in with his hair—much of it gone from his freckled scalp. Behind him were three older boys and a girl. As they walked, the red-scarfed man instructed, ". . . and, of course, lateness will not be tolerated. You men are here to work, and we will get a day's work from you. This woman, or one like her, will be by with a bucket for you to drink from every hour; as well, a woman will be by with a bucket, also every hour, into which anyone who has to may relieve himself. Once you are at your work, there should be no need to leave till we say so. Our first crew of barbarian loafers did more sipping and pissing and splashing of water over their heads than they did digging—*and* expected to get paid for it! But we've finally managed to locate a better breed for our wants here . . ."

As they passed, the girl looked at Pryn. I wonder, Pryn thought, if she thinks *I* shall be carrying a water pail or slop bucket?

Something brushed the front of Pryn's dress and struck Madame Keyne, a step ahead, full on the thigh. Madame Keyne raised her arm and looked down where the clot of mud—or worse—pulled from her skirt to fall to the dust. Madame Keyne looked off at the fence, beyond which barbarians massed. Someone pulled from the fence to hurry away in the closing crowd. Some of those around where he'd been were laughing.

Madame Keyne made a face, shook her skirt, and started walking again. "I'm afraid that's one of the inevitable unpleasantnesses of life outside my garden. It's also why I harbor my dislike of the Liberator."

"Was that one of the Liberator's men . . . ?"

"I doubt it," Madame Keyne said. "Much more likely it was some disgruntled creature with a mother to support, three sisters he has not yet married off, a wife, and uncountable children—a man whom we just failed to hire or, indeed, just fired for his laxness. Or it could be some mischievous youth, a cousin to our own Wild Ini, who has seen such a man as I described throw his clod (though he understand the reasons no more than a pampered aristocrat's brat) who merely finds such violations amusing. Unfortunately, though, a growing number of those men over there, including some of the clod throwers, think the Liberator is here for them."

"But I thought—" for all this seemed as confusing to Pryn as

 128

what had been going on within Madame Keyne's own walls—"the Liberator had come to free slaves."

"Slaves are men and women who labor for no pay. Over there are men who do no labor for no pay. The similarity is enough so that they might make the mistake themselves. If the Liberator makes the same mistake, I may well have reason to pay out full twelve and six to the next fanatic who asks." Madame Keyne sighed, her thoughts drifting somewhere else. Suddenly she announced "The thing Jade does *not* realize—" startling Pryn— "and that her position as my secretary, or perhaps my own love for her itself may prevent her from realizing, so that it is the one thing in our relationship for which I feel guilty, is that as one grows older, one lives more and more off the little signs of whatever community one moves through day to day and less and less off the gifts that fall out of individual relationships. If one does not prepare for this change in youth, then age becomes a bitter time. This is not to disparage the beauty of one's relationships with lover or friend. It is only to acknowledge what, for so many in the city, is a sad truth. Community can, however awkwardly, replace individual relationships. But individual relationships only grow poisonous and resentful if there is no community to support them. But we are *not* going to discuss this any more, my girl. Still—" Madame Keyne looked at Pryn without any smile at all—"I must tell you, if there was any motivation other than idle curiosity behind the disreputable act you caught me indulging with that clever, disreputable man on Black Avenue—and you are old enough, girl, to know no curiosity is really idle—it is only to protect my sense of that community, which includes, for me, equally the man who flung his clod, you, all those who wear my red scarf, Ini, and Jade, and, yes, the whole of this city ... the nation to whom I make my gift, here, as well as those neighbors of mine in Sallese whom I would not dream of inviting to a small, private supper with any of the ones of you I have mentioned, for fear the resultant hostilities and intolerances would render the whole notion of community ludicrous, if not barbaric."

Another clod landed a few feet before them.

Behind the fence was some kind of scuffle. The men ahead of them noticed; one, a great strapping fellow, turned back toward Madame Keyne.

"But what about *his* sense of community," Pryn asked. "I mean the Liberator's—"

"The Liberator, 'ey, Madame Keyne?" The big man who stepped up had the same green eyes, Pryn realized, as Gorgik. For a moment, Pryn wondered if, under the scarf about his neck, was the Liberator's collar.

Pryn blinked.

The face was unscarred.

And his forty-five or fifty years sat among the muscles, calluses, and the general heft of his body more easily than they had rested on iron-collared Gorgik's. "Are those dogs acting up again?" He bawled over the fence: "Have you no respect for a woman of Madame Keyne's standing in this city?" Shaking his head, he looked back. "You may be sure nobody wants any 'Liberator' on *this* side, Madame."

"Hello, Ergi," Madame Keyne said. "I'm glad to see my best foreman is on the job." She turned again to Pryn. "The men who work over here find the idea of the Liberator mildly uncomfortable—no doubt because they make the same mistake as the men outside."

"These fellows here don't want to lose their jobs to the men out there," declared Ergi. "If this Liberator is for the unemployed, then he can't very well be for the employed, too. Hey, you!" Ergi bawled again, waving his fist. "Over there—over *there* with that scaffolding! Not there!" He shook his head. "There's muscle a-plenty around here, Madame Keyne. But I don't think a man in the place can think two thoughts that follow one from the other. Is this your new secretary?"

Startled, Pryn looked up to see Madame Keyne at least looked surprised.

"Possibly," Madame Keyne replied. "And possibly not. I haven't decided whether I need one. This young woman reads and writes—"

"More than I can do!" Ergi laughed.

"—and she listens. As for what she thinks about what she hears—" Madame Keyne's dark, dry face took on its amused and curious smile—"that we have yet to determine."

"Well, you don't have to worry about what anyone thinks of the Liberator on *this* site, Madame Keyne! That's for certain—Hey, there! *Hey*! I said put it—!"

"Yes," Madame Keyne went on. "But there are other confusions to be made, just as simple and just as interesting. For example—"

"Excuse me, Madame." Ergi hurried off to right some confusion ahead, shouting, waving.

"Just as a man who has no work and gets no money for it may think himself a slave, so a man who has work and gets only very little money for it may think the same. And that—I have no illusions about it, girl—is very much the workers, men and women, on *this* side of the fence."

They had almost crossed the dust and gravel, which Pryn had finally been able to reread as a thriving market. What they approached now, however, baffled her.

In an area at least as large as the market proper, there were more workers than there were roaming the square. Clearly this was where Ergi's foremanship centered. Pryn glimpsed him off amidst the excavations, hurrying some naked men from one pit to another. Though some scaffolding had indeed been set up, most of the workers (and only the foremen, Pryn saw now, wore Madame Keyne's scarves) were digging out large, rectangular holes that left two- and three-meter walls of dirt between. "What will they be building here?" Pryn asked, as they started to walk along one.

"Here will be the warehouses, and administration offices, and archives, and market workers' barracks, and vendors' storage spaces, and ... well, all the buildings needed to house the functions that must accrue to any sizable market area. *These* are the buildings which will be mine! Mine to rent, to allot, to administer! Oh, believe me, though I disparage it, I've examined the Old Market as carefully as anyone in Kolhari. And I've learned precisely what keeps it so small. I am prepared to see that the New Market is successful, that it grows, and that I profit both by that success and growth."

The image of the market as a map of the nation returned to Pryn, to be shattered a moment later by her sudden apprehension of this neighborhood of storage spaces and warehouses beside the market as a map of the market to come. And though none of it had yet been filled in, nevertheless it would control the very shape and pace, the movement and organization of that market as surely as Madame Keyne controlled the comings and goings of her red-scarfed employees.

As they made their way over the site, one or another worker looked up to recognize Madame Keyne. The woman seemed to know most of them by name. "Morning, Terkin," she called as one man paused to grin up. She turned to another. "You swing your shovel that hard, Orget, and you'll wear it out!" which made Orget, already working furiously, laugh and redouble his effort.

Pryn looked down into the excavation on their left.

A young woman climbed, step at a time, up the wide ladder. By rope handles, one in each fist, she held a ceramic bucket, filled with urine and darkened with feces. She gained the wall and put the buckets carefully on the uneven dirt.

Urine spilled the sloping clay.

With similar buckets of clear water, around which bobbed half a dozen cups hooked over the rim by their handles, another woman stepped between Pryn and Madame Keyne to halt by the ladder top, waiting for the other to move off so she might climb down.

"Over there—" Madame Keyne pointed between the scaffolds and the workers rolling their carts of dirt along the ridges—"is the sea ... though one can hardly see the waterfront for all the confusion between us and it. Nevertheless, imports from the east and south will have easy access to my warehouses, and thus will have easy access to the entire web of commerce centering here."

Pryn looked down into the excavation on their right.

Dark haired, dark-skinned, arched backs running with water like the falls in Madame Keyne's garden, most of the laborers had abandoned all clothes, though two or three still wore a loin cloth, a leg band, or a leather bracelet.

"Morning, Silit—and that must be young Iryg, who you said you'd bring us today. Work hard as your friend Silit, Iryg, and you'll do well by us!" Madame Keyne stooped to take the wet, callused hand of a sweating man who ran up to tell her some story about his daughter, a lame ox, and a grain jar, to which Madame Keyne nodded and nodded with concern. As she stood, some joke came from the other side of the excavation—a very old joke, too, because Pryn had heard it even in Ellamon. But Madame Keyne tossed a jibe over her shoulder that made the diggers rest their shovels and the water carrier lower her buckets. All howled—till a foreman, passing on the far wall, shouted them back to work.

Several times since their early garden encounter, Pryn had told herself she had no complete picture of this woman. Hour by hour that 'non-picture' had suffered its changes. But, whoever she is, Pryn thought, here seems her home—no matter how much she enjoys her flowers. She might even swing a pick—or carry a bucket—for Madame Keyne had just stopped a slops carrier who'd been walking before them with a limp; she searched through the folds of her skirt, found her purse, and tucked a small coin into the shift, which was turned down and bunched at the dry-haired woman's waist. Then she called the foreman over. "Take Malika here back to the water cask and put her on the filling detail—where she won't have to walk on that foot so much." As Madame Keyne watched the older water-carrier and the younger foreman walk—and limp—off, Pryn thought: She really seems *more* comfortable here.

Madame Keyne paused at a pit to inquire of a balding barrow-pusher after the progress of his wife's illness; at another she stooped to ask a white-haired worker to show her his bandaged shoulder. "If it still pains you, Fenya, I don't want you straining yourself. The bones of dead laborers are not the proper foundations for these cellars."

"Oh, it's nothing, Madame Keyne! Don't trouble yourself over it!"

"The people who work for you, Madame ...?"

Standing, Madame Keyne looked around.

"Even when they have problems, they seem so . . . content!"

As they turned at the corner of another cellar, Madame Keyne took Pryn's arm. "That's because they have the discontented example of the barbarians on the other side of the fence to instruct them."

"You don't use nearly as many women as you do men." Looking over the workers around the site, Pryn pictured herself coming into the city—by some other road, as it were—arriving at the market as a seeker after work rather than as the owner's guest.

"Jade is always after me to hire more women," Madame Keyne commented. "I've actually entertained the notion—certainly I've known all too many women who can work as hard as a man and feel twice the drive to prove it. The idea has always struck me, however, as a thrilling transgression. But I'm afraid this side of fifty I react to such thrills as though they were simple stabs of fear—as though, if I did so, something terrible might happen. Even though I cannot think what. It is as if I want my construction site to look even more like the sites owned by the powerful men in this city than—well, than those sites do themselves. I am not the most powerful person in Kolhari by any means. Forces other than I have created a customary proportion in the sexual division of our labor, and I fear to deviate from it as though it might evoke some vast and crushing disapproval. That fear, you know, is not the disapproval of those whom I am equal to or whom I am above, but rather some fancied disapproval from those above me—men, and they are almost all men, who would never deign even to notice me and whom, when all is said and done, I do no more than glimpse from year end to year end, now as one passes in an elegant carriage, now as one enters some fine-gated mansion, their very absence vouching safe their powers over my actions far more than any adversary present to voice or hand."

"But you *are* a powerful woman!" Pryn declared, for her attention had wandered. "I hadn't realized you were . . . well, *this* powerful! How did you become so? I mean, how did you ever . . . ?" (We write, you see, of a more primitive time when civilization's inhibitions were fewer; so that those delicate questions whose very contemplation might throw the likes of you and me into hot-cheeked stammering or moist-palmed silence were easier to ask, at least for a mountain girl such as Pryn.) "You must tell me!"

"Would you like me to? Sometimes I wish it were more complicated than it is." Madame Keyne found the purse in her skirts' folds. Digging inside, first with two fingers, then with three, she removed two coins, then let the purse fall back. She held them up, one in each hand. The larger was a gold piece that flashed and

133

glimmered. "Here," Madame Keyne said, holding out the gold for Pryn to examine, "is the money with which I finance my projects—the money against which I make my loans, the money I cite when I bargain over lands, the money I have at my beck and call when I arrange prices for materials and labor, the money those who know I am a wealthy woman know I possess." The gold coin was stamped with a likeness of the Child Empress. "While this—" Madame Keyne held out the smaller iron coin—"is the money I am actually prepared to pay out for those unavoidable day-to-day expenses, expenses which include the wages for Ergi, for Jade, for Clyton, as well as for those sweating, naked men and women who dig and carry here—not to mention the six and two I spent back on Black Avenue." The iron piece bore the face of a man whose name and office Pryn did not know—though his coin was far the more common.

"Where do you keep this money?" Pryn asked, for she was beginning to sense just how much such a project as this market and these warehouses must require.

"Ah, it's hidden!" replied Madame Keyne, who, rather than taking offense at the question, seemed delighted. "It's hidden, carefully, throughout the city, where it's protected as much by the accounting acumen of the financially astute as it is by the monetary ignorance of the general populace. Really—" She looked from one coin to the other—"there is nothing complicated in it. You know, girl, there's something I've been more or less aware of since I was a child: if events ever struck me from the position of affluence and prestige that, certainly, my family secured for me far more than I did, as long as the world in general and the city in particular are organized along the lines they are today I could climb back, simply because I know *where* the ladders' feet are located—though I confess, the thought of having to make such a climb again becomes less and less appealing, if only because of my age and energies. But these smiling, sweating, impoverished creatures below us do *not* know—so that the ladders themselves will always be comparatively free of traffic for those of my class who require them. The men here love me—oh, by love I mean nothing profound or passionate; only love at that level of community that we must all indulge for a satisfying life—the women, I fear, do not love me *quite* so much. They are too concerned with how I treat the men and often do not notice my special concern for them: those women in extra need I will often give extra money to directly. I hear the foremen joke about it. But I have been to the homes of many of my workers, men and women—and I know the extra needs of a woman working in this city. I do not claim to hire an equitable number of men from all who need jobs. And I hire less women. But those I

134

hire, I treat well. To do otherwise would be irresponsible to the community which is my concern. Now those men—and women—on the other side of the fence, they are jobless and they hate me—and hate too those that now work. I console myself by remembering that, the odd clod aside, their hate is no more passionate than the love we share over here. Still, if only because I *do* know how real the one is, I must keep my eye open to the other.

"Those men over there, they wait for the Liberator to liberate them—into jobs indistinguishable from the jobs here. I watch them all and find myself smiling.

"There are ladders all about them that they step over and brush against and push aside. But without the training, and—yes—the vision needed to climb them, I suspect they cannot even see them, much less see where they branch, or where one must hurry or halt as one mounts.

"As I've grown older, however, I've had my anxious moments. The anxiety arrives along with a kind of alternative dream, the vision of a world arranged very differently, without any such ladders at all, where no privileges such as mine exist, nor such hardship as theirs: rather it is a dream of an equitable division of goods and services into which all would be born, within which all would be raised, and the paths from one point to the other would be set out by like and dislike, temperament and desire, rather than inscribed on a mystified map whose blotted and improperly marked directions are all plotted between poverty and power, wealth and weakness.

"The anxiety comes with it, however, when I hear report of some new political upstart, such as—yes—our latest Liberator, who declares his own muzzy dream of equality, freedom, and joy. I have watched governments come and go, some led by liberators, some by despots, and I realize that the workers on this side of the fence and the out-of-work on that side—as well as the Liberator they oppose and support—share, all of them, one common mesconnaissance: they think the enemy is Nevèrÿon, and that Nevèrÿon *is* the system of privileges and powers such as mine that supports it, or the privileges and powers such as the Child Empress's (whose reign is, after all, benign and bureaucratic) which rule it. As long as they do not realize that the true enemy is what holds those places of privilege—and the ladders of power to them—in place, that at once anchors them on all sides, keeps the rungs clear, yet assures their bottoms will remain invisible from anywhere other than their tops, then my position in the system is, if not secure, at least always accessible should I, personally, become dislodged."

"Then what is this ... *their* enemy?" Pryn asked. "I mean the true one?"

"You really ask me that, girl?" Madame Keyne laughed sharply. "You actually want me to name it—now? here?" The gesture with which Madame Keyne accompanied the laugh caused the gold coin, which by then was merely lying in her open hand, to fly up into the sun. It soared, it spun—and landed on the hard ground, rolling along the embankment, where it finally swerved and fell in.

"Look there, man!" Madame Keyne called down to one of the laborers. "Bring that back like a good fellow."

Wiping his forehead, the man blinked up. Looking about, he saw the coin, planted his shovel, and went to get it, then vaulted up to crouch on the embankment's edge. "You dropped this, Madame Keyne?" The rough hand, with its horny fingers and scarred knuckles (one nail blackened from a recent mishap), held out the gold. "There you are."

"And this," Madame Keyne said as she accepted the gold in her own dark fingers, "is for you." She handed him the iron coin that had remained with her. "For your trouble. Tell me your name. You're a good worker, I can see that."

The barbarian—this particular worker was a barbarian—squinted up at his employer, sun and surprise deepening the wrinkles about his ugly eyes. Suddenly he let a muffled guffaw. Pryn heard in it the nervous overtones of a man used to laughing openly. "Well, Madame Keyne, Ugrik will work for you any day! Ugrik, that's me!" His accent was as light as Jade's, as if he'd been in the city a long while. "Yes, I'll certainly work for you!" His fist closed on the small iron. Bobbing his bearded head and without ever really standing erect, he dropped back over the embankment and went for his shovel. "Yes, Madame Keyne," he called up, "I certainly will!"

Madame Keyne laughed with him, and walked on.

Coming with her, Pryn only wondered—as Ugrik seized up his shovel with his free hand—where he would put his coin; he was one of the workers who had already given up all clothing in his pursuit of labor.

"Do you see?" Madame Keyne raised the hand in which she again held the gold to shield her eyes. The confidence in her tone was both exciting and confusing. "You see how money that goes out comes back to me? And, you must admit, it costs very little. So now you have the whole system of enterprise, profit, and wages laid out for your inspection, girl. No wonder the Empress and the Liberator both decry slavery, when *this* is such a far more efficient system. You know where most of the iron for these little moneys come from, don't you? It's melted down from the old, no-longer-used collars once worn by—"

"But Madame," protested Pryn, who was both a logical and

136

excitable young woman, "you *lost* money in that transaction! Money went out—and you had to pay to get it back!"

Madame Keyne glanced up at the gold. "Little mountain waif—" she seemed intensely amused—"if you think I *lost* in that transaction, then you do not know what the enemy is, nor, I doubt, will you ever. But if you can see the real gain on my part, then—perhaps! —you have seen your enemy and may yet again recognize her glittering features." She turned the large coin so that sun slid across the likeness of the Empress till the blind-white flare made Pryn look away.

At the same moment a breeze blew some sand grains in Pryn's face, so that she stopped to rub her eyes. When Pryn looked up, Madame Keyne was walking ahead, now laying her hand on the shoulder of another slops carrier, now nodding to another barrow pusher. "Ergi! Ergi!" She called as Pryn came up. "Ergi, I want to talk to you!"

Down in an excavation, the foreman finished setting some sweating men to a new mound of rock and dirt, then came across the pebbles and dust, by now as wet himself as any of his workers.

"Earlier today, Ergi, out on Black Avenue," Madame Keyne called down, "I saw a woman try to deliver some very interesting bricks to a slug-a-bed not yet up to receive his shipment. These bricks were yellow—not your usual red. I want you to find out everything you can about them: their manufacture, functionality, durability, cost, maintenance—everything that contours their value, in any and every direction. See if they'd be good for paving. Then report back to me . . ."

The cart trundled along the tree-shaded avenue by the stone walls of the Sallese estates. It was past the hottest part of the day. Pryn sat beside the older woman, feeling an astonishing exuberance. Commerce and construction? These seemed the centers of life—far more central, certainly, than protest and liberation. On the rumbling cart Pryn could almost let herself think that these, indeed, were what she had taken off on her dragon to find.

Madame Keyne had been pleased and elated since she'd left the New Market. The streets were less crowded, and the drive back easier. By the time they'd reached the suburbs, both had fallen into a pleased silence. Pryn's, however, contained within it all the excitement of her encounter with project and enterprise. Madame Keyne's, as she guided the cart along, seemed—to Pryn at any rate—more pensive. In the moments when her own excitement lulled, Pryn wondered if the prospect of returning to her own embattled garden had quieted the older woman.

Suddenly Madame Keyne announced: "I know what *he* thinks is his enemy. What I must learn, though, is who he thinks to be his allies!"

Pryn looked at her questioningly.

For answer, Madame Keyne nodded toward the broad way the cart was just rolling past. At the end of the shaggy pines was the stone wall with its heavy gate, its leather-helmeted guards, and, behind it, the cracked and indifferently patrolled roof. As they passed, Pryn could see a rider had just come clattering up who now bawled out, so they could hear even at this distance: "Go inside and tell your master, the Liberator, Gorgik, that the Iron Hawk has come to join his ranks!"

The rider cantered off toward the city. Pryn had not been able to tell from the voice, raucous and high-pitched as it was, if it were a man's or a woman's.

Pryn asked, "What do you mean, his allies?"

Madame Keyne flicked the reins. "I want to know: when he runs out of slaves to liberate, will he choose the men on my side or on the far side of the fence as his next cause? Whatever his political program, the Liberator's is an image in our city both sincere and seductive. Whichever side he chooses, he may well succeed."

Ahead, Pryn could see Madame Keyne's gate. "Do you want me to get the answer?"

Madame Keyne raised an eyebrow. "How would you get an answer to that question in this city—" the brow lowered—"other than by asking?"

"But you don't understand!" Pryn said. Somehow she could no longer repress it. "I've ridden a dragon! And I—"

"Have you now? So—" Madame Keyne's smile took on its familiar ambiguity—"you, my dragon-riding ambassador, will lay my anxieties at the Liberator's feet? Under our present Empress, whose reign is clever and calculating, dragons have not been *that* popular."

"I can find out for you!" The cart rolled toward the gate. "I can!"

"I believe," Madame Keyne said as the studded planks swung in, and, between tugging fingertips, Samo's face peered around the edge, "that you believe you can. And belief is a powerful force in these basic and barbaric times." She chuckled as they rolled up the drive. The horse halted under the young fruit trees. Madame Keyne climbed down. Pryn climbed after her.

As she stepped from the bottom rung of the carriage's ladder, Pryn saw Ini coming from the house. She stalked over the grass with the gleeful smile of a child about to surprise a returning parent.

Then Radiant Jade stepped from behind the house's corner, one hand up as if to lean against it—the same gesture Pryn had noticed at their departure.

Madame Keyne went forward to pat the horse's head.

Hands behind her back, Ini reached the first tree. Pryn had a memory of a young cousin coming up to see what present she'd been brought—

Then Radiant Jade ran forward!

She ran with fist-pumping urgency. She ran like a contestant in a year-end festival race. She snatched up her shift in one hand, shouting, "No ...!" Steps behind Ini, she flung herself at the cream-haired girl.

Half a dozen feet from Pryn and Madame Keyne, Ini hardly had time to look back. Jade collided with her. Ini staggered, grunted, and fell under Jade's assault.

The two rolled on the grass ...

... and Pryn saw the knife Jade struggled to tear from Ini's fist. (Pryn remembered Ini's strength with the rearing horse and caught her breath.) Jade gasped and shouted: "No! No—you can't ... We *can't!* I've changed my mind! ... *No!* ... We mustn't—"

The knife, Pryn realized, had been drawn behind Ini's back all through the smiling approach.

Madame Keyne held the bridle in a shock as impassive as the roan's calm. Suddenly she flung the horse's head away—so that the beast stepped twice, three times, taking the cart with her—and strode forward. With one hand she yanked the knife from Ini's hand. With the other she began to strike about at the struggling pair. "Stop it! Stop it, I say! You are animals! Now stop it ...!"

In a kind of oblivious horror, Pryn stepped—nearer, as it turned out, but it could as easily have been away.

Ini finally rolled from Jade, to sit, brushing grass and dirt from her arms. "Oh, all *right...!*"

On all fours, with head hanging, Jade gasped with the effort of the fight.

Madame Keyne held the knife, awkwardly, above her head. Now that Jade and Ini had stopped, her other hand went to her neck, and her own breathing grew more erratic as Jade's gasps stilled.

"Madame Keyne," Pryn exclaimed, "they were going to kill you ...?"

"My dear—" Madame Keyne took another breath in which Pryn could hear the anger—"they were going to kill *you.* Ah—!" She brought the knife down sharply to her side. "They *weren't* going to kill you—they were only going to try and hurt you! But I *said* I wouldn't let that happen! I said I— They were only trying to scare

139

you! That was all they were doing!" She looked at Jade and Ini. "Tell me that was all you were doing! Say it!"

"That's all we were doing." Ini picked a dead leaf from her elbow. "Jade just wanted to scare her."

That was when Pryn realized the four of them were, now, surrounded by a peering circle of women and men, all of whom seemed, at first, strangers. But one was the heavy-set cook in her red scarf; and one was blinking Samo; and the three new kitchen girls; and over there, the gardener Clyton—among another five or six Pryn hadn't even seen yet on the grounds.

"I wouldn't have done it!" Radiant Jade gasped. "I wouldn't have ... I told *her* to do it! Yes. To scare her. But you see ... I wouldn't have really *let* her! You see, I *stopped* her! I stopped her ..."

"Get up!" Madame Keyne said. "Get up, I say!"

Ini stood, bending to brush grass from her knees.

Jade began to cry. Her head sank even lower. "I have nothing! Don't you see, Rylla, I have nothing. You have everything! You have money, a fine home, servants, respect! I, I have nothing—I *am* nothing! Now you would take even the little I have from me and give it—"

"Oh, stop it!" Madame Keyne declared.

"You are an empress here; you are a woman of high standing in the city—whereas I am totally at the mercy of your every whim and caprice—"

"I—?" Madame Keyne declared. In her laugh was anger. "I, empress? No, my dear. *You* rule here, despotically and completely! I loved you—and love you still; and I have been tyrannized for it. You order this room decorated thus, object to the decor in that one. And we all know we must comply, or suffer your sulkings and poutings till we are made miserable with them! You come from your room in the morning, and both servants and houseguests fall silent, waiting to see if you are in a mood or a pet over this or that. If you are, any one of us may be snapped at, snubbed, insulted, or—most mercifully—ignored; which allows us, at least, I suppose, to go on with our day. But sometimes I am silly enough to want something more than to be ignored!"

"Nothing! Nothing at all!" Radiant Jade cried. "Nothing! I hate myself. I loathe myself. You *are* right, Rylla. You are right about everything. You are *always* right! I cannot *live* with your insufferable rightness—"

"Oh, put it up, Jade!"

"But it *is* terrible to live with! Yes, I treat you, the servants, everyone, horribly! And you would destroy the one bit of self-esteem I have left by depriving me of my position and giving it to

this ... this awful girl! She doesn't belong here! Look at her, she should be in the forests, in the mountains, on the sea—anywhere but here!" (Pryn frowned at that but was too surprised to question it.) "She isn't worthy of us—of you, Rylla. Oh, *why* did you bring her here? Why!"

Madame Keyne took a deep breath, the knife out from her side. "You silly, silly woman!" She ordered Ini: "Help her up!"

"I will go," Jade declared, still on the ground. "I won't be *put* out—I couldn't stand that. But I'll go of my own accord. You needn't ask me ..."

"I am *not* making Pryn my new secretary," Madame Keyne said. "Your position here is secure."

Radiant Jade clutched unsteadily at the Ini's knees as the pale-haired young woman reached down to help.

"Of course I'm not!" Madame Keyne went on. "Oh, you *are* silly! I am making Pryn my ... my ambassador. She is going to go on a mission—"

Had it not been for the circle of servants, Pryn might have run off then, somewhere, to hide.

"A dangerous mission which she has volunteered for and from which she *does* return, then ... we shall reward her and send her on her way!"

"You're sending her away?" On her knees, Jade lay her head against Ini's hip; Ini still tried to pull her to her feet. "You're not going to replace me—"

"Pryn was not brought here with her own consent. I could no more keep her here than ..." Madame Keyne took another breath— "... than you could harm her for no reason."

Radiant Jade finally got her feet under her. One arm around Ini's shoulder, her head still hung. Her hair had come partially loose. Pryn, who had always kept her own hair fairly short, was surprised there was so much of it. Jade brushed her hand over her forehead. More hair fell.

"All right!" Madame Keyne said. "I want to go and walk in my garden. I want you three to come with me—where we can talk."

"All right!" Radiant Jade took a breath that seemed a kind of imitation of Madame Keyne's. The phrase, Pryn realized, was to the servants. "To your jobs now! There's no reason to stand around gawking at the misery of your masters! Go on with you, I say!"

Glancing at each other, the servants broke their ring.

"Yes," Madame Keyne said. "Please, go now. Back to your work. Everything is ... all right."

Her arm tightly about Ini's shoulder so that she moved the young

woman, unsteadily, with her, Radiant Jade began to walk—unsteadily—forward.

In a voice devoid of all the edges Pryn associated with it, Ini said, "Why do you lean against me so?" It was a rather caressing voice. Ini's arm was firmly about Jade's shoulders as she helped the barbarian along. "I do not like the touch of your body, Jade. I generally do not like the touch of women's bodies. For touching, I think I would prefer the bodies of men." With her free hand Ini reached around to push the straggling hair from Jade's face. "I have told you that, and told you again: I do not love women the way that you—and Madame Keyne—do. For that kind of love, yes, just as with killing, I prefer men." Ini laid her cheek against the secretary's, which was now, Pryn saw, tear-wet. "I do not love you. I do not even want to love you—not in the way you want to love me. I've told you that, you know. Many times." She moved her cheek against the secretary's. "I've told you."

Here Madame Keyne took Pryn's arm firmly. At another moment the gesture would have seemed simple friendship, but now it seemed protective. Caught up in a political massacre and menaced by a street hoodlum, Pryn could not help thinking that whatever danger still waited for her here was probably intriguingly minuscule. Indeed, it had much the same air about it as the scarred Fox's straying hand—something that, however unpleasant, could be gotten through, at least with Madame Keyne's help. Yet once it *were* gotten through, what might lay beyond it seemed just as great a mystery as the one her initial arrival had presented. For better or for worse, she found herself putting aside fear in favor of curiosity.

The red brick path they walked up was the one Pryn had mounted with Madame Keyne that morning. As they reached the sudden and surprising stone hut at the top, Ini finally shrugged away from Jade. It was only then that Pryn pulled her own arm from Madame Keyne's and called ahead: "But *why* did you want to kill me?"

With her calm and questioning smile, Ini turned. "I saved your life yesterday." Suddenly she sat on the grass, locking her arms about her knees, swaying. "Today I thought to throw a life away—yours? But why not." Ini frowned at Jade. "I *told* you I don't like to kill women! I told you that. And you wanted me to do it anyway! But I didn't care."

Jade's attention had gone from the Liberator's headquarters behind to the cityscape before them. Now she looked back at Ini—whose eyes, over the same seconds, had fixed on some deliquescent city in the clouds, its destruction, before high winds undetectable here at the ground, hugely attenuated by size and distance.

"I must talk to you," Madame Keyne repeated. "I must talk to you all. And I don't believe any of you are listening." She lowered herself to the stone bench against the hut's back wall. "But I *will* talk. It's my own garden. That's the least I should be allowed to do in it—to talk."

Because she felt nervous, Pryn sat, too, on the grass—somewhat away from Ini.

Jade still stood—there was room for her on the bench. Madame Keyne looked as if she expected Jade to sit beside her. But Jade swayed, nervously, looking at Ini, looking at the city again.

"I am sending you away, Pryn." Madame Keyne said. "You understand, now. I must."

"Yes . . ." Pryn nodded.

"This evening," Madame Keyne continued. "You must go to the Liberator for me and ask him my question. When you bring me an answer, I shall give you a gold piece—or, at any rate, its equal in small moneys. A girl your age shouldn't be showing gold about, trying to get it changed. Then I shall put you on the road again to continue your travels. Jade, Ini, do you hear? She is my ambassador to the Liberator—*not* my new secretary! And when she completes her mission, she shall go!"

"She will really leave?" Jade asked. "You really will send her away? Why can't she leave now!"

"If I *do* send her away, now—" The smile came to Madame Keyne's face with another emotion that seemed more serious than either curiosity or amusement—"will *you* send away your Ini—?"

"Oh, Rylla, *will* you persist in . . . Oh, I *can't!* I mustn't! I won't! You *know* how I feel about Ini. I would simply die if I had to—"

"Cease this!" Madame Keyne half-stood. "Cease!" She took a breath and dropped back to the bench. "You do *not* have to send away your Ini. And I *will* send away Pryn, I tell you. This evening."

Radiant Jade blinked about the clearing. "Then let me return to the house. I cannot stay here. I am exhausted by all this . . ."

"While I, no doubt, am invigorated . . . ! Of *course* you may go," Madame Keyne's voice had become somewhat shrill. "Why should you stay longer? You have everything you want."

"I? I have nothing! And you would ask me to give up even that. You have all the power, Rylla. All of it. I? I only want one thing." She turned suddenly to Pryn. "I want you *gone!*" (Pryn flinched—but from surprise; fear, as it seemed to more and more these days, had almost left.) "And I want you gone *now.* . . ! But I can't have that, can I?" She turned, listlessly, away. "So. Once again, Rylla, we shall do it *your* way." Jade walked off along the red brick.

"Oh, yes! I understand!" Madame Keyne's voice went even shrill-

143

er. "You are too distraught to hear anything I might have to say now! You've heard what you wanted to hear. Now you'll wander off into your own fantasies which, in spite of all our attempts at sanity, we find ourselves conforming to more and more each day—"

"Please, Rylla . . ." Jade said, not looking.

"You have what you want. Why must you do anything else? Now you leave us with the responsibility of carrying out your desires—"

Jade suddenly drew herself up and turned back angrily. "What do you want me to *do*!"

"What do I want you to do . . . ?" Then Madame Keyne sighed. "I want you to do what you always do: whatever you want. You may go."

Her anger again losing focus, Jade turned again to walk away on the red brick path, between shrubs, flowers, trees . . .

"Madame Keyne," Pryn said after a moment, uncertainly, glancing at the still seated Ini. "I'm happy to do your mission for you. Before, I didn't know whether you believed I could or not." She felt oddly distanced, almost light-headed.

"Before," Madame Keyne said, "neither did I."

Pryn frowned. "Are you . . . *really* that interested in the answer the Liberator will give about his allies?"

"I am interested in the answer," Madame Keyne said. "The question, however—no—does not interest me." She sighed. "But you must still go. At the far corner of my garden there is a break in the wall. I told Ini about it once, and I believe she has been working up her courage to try it. This evening, when it grows dark—"

Ini suddenly ceased her rocking, released her knees, and said: "She *is* a silly woman, isn't she, Madame Keyne."

"Jade?" Madame Keyne turned on her bench to regard the seated murderess. "Oh, I call her that in anger. But she's not really. I don't think she's silly at all."

"She's very upset now." Ini pulled her feet beneath her. "She's very unhappy and confused."

"Oh, I don't know." Madame Keyne shook her head. "No. I rather doubt it."

"You know how she feels about me." Ini pushed herself to her feet. "It would be best if I went to her."

"No." Madame Keyne mused. "Going to her now might not be the *worst* thing you could do. But it's definitely *not* the best."

Ini brushed grass blades from her hip, then turned off along the red brick. "I think, though, I will go to her . . ." She strode off down the path.

"I really think—" Madame Keyne picked up the knife from where she'd placed it beside her on the bench and turned it about—"our little Ini would like to be a caring person. But it's so foreign to her nature, she can only imitate the gestures. And she's bewildered at the idea that one or two such gestures might better serve the impulse behind them by being indulged only after reasonable forethought." She looked up. "Are you glad to be leaving us?"

"I ... suppose I am. Still, I wish I were leaving with more certainty as to why I had been brought."

Madame Keyne put the knife down in her lap. "I shall make a bargain with you. I'll tell you why you were brought here if you'll tell me why you came."

"Why I *came*? But you sent Ini to bring me! And I was on the bridge with that man—"

Madame Keyne raised her hand. "No, my dear. Those brutal and barbaric notions with which my secretary keeps order in my life and in hers may someday overwhelm our peaceful and placid civilization. Till then, however, we can admit that they are only stories." Madame Keyne frowned. "Or could it be that in the mountains around fabled Ellamon they believe that there are great powers and small powers and that the great ones always win and the small always lose, and thus smallness can be counted for nothing? No. Not if the fables I've heard about the weak and wondrous dragons are to be believed. My dear, sometimes *I* believe we shall lose all contact with magic. When that happens, civilization will have to be written of with other signs entirely."

"But what *is* this magic you are talking about again?" Pryn demanded. "You said it was power. But you don't seem very powerful now ..."

"And yet I speak of magic, claim to know it, claim to have it ..." Madame Keyne sighed. "Once I had a friend. Her name was Venn—one of those brilliant women from the Ulvayn islands. I met her here in Nevèrÿon when I was much younger. She had quite the most astonishing mind I'd ever encountered. I was rich and she was poor—but riches or poverty, neither one really concerned Venn. She traveled throughout Nevèrÿon and finally returned to her island. When I was older, I visited her there several times, and she took me around with her to see the tribes that lived in the island's center, describing to me their ways and customs—she had lived among them once, even borne a son by one of their hunters. She walked with me at night by one of the famous boatyards where they build those ships that are the wonder of Nevèrÿon's seas, pointing out over the fence which, among the skeletal hulks, were modeled from her own designs. On a rise above the island-edge village, her little shack was a storehouse of marvels. Once, when she was first here, she gave us a marvel to keep. It stays in this

hut—oh, but that must have been thirty years ago. No, forty. Ah—!" She touched her fingertips to her cheek. Bangles jangled to her elbow. "*More* than forty years ago—because I couldn't have been fourteen yet. Really, she gave it to my father, though I've always thought of it as mine. It was back when this was the barbarian inventor Belham's hut. I keep it in here." Madame Keyne suddenly stood. "Would you like to see it?"

"Yes—!" Pryn said, though it was, of course, the name of her great aunt's onetime friend that prompted her answer, rather than the divagation on the unknown island woman. Pryn stood and followed Madame Keyne around the hut's corner to the inset planks. As Madame Keyne took a metal key out of her purse, Pryn's mind tumbled with images both about her aunt and from her aunt's tales. Madame Keyne inserted the key in the lock, turned it, jiggled it back and forth a few times, turned it again. She pulled. Grating on the stone sill, the door slid open. And Pryn, moving behind her, was momentarily sure, if only on the most tenuous evidence of a sign not even written but mentioned, that she would find within something of her home, if not her vanished father!

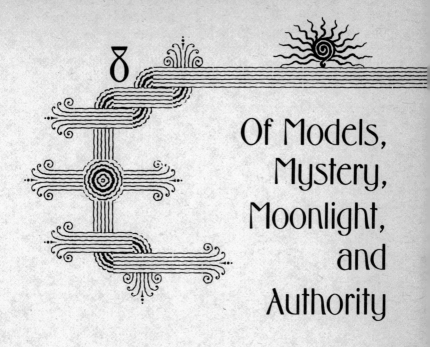

Of Models,
Mystery,
Moonlight,
and
Authority

The central thesis of this chapter is that usually, when we speak of "information," we should use the word "form." The scalar measure of information (e.g., energy and entropy in thermodynamics) should be geometrically interpreted as the topological complexity of a form.... Thus energy appears as the complexity relative to the largest system in which the given system can be embedded, and is the complexity which retains its meaning in every interaction with the external world; it is the *passe partout* parameter and so contains the least information about complexity.... Another example can be cited from biology: plants take in through their chloroplasts the grossest complexity of light, namely energy, whereas animals extract, through their retinas, the correlation of forms, or the information that they need to obtain their food, and thus their energy.

Let us now deal with the technical difficulties of defining the complexity of form.

—René Thom/*Structural Stability and Morphogenesis*

Pryn followed Madame Keyne over the worn doorstep. Grilles high in the corners let in light. On a large table by one wall, Pryn made out what first looked like piles of something green; other colors, here and there, flecked about it. In the middle of it was a ... house! ... a toy house! Pryn blinked. And toy trees! And toy statues! Around it all ran a stone wall, about eight inches high.

Pryn exclaimed: "It's ... your home!"

"And my garden," Madame Keyne pointed out. "And my wall. And my waterfall. And my bridge. And my fountains—watch!"

Madame Keyne went to the hut wall, where various containers and conduits were fixed. Standing on tiptoe, she checked if one were filled. She examined another, then pulled a small lever.

Pryn had gone up to the table's edge. The model's precision was, indeed, magical, as if one might find the break in the wall at the corner—or the rotten bars at the stream entrance. On one tree-shaded rise Pryn saw a tiny stone hut, a path of tiny red bricks

149

winding up to it and a tiny bench against its back, its wooden door indeed set ajar, so that she *had* to imagine two diminutive female figures had just stepped over its threshold, one of whom, even now, at a miniature table's edge, leaned over a tinier rise, atop which stood a tinier hut, its tinier door ajar, and over whose tinier threshold had just stepped—

A splashing made Pryn look up.

On the far rise, water sluiced through the arched grate (had the bars rusted through? The water covered them, and Pryn couldn't tell), ran along the stream bed, moved out along the four brick-lined tributaries to fill one, then two more, then the last of the brick-rimmed pools.

Water reached the falls and broke on fish, dolphin, kraken, and octopus. It swirled the rocks between the banks at the falls' bottom. As it swept beneath the bridge, one, then two more, then the last of the fountains at the bridge's corners sprayed, left and right, into the little stream. Water wound by bowers and benches, beneath over-hanging branches of shade tree and willow, around the house, divided in three at a stone clearly carved for the purpose, and rushed on.

"Did your ... *friend* make this?" The delicacy of the model was as close to magic as Pryn could conceive.

Madame Keyne pulled another lever. A contraption on the wall, with angled paddles, began to turn. "No. This, actually, was made by Belham—he was the inventor of the fountain and the architect for many gardens about Sallese and Neveryóna, you know."

Pryn breathed. "Oh ... !"

Leaves on the miniature trees fluttered; miniature willow fronds above the stream began to flitter fishbone shadows over the water in the sunlight barred by the high grilles. Waves of darker green played across whatever had been used to imitate grass.

"A map of the garden ... ?"

"Yes," Madame Keyne said. "You might say that. Did you see the fountains?"

"Oh, yes! They work, too! That's wonderful!"

"Have you determined *how* they work?"

Pryn frowned. "I just assumed that ... up there, the water in those four pools runs down through some kind of pipes to the four fountains on the bridge below the falls ... ?"

"Can you say *why* the fountains spurt into the air—instead of merely dribbling out in an uninteresting spill?"

"I suppose—" and, to be fair, Pryn had seen the fountains through the gates around the grounds of the Suzerain of Vanar's High Hold and had even once delivered lunch to an uncle and

cousin who had been called in with a work crew to repair one in much the same manner as Clyton had repaired Madame Keyne's— "it's because the tributary pools are so much higher. The water remembers its higher position and leaps up ... to regain the level of the source!" That is what she'd heard her great-aunt say.

"A good explanation! Almost the exact words of the barbarian who built it—so exact, I am tempted to think that brilliant and tragic man spent time in your own neighborhood. But no matter." Madame Keyne folded her arms. "It was when Belham was building these fountains and working in this hut that Venn first came from the Ulvayn islands to visit my family. Belham had finished this model, but was still supervising the workers at the falls itself. He showed Venn his model, here; and she spent a long time examining it, coming back to look at it by herself, and generally playing with it when the barbarian was not actually using it for his measures. Sometimes she would go right from here to examine the bottom of the real falls down below. (Belham thought she was a very eccentric woman and often complained about her inquisitiveness.) Finally she told my father, 'I am going to build you something.' And she moved in here for several days, during which Belham fumed and stayed in the main house with us. After perhaps a week, she had built—" Madame Keyne turned away from the miniature garden— "this."

Pryn turned with her, to confront the shadowy construct on the far side of the hut.

Madame Keyne stepped across the dusty flags.

Pryn, after a moment, stepped after.

On a stand, that put it about eye-level, sat a large bronze bowl. Leaded to the bowl's side was a copper tube that curved down and around to end at the edge of another large bowl set on a lower part of the stand; the second bowl's bronze rim came just below Pryn's knee.

"What will happen if I fill up the top bowl with water?" Madame Keyne asked.

"Water, I suppose, will run out the tube and down and around and into the bottom bowl." Pryn spoke with confidence but tried to preserve margin for any correction that might turn out to be the mysterious point of it all.

"Just as in the fountain," Madame Keyne confirmed. "And, as with the fountain, the water remembers its higher position and tries to leap back up. However, you will notice that the tube leaving from the upper bowl does not leave from its bottom, as do the pipes from the tributary pools; rather it leaves from low on the bowl's side. And in the bottom bowl, the tube end does not point straight up, as in a fountain, but spills in—also from the side. Now look more closely in the top bowl."

Pryn stepped up to peer over the top bowl's rim; it had been filled with some kind of plaster, from which a shape, with all sorts of grooves, gullies, and irregularities had been gouged. The plaster had dried—it looked as if a single hand had, in a one motion, scooped out the hollow.

"... and at the bottom bowl."

That bowl, Pryn saw when she bent to look, was filled to the brim with fine sand. The surface was quite smooth.

"Now—" Madame Keyne stepped away to more containers and levers on the wall— "I'm going to fill the upper bowl with water." A lever squeaked.

From a spigot just above the whole contraption, water sloshed down into the top bowl among the irregular plaster shapes.

From the tarnished tube at the rim of the bottom bowl, Pryn saw, moments later, water spurt across the sand, dig into it, wash some of it away, spread, dig, spread again. Sand and water overflowed the rim—to be caught in the trays and filters and drains set beneath it. In the lower bowl, second by second, sand gouged away; crevices and gulleys deepened.

"There." Madame Keyne said: "That's enough." She threw the lever back.

The water in the upper bowl lowered, clearing wet peaks and valleys.

The shimmer across the lower bowl, still filled, stilled.

"Now," Madame Keyne instructed, "examine both."

Pryn looked into the upper: wet pink plaster, small puddles in the deepest depressions—the impression of a single hand-swipe was even stronger. She could make out the clear tracks of the four fingers, the angled gouge of the thumb. Halfway across, all turned to the left. A few inches further on, there was another crater as if, in the hand's pulling loose, some extra clot had come out too.

Pryn bent to look at the bottom bowl. The water seemed to have scooped out quite a gouge. Under the bowl, on the filter tray, sand stood in wet piles. Sand streaked the bottom bowl's bronze sides.

Pryn looked in.

Beneath the water, Pryn saw four distinct troughs in the remaining sand, with a fifth angled from the side. Halfway across, all turned to the left. Then, a few inches on, a crater ...

"It's the same!" Pryn exclaimed, seeing as she said so that it was not *exactly* the same; shapes were gentler, some were less distinct. "It's *almost* exactly ..."

Madame Keyne nodded. "Not only does the water remember its

height in that top bowl, it remembers the entire shape within that bowl, remembers it all the way down the length of the tube through which it runs, remembers it well enough to recreate that shape when it runs into conditions that allow it to demonstrate what it remembers." Madame Keyne turned toward the hut's still open door. "What is below is an ... *almost* perfect map of what is above, as the model of my garden is an almost perfect map of the garden itself."

Between astonishment and the desire to demand a repeat demonstration, Pryn followed.

"After Venn showed us that—" Madame Keyne stepped into the doorway light—"and we were all as astonished as you—Belham, my father, my brother, myself—Venn said, and I shall never forget the equally astonishing humility on her island face as she said it, 'Any barbarian can look at the bottom of a falls and see in the rising splash the principle of the fountain. But what I have seen, what I have devised a way to show to you, so that you have seen it too, will remain a wonder till the globe of the world and the globe of the sun meet in their common center, and the one consume the other. This wonder humankind will know and forget, know and forget, know and forget again. And that knowing and forgetting will approximate the peaks and depths of civilization as close as the plaster rises and valleys of Belham's model approximate the rises and valleys of your garden.'" Madame Keyne paused in the doorway, her arms folded, looking down. "The house, of course, is in a valley. I was standing in this doorway, here, watching Venn, outside, talking. And I thought: 'Moving from place to place in society, power remembers ...'" She laughed. "And I think that was the beginning of my interests in magic, of the sort you have seen me engaged in at the New Market."

Pryn stepped out into the leaf-splayed light after Madame Keyne.

"That afternoon, Venn quit our house for the south. Belham was very upset, I recall. He got terribly drunk that night, and made a great bother of himself all about the grounds ... he'd been commissioned by several other families to make fountains in *their* gardens, too. Myself, I've always felt that ours were the nicest." Madame Keyne did not close the hut door but walked back to the bench and, with a little sigh, sat. Ini's knife still lay on the stone. Pryn looked at the woman, who, at this point, seemed both frailer and more wondrous.

"The purport of magic is so simple, it's odd that it is not as obvious as ... But then, what was obvious to Venn was not obvious to Belham. Still, in any encounter there is always a stronger side *and* a weaker side—and both sides *always* have power. But

because there is magic loose in the world, the stronger had best pay attention to the weaker if the stronger wishes to retain its position. You are not in a terribly strong position. I am not in a terribly weak 'one. We are not arguing, you and I, about which of us holds which place. You want to know my reasons for bringing you here. I want to know your reasons for coming. It only seems fair to me to ask, since you, at this point, know so much of me!"

Once more Pryn sat down on the grass—and felt the cloth of her dress, rumpled beneath one buttock, and a twig, nipping her under the other. "Let me use what little power I have, then: you tell me first."

Madame Keyne's smile took on its familiar ambiguity. "But you know already. I brought you here because I was jealous."

"Jealous of . . . ?"

"Jealous of Jade." Madame Keyne's shoulders lowered; her hands moved back on blue covered knees. "I suppose it's been three months now since Jade found her Wild Ini—in the public park, too, not a bench away from where, two and a half years before, I myself found Jade. Jade makes friends easily. Ini talked to Jade—Ini took her about the Spur, Ini fascinated her, Ini visited her here at our home. I talked to Ini, I took Ini about our garden, I fascinated Ini. Soon her talents were unofficially in my employ. Jade and Ini's relationship is precisely as you see it—nothing to grow jealous of, now, is it? And yet I grow jealous. In my jealousy I resolved to take the first beautiful street girl I saw for my own."

"—and that was me?"

"You are *not* traditionally beautiful, you know—"

"Radiant Jade is very beautiful."

"Yes." Madame Keyne sighed. "She's quite beautiful. Often I have thought her quite the most beautiful woman I've ever known."

"I don't have the set of features and lineaments that . . . threaten to spill you over into the silence of death?"

Madame Keyne laughed. "But for me, my dear, there *are* no such features and lineament—whereas Jade simply does not know what hers are." Madame Keyne's smile seemed to mock itself. "Of course, everyone else who knows her does: little street girls just into town with the memory of murder in their faces—"

Pryn felt herself stiffen. But Madame Keyne hadn't known—*couldn't* have known about the man in the cellar . . .

"There," Madame Keyne said. "Just what you did—just now. A kind of sulkiness, a kind of suspicion."

And Pryn laughed. "It isn't fair, Madame—" laughing seemed all there was to do—"the way Jade feels about Ini. I mean, along with the way she feels about your bringing *me* here."

The laughter made Madame Keyne smile again. "That kind of

fairness doesn't exist—or rather is for children buying lengths of sugar cane from the vendor in the Old Market, whining to daddy, whose concern is always elsewhere, about who has gotten the bigger piece. The potter god who glazed us did not paint us all evenly, nor even all with the same glaze; nor were we all fired at the same temperature."

"So I must go . . . ?"

"Girl, I had no more notion of using you to replace Jade as my secretary than I had of riding a dragon! But it so happens you *do* read and write. More and more people can, these days. I didn't know it when I first saw you—though Jade will never believe it wasn't part of my plan from the beginning. But then, *I* shall never believe it was merely concern for the secretarial aspect of her situation that impelled all Jade's actions toward you—though in an hour or a week she will be insisting that was all there was to it. Oh, well; I suppose she's no different from Ergi, who thinks that every young woman he sees me with shall henceforth be moved into my house and made heir to my worldly property. Such misreadings are very common—more, they are very powerful, almost as powerful as the proper ones."

"What will you do with Ini?"

"She will stay in my official employ until it is time for her to leave. But that is something Jade and I—and the Ini—will have to decide."

"It seems so strange." Pryn sighed. "I mean that you only brought me here to make Jade jealous—"

"Did I say that?" Madame Keyne leaned forward, looking a little surprised. "Certainly, I didn't say—"

"No, but I thought that's what you meant. I mean, when you said . . ."

Madame Keyne frowned. "Do you think so?" She pursed her lips. "Now myself, that had never occurred to me. Make Jade jealous . . . of me? But perhaps it occurred to Jade . . . ? No wonder she is so pained by your presence, then, for it must seem a very intentional hurt. The pain inflicted by a loved one that we believe inadvertent, to the extent we love truly, is bearable. But the pain we suspect is inflicted because we are considered not really human and therefore fit to be hurt, that makes us ache to the depths of our most human bowels." She pondered a moment. "Ergi would think as you did—Why shouldn't Jade? But no. I was not jealous of what Jade had—*have* the Ini? In any way one might reasonably want her, I *do* have her. No, I wanted to do what Jade did. I wanted to be *free* to do it. I brought you here to be free. That's all." She smiled. "I wanted to do what Jade did. And I have discovered, by trying, that . . . it is not within my power."

"Madame Keyne," Pryn said, "before I came here, my life was caught up in a world of men, where everything was purpose, plan, and plot—yet I was always outside it. But here, where everything is nuance, emotion, and jealousy, somehow I have found myself at the most uncomfortable and precarious center—where I feel just as excluded!"

"Are you saying you are some sort of mystic and are prepared to abandon both the worlds of men and of women for the world of magic and marvels? You *are* a special young woman, I can tell. Still, that is not what I would have thought you most suited for. But now I have told you why I brought you here. You must tell me why you came."

"I came here because I ..." Pryn looked down. "Because I was looking for a friend."

"A friend?" Madame Keyne regarded the girl curiously. "I dare say we haven't distinguished ourselves much in the friendship area. Though, who knows: perhaps one day you will be able to think of us as friends ..."

"She was a woman I heard about, once," Pryn went on. "She wore blue beads in her hair and carried a double blade—"

"The Western Crevasse!" exclaimed Madame Keyne. "Your friend was a woman of the Western Crevasse, where men serve and women rule and do all that men do in Nevèrÿon. Where did you meet this wondrous creature?"

"I never met her," Pryn explained. "I only heard about her."

"Only heard about her ... ?" Madame Keyne frowned. "Only heard? Ah, child, let me tell you something. When I was a girl, I, too, used to hear of those marvelous and mysterious fighting women of the Western Crevasse. Now and again someone would report that their red ships had pulled into the Kolhari docks. When I was a girl, I would hear my brother whispering to my father; that week no one would let me go down to the port, and I would be sure those wonderful women were what they were whispering of. When I was older, once or twice I sneaked down into the city when I heard that their strange ships were supposed to be in. And as I wandered among the children bouncing their rubber balls, some-times I would find a fishing ship from the Ulvayn islands, which occasionally employed a woman or three among its hands. But I never did see any of those double-bladed warriors. Let me tell you, girl. The warrior women of the Western Crevasse do not exist. Nor have they ever existed. They only grew up in stories because women like you—and me—from time to time wished they existed, because men like my father and brother were terrified they might. I think we use them as a kind of model. A model for thinking. But

156

the truth, I'm afraid, is that the closest thing you and I will ever find to those raven-haired legends is our own pale-haired Ini. After all, we want them to do all the things for us Ini does. But we want them to do them out of a profound, moral innocence that obliterates all the darkness and rescinds all the terror that our own little monster carries about with her everywhere she goes. Well, you can't have that kind of innocence any more than you have the kind of fairness that gives each child the same size piece of cane down to the centimeter. Your blue-beaded, double-bladed hero, coming to save you from the hands of wily men—and women—, who can perform any degree of violence in the course of its accomplishment yet with never a selfish thought, does not exist. Indeed, she would be quite terrifying if she did. Indeed, *if* she did, she would not be tall, but short, she would not be dark-haired but blonde, and she would be horribly wounded, a hopelessly mad and poisonous little white gillyflower of a girl. And at least we—or my poor Radiant Jade, at any rate—accept our Ini for what she is. Whether she wear my scarf or no, she does *not* accept us. But we have a compensation which, in the long run, is denied her. It is, simply and insipidly, love. As confused with other motives as it may be, deferred, displaced, speaking in codes when it would speak at all, written in shaky signs in shadowy ill-lit corners, it is still what brought you here. Somewhat purified, somewhat clarified, somewhat analyzed—and that is all any one of us can ask it to become—it is what sends you on your way." She joined her hands in her lap. "Girl, you have been swept up in this wildest of gardens by a great and real power. Now that you are about to leave, you may be tempted to shrug off the whole experience as an unfortunate irrelevance, best put out of current thought, best expunged from future memory. But you must know, as you make your way in the wider world, the same play of power and desire rages in all men and women, contouring all acts, aligning all motivations, no matter what the object. Nor will your own soul be free of that play. That play *is* desire, in all its myriad forms. And as you look back on us from time to time to judge or to rejudge us—and you will—do *not* be kind. All I would have you do is remember that we, in this garden, have been a bit more responsible, a bit more honest than most. Do not praise us for it, in these passionate and primitive times. But do not dismiss us heedlessly, either by forgetfulness or too-quick censure." Madame Keyne searched in her skirts with jangling wrists. Finding her purse, she pulled and plucked it open, went into it with one and another finger, teasing out one, a second, a handful of coins. "Here—this is for your coming efforts on my behalf to question the Liberator. No . . . I think it better to pay in advance in such cases. After all, there *is* the chance you won't return. Take it, take it right now. Yes, you have pockets in that dress. Go on." (Pryn took the iron coins uncertainly.) "Now come, girl, and give me a kiss."

"Madame Keyne," Pryn declared, for, though she was by nature affectionate, not only had she seen something of fountains in her own home, she had also seen prostitutes in the Ellamon market and had whispered and giggled with the other children about them, "you take me from the Bridge of Lost Desire, you give me a handful of coins, then you ask for a kiss . . . ?"

"—like a kiss from a daughter, my dear, expressing her affection to a mother, before she leaves on some necessary journey out into the world, with a coin or two diligently saved and given with concern."

"Well," Pryn said, "I never got along very well with *my* mother. I didn't really see much of her."

"Very well, then, to a father—if you must; a long-lost father, returning from the wars, in time to catch a peck and a hug before his daughter begins her own eccentric or domestic adventures along whatever courses her own lifetime may take her."

Though Pryn had not had a father, she had wanted one; but she hesitated a moment more. Finding the pockets, she dropped in the coins, stepped forward, bent, and, blinking, kissed the brown cheek.

One moment, lost in the desert of that warm, dry skin, Pryn thought she understood what had occurred; she let her mouth, then her cheek, stay against Madame Keyne's, thinking all the time that a tremor would pass through the woman any moment—or at least expecting to see, as she stepped back now, a tear make an oasis somewhere on that cheek.

Madame Keyne was smiling.

Though not particularly at Pryn.

"Well," Madame Keyne said after a breath. "You gave me that contact, that touch, that communion on your own—freely. Despite all exchanges, which always occur. Nothing compelled you, nothing coerced you. And I shall live off that freedom of yours for . . . a minute? A month? A lifetime?" She laughed softly. "It was, in its quiet way, as glorious as if I rode some wild and winged beast, soaring against sun-silvered clouds. Certainly it is worth as much as the caresses Jade wheedles, tricks, blackmails, and cajoles from the Ini." Madame Keyne raised an eyebrow, as though responding to a surprise on Pryn's face that Pryn, at any rate, hadn't felt. "Oh, yes—because I know how innocent we are, I have a measure of how innocent they are. Even if *they* don't know it—Oh, you may mark it on vellum! Now go. Down to the kitchen with you. You remember Gya, who oversaw your bath and bedding when Ini

brought you in last night? She will give you a supper basket at the kitchen door—I think Jade and I shall dine by ourselves tonight. Or, if not, I shall dine alone. Later, when the sun is fully down, you may take this—" Madame Keyne picked up the knife and held it out to Pryn— "to the break in the corner of my garden that leads through into the garden of the Liberator. If you can contrive an audience with him, ask my question, and return—"

"But Madame—"

"Oh, don't mind about the knife. You should have some small weapon with you. In these vicious and violent times it won't be taken amiss. Ini has more of them than she needs. One less from her collection is one more bit of trouble I don't have to worry about her getting into."

"Oh, no, Madame—" Pryn took the weapon and immediately felt uncomfortable holding it. "It's just that the Liberator isn't *in* his . . ." She stopped. Her meager knowledge—her tiny bit of power—seemed too precious to squander here. "Madame Keyne, if you want me to ask the Liberator your question, you must return me to the middle of the city, at the mouth of the Bridge of Lost Desire. From there I'll be able to find my way to—"

"My dear girl, if *that's* what I must do to have an answer, then I shall do without! Here we have been talking of responsibility, and you would have me turn you out into the same dangers from which I plucked you? No!"

"But Madame Keyne—"

"You've come near getting killed once since you've been in my charge. I am not about to repeat the possibility. You will do it my way, or you will *not* do it! I want no more protests, girl. As I told you already, and as Jade herself suspects, the answer is simply not *that* important!"

They sat together in the small, open-roofed chamber. On the counters about them lay clay tablets, shells with styli sticking from them, chisels, brushes. Reeds in bunches soaked in shallow trays of alum water. Rubbed and unrubbed parchment lay piled about, held down from the breeze by small pumice blocks. Against the wall leaned boards covered with yellow wax, boards covered with pink wax, tablet molds, piles of clay tokens, blocks of ink.

The little tripod had not yet been lighted.

"I thought, because we didn't get much work done today, you might like to eat in here." Jade replaced a flower, fallen to the white cloth, in its vase. "We might work later. Here. Together."

"Yes." Madame Keyne reached into the basket and pulled loose

159

the red scarf tucked about the wicker. "A useful idea. A pleasant idea!"

"Here, let me do that for you!" Jade took the scarf end from Madame Keyne's hand and pulled it loose—from large, succulent fruits. "And let me see, now. Yes. Gya has given us some of her wonderful small loaves!" Jade pulled loose a second scarf from a second basket. "I asked her to make them when I was dithering about this afternoon. I know how much you like them—Oh, Rylla, I'm afraid I got *no* work done today!"

"You asked cook . . . ? Thank you, Jade! I certainly didn't do very much work myself. Though I suppose I did get into town and review the construction earlier on this morning. I have been putting that off for so long. Now I don't have to think about that for another three days."

Jade touched a third scarf over a third basket, this one somewhat spotted. It came half away from a cut of meat, gray and rose. Jade paused. "You worked today. I did not. Somehow, everything you say indicts me. There is nothing I can do for you that means anything . . . !"

Madame Keyne was silent a moment. Then she reached out and put her hand on top of Jade's. "I would have nothing meaningful in my life if I did not have you and all that you do for me, all that you are to me."

Their joined hands pulled away the scarf. Jade had washed the clay from her fingers. Only a bit clung about her nails. "Sometimes, Rylla—" Jade held Madame Keyne's hand more firmly, then more gently—"you are very cruel."

"Because I love you?"

"Because when I become resentful, become confused, when I become frightened and lash out, at you, at myself, at everyone, you do not stop me." Looking down, she withdrew her fingers to the white cloth's edge.

"How could I . . . ?" Madame Keyne looked bewildered.

"You could say, in the middle of it, or before it even began, at any point . . ." Jade looked away from the table. "Oh, it *is* hard to say! *I* cannot say it. It would be easier to write it—! You could say—" She blinked at Madame Keyne—" 'Jade, I love you.' " Shaking her head, the secretary suddenly, quietly smiled. "Is it so surprising that when I am at my least lovable that is when I most need to know your love? If only I could hear that from you during those terrible times, then I could become myself again."

"You have said that before. Yet it always surprises me."

"You have acted on it before. If you never had, I could not have stayed in this confining garden. And yet, because from time to time

you withold it, it is hard for me not to feel that—from time to time—my humiliation is something you inflict on me, you create in me, you exploit for purposes that are beyond me to understand—"

"Oh, Jade!" Madame Keyne leaned forward and took both her secretary's hands, drawing them across the table top. A bracelet clinked against the vase. "No . . ." (The replaced flower fell again to the cloth-covered table.) The women leaned forward from their backless stools. "It is hard for me, Jade, in a circle of my own servants, with Ini there, with that girl, Pryn, simply to *say* such things—"

"It is hard for you, with me rolling and screaming in the dirt, to *feel* such things—"

"No . . ." Madame Keyne sat back. "No, I feel them. It is only as I said."

"Yet that is still what I hear when you say it."

"And because I know that is how you read it, I must take the responsibility for it as though I had actually marked it on vellum myself." There was something of questioning, something of dismay in Madame Keyne's inflection. But who could say what the proportions were.

"You could have stopped me," Jade repeated.

"You stopped the Ini. That was the important thing. As for the rest . . ." Madame Keyne shrugged. Then she shook her head. "My poor, my dear, my most radiant Jade. You have your bad habits. I have mine. And there are, alas, some things it is simply—and habitually—hard for me to do, in public."

"Public? But we are all within your garden walls! You have brought us all here—the servants, even the Ini, even that girl. What public is that?"

"I have allowed each of you to come, for your own reasons—and mine. To each, I have my responsibilities, which again involve my reasons with theirs—and yours. Were I some crazed aristocrat, living a neighborhood away, I might read into such a situation some absolute power to influence all about me unto life and death. But I'm not, and I can't. Oh, certainly I can abuse the power I have. If a servant's face or gait displease me, I may say, 'Your work is performed not quite to the style that I desire,' and dismiss him. If some housegirl's manners or politics are too unsettling or too loud, I might—depending on her gait and face—say much the same. But the nameless gods have decreed that there will be enough young women both comely, intelligent, and poor so that the rich and powerful can exploit desire in the name of labor—the rich who can read and decipher desire's complex signs—in such a way that power here will reproduce itself there, and we may learn from those paupers at once beautiful and egregious—"

"But it's true, Rylla! You *are* always in public—even within your own gardens: you are always prepared for some fancied spy to observe you from the bushes, overhear you from the eaves."

"And you, Jade, are always in private, terrified lest someone see you, someone judge you, someone condemn you; and your better nature is paralyzed under expectation of that perpetual gaze, that eternal acuteness that is everywhere about to break in on your privacy and fill it with anxiety. Only when you feel shored up against all such eyes and ears can your better nature speak."

"But because *you* are always within the publicity of your servants, your employees, your acquaintances, your friends, and—yes—your lover, you are condemned to *have* no better nature. I know that you are a very lonely woman, Rylla. And your loneliness is not what I love about you—it is too much like mine. I think what I love is the illusion of an inner privacy that might, somehow, be *made* public . . ."

When Jade was silent a while, Madame Keyne said: "When your illusions collapse—or when mine do—then we both need to hear, 'I love you,' from the other. No, it is not so much to ask: that we speak our truest thought clearly."

Jade smiled again. "Do you remember, Rylla, when you took me on that business trip to the south?"

"Ah!" Madame Keyne rocked back on her stool. Coming forward, she seized her secretary's hands again with a desperate eagerness. "How could I forget!"

In her own eagerness, Jade pulled one hand away to gesture. "Remember, we stopped at that inn where that bandit gang had also taken rooms for the night?"

"I thought they were slavers, or only young smugglers—and there were no more than three!—who had sold off their wares and thought it would look more respectable to appear as honest highwaymen!" Madame Keyne laughed.

"I was so terrified! And they had the room right beside ours, with the thinnest wall between. They drank so loudly and made so much noise! I was afraid to speak, even in a whisper, for fear we should be overheard—"

"Ah, yes!" Madame Keyne sat back. "But we had our business that had to be gone over that night. So I took a waxed writing board and scratched you a note—"

"—and, trembling, I scratched one back to you." Jade smiled. "I was sure they would hear the stylus in the wax itself and be able to know just from the sound what we exchanged between us!"

"*Exactly* what you wrote me! I was quite surprised."

"And you wrote back: 'I love you more than life and wealth and they will never know of it.' Or was it 'wealth and life'—?"

"I think it was 'breath and wealth.' Or was it 'light and breath'—? No matter; it was the right matter for the time!"

"It was the right matter to calm my fear—enough so I could tell you of my terror."

"My wonderful Jade—you used to be terrified of so many things, back then. Slavers who were bandits; bandits who might be slavers—"

"Yet as we sat on the edge of the bed, passing the board back and forth, concentrating so hard on what we glyphed into its surface, now rolling the scrapings away and sticking them to the board's bottom, staring at the board in the candlelight without even looking at each other, stopping to thumb out an ill-scribed sign—"

"Oh, I always watched you, Jade—at least when I wasn't writing!"

"—yet our questions and answers seemed to go so quickly by and through our business for the night . . . and moved on to other things, other thoughts, till at last we were writing back and forth of our most intimate feelings, our most intimate fears. It was as if the stylus itself were aimed at just those hidden parts of our souls. It was as though the wax already bore the signs and only waited for us to scratch the excess away to reveal the truth. And all the while, those evil folk in the next room laughed and listened, listened and laughed!"

Laughing, Madame Keyne said: "*I* thought they were too busy laughing to hear a thing! Though it's true, writing to you across that little gulf that you could not speak over for your reasons and I would not for mine, for all the sinister laughter about us—and bandits, slavers, or smugglers, it was certainly sinister enough!—I have never felt so intimate with another human as I did that night, nor felt I could be more honest, or more—"

"Ah!" Jade threw up a hand. "You just cannot admit you are wrong!"

Madame Keyne looked puzzled.

"They were *not* slavers! Or smugglers! They were bandits. And they listened to every word we said, determined to rob us on the least pretext!"

"Quite probably they *were* bandits!" declared Madame Keyne. "Most likely I *was* wrong. Rob us? No doubt they needed no pretext at all!"

"We were in the south," declared Jade. "The south is my country, not yours!"

"We were indeed thirty, almost forty, stades south of Kolhari." Madame Keyne shook her head again, again smiling. "And the next morning, you made us leave the inn and return to the city—it was too dangerous, you said. So we never did complete our business that trip."

"See! You can*not* admit you were wrong," Jade cried. "You must always be right!"

"It is very easy for me not to be right—most probably I was not right. There is a definite possibility I was—definitely—wrong. There is a definite possibility that the probability was large, huge, over-whelming. Certainly there was no need to take chances. I admit to it all! The only thing I can*not* admit to is that ... I believe what I don't believe!"

"I hate that in you!"

"I do not love it in you, either!"

Jade looked down. "But you went back, two weeks later, and completed what business you had. Alone."

"Yes." Madame Keyne sighed. "I did. Ah, I missed you on that trip. All the bandits and slavers and smugglers seemed to have melted away. And there was no one to sit on the bed's edge with in the lamplight at evening and write notes to. Without you, it was only dull business."

"I do not like to travel," Jade said. "Business trips, the rushing, the inconvenience, being gawked at by strangers, the small talk with new acquaintances that one will forget ever having known in a week—that is for you. It's not to my taste. When I come to a new town, a new city, I like to stay in one place for a time, to live there, to meet the street girls and talk to the market vendors, to learn the names of its alleys and avenues; I like to find myself a little garden and walk in it a while. You, Rylla, you run through cities and towns and villages as if they were all suburbs of one great city in which you could never quite find your home. It's as if you were afraid to hear what your own thoughts might say to you were you to move slowly enough for them to overtake you."

"I think it is fear that I might have to read the results of my own actions inscribed on the pliable wax of the world." Madame Keyne sighed again.

"You talk too much and travel too fast," Jade said. "That's why you're so unhappy."

"I suppose, when I am unhappy, that is, indeed, the reason. But what was so important on that trip we took together was not the sort of things we say to each other now, but rather what, that night, you wrote to me, what I wrote to you. There, outside my garden walls, I think I felt that what I wrote was, finally and nakedly, private, safe from any spy—"

"There, hemmed in by the fear of all I did not know about me, I

thought that what I felt was nakedly, totally public, overseen by all eyes, overheard by all ears—"

"Yet it was honest. You felt that, didn't you? That it was honest?"

"Though I may have been impelled to honesty through fear for my life, yes, it was more honest than I had ever felt I could be with another person." Jade smiled. "But your writing, Rylla, in the shaping of your signs, *is* atrocious! There were words I was not even sure of that night!"

"As you wrote to me. Several times. And I've tried to do better." Madame Keyne laughed. "But that is why I need a secretary. And you suffered to read my messages, and responded with your own, as beautiful as the script in which you scribed them; you struggled to make out whatever, and however, clumsily I meant."

Jade sighed. "I have often wondered if simply because of those frightening men in the next room, you were not just driven, like some slave lashed on by an overseer's whip, to come closer to your own real thoughts while we wrote to one another that night—"

"And I have often wondered if, because writing is so different from speaking, so much slower, so much more considered, if you weren't forced to consider, slowly, what you really felt—"

"Well," Jade said, "I suppose it's the same thing—"

"—produces the same results," Madame Keyne said. "Works the same way."

"It was wonderful, certainly! And yet so strange—" Jade gave a little shudder. "But you are right, Rylla. I feel as though I am at all times observed; and I am paralyzed by those eternally judging eyes—or, when I am not paralyzed, I am frightened to the point of anger, of incoherence, of rage. Often I've even felt that it was you who observed me, you who judged me. And then I have been at my worst, certainly. At least to you. But I know, and always have known, finally, that it was not you. You, too, feel you are always observed; but you read in that fancied attention the benevolence, the approval, the applause of the market for the mummers. Your life seems to all about you nothing but success—and without your successes, there would be only failure for me. Often I think it isn't fair."

"You are right." Madame Keyne said. "It isn't."

"At other times, I only wish I could confront, once and for all, the stranger who is always gazing at me, just out of my line of sight, who is always overhearing what I say and finding it silly or selfish or wrong. If I could truly create such a confrontation, I would be rid of it forever! That I try, so often and so hard, sometimes seems to be the only thing in the world that makes my life worth living."

"You are right," Madame Keyne said. "There is nothing more

important than that perpetual and repeated confrontation with the nameless ones. Otherwise one can never become free, can never remain free."

"And sometimes I think the difference between you and me is that I *have* at least tried to engage them directly, that I have at least tried, however frightened I was, to look at them, whereas you have not—not really. You have never listened intently to their breathing just behind your shoulder. You have never turned suddenly to stare one in the face. If you did, if you could see them, truly know that they were there, you would be as terrified as I, and would know your own weakness, know how unhappy you are."

"Again, I think you may be right."

"No . . ." Jade shook her head. "Though I love you, I know you do not believe me. Again, because you cannot admit that you are wrong—"

Somewhere a branch fell, off in the bushes. One or the other of the two women glanced up from the table with vague curiosity. The other went on talking.

Certainly it was no more than a branch.

But it made Pryn pull sharply back from the window's edge. She looked about the hedges. She looked back at the window. (Inside, one of them said: "I love you, and I know that you love me. That is all I know. That is all I need to know . . ." But the voice spoke so softly Pryn did not catch which woman it was, so that the words seemed like a message glimpsed on a discarded clay tablet without any initialed name above or below, sender and destination forgotten.) The gauze hanging to the sill was as gray as the wall around it. No sun fell through at this hour. Doubtless the women inside, had they looked, could have seen out as easily as Pryn could see in. Really, she must not stay any longer. It just wouldn't do to be caught here.

Pryn walked along close to the house. Turning the corner, she let herself move out between the bushes.

As she came around by the back door of the kitchen, Gya shoved aside the woven hangings and stepped out. The red scarf around her head was blotched with perspiration. "Here's your supper!" She handed out a basket. Things in it were wrapped in large leaves.

Pryn pulled one loose: strips of celery, cut turnips, and carrots fell out. And a sizable piece of roasted meat. There was a jar with a wooden stopper, whose surface was still damp and about which she could smell apples. Could it be cider . . . ? There was also a small, dark loaf. "Thank you!"

The housekeeper stood on the doorstep, scratching at the hip of her skirt.

Pryn broke off a piece of the loaf and put it in her mouth, to be astonished at its sweetness. (She had tasted neither corn flour nor banana bread before, both of which these were.) She broke off another piece and ate it.

"And if you see the other, white-headed one, tell her to come and get hers too," the hefty woman called. She turned back to the hanging raffia. "Though sometimes I do believe that one doesn't eat at all!"

"Yes," Pryn called again. "Thank you! I will!"

Now and again the moon shone blue-white between coursing clouds. Brambles bent and whispered around her. She pulled a branch from dark stone to reveal the darker opening. Had the far end been blocked up? But she squeezed herself, crouching, into the fissure. She slipped through a memory of narrow, underground corridors. Then moonlight speckled brambles outside the rocks just beyond her left eye. Slipping out sideways, she pushed away chattering branches and stood up in the heavy growth. Pryn gazed over brush that darkened under a cloud, then paled to mottled blue as the cloud dragged off.

There was no light in the great house across the cluttered wilds. Somewhere beyond the house itself, a campfire fluttered beside some outbuilding's door.

Was that a soldier moving along the great house's roof? No, Pryn decided. This evening the upper cornices were patrolled only by changes in the moonlight along the cracked balustrade. Dark, the house seemed far bigger than Madame Keyne's.

Pryn pushed forward, clenching her jaw at the rattling brush.

She was approaching a clear space—and struck her shin.

Hopping back, looking down, holding aside leaves, she saw a stone expanse, which, she realized looking out over it, was why there *was* a clearing. She stepped up on the stone lip.

Across the mossy rock, she saw the sculpted stands, each topped with carved shells, like the ones at the corners of Madame Keyne's bridge.

She was standing at the edge of a great fountain that no longer worked at all. She looked about for higher ground. In the wild rises around, had time clogged conduits and tributaries with refuse in the same way a little murderess had packed the emblem of her service down a drain?

What am I doing here? she thought, stepped from the lip, and moved around it toward the house. But *he's* not there . . .

That was what she knew.

That knowledge had led her to volunteer her services in the first place. But here she was, on the strength of that knowledge charged with a mission which that knowledge, precisely, assured her could not succeed.

This is ridiculous, she mouthed for the seventh time, freeing a twig caught in the coin-filled pocket at one side of her dress, moving a branch that snagged on the knife at the other, now pulling back from thorns that scraped her calf where she'd hiked the dress up for easier maneuvering.

She reached the end of brush and bramble and stepped into what was merely waist-high grass.

That back window—were those cloth hangings inside it? She could climb in. Coming closer, her gaze rose to the roof, whose cracked and crumbled balustrade, as she walked up, approached her in some infinitely delayed topple.

A texture change in the earth underfoot made her look down—at the window, now before her, with its dark drapes.

Pryn vaulted to the sill, got her feet up, dropped one foot over, pushing back hangings. The cloth was incredibly gritty—she heard it tear. As she jumped down, another cloud drifted from the moon. Light fell through the open roof into the inner court—very like Madame Keyne's.

Might this, Pryn wondered, be what Madame Keyne's home would look like in ruins years hence? All furniture had been taken out, the floor tiles broken—five or six benches had been up-ended against the wall—

Footsteps!

Pryn crouched beside one as a thick-necked soldier walked from the stairway across the floor, glanced up at the moon, then went to the doorway, where he paused in the shadow—a moment later his urine hissed against the door post. Still barefoot, Pryn resolved she would leave by the window she'd entered.

The soldier—no doubt the one she'd thought mere moonlight on the cornice—went.

Slowly, Pryn stood.

There's no one in the house, she thought. At least no one important. I am alone with the absent Liberator. It was preternaturally silent. She felt like the central figure in a complex joke whose humor was just beyond her; she also felt exorbitantly free, as if her knowledge allowed her to wander, to run, to fly on spined wings anywhere in the moonstruck dark—as long as she flew quietly. She stepped from behind the bench. The dead barbarian . . . ?

Lusts as depraved as . . . Unanswerable questions glittered in her mind like mummers' gibes in a market skit before which a shadow audience howled silent laughter.

Pryn walked across the court and climbed the steps down which the soldier had come. As she entered the archway at the top, the house reached the end of any similarity with Madame Keyne's.

In the corner of the large room a ladder led to a hole in the roof; moonlight spilled in. Was this how soldiers went up for their theatrical patrol during the day?

Pryn smiled at the lack of attempt to maintain even the fiction of a dweller in this space. She walked over the tile floor and through another arch: another bare room. Narrow windows along the wall let slats of silver. She went up to one and looked, carefully, out. At the outbuilding men stood or sat about the fire. Someone added a log.

In the breeze, branches dipped and rose between the window and what she looked at, so she moved to the next sill. Two men came in through the small door in the plank gate, stopping to joke with two others leaving.

Hand on the knife at her hip, Pryn turned to cross the high-ceilinged room.

What shall I tell Madame Keyne when I go back? she wondered. And why should I go back at all? Pryn stepped through another archway, the floor all shadow-dappled from, this time, a wide and generous window beyond which hung more branches. Was this how a queen, or maybe even an empress, felt, moving through her own castle?

On her third step, she saw.

He stood at the edge of shaking light.

Truly frightened, Pryn fought back nervous laughter. At the same time, part of her wondered, quite coolly, what she might say to this guard, seconds from now; what might he say to her—certainly he had seen her. She was standing in a clear swatch of moon.

The man—the big man—stepped forward.

And Pryn got chills.

Chills surged the backs of her shoulders, tickled her thighs. She wanted very much to be somewhere else, and at the same time to move seemed impossible—which only made the feeling more intense, more unsettling.

The chills came on and on.

"What are *you* doing here . . . ?" she whispered. "I mean, how . . . did you get *in!*"

He gave a snort. "These old Neveryóna mansions have their cisterns too." Heavy features shifted about the scar. "The one here's been empty as long as the one down in the Spur. What am I doing here? Well . . . we had some more trouble, earlier today, of the same sort we had the last time you were with us. This seemed

169

as good a place as any to retreat. Now. What are *you* doing here? And how did *you* get in?"

"I ..." Pryn swallowed. "Well, I came in the window—looking ... for you! Only you weren't supposed to *be* here—"

A sound across the room—

A figure blocked more moonlight under a far arch, then darted to the Liberator's side, to crouch, looking up at Gorgik, looking over at Pryn. Black hair straggled the bony forehead. The single eye blinked.

Gorgik's great hand dropped to the one-eyed bandit's shoulder. As if those fingers and knuckles and nails were too heavy to bear, Noyeed sank to one knee. "Is that the spy, Master ... ?"

"Me," Pryn started, "a spy ... ?" She could not tell, in the flickering through the branches, if any irony had worked its way into the Liberator's scarred face.

"You disappeared in the middle of the last little fracas we had, Blue Heron—then, when it was over, some of the new men, the Wolf and the Fox, told me how they'd known you before. They said they'd suspected you of spying even then."

"But I—"

"Blue Heron," Gorgik said, "can you honestly tell me that you know nothing of the red-bearded demon with the jangling ankles who attacked us in our underground cellars this afternoon? Can you say truthfully that you were not sent here by powerful merchants to ply me with questions of strategy, alliances, and policies, the answers to which you will report back for a handful of coins?"

"I—?"

"Master," Noyeed hissed, "I think she's lying!"

"*You'd* think the first words of a mother to her child were riddled with untruths, little savior." Gorgik jogged the bandit. "From the life you've led, who'd blame you? Still, I've told her my reasons for coming here. Now I want her to tell me hers." He looked at Pryn. "You say you came, looking for me—and, however unexpectedly, you've found me. What is your mission?"

"I only wanted ..."

Noyeed's eye batted and glittered.

"I only wanted to ... say good-bye. I am leaving this strange and terrible city! I am leaving Kolhari! I wanted to ... thank you. For being friendly to me on the bridge. And to say good-bye."

"I see." The Liberator settled his weight more on one hip. "Is that all?"

"Yes. And to ..." Pryn looked down. "... to ask you a question."

Gorgik dropped his hand from Noyeed's shoulder. Noyeed reached

up to scratch it. There was something loose around his neck. In the moon-dapple, Pryn was not sure what it was.

"What did you want to ask?"

"It's only a question for myself." Pryn blinked. "That barbarian, the one your ... friend there killed. Before he died, he said you ... *sold* him. As a slave. Was that true?"

"Yes."

"But that's terrible!" Pryn frowned. "You're the Liberator? Why did you do it?"

"Actually I sold him—as a slave—on a dozen different occasions. As I recall, he sold me—to slavers and to private owners also—well over half a dozen times."

Pryn's frown had begun as condemnation; it crumbled into bewilderment. "But I *don't* understand ...!"

"It was the nature of our relationship—when we had a relationship." Gorgik shrugged. "That's the trouble with spies, you know. It's not that they carry information. It's that they carry fragmentary information, out of context, misconstrued, badly interpreted, incomplete, and misread."

"I'm *not* a spy!" Pryn said. "I just don't understand—"

"You know that we were slavery-fighters together. It was simply more efficient to have one of us working from within the slave gangs."

"Yes," Pryn said. "But certainly *that's* not what he meant by ..."

Gorgik looked with dappled face at the dappled floor. "It's hard to say, with someone like Prince Sarg, what he meant. Nor is he here to clarify it for us. But there are as many ways to read the iron collar, the chain, and the whip as there are to read the words a woman or a man whispers under the tent's shadow with the moonlight outside. But you're too young to—"

"Oh, no!" Pryn protested. "No. I'm not!"

The giant looked up. "Well, *perhaps* not." He smiled—though the scar, like a careless mark scrawled across eye, cheek, and lip, confused that smile's meaning. "You've heard camel drivers in the market, cursing their beasts, one another, and the whole inconvenient and crowded world of commerce through which they must drive their herd? The brutal repetition in their invention and invective alone keeps such curses from being true poetry."

She wasn't sure how poetic curses were, but she knew camel drivers were foul-mouthed. Pryn nodded.

"Are you too young to have heard, little Heron, that some of these same men, alone in their tents at night with their women, may implore, plead, beg their mistresses to whisper these same phrases to them, or plead to be allowed to whisper them back,

phrases which now, instead of conveying ire and frustration, transport them, and sometimes the women, too, to heights of pleasure?"

Though Pryn had never heard it put so bluntly before, she knew enough to suspect the process existed, and nodded quickly lest she be thought less worldly than she was.

The giant's smile broadened. "Now there are some, who, wishing to see the world more unified than common sense suggests it could possibly be, say that to use terms of anger and rage in the throes of desire indicates some great malaise, not only of camel drivers but of the whole world; that desire itself must be a form of anger and is thus invalid as an adjunct to love—"

"*I* would say," Pryn said, who after all had heard her share of camel drivers taking their herds from prairie to desert over the rough Falthas, "the sickness is using terms of desire in the throes of anger and rage. Most curses are just words for women's genitals, men's excreta, and cooking implements hooked up in preposterous ways."

"A theory the most intelligent and high-minded of our young have always been fond of. But both arguments are very much of the same form. Both assume that signs thought about in one way and felt to mean one thing mean other feelings that are not felt and other thoughts that are not in the mind. Since the true meanings in both arguments are absent from the intentions of the man or woman speaking, one finally ends with a world in which neither love nor anger can really be condoned, since neither is ever pure. The inappropriate signs do not enrich the reading; they pollute it. And it's surprising how fast one argument becomes the other—as the most intelligent and high-minded of our young grow older. But there's another way to read."

Pryn's frown questioned the wavering leaf-light the moon threw about the room. Here and there a twig's or branch's shadow was doubled on the bare plaster by leafy refraction.

"Even the most foul-mouthed camel driver knows a curse from a kiss, whatever signs accompany it." Gorgik snorted. "Enriched pleasure is still pleasure. Enriched anger is still anger." Along with the quiet tenor of his city voice, the scar and moon-dapple inflected his features toward some other meaning than the anger she kept reading there. "A word spoken in the noon sun does not necessarily mean the same as it does when uttered in the moonlight. The words by which we indicate a woman's genitals, men's excreta, or cooking implements are not, in themselves, lusty. They simply can be used in many ways—among many others."

With adolescence, Pryn had certainly taken on the sometimes troubling knowledge that almost anything with an outside and an

inside supporting movement from one to the other could be sexually suggestive. "But what does this have to do with your ... friend who tried to kill you?"

The Liberator sighed. "The signs by which slavery manifests itself in the world in many ways resemble the camel driver's curse." The great hand had strayed to the bandit's neck. Gorgik hooked a forefinger around ... it was an iron collar that hung there. "The collar itself may be a sign of all social oppression—yet its wearing can also be an adjunct of pleasure. My little barbarian prince, while we fought and loved together, was very much one out to have the world more unified—while I, in such matters, am ... a camel driver." Gorgik's laugh had a nervous relief that Pryn wondered at. "Sarg claimed he felt no bodily pleasure in the collar. Under the sun he and I wore it to advance our fight against slavery, to infiltrate and obliterate it. At night? Well, he tolerated it—at first. Sometimes he laughed at it. Later he began to argue against it; and it was an argument much like the one I—and you—have sketched out: its oppressive meaning debased love; its sexual meaning made of slavery itself an even more terrifying mystery. Finally he refused to wear it any longer. Nor did I press him to it—since he allowed it to me. But as Sarge wore the collar less and less by night, I could not help notice the change in the *way* he wore it by day. That he wore it much *more* by day, while that is true, is not so much the point as that he now *insisted* on wearing it. Several times when we were camped outside a town, he wore the collar into the local market while he bought our supplies, whereupon he would brazenly insult, or cheat, or anger someone, then, at their complaint, bring them back to his 'master'—me—and I would have to promise to discipline my 'slave.' Then, when the offended party was gone, he would laugh, finding it all a great joke that we should now share. The first time, I read it as a boy's high spirits and laughed—uneasily—with him. The second time, it was a bother; and I was simply silent while he laughed alone. The third time, I grew angry and *told* him it was a bother—and a dangerous bother at that! He grew angry in return. That, indeed, was one of our first arguments over the slippery meaning of the iron ring. But from then on, in our forays against the slavers of the west, more and more he demanded to be the one to play the slave—because, as he would now chide me, first jokingly, then seriously, I could not be trusted in the role. For me, you see, it was *too* charged a sign. Yet as soon as he had the collar on, as soon as he had been 'sold' and had gained admittance into the slave pens, he would needlessly prolong his time there, sometimes boasting to the bored guards, sometimes to the confused slaves, of his exploits outside ... before, together, we would let them know

why he—and I—had come! Sometimes he would ignore our plans and signals altogether, so that I would not know what had happened to him. Later, laughing, he would say it did not matter if we began an hour or three hours after I, waiting for him outside, had expected. For hadn't we succeeded? Often, as I left after selling him, I would see him turn to taunt the overseers, drawing attention to himself and his collar at precisely the moments when he should have remained most inconspicuous. Several times by such behavior he put his own life and mine in danger—his reasoning was that whatever eccentricities he indulged within the iron band, they were better than any actions I might perform, as his were not contaminated by the secret productions of lust. Yet to put on the collar and walk into a group of slaves and their masters seemed to throw Sarg into a kind of trance, a strangely reckless state where ecstasy and obliviousness, daring and distraction, were one with bravery itself. I did not want to fault him then—and do not now. Many times—bravely—he saved my life. Many times I saved his. But that was the situation, and to talk about it with him was to enter an endless maze of anger, recriminations, and resentments where it was always *my* overvaluation of the collar that was to blame for any fault I found in *his* actions while he wore it. Carelessness? Forgetfulness? Heedless braggadocio? What did any of them matter if we were still alive—if we could still free slaves? If we ourselves were truly free? I loved him. And I believe he loved me—certainly he was honestly and infinitely grateful to me, for he would have been a true slave without me; and we both knew it. Had we been embarked on an enterprise where only our own desires were at stake, I think I would have stayed with him, would have fought to keep him, would have risked my life and possibly lost it—fought for my own values and through whatever the world set between us so that we might remain together. But we had a cause that I felt was more important than my own life or safety; and so, possibly all too conveniently, I felt that cause was more important than what we might have won for ourselves by solving such problems.

"That day we had camped outside a provincial, western hold. Over the previous nights we had freed several gangs of slaves in the area, and I was growing wary that our next strike might be anticipated, since we used basically the same tactics each time. Perhaps we should wait? Or move on? But no, Sarg said; why *not* strike again—I didn't *want* him to wear the collar, he claimed, laughing. Obviously I was jealous of his wearing it. I took the iron to fasten it around Sarg's neck. He took it from my hands, I recall, and put it on himself. Wearing the leather apron and fur cape many slavers sported in those climes, I led him to the buyers we had singled out: three men who had managed to bring together, through cunning raids and careful bargaining, a gang of men and women whom they were taking off to some killing labor in a desert mogul's great cave-carving project, where, to create those incredible columns and corridors that are palaces for five or seven generations and then, for the next thousand years, become the haunts of beggars, slaves toil in near-darkness by the hundreds and die by tens and twenties each week. Of course Sarg would not come to the selling board with his head bowed and his shoulders hunched, as most slaves would. Rather he wandered up ahead of me, looking about, grinning and curious—for he claimed, and with some justification, that slaves all observe their masters carefully but that masters pay no attention whatsoever to their slaves. The chief slaver pounded Sarg's back, ran his thumb under Sarg's upper and lower lip, now into one cheek, now into the other, to see how many of his teeth were loose. Sarg was a strong lad, with a sound mouth, and well-muscled, the kind of worker they like for gang labor. I received my handful of iron coins and left him there, grumbling over falling prices in flesh—and immediately turned aside to go off behind the rocks and climb to the overhang from which I could look down and coordinate my attack from without with Sarg's from within. Hidden in the bushes, I watched as he was led back to the other wretches, who stood peg-linked to the plank they carried on their shoulders. Their heads hung. Their feet shuffled in the dust. Sarg was already strutting and laughing. 'You think I'm an ordinary slave?' he called, as if—I always felt when he did it—to me. 'Ha! You think, just because I wear the iron, I am an ordinary slave. You don't know who I am at all!' They did not hit him—one shoved him a little, toward the gang. Many times, you must understand, he had explained to me, when I had chided him on such behavior, 'If I rave thus, they only think me crazy. And if masters pay little attention to slaves, they ignore completely those slaves they think mad. Besides, it sets an example of defiance to the other slaves, and I get pleasure from it. A pleasure of the mind, *not* the body! *You* should see in such taunts that bravery which, if all slaves showed at once and together, would crumble the institution and there would be no need for liberators like us! Given the pleasure that the collar brings *you*, you would deny *me* my joy in such outbursts . . . ?' This time I saw the slaver narrow his eyes at Sarg. And I had seen slavers narrow their eyes at him before. The slaver called over one of the others. I had seen slavers point Sarg out before to one another and laugh. This man did not laugh. He nodded at a whispered instruction from his fellow, then turned to leave the encampment. Our plan was to wait for nightfall, when Sarg would have gotten a chance to decide which slaves we could trust to aid us and which would be too frightened. But twenty minutes later, from my vantage, I saw the man returning—with twenty imperial guardsmen. They were down the road, out of the line of sight of the camp. My first thought was to give Sarg our signal—the wail of a wild dog— and at least throw down to him a blade I kept for him under my furs and begin the attack at once. But as I raised my hands to my mouth to howl, there was a rustle in the brush beside me, and three other guardsmen stepped out. I thought they knew who I was and was only a moment from rashness. But seeing my leather apron and cape, one turned to the others and said: 'See, they hire us to patrol this campsite till dawn, and already they've posted a lookout here against these accursed Liberators,' and nodded to me. 'Let's move further on.' I nodded back, trying to look as much like a lookout as possible. There were other guards, I saw, moving behind the trees. Sarg, down in the campsite, did not see, nor was he even looking. For two men to fight with the help of twenty slaves against three slavers is a viable battle. For two men to fight twenty or more armed guards expecting an attack is not. Should I have thrown him his sword then? He would have fought then—and died. Perhaps he wanted to die. But though all his actions seemed to say so, I still think such a reading of them was not mine to make. What I did, after a moment's thought, was to turn away and leave the site—leave the west and make my way back toward Kolhari, to redouble my efforts where slavery was already at its weakest, and thus establish a position to move back into those areas where it is still strong. I left Small Sarg, my barbarian prince. I did not even think about returning to the guarded site that night. I do not even know if Sarg ever knew that the guards were there. Or that his own actions had called them in. I left him a true slave, without a weapon. Yet, for the week, for the month, and still sometimes on such moonlit nights as this, I can hear his argument. 'You *wanted* to get rid of me. The guards were only an excuse to abandon me because you did not like my fighting manner, which was no more than high-spirited bravery itself. You wanted to be free of my recriminations in order to pursue your own desires. Your only real objection to my carryings on were that I did not act *enough* the slave to appease your lustful fantasies. And it was *your* desire to see me in the collar that made me a slave—that now abandoned me to slavery.' " The Liberator shrugged. "How does one refute such an argument? I'm only glad I had a cause to help me put such recriminations aside."

"It's as if," Pryn said, suddenly, "he felt all those desires secretly that you felt openly! But because his were secret, even from him-

176

self, they took control of him and led him to those foolish and dangerous actions, while your desires were known and acknowledged, and so, if anything, you were the better Liberator for it . . . ?"

Gorgik snorted again. "It would be a lie if I said I had not thought the same from time to time. But what I let myself think idly, I do not necessarily believe." He lifted the collar on his finger so that it tugged Noyeed's head to the side. Then he let the iron fall to the little man's neck. "Sarg said he felt no lust within the iron. I say I do. Why should I assume he spoke any less truly of his feelings than I speak of mine? If such a sign can shift so easily from oppression to desire, it can shift in other ways—toward power, perhaps, and aggression, toward the bitterness of misjudged freedoms by one who must work outside the civil structure. We killed many slavers, Sarg and I—he was only a boy, really. I do not think dealing death makes the best life for the young. The chance organization of my inner life and those situations life has thrown me into have taught me, painfully, a sign can slide from meaning to meaning. What prevented it from sliding another way for Sarg? For me, the collar worn against the will meant social oppression, and the collar worn willfully meant desire. For Sarg, the collar *was* social oppression, as well as all asocial freedom. Nothing in our lives, save my anger, challenged that meaning for him. And my anger was a lover's anger, which too often feels to the loved one as oppresive as a parent's. We fought—the two of us—for a vision of society, and yet we lived outside society—like soldiers fighting for a beautiful and wondrous city whose walls they have nevertheless been forbidden to enter. Sarg did not have the meanings I had to help him hold his own meanings stable. That is all. And my desire's position in this blind and brutal land means only that I know desire's workings better than some—but it does not make me either a better *or* a worse Liberator. Only what I do with my understanding changes that. Do *you* understand a little more now?"

Pryn nodded. "Perhaps. A little."

"And do you think, now, you might be able to write a clearer account of it?"

"Oh, yes, I—" Then she realized he meant an account for some absent master and her possible spying. Pryn felt her face redden in the half-dark.

"Well, perhaps I do too—now." Gorgik snorted again. "Perhaps I, too, saw in myself that other meaning, Sarg's meaning, when I left him. Certainly, when he swung down from that balcony at me, across the cellar, I saw all the dangers of such asocial freedom descending upon me—and they were indeed as terrifying and as paralyzing as the first and sudden discovery in one's own body of

177

lusts which have no name. You say you're leaving the city? Probably that's wise. Tell me, girl, which way are you heading?"

"I came down from the northern mountains," Pryn said. "I suppose I'll head . . . south."

"Ah, the monstrous and mysterious south! I remember my time there well. I hope you learn as much about the workings of power while you are there as I did." The Liberator's free hand moved absently to his broad chest, where his bronze disk hung. The broad thumb slid over the marked verdigris, as if the hard flesh might read what was inscribed there by touch: certainly the shifting leaf blotches made it impossible to decipher those signs by sight. "Tomorrow I have my meeting with the minister of the Empress. The denizens of the High Court have little love for the south. I'm afraid this astrolabe is, in its way, a map of just that southern-most peninsula which those now in power have traditionally seen as their nemesis. To enter new territory displaying the wrong map is not the way to learn the present paths that might prove propitious." Thick fingers moved from the disk to the chain it hung from. Gorgik suddenly bent his head to loose the links from under his hair. Pryn saw his own collar was gone . . . and now realized it was the Liberator's that hung around the bandit's neck, ludicrously too large and lopsided on the jutting collarbones. "When I was a boy in this city—" the Liberator raised his head—"half your age, if not younger—oh, much younger than you—my father brought me to visit a house in Sallese. I remember a garden, some statues, I think a fountain . . . maybe some fountains near running water." The Liberator laughed. "When I heard this house was for rent, I was told it was *in* Sallese—and I felt the return of old joy to think I might be taking for my headquarters the very home I had visited as a child. It *isn't* in Sallese, you know. It's right next to Sallese, in the suburb called Neveryóna, where the titled aristocracy have their city homes— those who are not staying at the High Court of Eagles itself. Once, they actually tried to call the whole city Neveryóna, but that never went over very well, and when the Child Empress came to power . . ." His mind seemed to reach for the distant time, while moonlight spilled its shadow over his face's rough landscape. "It seems an irony to be here rather than there—though it's not ironic enough to make me truly laugh. Here, girl." Gorgik gestured with his two fists, below which, in moon dapple, the chained disk turned and turned back. "If you knew the trouble this has guided me through, you might not take it. Yet I suspect the trouble I have got through under its weight is trouble I have lifted from the neck of all Neverÿon—an illusion, perhaps; but then, perhaps the fact that it is an illusion I believe in is why I am signed and sign myself 'Liberator.' "

Pryn stepped forward.

Gorgik raised the astrolabe.

Noyeed reached between his legs to scratch—and blinked.

As she neared them, moonlight flittered over Pryn. She felt a growing sense both of disgust and trust. Had she not just spent the time with Madame Keyne—and the Wild Ini—she might have thought that the trust was all for Gorgik and the disgust all for Noyeed. But in the conflict and complication, the chills, which had never really ceased, resurged. Was this fear? Was it more? It seemed to have lost all boundary; it filled the room, the house, the city the way the flicker and glitter of moonlight filled her very eyeballs.

Gorgik passed the chain over her head. Tale fragments of the crowning of queens returned to her. Links, warmed through the day against the Liberator's neck, touched the back and sides of hers—and a memory rose to startle: jerking the twisted vines up over a scaly head . . .

Fear was replaced by terror. Pryn had a moment's vision of herself in a complex and appalling game where Madame Keyne, the Liberator, the Child Empress Ynelgo, perhaps the nameless gods themselves, were all players, while she was as powerless as some wooden doll, set down in the midst of an elaborate miniature garden.

Something grappled her wrist.

She looked down—all the motion she could muster. And the moment's fear was gone. Noyeed held her forearm with hard fingers.

The eye turned from Pryn to Gorgik—the Liberator was looking down with the same questioning Pryn fancied on her own face.

"She has a knife, master!" Noyeed's gappy gums opened over his words like a mask of Pryn's own former fear: he looked as if he were avoiding a blow. "See—at her waist? The spy has a blade! I was *only* protecting your life, master—protecting it as I have protected it before, as I will always protect it!"

Pryn wanted to laugh and only waited for the Liberator's great and generous laughter to release hers.

"Very well then, Blue Heron." Gorgik did not laugh. "Take my gift, with your blade, into the south."

Pryn jerked her arm from Noyeed's grip. The little man, squatting at their feet, almost lost balance. She stepped back. The chain pulled from the Liberator's hands. The astrolabe fell against her breasts.

"No one can say for certain what confusion I give you." (Gorgik's perturbation seemed far from her own. And where, a moment back, she had felt at one with him, a oneness inscribed in wonder and fear, now she felt only annoyance inscribed on more annoy-

179

ance.) "Tomorrow I shall go to the High Court of Eagles for ... the first time? Does anyone in this strange and terrible land ever go anywhere, without having been there before in myth or dream? The minister with whom I shall confer will ask me a simple question. Beyond my campaign to free Nevèrÿon's slaves, whom will I ally myself with next? Will I take up the cause of the workers who toil for wages only a step above slavery? Or will I take up the marginal workless wretches who, without wages at all, live a step below? Shall I ally myself with those women who find themselves caught up, laboring without wages, for the male population among both groups? For they are, all of them—these free men and women— caught in a freedom that, despite the name it bears, makes movement through society impossible, that makes the quality of life miserable, that allows no chance and little choice in any aspect of the human not written by the presence or elision of the sign for production. This is what Lord Krodar will ask me. And I shall answer ..."

Balancing on the balls of her feet, Pryn felt as unsteady as little Noyeed, crouched and blinking, looked.

"I shall answer that I do not know." Gorgik's hand found the little man's shoulder; the horny forefinger hooked again over the collar. Noyeed, at any rate, seemed steadied. "I shall say that, because I spent my real youth as a real slave in your most real and royal obsidian mines, the machinery of my desire is caught up within the workings of the iron hinge. Slavery is, for me, not a word in a string of words, wrought carefully for the voice that will enunciate it for the play of glow and shade it can initiate in the playful mind. I cannot tell this minister what slavery means, for me, beyond slavery— not because desire clouds my judgment, but because I had the misfortune once to *be* a slave."

Elation triumphed over all fear; annoyance was gone. And joy seemed a small thing to sacrifice before what Pryn suddenly recognized as the absolute freedom of the real, a freedom that, in its intensity, had only been intimated by the truth of dragons.

She turned, started for the archway.

"Where are you going ... ?" which was the one-eyed bandit.

"To the south!" Pryn called.

Gorgik laughed.

And Pryn ran through moon-slashed rooms, down leaf-loud steps, across the unroofed court. Climbing through the window, she laughed to be leaving by the way she'd entered because of something so indistinguishable from habit when one was *this* free that habit seemed ... But she did not know *what* it seemed; and crashed through grass and garden brambles, rushed by a stifled fountain, pushed back branches at the wall, felt along stone for the opening, found it, wedged herself into darkness—

Her shift snagged as she slid by rock. She pulled—and heard something tear. Still, she managed to get one arm out, then her head—

"Give me my knife!"

Fingers grappled her hair; and her arm, yanking.

9

Of Night,
Noon,
Time, and
Transition

To attempt to define more precisely the 'city' is pointless; it is
'civilization' itself we must define.

—Ruth Whitehouse/*The First Cities*

"**G**ive it to me, little spy!"

Pryn jerked away and, with a foot she'd gotten free, kicked at the
Ini, missed—struggling, she glimpsed the dark face, backlit by
moonlight through pale hair.

"Give it to me! *You* don't know how to use it! It will only get you
in trouble! It's mine . . . !"

Still wedged into the opening, Pryn felt for the knife with her free
hand and jerked the other loose from Ini. Between the rocks, she
could not get it out—and wedged in further to escape the Ini's
yanks and punches.

"Give it to me now! *I* saw you spying on Madame Keyne! Jade
and Madame Keyne! This morning *and* this evening—didn't you
think I saw you? When I tell Madame, *she'll* know what you are!
Give it to me—No, *don't* go back in there! No, it's dangerous in
there! It's terrible! Horrible! Anything might happen—come back
with my . . ."

But Pryn was again out the other side, standing, stumbling back
in brambles, waiting for the white-blond head to emerge. She
breathed, hissing between her teeth. Her side had begun to ache
again. She took another breath . . .

Silence.

She waited.

But the Ini, murderous to those she thought powerless—again,
Madame Keyne had been right—was terrified of anything she perceived as authority. And this untenanted house of power and all the
grounds around it had become, at least for the dwellers over the
garden wall, the authoritative center of the city.

Pryn wondered if she ought to throw the knife back through the
hole; but she was afraid to get too close, in case that was the
moment Ini chose to overcome terror and emerge.

185

If I see her, Pryn thought viciously, I'll kick her head—

She didn't see anything.

At least not coming out of the wall.

Calmer now, with none of the elation she'd felt before, Pryn made her way along the rock, her hand on the knife in her sash, now and again glancing over her shoulder.

If there were breaks in Madame Keyne's walls, given the conditions here, there must be great gaps leading out every which way ...

After the wall turned, many meters along (it *must* be facing on the main avenue by now, she thought; and still wasn't sure), Pryn found a place where, indeed, some stones had fallen and a tree had grown up close enough to allow her to climb. And she was too tired to search further.

She climbed, clambered across leaves fallen on the top stones, knocked small pebbles to the ground, and jumped.

On the high road in the moonlight, she brushed off her dirty hands, rubbed her sore knees, and looked about at the groves of palms, at the walls around her, at the roofs beyond them.

... to the south? Pryn laughed on the empty avenue; and walked, not sure whether she were wandering into or out of the city. For all her tiredness, she felt quite lucid. She could write down the salient points of her situation clearly tonight. She was a mountain girl, new in the city, with a strange astrolabe, a few coins, and a stolen knife at her belt. Adventurer, warrior, thief ...? (True she *wasn't* sure which way she was going.) It would be exciting to leave the city by some unknown direction, turned out onto the land to wander wherever she might ...

Forty minutes later, she knew she was definitely moving toward the city's center. Once she turned up a dark street she thought looked familiar. Several times she turned up others that were completely unknown. Then, from an unexpected direction, she came out of an alley at the familiar bridge.

As she strolled onto it, the moon hung just over the ragged roofs beyond.

The bridge was nearly deserted.

All that actually lived in the city seemed to have retired for the night. She looked down over the stone wall at the water, to see moon-flicker here and there between rocks. From somewhere she remembered an old tale of night in Kolhari with throngs of merrymakers, high-held torches, songs in the alleys, revelers moving from party to party, house to house ... What traveler in the Ellamon market had she overheard voicing such lies? Certainly that was not this city, nor this night, nor this neighborhood.

 186

Ahead, by the wall, she saw two women in tense, quiet converse. The younger kept touching the broad white collar-cover worn by the older, then dropping her head to shake dark hair, which now and again the older would stroke with a wide, work-scarred hand.

She heard footsteps behind her and male voices, slowly overtaking her. For moments she was sure that she would be grabbed, that someone would push her down on the stone, that the coins would be ripped from her pocket—the men broke around her—boys, really, she saw now, though no less frightening because of it—and passed ahead.

They continued, walking, talking.

On the other side of the bridge she saw a man, unsteady with drink, stop and look at her. In the same way she had felt herself the center of attention with the unseen boys who'd come up behind, now she tried to tell herself that, no, he wasn't really staring at her. As she passed, he turned, looking. The moment he was out of eye-sight, Pryn felt an overwhelming urge to look back and see if he were following—and at the same moment felt that *that,* above all, was what she must not do. It would only make some horrible and unnamable and inexplicable thing occur.

As she walked on, the conflict inside her grew, filling up her head, then her whole body, reaching toward some unbearable level till she groped for her knife—

He ran around the newel ahead of her, came a dozen steps onto the bridge, stopped a dozen steps in front of her—a naked barbarian boy. Suspended in a moment of astonishment, he paused, like someone running to keep an appointment only to realize, on arrival, that the person ambling by the appointed corner is not the expected party but only a passing stranger—that, indeed, the appointment itself was for a different day, if not a different street, at a different hour, in a different town altogether.

The boy blinked, turned, and ran off down the Spur-side quay. Carefully, Pryn looked behind her. (Her hand had gone up from her knife hilt. Her knuckles knocked bronze.) The drunken man was walking away unsteadily.

Here, thought Pryn, I can follow every story, image, and bit of misinformation to its source in memory; yet I have no notion where such contradictions come from. Not look *back?* I'd best learn when to, or—better—just shake such contradictions from my head; if I don't, and still I stay in such cities, I shall be dead of them!

Pryn walked from the bridge out onto the empty market's worn brick. (She could be afraid. But what was it she must learn to fight . . . ?) Crossing the square in the night-breeze, she stopped by the stone fountain, bent, drank, then looked up, trying to decide which of the hills about her fed this foaming basin.

She bent to drink again.

Were this another story, what we have told of Pryn's adventures till now might well have been elided or omitted altogether as unbelievable or, at any rate, as uncharacteristic. In that other story, Pryn's next few weeks might easily have filled the bulk of these pages.

Such pages would tell of a dawn's waking in the public park. They would recount a day of watching beggars along the waterfront—and the three not very profitable hours Pryn spent begging herself. The coins Madame Keyne had given her, without hope of adding to them, did not seem much to live on. Those pages would chronicle the evening she carried baskets of yams and sacks of grain from store to kitchen in a large eating establishment frequented by doggedly hungry, dirty men, most among them barbarian laborers who'd managed to secure jobs in the New Market. (The food most popular among them was a kind of vegetable stew which, when Pryn tasted it, proved almost inedible because of some pungent spice whose flavor glimmered all through it.) They would describe the two young women Pryn met working there, who dissuaded her from her plan for the next day: to go to the New Market and ask for a job as a bucket carrier. For didn't Pryn know? Only barbarian women took such jobs. That was no way to climb the social ladder.

One, about twenty, was a short redhead with immense energy and a thick accent (non-barbarian) who would not say where she was from. Her name was Vatry, and she told Pryn she was a dancer. The other was taller, older, heavier, slower, less insistently friendly; still, Pryn found herself taking to her. She was a second cousin, or a friend of a second cousin, of the woman who managed, but did not own, the eating hall. Much later, when Pryn was quite exhausted and had been assured neither she nor Vatry could work there tomorrow because the two brothers who usually did the job would be returning the next day from a family funeral out of town, it was she who said, once she discovered that Pryn had *some* money of her own, that Pryn could come with her and sleep in her room.

Vatry seemed relieved.

Since there was an extra pallet and lots of blankets, it turned out to be as comfortable a sleep as Pryn had gotten in a while.

That story would tell how Pryn met Vatry, as planned, the next afternoon in the Old Market. Vatry knew the mummers who performed their skits there. Pryn and Vatry watched one of the comic extravaganzas from inside the mummers' prop wagon, crouched among old musical instruments, with mountains and flowers and clouds and waves painted on leather and canvas roped to wooden frames and stacked about them. Actors offstage pulled cords to make an artificial beast with jeweled eyes open and close its mouth—while another offstage actor roared—then lowered a wooden eagle whose wings could be flapped by other actors pulling other cords. (A girl, who, in false white hair and beard at the beginning of the skit, had hobbled about the platform in a very funny imitation of a crippled old geezer, crouched beside them now, hands cupped to her mouth, cawing and shrieking and cawing.) It would tell how Vatry, five years older and a head shorter than Pryn—who, after all, was not tall—performed for the mummers between two skits. The performance was called an "audition." Pryn was given a clay drum with a leather head to pound, and sat, pounding it, with the other musicians at the stage edge, making simple rhythmic music, while Vatry grinned and gaped and bounced and bent and turned impressive cartwheels and finished with an astonishing backflip. Later, Pryn must have asked her twenty-five times how she did it and where she'd learned it; but Vatry just laughed. Everyone was very friendly and told Vatry to go walk about the market for an hour while they made their decision. Pryn was nervous, but Vatry thought the whole situation very funny and kept darting off to look at that or this—Pryn once used the opportunity to buy a piece of sugar cane for herself. Then she decided that had been a silly way to spend one of her coins; but it was done. Once Vatry ran up holding a chain on which was ... Pryn's astrolabe! She explained that, while, minutes ago, the two of them had been watching a man with a trained bear, Vatry had seen someone lightly lift it from where Pryn had stuck it into her sash that morning and make off with it. Vatry had gone after him and, as lightly, lifted it back! To Vatry it all seemed amusing, but Pryn found herself wondering, as she put the chain once more around her neck, if the tiny, energetic redhead weren't more talented as a pickpocket than as a dancer. She gave Vatry the last of her cane. Then they returned to the mummers, where, as they stepped up on the by now half-dismantled platform, the corpulent man, who had done a silly dance himself in the first skit with a tall woman who could bend every which way, announced perfunctorily: "More cartwheels and flips; less bumping and bouncing. If you want supper, go back to the wagon there. You can take your friend," which meant Vatry had been hired. Pryn ate that evening with the mummers, terribly excited about Vatry's coming tour—which is mostly what the other mummers talked of as they passed food along the benches under the darkening sky, bruised green and copper along the market's western edge. Vatry herself did a lot of complaining, mostly under her breath and to Pryn,

about the director's instructions. "Does he think I sell my dances the way a prostitute sells her body on the bridge at the other side of the market? What he wants me to cut out are all the magic parts, the truly wondrous parts! But nobody understands magic in this vicious and vulgar city!" The troupe, apparently, would soon travel to markets throughout Nevèrÿon. What wonderful people, Pryn thought as she leaned on her knees and ate fruit and a mush of grain and fried fat that the leading lady said was practically *all* they ate in *her* home town when *she* was growing up, though Pryn was as unsure where that was as she was of Vatry's origins. They drank beer from clay buckets and passed around platters of roasted potatoes. Indeed, the only thing that seemed to interest these odd and exciting people more than travel, past and to come, was sex, about which they joked constantly and in several languages. But the jokes—the ones she could understand—made Pryn laugh, and only now and again did she feel any apprehension about what the night might bring.

Though she'd eaten with the mummers, it wasn't Pryn who had been hired to dance, or who could now blanket off a section of one of the cramped prop wagons to sleep, or who had the wonders of all Nevèrÿon's markets promised her for the season.

What the night brought was mass confusion.

Pryn went back to her other friend's room and was just at the door when she heard scuffling inside. At first she started to move away. Then she heard her friend cry out. Pryn pushed the door open and ran in. A very drunken man was hitting her friend, who had a large yellow and red bruise on her face already and who was making a piteous sound. Pryn opened her mouth and grabbed her knife, both without thinking. She cut the man deeply on the arm and not so deeply on the buttock—and when he tried to grab a workhammer with which he'd already hit the woman, or at least had been threatening to, Pryn slashed the back of his shoulder. This time he got out the door and stumbled down the steps. Her friend was very upset and said they couldn't stay there because, first, he might come back and, second, there was blood all over everything and, third, the landlord, if he saw any of it, would throw them both out—so they went to the room of one of the woman's friends, three streets away.

The story would certainly tell of the two young men Pryn met who were also visiting there that evening. It would, no doubt, record the intense conversation, much later that night among all the young people, about the city's violence. "You say you're scared every time you hear people walking up behind you on the street?" said the younger of the two men, who had a Kolhari accent so thick that for the first minutes Pryn had to restrain herself from laughing, for it sounded like something you might hear from a mummer in a comic skit. "You can't live like that! You have to develop strategies. Now you—" he pointed to the woman who worked in a harness house and whose room it was—"suppose *you* were walking along, at night, and you heard footsteps behind you. What would you do?" Pryn didn't know and, with the young woman addressed, said so. "You'd *listen*, that's what!" the young man cried. "And if the people were talking among themselves, men alone or mixed men and women, you'd know it was all right. If they *weren't* talking, *then* you'd move!"

"What if they're talking about you?" asked a pretty girl who'd given Pryn's friend a rag dampened with vinegar told hold against her bruise.

For some reason, that made everybody laugh—except the girl who'd said it and Pryn's friend. (The vinegar made the whole cramped room smell.) "Most of the time they *will* be talking, too," the Kolhari youth went on. (For the two young men, at any rate, the laughter seemed to have dealt with the objection.) "But you have to learn things like that, otherwise you'll be too scared to go out in the street!"

Pryn, who'd never thought about such strategies in Ellamon, was impressed—the objection notwithstanding—and resolved at least to try it.

The story would tell how the two young men that night said they were planning to take a cartload of something they didn't want to talk about too much someplace in the south they didn't want to name; and since, with whichever strategies, Pryn didn't want to wander about in streets about in which also wandered some half-mad creature whom she had considerably injured, she asked if she could go with them.

The young men thought it was a fine idea.

The story would tell how the night before they actually left— several days after they'd planned to, which gave Pryn a chance to practice her "strategy," and find that, more or les, it worked—there was some festival in a neighborhood of the city Pryn had never been in before, but where the younger one (with the comic accent— though he was getting easier for her to follow each day, if not hour, she spent in the city) said he had some friends. That night people crowded the streets. Bonfires blazed over a small square; and the smell of roasted pig and barbecued goat drifted down every alley.

Pryn and the two youths walked through the throng, passing under high-held torches. And though they never did find the younger man's friends, twice they were taken into people's houses and given lots of beer and, once, some roasted pork. The elder now and again met several people he knew; once Pryn thought she glimpsed the man she'd cut. But that was better than the first day, when she'd seen him every twenty minutes, now turning this corner, now standing in that doorway—which finally was what was wrong with strategy, since it didn't cover that. Still later, over the heads of the crowd, Pryn caught sight of the mummers' wagon, with its raised stage and torches flaming along its upper edge. Yes, there was Vatry, turning her cartwheels and doing her backflips and, indeed, looking better than she had in her audition, because, for one thing, she now wore lots of small bells around her wrists and trailed green and yellow scarves from her waist and neck. At Pryn's urging, the three of them tried to work closer to the stage. Pryn was sure Vatry had smiled at her—indeed, the little dancer was always moving stage front and winking here or waving there. Certainly, Pryn maintained, someone like Vatry would have many friends all over Kolhari, all over Nevèrÿon! But the elder youth just laughed and said that was the way with mummers. And he had known his share. Besides, the crowd was too thick to get any nearer. And so was Pryn, quipped the younger one in his Kolhari twang. (He was blond and extremely thin.) Pryn smiled and wished he hadn't said it. Finally they found a place by one of the fires, beside which some orange-robed women stood together singing a mournful song in a strange language.

The three young people felt mildly embarrassed—but happy. They all thought the song was moving, even though they didn't know what it was about. And Pryn, for herself, decided night in the city was not so bad after all. But why, she wondered, were they leaving it tomorrow at sunrise?

The story would certainly tell how the elder of the two youths had, till six months ago, worked on a farm half a day's ride from town. He was twenty-three and, despite his bearded, pock-marked face and huge, apparently uncleanable farmer's hands, seemed to Pryn the sweetest, gentlest, funniest person she had ever met.

With his comic drawl, nineteen and still no beard yet—and a slight cast in one eye that sometimes reminded Pryn of Noyeed—the scrawny youngster, sunburned and golden-haired, had not so long back been a pipe-fitter's apprentice in a shop off Bronzesmith Row.

Both youths had left their jobs under ignominious circumstances, of which they seemed, nevertheless, quite proud. Both would sit for hours, in company or just with Pryn, alternating anecdotes that dramatized, in the case of the younger, his complete detestation of, and, in the case of the elder his complete incompetence at, anything resembling work. Yet Pryn soon saw, when their canvas-covered cart came to any stream or stretch of rough road, however much he claimed to detest it, the scrawny, wall-eyed one labored with an energic earnestness that should have shamed his bigger, bearded, pit-cheeked companion. In the evening around their camp-fire, the elder's arm about her shoulder, Pryn also learned that the younger had the most repugnant ideas about women and sex she'd encountered since the late Nynx. She leaned against the elder, while across the fire the younger outlined interminable schemes involving women and money, women and money, the one taking the place of the other in his discourse more rapidly even than they might on the Bridge of Lost Desire. At first Pryn tried to argue with him. Later she only half-listened, or tried not to listen at all. Also, now, the elder did not talk as much, nor tell his funny, self-deprecating tales, but sat, staring into the flames, while, in the orange flicker, Pryn looked back and forth between the fire and his ruined, romantic face, trying to imagine what he saw—trying also to shut out the other's droning on about wealth and parts of women's bodies; for he seemed truly incapable, Pryn finally decid-ed, of talking of women at any one time as other than breasts or eyes or legs or genitals or knees or buttocks or arms or hair. (He had this thing about women's knees, which he was always explain-ing.) Occasionally she mustered an amused tolerance for him and his more grotesque strategies. (For every one he had to acquire quick money or avoid urban danger, he had six to start conversa-tions with strange women—each of which he seemed unshakably convinced was as fascinating to Pryn as to himself.) More often, however, she felt simply a quiet disgust. She was thankful that he was only nineteen and had not yet found opportunity to try out any of his more bizarre plans—at least not on the scale he envisioned. She wondered how the elder, whose shoulder she leaned so sleep-ily against, could tolerate, much less cherish, this distressing youth's friendship. When she mentioned it during some rare minute when they were alone, he shrugged it off, saying that his friend was really a good sort and worked hard.

The last, certainly, was true.

On the third evening out, when the mutton and dried fruit prepared back in Kolhari for the first two days was gone, Pryn waited to see how the cooking duties would be divided. At her great-aunt's, she'd done a good deal of it, and after they made camp she was ready to volunteer. But the wall-eyed blond had already taken out crocks and pots and had apparently, earlier in the afternoon, put salted cod to soak in a jar at the back of the wagon, and was now cutting turnips and already quite efficiently into the preparation of the food they had brought for later meals. So Pryn horsed about with the bearded elder, who didn't seem inclined to help at all—until the wall-eyed one made his third (twangy, nearly incomprehensible, but definitely dirty) joke about women too lazy to cook. Pryn said angrily: "Why do you say that! I was *going* to help ..." The elder took her part—while the younger went on cooking and grinning his disfocused grin. The next evening, how-ever, Pryn insisted on helping, and after a few (disfocused) protests that her help wasn't needed, the wall-eyed one accepted her aid. This became their pattern of food preparation for all the meals they fixed outdoors. Pryn and the younger chopped and soaked and sauteed and fried, Pryn muttering *nivu* under her breath like an unknown word from a poem overheard in another language. The elder would sit, not watching—once he fixed something on the cart. Sometimes he would get wood. More often he just lounged or ambled about. No one complained. But one reason Pryn kept at it was because when the wall-eyed one cooked was the only time he wasn't talking about women's bodies, and Pryn had decided that if they were to be any sort of friends, she'd best do something with him then.

The story would doubtless tell how Pryn finally made love to the elder youth, several times over several days. "I love you, and I know that you love me," she told him—several times through that glori-ous season. He liked hearing it, too: it made him smile. (The younger one, when he overheard her once or twice, seemed to like it just as much and smiled just as broadly.) "That is all I know. That is all I need to know," she would finish; but when she had, she always felt caught up in some play of preposterous contradictions, as if it were a line from a mummer's skit she could never read aloud with the proper inflection. That was probably why, she decided later, she said it as many times as she did. Still, with sunlight on his bearded, broken face, the elder would smile at her, or nuzzle her neck, or walk with her among the trees, his arm about her shoulder.

He never, however, said much of anything back.

As we have noted, it wasn't the first time Pryn had had sex, for in mountain towns of the sort she'd grown up in such intercourse was frequently accomplished at an even earlier age than in the cities. But it was not yet her tenth time, either; and it was certainly her first time with someone only two weeks away from a total stranger— and without the support of a society ready with rituals, traditions, and the coercive wisdom necessary to turn the passing pleasure of adolescence straightway into a family at any sign of natal conse-quence. The story would also tell how, nights later, when they'd decided to stay over at an inn, the wall-eyed one brought back to

Pryn's room two of the Empress's soldiers from a garrison housed in an old barracks outside the town and argued with her for a solid hour, not loudly but with the same earnest perseverance she'd seen him use to free a cart wheel in a stream when it had caught on a submerged root. Finally she agreed to make love to them.

Synopsized, the hour's whispered conclave had run:

The elder youth had spent too much money on beer in the inn's tavern that evening, so that now, even with Pryn's remaining coins, they did not have enough to pay for their rooms; nor was this civilized Kolhari, where they might be turned out with a scolding on account of their youth or made to stay and work off the debt. It was a backwater province where everyone was related to everyone else and where the locals had proved themselves hostile to strangers in a dozen ways already.

Anything might happen here.

The money the soldiers would give her was the only way the three of them would have enough to pay for their lodging next morning.

It wasn't—quite.

But the inn keeper finally agreed—angrily—to forfeit the small difference and sent them off. Clearly he did not wish to see them return.

Certainly the story would tell how, some three hours after they were on the road, Pryn managed to get into an angry and perfectly ridiculous argument with the elder—indeed, the argument was so idiotic that, after she'd stalked off in a rage, leaving both of them for good, she was sure, she could not even reconstruct what its point had been. (It wasn't because of the soldiers. *He* didn't even know about *them,* having been sleeping too soundly because of the beer. And the wall-eyed one had *promised* . . .!) She only knew she was glad to leave him, glad to leave the both of them! Then, after tramping for two more hours along the sun-dappled, dusty road, Pryn began to cry.

She was thinking about being pregnant.

Indeed, Pryn now admitted to herself, she had been thinking about almost nothing else for several days, though before last night it had seemed a hazy daydream involving going back to Kolhari, or even Ellamon, with the elder friend, while the younger, in the dream, remained in the south—or vanished!

But now, somehow, there was nothing pleasant left to it. The pock-marked youth from the farm was lazy and the wall-eyed one from the city impossible; and she knew they would not cease their smuggling or dissolve their friendship over some child by her.

The story would tell how, over the next three days, practically

every six hours Pryn broke out crying—suddenly and surprisingly, whether she was by herself walking in the woods or passing a yard with people in it.

Once a man said she could ride downriver with him in his boat if she would help him with the fishing. She got into the shallow skiff and sat, looking at the woven reed lining. His brown hair thinning in front and tied with a thong behind one ear, the fisherman pulled on the wide wooden oars. Pryn looked about the boat's floor at the coils and tangles of line, the bone hooks stuck along a piece of branch, the woven nets heaped around; suddenly she felt a surge of useless-ness and a second surge of exhaustion, which surges battled, burning, in her eyes—tears, for the tenth or the hundredth time, spilled her puffy cheeks.

She sat in the boat, crying, while the fisherman, with his big-knuckled, pitch-stained hands, rowed and watched her, saying nothing.

Finally Pryn coughed, pulled her own hands back into her lap, and blinked. "My name is Pryn," she got out, "and I can . . . I'm going to have a *baby*!"

Despite his thinning hair, the fisherman looked no more than twenty-four. He pulled and leaned, pulled and leaned, pulled and leaned. With three bronze claws fastened to the rag wrapped around his waist and between his very hairy legs, the wide strap over his right shoulder went taut, then slack, taut, then slack, over the sunken well in his narrow, near-bald chest. "My name is Tratsin," he said after a while. "I'm going to have one, too."

Pryn looked quite startled.

Tratsin pulled on the oars. "My wife," he added, by way of explanation, "I mean. She's having it. For me." Taut; slack. "It's been all girls so far—this will be my third. Well, four, actually. The first was a boy, but she lost him. That was even before she would live with me. In these parts they say it's a curse to have girls. But you know who takes in the aged parents? The girls, that's who. My parents lived with my sisters. My wife wouldn't live with me until after her father passed—though my boy died only a month later. I think that's because he needed his own father—me. And when I get too old to work, I'll live with one or the other of my girls, I'll bet you. And I'll be a father they'll *want* to have live with them. That's important. Come home with me, girl. Come home. My wife's name is Bragan. She's a good girl. About your age, I'd bet. But skinnier. At least she used to be. Certainly no more than two or three years older. Come home, now . . ."

Somewhere in all this Pryn started crying again.

Over the stades they rowed downstream, three times Tratsin

stopped to fish. In the course of it, Pryn learned he was not really a fisherman, but a benchmaker. He'd taken his two days off for the month to travel north, had rented one of the reed-lined boats, and was fishing downstream over the second day toward home. A man has to get away from the women sometimes, he said—though he seemed happy enough for Pryn's company. He said: His wife, Bragan, was seven months along toward another child. He *hoped* it might be a boy, but a girl would be all right. Girls could work, too. His younger brother, till only weeks ago, had lived with them— Malot, now he'd been a strange boy. He'd worked at the quarry, but he'd run off to the city. At any rate, that's what everyone assumed— it was all he'd talked of for the six months before he and Bragan's household money had disappeared one day. It had wounded Tratsin deeply, his brother's running away. Wounded him to the heart. They lived, Tratsin and his family, in the town of ... but Pryn missed the name: she'd begun to cry again. Probably Malot would come to a bad end, Tratsin went on. (Pryn sniffled and tried to listen.) His wife's cousin, Gutryd? She lived with them, too. And spoiled the girls and was a silly girl herself. He didn't understand Gutryd. He didn't think she was happy.

His boss was good, though.

His working conditions were good.

His wife was a good girl: she let him go fishing on his two days a month off.

He was a happy man, Tratsin reasoned.

With six freshwater perch, one of which Pryn caught herself when Tratsin let her throw in the line, and seven or eight brook trout—they threw back lots of little palm-sized fish he said wouldn't taste good at all—they came that evening to a bank loud with crickets. They pulled up at a muddy beach where half a dozen boats with woven linings had been tied to branches so that their prows were lifted clear of the water. The sky was deep blue, halfway into night. The air was dry and cool. Now and again the bushes and shacks about them flickered into full daylight with hazy lightning.

"Come with me, now." Tratsin's bare feet sank in black mud, breaking cracks around in it. "Come. You'll like Bragan. She's a good girl. And she'll help you. You'll see." Thunder trundled somewhere in the cool summer sky. Again lightning flickered. "Come. This way."

Pryn did like Bragan, who pushed aside the hanging in the shack doorway and, after Tratsin whispered to her briefly, declared: "You're having a baby!" She clapped her hands to the sides of her own seven-and-a-half-month belly under the sleeveless brown shift while the hanging fell against her shoulder. "Come in, now! Come in!

Your first weeks? You must be dead tired. My two girls—oh, I carried both of them easily enough. But *this* one?" Firelight flickered in her frizzy hair. "Well, I was sick as a poisoned dog for the whole first month and a half! That's why I think it's going to be a boy—Ah! I want it to be a boy so badly! I had a boy first, but he died, poor little thing. Boys carry harder and higher, they say. Or is it girls? I never can remember! But come in! Come in!"

The shack's single room was comically crowded, and Pryn was too tired to remember who was who, other than that the heavy one with the dead black hair and beard—Kurvan—was Tratsin's best friend.

"You working yet?" were Tratsin's first words to him.

"I wasn't working yesterday morning when you left." Leaning against the wall, Kurvan folded his arms over his fleshy chest. "What makes you think I'd be working when you got back?"

"You haven't been working for almost three weeks." Bragan stepped around a baby basket on the floor. "You should have a job!"

"Until *he* came home you were happy enough to let me lounge and gossip by your fireplace!" Kurvan laughed. "Now you *both* start in on me!"

"You *should* have a job," Tratsin said. "I could get you a job. Since Malot's gone, they need another man at the stone pit. I could speak to—" But that actually seemed to get black-bearded Kurvan annoyed.

So Bragan cried: "Let's get this young woman some soup!" She put her arm around Pryn, heading her around the end of a bench toward the corner fireplace.

"Get her some beer," Kurvan said. "Beer's good for pregnant women. We have fine beer here. It comes from the breweries down on the coast," and he turned to help himself from a dripping barrel set back between two plank beds.

"Soup!" protested Bragan, then turned to Pryn. "Unless you'd rather not—with this one, I couldn't eat a thing, night or day, for the first six weeks. Though my sister said that's only supposed to last for three. Ahh! and in the morning! Everything I tried to get down—?" She made a spewing gesture. "What a mess!"

A baby began to cry. The other woman in the room—the sister? Gutryd?—went to see about it, while Bragan ladled soup, thick as stew, first from one pot, then from another, into one red clay bowl and the next.

The stuff in the first cauldron was brown and meaty; the stuff in the second, which Bragan spilled on top of it so that the two made ribbons across one another in the bowl, was creamy and dotted with yellow vegetables. Filled with the two of them, the red clay heated Pryn's palm to burning as she raised the bowl to her mouth—to be struck by a memory out of childhood:

The gray-veiled woman traveler from the Ellamon market, who wore the wide silver rings, had told her aunt, "And their double soups? The glory of southern cookery, I say—though you must know the people to find any. They won't serve it at the inns." And her aunt had said, "Chemistry, medicine, alchemy, and the other branches of charlatanry that sap the purse of our Suzerain today at the wheedling of clever men, they're all forms of the woman's science of cuisine—especially that part of it concerned with mid-wifery. Belham told me that. Do you know of Belham, the barbarian inventor from the south? He stayed here in fabled Ellamon—oh, it was many, many years back—"

Kurvan handed Pryn a piece of bread, burned in spots on the crust but with (as she took the third bite, she realized) dough still raw in it. She ate hungrily, nevertheless, thinking that it was the kind of loaf people had brought back to her cousin in outrage (or begrudging sympathy) during the first months of his bakery. With it she shoveled soup into her mouth.

The soup *was* wonderful!

"That woman is hungry!" Holding his own bowl, Kurvan squatted down in a clear spot on the floor mat. "She'll have a fat and healthy youngster, with good bones and a worker's back, if she eats that way."

"You should have a job, Kurvan," Gutryd said sitting on the bench next to Tratsin, who was almost finished with his bowl. "Three weeks without work? Bragan's right. It isn't good for you or your family." She reached down for the loaf leaning against the baby's basket. "You want to be able to marry and have a fine family of healthy children now, like Tratsin and Bragan, don't you?"

To wake with straw tickling her cheek and ankle and the smell of damp thatch and babies and last night's cooking, the pallet below the straw hard under one shoulder and water dripping somewhere from the torrents that had poured loud enough to wake her just before sunrise (Pryn did not open her eyes), was to realize that, before she'd started these adventurings, she'd spent most of her life in such a shack. It was to realize that whenever these adventurings were through, no matter how far away they deposited her, unless life for her went very differently from what she or anyone else might expect, she was likely to spend most of her life to come in such a shack—however better insulated she might make it.

A clay top moved on a clay jar. A woman whispered. A man's

bare feet crunched the floor mats. He said, answering a question Pryn hadn't heard: "Well, it was time to get up. Who sleeps when there's work to do?"

Pryn rolled over, stretched her feet onto the floor, rubbing her hands' heels on her eyes.

The woman spoke now. "I just thought they might like to sleep a *little* more, that's all. Especially the girl you brought in last night, since she's . . . you know."

Pryn let her hands stay over her eyes.

"Sleep instead of work?" The man laughed. "Now, who would want to do that—except, well, let's see . . . a few I could name!" His next laugh was louder. "Besides, the girl's not sick. She's only having a baby! You get her to help you with the chores. See, *she's* awake at least. Not like this other lazy good-for-nothing."

Fingering the corners of her eyes, Pryn looked up.

Squatting naked, with her knees wide and her great belly between them, Bragan was doing something at the fire.

Tratsin was bending over her with his hand on her shoulder, the sides of his narrow buttocks hollow, the ligaments standing out at the backs of his hairy knees. "Now don't be afraid to ask her to help you. She's a good girl—like you!"

At which point a baby cried.

Like a man reminded of a pressing duty, Tratsin lunged for his loin rag, winding it about his hips, tucking it in on itself here and there, getting it between his legs, while making for the door. Bragan got even busier poking up the coals under the pot and blowing them to brightness.

The cry ran out of breath; in the pause, Pryn pictured the tiny chest filling itself mightily. She looked around, thinking to go to the baby herself. But Gutryd came in through the back door-hanging. The brush of hemlock twigs on the bottom to keep out insects swung in over the mat. Gutryd's dress was bunched down around her waist, and her hair was wet. She seized the child's basket up from the corner, to shake it back and forth. The next cry was notably quieter, with, somewhere in it, a movement toward relief.

At the fire Bragan said: "Gutryd, get her! Please!"

"There, there!" Gutryd said, though whether it was to child or adults, Pryn was not sure. "I have her! I have her!"

Pryn stood up on the rush mats and started forward to volunteer her help to Bragan—as the toddler toddled before her. Pryn stepped wide; her foot landed on the corner of a blanket, largely wrapped around large Kurvan. Broad, cracked feet stuck from the blanket's edge, confirming what last night Pryn had only suspected: she'd been given the pallet Kurvan usually slept on when he stayed over.

 200

Then, for some reason known only to those under three, the crawling girl sat back on her haunches, twisted up her face, and let a wail that carried within its knife-tones the anguish of a god before a clumsy, foolish, ill-made, skilless, cracked, and useless world. The pain at that cry's core seemed something that might be looked away from, more likely suppressed, but that could never be assuaged.

"Oh, little one," Kurvan said from under his blanket, "*do* shut up!" He rolled away, tugging more blanket over his black, bushy head.

As the blanket corner pulled from under her heel, Pryn took another ungainly step to avoid the baby's hand and Kurvan's feet. At which point Kurvan rolled back, thrust his naked arms out, seized the wailing child, and pulled her to him with all the compassion of a man who'd spent a lifetime in such world-sorrow as she now howled of. "Oh, I'm sorry, honey!" He cuddled and rocked with her on the floor, as if he were personally responsible for the profound and universal disorder by which she had just been shattered. "I'm *sorry!*"

Pryn started toward Bragan, who had suddenly become very involved with the fire, food, and crockery in much the same way she'd increased her involvement in the ashes when the baby had first cried.

So Pryn veered toward the door, out which Tratsin was leaving.

She caught the hide hanging as it swung across the doorway. Hemlock leaves, from the branch tied for weight and bugs along its bottom, brushed the door stone.

She stepped outside.

Coppery sun burned on wet leaves.

Other shacks stood near; still others stood across the muddy path down the slope.

Through the break in the brush the river looked substantially narrower at dawn than it had in evening's half-dark.

More shacks sat on the far bank, a few stone huts among them—in short, the farther shore was much like this one. Tratsin stood a little off on some rocks around which the grass had worn away. He scratched at his thinning scalp so that thong and bound hair shook behind his ear.

Down the slope, someone guffawed in the next cottage. A woman yelled. The other person laughed.

Hemlock leaves shushed.

Naked and disheveled, but without the child, Kurvan stepped out.

Branches dipped slowly across the road, then turned up all their whispering leaves to show gray. The breeze reached a tree near the door.

Droplets hit Pryn's cheek.

And Kurvan said something like, "Aargchh ...!" rubbing the splatter from his face and shoulders while Tratsin laughed and pointed. Pryn grinned—as Kurvan's stubby genitals contracted within the black hair below the crease under his broad belly. "That's right!" he announced. "Everyone else gets a few drops, but Kurvan gets the soaking!"

"What *you'd* better get," said Tratsin, "is a job!" He laughed again.

"Oh, yes—" Suddenly Kurvan's annoyance and brushing turned into a great, open laugh so that his big chest shook. "I get the soaking? Well, sometimes I think my job is to give you and your family something to laugh at! Oh, it's not such a bad vocation. The hours are long. The pay is mostly in kind—" Here he leaned toward Pryn in a mocking aside—"though he lets me hit him up for an iron coin or two." He dropped his hand to his knee to scratch. "But I suppose the work has its higher profits—"

Which made Tratsin laugh again. "You mean all the food we let you eat?" He turned, shaking his head and smiling. "What you don't understand, Kurvan, is the value of work itself. To do work—of any sort, of any kind, under whatever conditions—is important in itself. A body whole, healthy, and able to toil is the most wonderful and carefully crafted of gifts the nameless gods can give. Work is what makes you human. To do, to make, to change something with your hands—"

"Certainly any slave must feel better for his slaving, eh?"

"Well," said Tratsin, "that's what you always say to me when we have this argument. And I will say what I always say back: we have no slaves in Enoch, and because one can work—here—as a free man rather than a slave, we have—here—the final sanding and varnishing on an already beautifully constructed thing: labor itself."

Coming up the muddy road, two men carried a wooden bench, one lugging each end. It was very like the bench Pryn had once sat on against the building her first day in the city, or the bench at Madame Keyne's reproduced in stone at the back of the hut on the rise in her garden, or the one in Tratsin's hut. Sunlight through the trees splattered and spilled over and off its seat and carved back.

Running up behind the bench carriers, the knees of his bowed legs knocking forward a leather apron, the leather bib sagging from the strap about his neck, came a third man ...

Man?

Boy?

Pryn blinked.

He was substantially shorter than Pryn, though his face held

thirty-five or forty years above that sparse gray beard. His forehead was wider and broader than either Kurvan's or Tratsin's. He grabbed up the bench in the middle to help carry. His shoulder was as high as the others' waists.

Tratsin said, oddly soft, to Pryn: "That's some of my work there . . ."

The dwarf—for it was a dwarf in the leather apron—turned over his shoulder to look up the slope. "Hey, Tratsin, come down here and help us carry this back to the shop! That rain last night? They won't be along the river road to pick this up till evening, now. I don't want it sitting in that leaky riverside storehouse all day. If it rains again, the roof will cave in on it in that place!"

"Hey, Froc! I haven't had my breakfast yet!" Tratsin glanced again at Pryn. "And the little man there is my boss—a good boss too."

"Aw, what's breakfast to a worker like you? Let your woman bring you an extra apple with dinner. Come on, now! Don't be like that! We need you!"

Tratsin chuckled, shaking his head again. "Tell Bragan I had to go in early, will you? A worker in Frocsin's shop sometimes plays the woodpecker—and sometimes the ox. Hey, Bragan . . .!"

Inside the hut, the baby cried again.

"*You* tell her I'm gone!" Tratsin started down the slope. (Pryn wondered whether the instruction were to Kurvan or to her.) At the bottom he slogged onto the muddy road and grabbed up the bench edge. The dwarf stepped back. "There you go—there . . . ! Watch out for it, now!" They moved on up the road.

Standing beside Kurvan, Pryn watched them.

"You know," Kurvan said after a moment, "the cut-down one there *isn't* Tratsin's boss."

Pryn glanced at him, frowning.

"Froc is just his foreman. Now Frocsin would probably make a better boss than the one he's got. But he isn't the boss, much as Trat would like to think so."

Pryn looked at Kurvan, questioning.

Leaves hissed above them. More drops. But Kurvan did not rub or complain.

"The boss's name is Marg, and he has a belly bigger than mine and less hair than Tratsin's father, and he lives two villages away. He rides by to check out the workshop on Tuesdays and Fridays, and says along with everyone else what a little jewel he has in Froc—Marg says it and his workers say it too. But Frocsin's no more the boss of that shop than I am!"

Pryn wondered at the bushy bearded man's insistence. "Tratsin

203

seems like a happy man," she offered idly. "And he's a good man, too."

"A good man, yes. They don't make better. But happy?" Kurvan grunted. "Well, he's happy *now*. But he wasn't happy a year ago. And I don't know how happy he'll be in another year." Suddenly he snorted and rubbed his thumb knuckle hard under his nose, leaving his moustache a black cloud with no shape at all. "Myself, I'm a simple man—simpler than Tratsin, I think. I don't like work. I like play—and I only do the one when there's no way else to pay for the other. But I can remember what happened yesterday, and I can figure a little of what's coming tomorrow. . . . And that's never the way to be happy, is it?"

"What do you think is going to come?" Pryn asked. "For Tratsin? What was it like for him before—last year, I mean?"

Kurvan shrugged. "Most of the men hereabouts aren't bench-makers, you know." He nodded off toward the hills. "They work in the quarries up at Low Pass. Like Malot used to do."

Another shout came from the cottage across the road; a man stepped out the door, his head bowed between grizzled shoulders. Two workhammers hung from his leather girdle. Seconds later a boy hurried out after him, overtook him, turned back to wave him on—and became a girl! "Come on, Father. Run," she called. "We're already late!"

"*You* run," the man called back. "I'm walking!"

"Now Wujy, there, is a man like me! *Me,* off to work before I'd had my breakfast?" Kurvan laughed. "But Wujy there's been sick. Everyone else has been off to the quarry before sun-up—probably in that rain, too. Wujy goes in with his daughter two or three hours late every day. He's got permission, because of his age and infirmity. The girl picks up chips and gets paid one iron coin for every three days of work she puts in. And they let Wujy come in when he can and work as long or as short as he wants—Tratsin says its humane and just. Myself, I call it murder."

Pryn frowned.

"You get paid by the weight of rock you dig out. If a man is too sick to dig any more than a green boy can be expected to come up with on his first week at the job when he's still learning how to swing his hammer, then it's a green boy's wage he gets. Even if he's an old man sick to death."

"In the city—" Pryn remembered Madame Keyne's concern for the injured digger—"I met someone who was supposed to be a—" She began to say 'a Liberator.' But then, the Liberator was *only* interested in slaves . . .

"You get paid by the load *unless* you're part of the scaffolding

204

crew. Then, as Tratsin used to joke when he was a young scaffolder, you don't get paid at all! The scaffolders put up the wooden walkways and platforms against the rock faces for high work. Oh, they. get a steady wage—but it's lower than the pickers'. And we haven't gone a year without one or another eighteen- or nineteen-year-old wood roper falling to his death. Till a year ago, Tratsin swung up and down the rock face putting up scaffolds. I was his friend, and I knew he hated the work, was frightened of it, and was scared to make any moves in life because of it." Kurvan 'humphed.' "Ask him, and he'll say, 'It taught me the basics of woodworking—without which I couldn't do the job I do now.' " He rubbed his bushy chin. "Tratsin has the fine job he has now because a fat old tile-layer had a cousin who was a master woodworker who knew some wealthy families who were building new homes and who had taken a liking for a kind of benches they usually build further north. Marg said: 'Why not build them here?' and he had enough initiative to get his cousin and half a dozen carpenters—most of them, I might add, like Tratsin, out-of-work scaffolders—and an old grain storehouse and an industrious dwarf, and put them all together just on the other side of the bridge. And behold, a business!" Kurvan shook his head again. "And a happy Tratsin, for whom the only value in life is labor: profitable, satisfying, challenging—till all the orders are filled. And they *will* be filled, you know, inside a year. Tratsin, with another couple of squalling babies and maybe even a second wife, will go back to the quarry. But already his scaffolding skills have been refined into the delicate touch of a master benchmaker. But he will no longer be able to live on scaffolders' wages. He'll have to work as a common digger. His skills will turn rotten in his hands and arms. Oh, he'll stop talking of labor like some god among gods discoursing on his craft and begin to curse it like a man among men—though he'll wonder and ponder and fret and try to pretend he's a god still. For that's Tratsin. It's also half the workers in this village. Me, I wonder what Malot's doing in the city."

"Malot—?"

"Tratsin's crazy brother, who ran off from the quarry three weeks ago—always talking about the city—and who, when I'm thinking like this, doesn't seem so crazy." He laughed again. "But you were in Kolhari. And all it seems to have given you was a belly that'll be poking out even beyond mine in a few months, hey?" He smiled saying it; she knew he meant no harm with it. She felt her cheeks heat anyway. Pryn clamped her teeth and hoped tears wouldn't come.

"Well, you're probably better off than Malot. You're here; we like

you. That's something. Malot's there—and he hasn't Tratsin's brains or skills. Would you rather be a crudestone worker out of a job in the country or the city?"

Pryn blinked to find her memory flooded with images of the unhired laborers milling about the New Market.

"But I won't be surprised in a year when Tratsin and Bragan are off to the city too. That's the biggest—and the saddest—possibility, I think. Well, *I'm* off to do a little hunting—not animals. But I know half a dozen wild fruit trees that the local children haven't stripped yet. If I net together a vine-fiber sack and bring it back filled with pears, Bragan might make us a fine cobbler with supper this evening, and let that stand me for work—though the kids around here would call it play." (Pryn thought: You don't have to twist vines to net a fruit sack. She'd tied together many such sacks in the mountains ...) "Work makes a human being ...?" This time when Kurvan shook his head it was as though he'd suddenly discovered some notion caught all over his mind, like woodlice on rough fabric. "*Play* makes a human being! Work just means you don't have to feel guilty about playing, which I don't feel much anyway. Mainly work means I don't have to suffer the taunts of my friends who wonder why I'm playing as hard as I do! What's it like in Kolhari?"

"Oh, it's ..." Pryn hunched her shoulders. "It's different. Confusing. You can't understand much of anything there. I didn't, anyway. Maybe because I don't know what it used to be like. And I couldn't figure out what it was going to become."

"You're like me." Kurvan grinned. "You're not out to be happy either. And you're serious about your play. That's what it's like to be committed to playing. Only the ones who love labor would dare try for happiness. And luckily you'll be having a little one to take your mind off such difficulties. Well ..." He put his hands on his hips and looked around. "I'm into the woods to walk—and think about what's difficult. That's a kind of play, too." He wandered away, heavy-footed, over the grass.

Which left Pryn to go in and tell Bragan the men had gone.

She turned and pushed back the hanging—

At which point the shack floor rose into the air almost to her chin.

"Oh ...!" which was Bragan. "Catch it!"

Dust puffed from the matting, getting in Pryn's mouth. She stepped back against the wall.

"Catch it!" Bragan cried. "Catch it ...! Catch it!"

Pryn caught the mat's edge. Reed-ends rasped her palms. The mat settled heavily against her.

Wielding a stick lashed at its end with straw, Gutryd swept violently at the stones and dried mud beneath.

"There—no, pull it back further ..." which Pryn did. "That's it—now help me lift the other side ..." which began the morning's furious housework. Pryn was surprised it took so much energy to keep the little shack and the possessions of its three permanent adults and two children this side of clean and clutter. Amidst the brushing and scrubbing, the pushing and lugging, Pryn told Bragan that Tratsin and Kurvan were off.

"Together?" Bragan demanded, as if it were possible Tratsin had missed work to go with his jobless friend.

"Tratsin went to work." Pryn held a wet rag in one hand and some bowls under her other arm. "And Kurvan just ... went."

"Oh. Well." Bragan dried her wet elbow against the gray cloth she'd finally wrapped around herself. "That's better than Kurvan's hanging about all day and *talking*. Oh, he's a good man. But let him, and he'll explain everything in the world to you and how it relates to everything else. Then, when you tell him we're just poor working people here, he'll say it's because we won't consider such things that we stay poor." She laughed. "Now have you ever known anyone like that?"

Pryn thought of Gorgik, of Madame Keyne, and wondered how to speak of them; but, ducking in through the back door again, Gutryd said, "Here, Pryn. You can take that jar down to the river and bring some water for me, if you like ..."

Pryn made several trips to get water in a large clay jar. At the bank she watched five yellow-haired women, filling jars as large and handling them more easily. She carried hers, its neck dribbling, back between the shacks.

"You know, I always used to wish Tratsin could spend a day home with me." In the yard, Bragan wrung out a hank of cloth, then shook fold from wet fold to lay it over the basket's rim. "Only, when he does, it's always because he's sick, so it's just like having an extra baby in the house. Finally, I realized it wasn't Tratsin I wanted so much as the excitement of going off to the mountains to work, of hiking upriver to fish—something I thought he could bring just by staying here! But the moment I realized it, I realized—and it came practically with my next breath—*he* couldn't bring that! If I wanted such excitement, *I* would have to go out and seek it. And three days later, as I stand here—" She shook out more unbleached fabric—"I knew I was pregnant with this one!"

And inside, minutes later: "Ah, you see—" turning from Pryn, who stood now on the bench to rummage in the purple shadows of an upper shelf under the thatched roof—"always *I* must do the

scolding." Bragan snatched up the toddler from where she was about to crawl onto the hearth. "Tratsin, when he comes home, is either all hugs and cuddles, or he just ignores them; so *I'm* the bad parent." She came back, joggling her daughter, to stand by Pryn's knee, while afterimages of the sun with a branch through it glimmered before Pryn in shelved shadow. It smelled like figs. Dusty crocks. Bound straw dolls with clay heads and hands. Below: "He says he doesn't want to punish them because he wants them to love him. Which is all very fine, but children *must* be punished sometimes. So I'm left the great monster to plague their dreams as well as the dream itself they cling to, while *he* remains just human. Oh, I envy him the ways by which he shirks power and stays only a man. Can you find it?"

"I don't think it's here."

Then outside again, while Pryn handed Gutryd up the dripping garbage basket which Gutryd dumped over into the smelly cart: "So, you're pregnant. You and Bragan, a pair!" Standing on the log that ran along the cart's side, Gutryd pounded the basket's bottom. Perspiration glittered on her temple. (The cart's driver had very large, heavily veined ears sticking out of hair as bushy as Pryn's.) "You're quite different, of course, you two—I mean the way you act. But somehow I don't think that *makes* much difference, now, does it?" Which Pryn hadn't thought at all. The notion was surprising, if not worrying. (Six years older, she would simply have thought it wrong.) "I almost thought *I* was, three months ago! Pregnant, I mean. Well! When the full moon drove my blood out at last, I was a very happy woman! I don't think Malot was so crazy to go off to the city. After all, he was in trouble here—though you mustn't tell anyone I told you. Still, it surprised us all he actually went. One day he was here, and then—like magic—gone! I thought it *was* magic myself at first, but Kurvan said, no, he'd just run off to Kolhari. And Tratsin agreed. Well, no one will know him there—and often he wasn't a pleasant boy to know here. But you've *been* there. I'd like to go. Although I wouldn't like to have a baby there, from what I've heard."

And inside again, Bragan: "You haven't seen the abandoned huts up near the crossroads yet, have you?" It was a considered observation. Another mat collapsed between her hands, to be folded, bulkily, again, then again. "You can stay in one of them tonight— Kurvan or Tratsin will take you when they get back. But you see how crowded we are here. They're not as nice as this, of course, but then there'll only be one of you—at least for a few months more. You can fix it up as nicely as you like."

"Oh . . . !" It struck Pryn with the surprise of the inevitable. "Yes . . ." Feelings of rejection contended with feelings of gratitude.

"But you see how difficult it would be if you *did* stay with us. For too long. Oh, I don't mean you haven't been helpful." Bragan smiled apologetically. But she also looked relieved, as if she'd been contemplating saying this a while. "You understand."

"Oh," Pryn said again, "I do."

"It would be best, I think. And it's not very far away. Believe me, we'd help you just as much as you've helped us. Enoch is not a very big town. You don't get too far away from anyone here. Old, yes. But not big."

For the first time Pryn thought of it as an incipient city, a little one with a garbage service and a name and a riverside dock.

"I'll be honest. They're not so large." Bragan put the mat down—almost on the napping baby; she cried out, moved it aside, laughed, put her hand to her neck, blinked, and went on: "But you'll have a roof over you. That's better than nothing. You'll be near the quarry road. And that's not bad."

Which is when Gutryd stepped inside and said: "Really, it's not. From time to time, I've thought of moving there myself. Don't worry." (Pryn wondered just how long they'd been discussing her coming move.) "It all seems a little strange, I know. But you're used to the way we do almost everything here. And soon we'll be used to you."

Which made Pryn blink and smile.

"Ah!" as a memory assailed Bragan. "Tratsin didn't take his dinner—I haven't even *fixed* it! Now that's so like him." She sighed. "And me." She turned to the hearth, where Gutryd already sat on a wooden stump and, with two triple-tined wooden forks, was picking through a bit of wool, teasing it out, by small tugs, to fine fluff, now pausing to pinch loose a twig or leaf-bit, which she tossed viciously into the fireplace before falling back to her carding.

"Are you going to do that whole basketful?" Bragan asked. "Well, I suppose it has to be got through sometime. But once it's done, someone should spin it—because if it just sits here for three days, with these children, you know the shape it'll be in—"

Against the wool basket lay a flat stone with two irregular holes . . .

"Oh, I'll do it." Pryn did not like spinning. "I mean I can, if you don't have *any*thing else for me to do . . ." Still, she spun well. And Bragan didn't have any other job for her right then. So Pryn sat at the other side of the hearth from Gutryd, took up a lapful of carded fleece and the spinning stone, and twisted at one corner of the wool till she had a long enough thread to wrap through the spin-

dle's holes (not a very well balanced spindle, either) and began to knock its rough side with her palm, letting it twirl the fiber into a fine yarn, which she fed out evenly from her fist between bunched fingers.

"You do that very skillfully." Bragan laughed. "You're one of those women who does it so well you'd think you invented it yourself!" She turned to a wicker onion bin on top of which sat last night's loaf, still wrapped in a bread cloth, and began to busy herself with food. "Now me, when I spin, it's all thumbs and knots . . ."

Thinking of invention, Pryn said: "The soup . . ."

"Mmm?" Gutryd looked up, picking.

Pryn glanced at the two empty pots, which had been raised to higher hooks above the fireplace's ash-banked embers. "The soup we had, last night. I was just thinking—"

"Ah!" Bragan exclaimed, tugging the outer leaves down from something that looked like a leek. "If we had some more, I'd put a ladle of that in a bowl and send you off to Tratsin with it. He doesn't mind cold soup. But Kurvan eats enough for three. When he stays here, leftovers don't."

"What about the soup?" Gutryd looked back at her flying picks. "Do let her talk, Bragan. Get you alone and you're bad as Kurvan."

"In my home, in the mountains, in Ellamon, where my great-aunt lives—" Pryn brushed her hand at the rock's edge, its spin finally fast enough to steady its joggling—"it's very much like here. Oh, we knot the edging on our floor mats differently. And we don't scratch those funny designs into the base of our pots—the food we eat is different. Still, lots in Enoch is very much like home. Except the soup. The double soup, in the two pots, the way you make it."

"You don't have soup in the mountains?" Gutryd picked.

"We don't have soup like that, made in two pots and served in a single bowl. But you see, back in my town, oh, years ago, my aunt met a traveling woman once—she bought her some autumn apples and talked with her. My aunt always liked to talk to strangers—at least she used to. And the woman told us about your soup."

"*My* soup?" Bragan asked. "I learned to make it from my uncle. And Tratsin's cousin, Mordri, makes it much better than I do—but she won't tell me exactly what she puts in it. You'd think it was some kind of magic!"

"But that's just it!" Pryn spun the rock. "It *is* magic, or at least it almost is, to me. You see, there I was, out in the Ellamon market, sitting in the shade of the dyer's stall, maybe ten years old, with a little bit of sunlight through a hole in the thatch falling right into my eyes, while my aunt and the traveling woman sat on the benches out under the awnings, leaning together over large plates with a few bits of cut-up fruit. The woman traveled with a little boy, I remember, about my age, who may have been a slave—but I don't think so, because he wore lots of copper jewelry around his thighs and wrists and squatted out in the sun making patterns in the dust with a pouch full of colored stones. And she said, 'If you ever go to the south, I mean into the head of the barbarian lands beyond Kolhari, you must try their double soups—no, you can't get it at the inns. They think it's food only for peasants, not tourists. But in the people's homes, sometimes it's served. The glory of southern cookery . . . Vegetables cooked in one pot, and meat boiled almost to pieces in the other and thickened with goats' cream—' "

"*That's* what it is!" Bragan turned suddenly. "Of course—*that* must be what Mordri uses! And the rest of us, mixing a handful of ground wheat to thicken it—but then you can *get* goat's cream in Mordri's village! No one herds goats around here. If I sent Kurvan after some of the wild ones roaming in the hills—"

"Oh, Bragan," Gutryd said, "let her finish! She said something about magic!"

"It's as though on that odd afternoon, while I listened to the traveling woman in her rings and veils and watched her little boy play with his stones, something was fixed in my childhood by her description, that grew and changed and worked on me, worked secretly in the dark places below memory; her description of your soups here began working and working on me there, pulling me and guiding me, first away from my home, then through Kolhari, then on into the south, till I met Tratsin, and at last, in Tratsin's boat, here to—Enoch? Yes, to this old, old town." Pryn knocked the stone, watching it spin as she talked. "As if by magic I was led here . . . led here by the silent strength of that traveling woman's words—she sold pictures of the stars that she would make for you on pieces of wet clay, and for an extra iron coin, she would tell you what they had to say of you on the day of your birth—that is, if you knew it. If you didn't, she would guess at what day that must have been from the way you looked and the things you said, according to what the stars might suggest. Something worked and worked from her words to bring me here and finally to taste the soup, your soup, the soup here that she spoke of—"

"Ah!" Something in Pryn's eloquence (or perhaps in Pryn's spinning) seemed to catch Bragan up; she turned from turnips and green peppers.

With her own surprise at her recognition of Bragan's, Pryn thought: There's something very wrong with all that.

Trying hard to explain what she might have written (and what is,

in a world where many such tales have been read, easy to call 'her thoughts'), Pryn frowned. "But there's something wrong . . ."

Gutryd put her picks down and looked confused.

Bragan put down her knife and rag, looking both surprised and interested.

"All that happened—" Pryn stopped the spinning rock between thumb and forefinger; she lowered thread, spindle, and fluff to her lap—"is that a traveling woman in gray veils spoke within my hearing—spoke of something as many men and women have spoken of various things to me or near me—and years later, now, last night, something happened—among the many things that have happened to me . . . I ate your soup; which made me remember what she said, years ago—made it mean something."

"Made what the woman was saying *into* magic . . . ?" With her confused look, Gutryd suddenly struck Pryn as a woman who'd find anything to do with magic fascinating. "Or made the *soup* magic . . . ?"

"Made it into a tale," Bragan said. "Is that what you mean? Made it into a tale you could tell . . . the tale you just told?"

"That's right," Pryn said, surprised the understanding came from Bragan when she'd expected it from Gutryd. "Made it all into a story. I mean—" Here Pryn laughed and lifted her fleece till the rock rose from her lap; she set it spinning again—"sometimes I think there must be nothing to the world *except* stories and magic!" (She'd never thought anything like that before in her life!) "But I guess stories *are* more common—while magic is rare, I'm afraid. But until I questioned it, I'd just assumed it was the other way around. Which isn't to say anything *bad* of either one . . ."

"Well." Gutryd sounded disappointed. "I know something that certainly isn't a story. In two months you—" she nodded toward her cousin—"and in seven or eight months you—" she looked at Pryn—"will deliver yourselves of children. That's what's real. But perhaps it's magic, too—oh, this is all like Kurvan's talk—very clever, but I can't really understand it!"

"Oh, I don't know . . ." Bragan looked quite happy—indeed, the most familiar thing in the whole room to Pryn suddenly seemed Bragan's expression; because it was the one Pryn used to descry, among all her great-aunt's wrinkles, years ago, at the advent of an interesting stranger. "Well, let me finish this up." Bragan nodded toward Pryn. "You'd best get back to your spinning—and after you take this to Tratsin at the factory, you can come back and have something to eat. You'll eat supper with us here tonight, too, before you go . . . ? Oh, it will be fun to have you living in Enoch. Yes, it *is* like Kurvan's talk; and that's why I like Kurvan! Now the

trouble with Tratsin ..." and went on (turning all she'd said of her husband before into a tale, Pryn thought), while Gutryd carded and Pryn spun. Listening to all these familiar complaints, Pryn thought: So many things are thought but never spoken, such as this thought itself—which is exactly when the ache in the hand to hold a stylus comes. She let thread twist through her fingers, feeling the tug in her shoulder.

Gutryd's forks flew through the wool in her lap as she gazed at her work intently, just as if she saw some amazing magic in each marvelous, fluffing strand—at least, thought Pryn, that's the tale I'd tell of it.

"... *what* rock?" Pryn took the dinner bowl. "*What* bridge did you say?"

But Bragan was too preoccupied to notice Pryn's surprise. "... not along the river but up the stream," she repeated her instructions. "Like I said, you'll find him sitting under Belhams Bridge, right by Venns Rock." Both children were crying. "You take the ravine short-cut and you can't miss him," Bragan went on, joggling one baby and looking for the other. "He always waits for his food there—to be by himself a while, he says. Oh, it's just a—well, you go on now. I've got to take the girls to play with some friends—where they should have been an hour ago! Venns Rock, Belhams Bridge. I'll be home in a bit—and Gutryd should be home even sooner ..." So Pryn could only take the clay bowl with the leather cover strapped down over it out into the sunny yard and set off between the shacks. (The bowl reminded her of a mummer's drum.) And found the stream.

And started up it.

Shacks fell away, while trees and stone rose about her either side of the water to make the current into the bright flooring of a sun-splashed gorge. She walked over a slanted stone, matted with moss that became black mush in the ripples. Twisting here and untwisting there, a brown vine branched above her, beckoning her to climb the six meters to the leafy rim. She would have, too, if she'd been wandering alone in the mountains and not carrying dinner to a working man.

Perhaps she might put Tratsin's bowl down for a few minutes and explore that cut there where the gray rock turned out and, losing all vegetation, went russet. Nearing, she saw, it was as if some great block, the height of the ravine wall and meters wide, had been quarried away, revealing the earth's red marble muscle. As Pryn walked before the sheared face that sloped so steeply, she saw several grooves running the height of it, straight enough and

clean enough that they must have been tool made. She looked behind for some obvious stone by the stream to set the bowl near . . .

Then she saw the wood chips.

One, the length of her little finger, vaulted in the rush between two foam-lapped granite chunks, flushed against a third, then spun downstream—as another, and seconds later another, followed.

Pryn frowned; and decided, really, the red marble face was too steep to climb. She'd better go on with her journey. *Belham's* bridge . . . ? Venn's . . . ?

White wooden shavings, about three or five breaths apart, floated past her over shallow water floored with red and gray pebbles. She climbed across a log and went round a high slab, gray once more and grooveless.

The stream changed direction, and the ravine wedged out from four or five meters wide to six or seven times that. Rough with last night's rain, the water rushed back and forth across the ravine's floor, winding through the spread of round, gray stones.

Ahead, where the canyon grew wider still, she could see a man sitting on a large rock—yes, it was Tratsin.

Holding the leather-covered bowl in both hands, she walked on the sand between the stones. Pryn hesitated at a wide pool, then waded through. Water chilled her to the ankles.

She could see that Tratsin held a piece of wood in his lap. With a large knife—some bench-carving tool?—he was shaving at it. Near her, another chip floated past, turning over the water.

Above Tratsin, the stone bridge ran from one ravine lip to the other. Under it, behind him, irregular to the left, with a more or less flat surface to the right, a great rock rose like a squat mountain to form the bridge's central support. The shallow waters, here and there interrupted by boulders like the one Tratsin sat on, ran around both sides of the immense support.

The whole seemed like a more modest Bridge of Lost Desire, though at the stone rail it seemed to carry no traffic at all—at least for the present. Still, it was big enough to erase her picture of the little city and resketch a more complex one. To sport such a public work, Enoch had to be more than the few dozen shacks clustered near the river—which, as they were all she'd seen till now, were all she'd assumed there were.

As Pryn walked forward, Tratsin raised his knife and waved. "You been to the huts yet, where you'll be staying tonight?"

"What?" Pryn stepped over crumbly ground, where a plant the size and color of rockweed brushed her wet ankle. "Oh . . . no." Only its leaves were not the same star shape as rockweed leaves

at all, but thin and in tiny bunches. "Not yet." She looked at Tratsin, who was smiling. Apparently her coming relocation had been discussed at least as far back as the morning, before she'd awakened, if not whispered about on the previous night after she'd gone to sleep. "Bragan said you or Kurvan would take me there this evening." She came up to the ribbon of water that lay between his boulder and the sand.

"Oh." The blade caught under white wood. A chip curled on the metal, fell to hit his toe, then dropped to the water and drifted away. "It's not that far from here. Well, I guess when I get home . . ." He laid the wood beside him on the stone and put the darkly mottled blade with its leather-bound handle next to it. "Come. Show me what Bragan's sent me for dinner. You sit here." He patted the stone on the other side of the blade, then leaned his sunken chest forward to rest one forearm on his hairy knee. He reached out with his other hand.

As Pryn held out the bowl, she looked up. The dark stone bridge cut away clouds and blue sky—and the bowl was taken from her hand.

She looked back at Tratsin, who was pulling aside the cover strap. "Wonder what I got."

Pryn waded over the pebbly stream bed and climbed to the boulder beside him. The great knife—not very different from the broad sword the Liberator had swung in the cellars of the Spur, but turned into a tool by the wood beside it—lay between them.

Heels against the stone, Pryn put her head back as far as she could, straining her neck to feel her hair crushed against her back, till she could see the bridge, with clouds drifting a-slant it.

"You want some of this?"

Still looking up, Pryn shook her head. "That's Belham's bridge?"

"That's what we call it."

She dropped her head—and rubbed her neck; it had developed a sudden crick, which, in moments, drifted away like a wood chip. On the water, she saw the bottom of her own feet and beside them the bottom of Tratsin's; way below was the bridge's dark and dripping underside; and below that wavered the blue sky with its drifting clouds. "Is this Venn's rock we're sitting on?"

"No . . ."

Pryn looked up.

Tratsin was eating a handful of something oily with onions in it that dribbled down his wrist. "Back there, behind us." He gestured with his chin over his shoulder, and went back to chewing. "That's Venns Rock. The one holding up the bridge."

Pryn twisted around, getting up on one knee to see. In the

215

bridge's shadow, it was gray and irregular to one side; then, just behind her, it slanted back, revealing a red marble face. Running up it were those regular grooves. "Did this rock come from back down the stream?"

"It's supposed to."

Pryn looked up the six-meter block, almost as wide and nearly as thick. "She must have had some job getting it from there to here!"

" 'She' who?" Tratsin asked.

"Venn," Pryn said, surprised. She turned back.

Tratsin sucked first one finger, then another, watching her and looking almost as puzzled as she remembered him from the boat when all she'd been able to do was cry.

"I mean, if it's Venn's Rock, I just thought Venn must have had *some*thing to do with putting it here. Just like it's Belham's Bridge—" She looked up again. "Didn't Belham build it?"

Tratsin looked at her oddly, and ran another finger in his mouth. "I don't know. Was there someone named Belham? And Venn?"

"But you're *from* Enoch," Pryn said, "aren't you?"

"I was born here," Tratsin said. "So was my father. His father, too."

"Don't you know *anything* about this bridge? I mean who built it and all? Who got the rock up from downstream?"

"I know what we call them," Tratsin said. "But I never thought they might be people—real people, I mean. And a woman, too, you said?" He glanced back at the great stone support. "No, I don't think any woman put that there." He went digging in the dish on his lap with greasy fingers. "It doesn't seem too likely, no ..."

"What *do* you know about the bridge, then ...?" Pryn looked around and up. Somewhere, out of her aunt's stories overlaid with Madame Keyne's revelations, a tale had formed, almost without her knowing it, of some bygone Enoch residents who had called in the great Belham to construct a bridge across their ravine; and, after making his plans and drawings, the barbarian engineer and inventor had at last declared it would be impossible unless there was some support in the middle. But how to get one ...? Then the brilliant young woman from the islands had said, shyly, "Wait. Here ..." Somehow, through astonishingly ingenious contrivance, the rock had been hewn loose and moved. And a grateful but frustrated Belham had gone on to build his bridge ...

"I know lots of things about it," Tratsin said. "Just not who built it. How come you think you do?"

"Um ..." Pryn felt embarassed. Whatever hearsay knowledge she had, she felt terribly uneasy about squandering it here. "Well, I

... I suppose I don't really *know,* either. What do you know about it? You tell me."

Tratsin looked back at his bowl, empty now, and licked oil from his forearm. "I know when I was a boy they called in the soldiers, and they came marching across the bridge up there, to flush out the quarry workers who'd holed up in the hills—and they killed the leaders and carried their bodies, roped to long poles, back down across it, and we hung out watching from the bushes. Everybody thought they were going to put collars back on the rest of us like there used to be in my father's father's time. They hanged Kurvan's uncle and three of the others on ropes from the wall, so that their corpses dangled right down over where we're sitting. After a couple of days, you couldn't come down here to play any more, because it stunk too bad. And once—" he glanced up, then looked at Pryn— "about six years ago, when the women came over the bridge who worked in the—"

A breeze moved in Tratsin's thinning hair as he looked down again over the bowl in his lap. Trying to see his expression, which had changed again, Pryn remembered the Ini's account of her escape from the western slavers.

Then Pryn happened to glance at the water.

Someone was leaning over the rail above them. Broad head, narrow shoulders, the leather bib of a work apron—she recognized the dwarf with whom Tratsin had gone off that morning to work. Tratsin was watching him in the water, too. In the rippling surface the little foreman grinned at them, waiting to see how long it would take them to notice they were observed.

In the silence, Pryn grew uncomfortable, wondering if she ought to look up or not; or whether she ought to go on talking; or—

"Hey, Tratsin ...!" Finally the dwarf reached out his hand and waved. "Is that the mountain girl you said was going to move into the huts across the road from the shop?"

Tratsin looked up now—with an affable enough expression. "Hey, Froc! Yes, this is Pryn. Bragan sent her down here with my food."

Pryn squinted up at the rail.

Grinning, the dwarf bobbed his oversized, bald, and bearded head. "Pleased to meet you, there. Come on, Tratsin. Let's get on back to work, now? Marg doesn't pay you to sit in the shade and flirt with pretty pregnant strangers!" He waved again and was gone.

Pryn looked back down, with heat in her cheeks and knees, wondering if every one in Enoch knew about her and her baby.

On the other side of the blade, Tratsin was running his thumb along the bowl's edge for a last bit of food.

"You were talking about things ..." Pryn tried to ignore the

discomfort the dwarf's farewell had called up—"things that happened up on the bridge . . . ?"

Tratsin sucked his thumb. "Nobody wants to remember things like that," he said, shortly. "Except the soldiers, maybe. The soldiers won, after all." He looked at her with a rueful smile that may or may not have held sympathy for her discomfort. "But for the rest of us, such things are best forgotten." He put the bowl on the leather cover he'd dropped on the boulder. "You can't work your best with memories like that plaguing you. Why go over them? I wouldn't tell such stories to my own girls—nor to a son, either, if I had one. Why should I tell such things to you, eh?"

"Oh, but I *want* to know about the—"

"Now in the quarries—" Tratsin looked off toward the ravine wall, where Pryn saw dirt steps, shored with logs, leading to the rim— "from time to time the men will grumble about what went on in Enoch three or ten or thirty years ago—more often just make a joke of it. I don't like it when they joke. That's to mix the worst part of forgetting and remembering both. I come down here at lunch so I don't have to listen to such grumblings—or jokes—from the other men. They make a lot of them in these times, what with so many people going north to the city. But I just want to do my work, you see, and enjoy it as much as I can. Now Kurvan—" Tratsin chuckled—"*he* says what's wrong with Enoch is that we forget too much. He says it's a town with no memory at all, and that's where all our problems come from." Tratsin dropped his head to the side. "Though perhaps we have the names, we certainly don't remember anything *about* who built the bridge here!" Pryn started to say something about memory and writing. But in the same way she knew the alleys and hedges and the people in her great-aunt's neighborhood in Ellamon, she knew Tratsin and Bragan and Kurvan and Gutryd were illiterate; and she knew from her aunt's example how much hostility one could create by claiming to know too much among them.

"You know, I used to work in the quarries," Tratsin said, suddenly. "On the scaffolding crew. But you wouldn't know anything about that—"

"They put up the scaffolds and wooden walkways for high work . . ." Pryn quoted Kurvan from the morning.

Tratsin nodded, a little surprised. "Well, yes. They do. Anyway, in the last year I was working there, they were getting ready to send three crews up on the new cliffs for basalt blocks. We were working down from a ledge that hung over a drop that was, oh, a good three times the height of that wall there." He pointed to the ravine's lip where the bridge joined it. "The boys were roping wood together

218

and pegging it into the stone face. The digging crews weren't up yet. Just us scaffolders. There was a big overhang over the ledge where I'd gone up to take some short-planks so we would have them at work level later on. I was standing on a bushy little outcrop with all day down behind me, when I heard a crack and a rumble. Someone shouted, 'Tratsin!' I looked up, and saw big brown rocks tearing away from the mother face and sliding toward me—"

"What did you *do*?" Pryn asked.

"There wasn't anywhere to go left or right. And those falling rocks were pretty large ..." Tratsin paused meaningfully. (Pryn took a breath.) "So I jumped—right off the ledge! I remember being in the air and the sun in my right eye as I fell, and wondering what it was going to be like to be dead in a second, and whether I'd feel my bones snap on the rocks below. And then I hit—I felt it all right! But somehow I hit rolling; and balled up real tight. I swear I bounced down that slope! I heard a lot of thumps, but I don't know if they were me hitting earth or the rocks hitting around me. The next thing I knew I was lying against some tree with my back stinging like I'd been attacked by hornets; and my left thigh, too—I'd scraped both of them all up on small stones and twigs. The guys were running up. Everyone was trying to help me stand, and pointing up the cliff to the ledge I'd jumped from—it was very high, and the rocks piled all over it now looked very heavy. I didn't break one bone! Other than the scrapes, somehow I was all right!" Tratsin chuckled. "For the rest of the day, everybody kept on talking about 'Tratsin's leap,' and how it was certainly some kind of magic that skinny Tratsin was still alive after falling so far—what I'd looked like in the air, and which one of them had seen it happen, and which one hadn't, and which ones had seen scaffolders fall to their deaths before over less than half that distance. That kind of thing." Tratsin looked at his greasy fingers. "For three days they talked about it, pointing up at the ledge when anyone passed it. It was 'Tratsin's leap,' 'Tratsin's leap,' 'Tratsin's leap ...' For almost three days. I thought they were going to name the ledge 'Tratsin's leap,' only then they cleared the rocks off it—" Tratsin pushed himself forward to splash down into the shallow water before the boulder. He plunged his hands in the stream and brought them up covered with mud and sand. With one hand, then the other, he scoured his fingers and forearms. "It was just the upper ledge of the basalt face again. 'Wasn't that the one that skinny Tratsin almost got hurt on?' Then nobody even bothered to mention *that* any more." He rinsed his hands again. Mud made its own clouds around his wrists. Mud floated out about his ankles; and Pryn could no longer see the reflected bridge and sky. "For a while, though, I

thought they were going to name it after me—the ledge, I mean. It would have been nice if they had—for the girls, when they got older. Of course they weren't born when it happened. But if they knew that their father had jumped from a ledge—and lived. I don't even have a scar left from it—but then, skinny as I am, I've always healed well. Still, I thought it would've been a nice thing." Tratsin shook water from his hands. Bubbles floated back between his ankles where the hair was wet flat against his calves. "But then I guess whoever put up the bridge here might have liked to be remembered too. By more than their names, I mean." He squinted up at the stone structure. "I mean if those really *are* names ... Well, I want to get back to work." He paused a moment, then shook his head. "But it doesn't matter. It was years ago. Why should anybody call it 'Tratsin's leap' today?" Then he grinned. "But they *almost* did! Hey, take the bowl there back to Bragan for me ...?"

"Oh, I will!"

"That's a good girl." He reached up, took the knife, the wood, and started away.

Watching him, Pryn thought of her great-aunt, who might like to be remembered as something other than an old, odd woman claiming credit for impossible things. Pryn picked up the bowl, put the leather cover inside it, and slid down until her feet splashed into the hazed water.

Starting up the stairs to the ravine rim, Tratsin waved.

Pryn waved back and walked to the water's edge. She squatted where the current had cut a finger-deep shelf from the bank, took the leather out, and put it beside her. Digging up a handful of sand, she swished out the bowl with it, swirling the bowl itself in the water. So many things to remember, she thought. So many things to forget. Certainly Enoch, like Ellamon, would have its fables; and, staying here, she would eventually learn them. But fables were the tales a town or a city could bear to recall. Fables taught simple and clear lessons everyone could agree on. Fables were tales that could be put to immediate use, either to instruct or entertain a child, to remind adults of past glories or recurring dangers. But there were always the incidents on the bridge that no one could bear to recall, or Tratsin's leap that, for whatever reason, people just ... well, forgot, or women's talk before the fire, while they carded, cooked, or spun, that no one thought important enough to remember—

Pryn stopped and kneeled back on the sand. She'd been struck with a vision, clear as sunlight on the water before her. Somewhere in Enoch, she knew, watching over some bunch of digging, screeching, rolling children, Bragan would be saying to another Enoch

mother: "... this northern girl my Tratsin found up river, who's staying with us for a day or so—she's going to have a baby, poor thing. But do you know what she said about my soup—I mean the double soup we make here? She said that as far away as fabled Ellamon, it's all that anybody can talk of! Travelers speak of it in the markets! She said she's actually *heard* them talking—oh, they must be raving in markets all over Nevèrÿon. Imagine...!" Pryn rinsed the bowl again. Odd, she thought, how words must leave and return, bearing some trace of their journey, for that sort of memory to fix itself. Well, then, she'd done her part to see that something—at least a soup—was remembered.

Certainly it was good soup!

She put the bowl down and began to rinse the leather.

Supper that evening verged on the inedible. Bragan made a paste of yesterday's fish (a dubious notion to Pryn from the beginning; she'd caught trout at home in her strolls along mountain brooks) with various vegetables and breads and oils. Bragan sat in the corner by the fire with her bowl on her lap. Tratsin sat on the bench along the wall, eating his share with his fingers. He'd brought the carving knife home to work on a bench leg; it leaned against the wall. Gutryd and Kurvan sat on the floor, and Pryn sat on the pallet, eating. The babies took the odd finger full of fishy mush, now from Kurvan, now from their mother. Pear juice bubbled through cracks in the crust of the cobbler cooking at the fire's edge; now and again Bragan would reach over and turn another side of the bowl to the heat. It smelled quite wonderful. When it was served, though, and Pryn tasted it, she was thrown sharply back to the barbarian eating establishment where she'd worked that night in Kolhari. The spice that had ruined the barbarians' vegetable stew was all through the fruit. Pryn frowned, said nothing, and tried to eat it anyway.

"Is Bragan's cobbler good as her soup?" Kurvan wanted to know, handing Pryn up a refilled mug that Tratsin, by the beer keg, had just handed him. "Maybe her soup will get the same kind of reputation as the fine beers brewed in the south, 'ey?"

Pryn smiled; and drank beer; and nodded; and ate the unpleasant food. The beer, at any rate, she'd begun to enjoy; it made her feel strange and relaxed. There was apparently some joke in the family about Gutryd's drinking enough to get herself sick at last summer's Labor Festival. The first three times Kurvan or Bragan made laughing reference to it, Gutryd made jokes in return. But the next time Kurvan spoke of it, Gutryd's good humor broke. "I don't want some lazy, out of work indigent like *you* saying things like that

about *me*! It was years ago, now. Can't you forget *any*thing? Stop it, I say!" She turned sharply. "Oh, Tratsin, *tell* him to stop!"

"You don't have to tease her like that..." Tratsin said seriously to his unserious and grinning friend. Perhaps it was the tone, but the infant, on a pile of cloth in the corner, woke up at that moment long enough to give one cry in the firelight of the over-warm cabin, sigh, and go back to sleep, while the toddler, with mushy hands and dirty face, sat back on her heels in the middle of the floor and giggled. But Bragan pushed to her feet. "Now you've got to take Pryn over there soon," she said, looking about, "before there's no light left at all. Here, I'll put up some food for you, so you'll have something for the morning."

"Oh," Pryn said. "Yes. I guess we'd better go." She stood up, torn between the discomfort of rejection and the relief at leaving the hot, fishy shack. "I'm sure I'll be all right ..." she added, though no one had suggested otherwise.

Kurvan stood ponderously and picked up Tratsin's carving knife from against the wall. "Yes, we'd best be off." He swung it back and forth. "You never know what ogres, ghouls, and night monsters we might have to fight, making our way through the ancient and troubled streets of Enoch—"

"Not in the *house,* Kurvan!" A bowl in each hand, Bragan looked back and forth between them. With a glance at Pryn, she chose; "Because you won't have to bring this one back so soon," and began to fill it from the pot. "You've been awfully helpful while you were here. That was very nice of you. I mean in your condition—for the first month or so, sometimes, you just don't feel up to doing a thing!"

Five minutes later, after goodbyes and gratitude, Pryn pushed out the hide hanging where Tratsin and Kurvan had already gone.

Kurvan swung the blade and lunged over the grass, heavy and naked in the evening.

Tratsin said soberly: "That's not what it's for, Kurvan."

Kurvan walked back up the slope, testing the blade with his thumb. "So little happens around here, I bet you wish it *was* a sword, and you could go off with it after brigands and slavers and horrid beasts!"

Tratsin took it. "I need it to work. It's not for games. Come on." He started down the slope toward the road.

Kurvan gave Pryn a great grin. "No sense of play at all, I tell you!" He took the food bowl from her and, holding it against his hip, followed Tratsin down. "Must all the good people in the world be like that?"

Under twilight, they walked the same road Tratsin had gone off

to work on that morning. Tratsin and Kurvan fell into conversation about people Pryn didn't know, with problems whose backgrounds she didn't understand. Sometimes strolling beside one of them or the other, sometimes lingering a step or two behind, she realized that, leading neither to the river nor along the ravine, this road was revising her picture of Enoch again simply by passing through the little city itself. Now here was a row of five shacks almost touching. There were two stone houses with three horses tethered under a thatched awning between. Children crossed ahead, two together giggling, one alone dawdling. A man pushed back his door hanging to shout, "Stop your play and come in now, I say!"

Off among other huts a child answered, "I *said* I'll be there in a minute!" while a cart filled with gravel rolled up the street. The drivers made some joke with Kurvan that set all four men laughing. A dog trotted behind the clattering wheels.

They passed a partially paved area, with a tarpaulin over one section and a well in its corner, which, if Enoch were anything like Ellamon at all, would be the market area on specified days of the week. A few buildings here even had walls around them. Through more houses Pryn could see another length of wall that may once have enclosed a section of the town itself, or at least acted as a partial fortification.

Pale lightning flickered over the evening. Pryn looked up, remembering rain. When she looked down again, she said, surprised, "We're on the bridge . . . !"

"Belhams Bridge it is," said Kurvan, "propped on old Venns Rock."

Pryn looked over the stone rail at the ravine and its wide, shallow stream. No, it wasn't a large town at all. "Kurvan, do *you* know anything about who built the bridge here?"

"You mean Belham and Venn?" Kurvan said.

"Now you see," said Tratsin, "I've lived here all my life and I wasn't even sure they were people's names."

"I'm not *sure* they're names either," Kurvan said. "At least not of the bridge builders. I used to think they must be a pair of ancient quarry owners who pooled their money to have it put up—they'd be the only people from here rich enough to do it."

"Names," Tratsin said. "Really, that they were names never even occurred to me."

"They certainly don't sound like names from around Enoch. But then," Kurvan went on, "they may just be old barbarian words for animals or stone. 'Belham'—now that sounds like it could be a barbarian word. But up here, nobody has really spoken the old language since before the coming of the Child Empress, whose reign—" Kruvan ducked his head and touched the back of his fist to his forehead—"is just and generous. So we'll probably never know."

As they reached the bridge's center, Pryn stepped to the low wall and leaned over, trying to see the great support beneath. (Perhaps Belham had built the entire bridge first; then, after a few years, when it became apparent that it would soon crack from its own weight, clever Venn came and found a way to drag the supporting monolith from downstream to prop the bridge up ...) What she saw was her own dark head against the darkening sky, reflected on the shallows flowing around the boulders.

"That's where I work," Tratsin said.

Pryn stood up and looked.

He was pointing with his carving knife to a low, barracks-like building off beyond the bridge.

"That's where Tratsin works," Kurvan repeated, "and that—" he pointed to the other side of the road—"is where you'll be living."

"Where?" Pryn asked. With the bridge, certainly Enoch proper had ended. "Where do you mean?" Beyond were trees, a cross-roads, the workshop; and it was at the trees that Kurvan was pointing.

As they walked on over the bridge's leaf-scattered flags, Pryn was sure that to live on this side of Enoch, even if the quarry-men passed here in the morning, even if farms were scattered about, or a workshop sat here, or the odd abandoned huts—this was no longer to be within the town, this was no longer to be a part of the village, this was no longer to share in whatever characterized even the tiniest city.

Rejection had been a personal thing that Pryn had dealt with from a sense of practical strategy. But the feeling now as they came off the bridge was a sense of cutting loose, of disorienting freedom. She rubbed her stomach to knead away the discomfort that, having faded almost to nothing sometime before, returned. Yes, it was anger. But it was a kind of disfocused anger about which she could do nothing. That made her want to cry.

As they passed beyond the workshop, Pryn peered among the dark trees, still trying to see what Kurvan indicated.

Tratsin seemed to be having the same trouble, himself, finding these alleged 'abandoned huts,' because he laughed now. "They were here a couple of days ago, I know! Don't tell me someone came along and tore them down ..."

"Now up there's the north-south road," Kurvan said, as if orienting himself. "That direction would take you back north as far at least as Kolhari. Down there would take you into the barbarian lands. Along there, let me see ... that's the long way around to the stone works. But usually we go the short route back along the stream."

Pryn suddenly wondered if a joke were being played—if, really, she weren't sumarily being dismissed from the town ...

"*There* they are!" Tratsin said. He strode over the road, hacked his knife high into a thin tree at the road's edge, and, leaving it stuck there, stepped in among the bushes. "See them, in there? I just didn't remember them being so far in off the edge."

"An indication," declared Kurvan, "of how far the road's edge has shifted since you and I used to come here as boys!"

Pryn followed Tratsin in among the saplings. Transferring the food bowl to his other hip, Kurvan followed Pryn.

Saplings were widely spaced about the brush. Crickets chittered loudly. Without apparent source for the lightning, the sky flickered again.

"Oh, yes," Kurvan said behind her, "in two or three days, what with going for water in the ravine and walking in to market, you'll wear a natural path here. There was one about a year ago, I remember. But I guess it grew up."

Tratsin stopped in front of something that looked like a haystack, or perhaps a pile of leaves. It was about Pryn's height; and there was a dark hole low down in it. A few meters away was another such structure, and a few meters after that was half a one—part had collapsed in on itself. A little way from the one before which Tratsin stood were fireplace stones. Summer grasses spired between them.

Pryn looked at the dark hole, her head a little to the side.

She looked for a long time.

Once Kurvan stepped beside her, squatted, and put the food bowl down in the grass by the door. He looked up at Pryn, his smile giving way to curiosity. Then he stood and stepped back.

Tratsin said: "Sometimes kids come out here to play. But once they know someone's living here, they'll keep off mostly—except the one or two who come to stand across the road and gawk."

"Gawking doesn't hurt anyone," Kurvan added. "That'll only be at first. And there won't be much of it."

"Well." Pryn took a breath. "At least ... it will keep the rain off." She stooped and, not wanting to, squat-walked through the opening. Inside, the darkness around and above her was prickled with spots of evening light. (So much for the rain, Pryn thought.) She turned awkwardly, scraping her arm on twigs—a branch had fallen loose from the slanted wall. She grasped it and thrust it outside, with rattling leaves.

She heard Kurvan laugh.

 225

The ground under her was soft and, save the odd leaf, clean. She'd been expecting mustiness or mushiness; but the enclosure was dry and, astonishingly, odorless. And that, she went on thinking, is what makes it so unlike a home! Could one live here, have a baby here at the edge of the town? Running the words through her mind, she felt her stomach knot and her emotion swell, blurring the spots of light about her on the riddled walls. To keep back tears, she scrambled out the door again and stood. "You know, I could put some mud over it. And I have a way to mix the mud with oil, so that if I take a hollow reed and blow lots of bubbles into it—"

Kurvan stood a few steps away.

"Where's Tratsin?" Pryn asked.

"Oh," Kurvan said. "He's gone ..." He rubbed the side of his beard with the ham of his thumb. "To get some things for you. He'll be back. Later." He took a step toward her and smiled. "Well, I suppose it isn't much. But it's something." (Tratsin must have left running, Pryn thought. She couldn't have been inside half a minute!) "I know it's not so wonderful, but once you clear the grass from around it—here, I'll help!" He grasped some brush, tugged it loose, hurled it away, tugged loose some more.

"No," Pryn said. "No, you don't have to ..."

Kurvan stopped and looked at her, a little strangely.

Pryn looked back at the hut, which was too small to stand up in or stretch out in. To insulate it by her great aunt's method ...? Would it be worth it? She blinked and thought: No, I'm *not* going to cry. No, not this time.

"Um ..." Kurvan said, a little closer to her. "It won't be so bad. The quarry workers go by here every morning and evening. There was a woman who worked here for three years, once. She had a couple of children, too. And she was a lot older than you. She didn't do badly. There're always one or three men of an evening, with no wives of their own and an extra iron coin or so. You be nice to them, smile, let them stay for an hour—you'll get enough money to eat, maybe. Maybe even more. I thought—" Standing naked in the grass, heavy Kurvan looked at the ground and brushed his hands together, freeing them of the dirt from pulling up the brush— "Well, you might start by letting me stay for a while. And being nice to me. For just a bit." He looked up again, questioning. "Of course I don't have a coin for you. That's because I'm not working. So you might not want to. With me. I'd understand." He reached up and rubbed his beard again, hard. "But you're going to have a baby anyway ... so it wouldn't matter. Really, I could help you out around here a little, clearing things out, straightening things up ..."

Pryn stood before the hut, frowning. The realization of what she

was being asked to do—what she had been placed here to do—struck the tears from behind her eyes. "No," she said. "No. I don't want to—"

"Oh, I understand," Kurvan said, quickly. "My not having a job and all." He sounded almost relieved, as though some obligation had been lifted. Then he pursed his lips. "Are you sure? I mean, maybe you just want me to stay and argue a little. Some girls, I know, are like that—"

"No!" Pryn repeated, loudly. "I really don't want to. At all!" Whatever had struck away the tears had also struck away that partial sentence with which she'd begun to protest that it had nothing to do with his working, that she even liked him, that he misunderstood completely. But Kurvan had turned and started away.

Then he stopped. "Oh ..." he said, looking back. "Tratsin will be coming soon. With the things for you. He was going to stay away for about an hour. To give me time. Then he was going to come. Bragan, you know, isn't very interested in much right through here, so ... he's probably going to ask you too." He turned, stepped up on the road, and started back for the bridge.

When, Pryn wondered, had all these whispering plans been made about where she would go and what she would do when she got there, and who would come to her, and who would wait for whom to finish ...

The same times and places, of course, she answered her own query, that they were made in any other little town!

It wasn't anger. It wasn't embarrassment. It wasn't even hurt. Rather it was a tingling coldness that settled, nevertheless, in those places where embarrassment's fires could prickle: her cheeks, her knees, the small of her back. She stood before the hut, feeling terribly cold, till Kurvan had been out of sight for minutes. Then she walked to the road and took a few steps along it.

She could see the bridge over the ravine, the workshop this side of it, the houses beyond it. After a few moments, she said aloud: "But I don't *want* this town ...!" Certainly she did not want to be this town's roadside whore with a dirty baby squalling in the yard. She ran both hands slowly down the stomach of the shift Madame Keyne had given her. First the Fox's wandering hands, then the pimp on the Bridge of Lost Desire, the coins Madame Keyne had given her for a kiss—the two soldiers at the inn in the night ...! This is not where I want to be, she thought. Why has everything conspired to put me here?

Yes, this may be the town she had come from. It might even be the town where she would finally live most of her life. But it wasn't the town she wanted to be in now. Not the town to have a child in. And certainly not here, in these roadside hovels. The only reason, she realized, that she'd even considered staying was that momentary look of interest from Bragan, and she knew enough of Ellamon to know that Tratsin and Bragan (whether Tratsin stayed here another hour on his return or not) would be among the first friends she would lose if she stayed. Tratsin and Bragan? They were good people, kind people, generous people, both of them. But she was here, on this road, at this hut now, because she was a foreign girl about to have a baby, and they could think of no other place for her.

The thought came like sentences written on some parchment scrap thrust before her eyes to read:

My father once walked into a town like this.

My father once walked out of one, too.

Certainly he had walked into Ellamon, more or less a stranger. He had met her mother and left her with a child—Pryn. He had left, in his case, for the army and death by fever. But he *had* left, left just such a town as this. Just walked out of it. That was the thing. In her own way, hadn't Pryn followed him into Enoch? Well, then, she could just as well follow him out again. Of course, she was not leaving a child behind but taking one with her. Very well, she would have her baby where she might. But it would not be in this narrow-minded provincial hold, where all anyone and everyone could think of was labor. Of course there was no army to snatch her conveniently off to adventure—but there was no army to get a fever in, either. What were imaginary fathers for if you couldn't use them for *some*thing. . . . Blinking at the bridge, and the roofs and trees beyond it against the darkening sky, she had a memory of Tratsin that afternoon in the ravine below it: soldiers had once crossed it . . . ? Perhaps her real father, in the real Imperial Army, *had* walked into this town! And when he'd died his real death, she wondered, what real and unbearable memories had died with him? Somehow simply asking the question, simply realizing that she didn't have an imaginary father, but rather that she'd had a real one, real as Bragan or Tratsin or herself, leached all her resolve. Wherever he might have died, her own father—the real man she'd never known—had come from a town much like this, like her mother, like herself. Pryn put her arms across her stomach and turned—crying now—on the road. She was very tired. For all the warm, stormy night, she was cold.

If I stay, she thought, there must be work I can do other than this—carry water or slops or collect stone chips at the quarry; perhaps find a job with some richer town family in their garden or

house; perhaps I might take care of other children, teach them my lettering skills. (Her aunt had begun with her at age seven.) But these people who had placed her here would not give her their children, she knew, if only as punishment for having her own so far from home. The master and mistress of any rich home she might work in would cast their glances in this direction as surely as poor folk like Tratsin and Bragan. That was the way in such towns. And the path to the quarry would lead her by these huts daily. It was not even that they (or Pryn) had any inflated notion of the perniciousness of such work itself. Rather, she thought, it's that I've learned the forces that limit me to it all too well at Ellamon! They'd been cut into her the way so many small droplets running along the same path cut a ravine to the sea, so that once within it—as if caught in a wound slashed across one's own body—there was no leaving.

That was what terrified.

That was what paralyzed.

Shivering a little, tired, she walked back toward the road's edge.

Tratsin would be coming soon. With things for her. Tratsin was a good man, a kind man. Tratsin had certainly borne his wounds from Enoch's Margs and Malots, if not the soldiers on the bridge, and he seemed as resigned to them as a man might be who'd never considered the possibility of healing. Maybe she could tell him, and maybe he would understand, how lost she felt in this most familiar of cities. And maybe if he stayed a while it *would* be better than being so alone ...

Once more the sky flickered, this time rumbling.

And Pryn stopped.

The shadow flickered on the printed dust, among shadows of sparse leaves and twigs, flickering with the flickering sky.

It was the shadow of a sword on the ground, there the point, there the hilt. It was as if the weapon itself hung in the air. But the shadow—that was what had made her stop. Because there were *two* blades running off the hilt, each the same length, and set parallel.

Pryn looked up—at Tratsin's knife stuck in the thin tree above her. Not a weapon at all, it was only a carving tool. Still, the light falling through the leaves above it (most obligingly, the lightning flared again—yes, there it was on the road) was refracted through the spare leaves above so that, hitting it at the proper angle, it seemed to come from two sources, doubling the shadow that reached the ground.

A drop of rain hit Pryn's shoulder. She looked about. Perhaps three meters away, another drop cratered the road dust.

What she felt was a kind of chill. The food? No, it was inedible! Tratsin's tool? No, he needed it, and, besides, she still had the Ini's blade tucked at her waist. Once again it seemed that, of all the people she had met on her travels, Madame Keyne had again proved right: No, there were no masked women warriors waiting to save her with double swords. The blade was a man's, a man who would be returning for it soon. Still, its shadow was real enough for the use she needed to put it to. "I can't *stay* here ...!" she whispered. Then, very simply and not at all like a young woman who had just made an extraordinarily difficult decision, Pryn turned toward the crossroads and began to walk with long, quickening steps.

Were this an entirely different story, it would no doubt go on to tell how, later that night, when the sky blackened and the rain began to pour, Pryn found a stony niche off the road and lay in it with her back against rock and dry leaves high around her shoulders and knees, torrents thundering across the opening a foot before her face, the curtain of drops now and again gone glittering blue with lightning.

Presumably the tale would also tell how, the next morning, when she went off a little ways in the woods to urinate, the wet leaves with which she wiped herself were touched with blood.

She stood looking at them for a long while.

Then she cried again, this time with a kind of hiccuping relief.

She didn't cry much after that. Later that day, when the south road took her through another town, she saw the familiar canvas covered ox-cart, tied outside an inn. She stood, looking at it too, for a time. Then she walked on—only after a couple of minutes, she stopped, turned, and walked back. Ten minutes later, the three young people were laughing together in the inn-yard. The boys kept asking her what in the world had *happened*, and she kept laughing and saying *nothing*, really, she'd just decided to go off by herself for a few days; nothing had happened at all! The boys had gotten some money from somewhere, enough to pay for a fine dinner at the inn, where they'd stopped the night before, they told her, to escape the rain.

"Let's ask if they have the double soup—it's quite the best thing in the area, though the inns shy away from the common food. Some of it can be inedible!"

The innkeeper didn't have the soup, but made much of her for knowing about it. The boys didn't volunteer to tell Pryn where the money had come from, and once they got the cart under way Pryn decided not to inquire. Making camp that evening, they saw a few flickerings on the sky—but it looked as if, at least for a while, the summer nights were rained out. After cooking as usual with the younger, just as if she'd never been away, Pryn lay (as usual) in the arms of the elder, with his broken face beautiful beside her and his huge hands heavy on her back, thinking for rather a time.

Then, on the other side of the fire, the younger pushed up on his elbow and said in his heaviest city drawl: "Look, if you two don't hurry up and fuck, I won't *ever* get to sleep! How do you think I get *my* rocks off?"

"Shut up, you be-shitted goat's ass!" the elder shot back, sharply enough to startle Pryn, the exchange's intensity hinting of some recent argument between them that may well, she fancied, have had her as its topic.

The younger one chuckled and laid his blond head down. Soon Pryn heard his breathing across the fire take on the slower rhythms of sleep; then the lightly bullish flutter of snoring began from the youth warm against her—so Pryn slept too.

Light beyond her lids ...

She pushed from under blankets and a warm arm, into cool morning. Pryn rubbed her shoulder, pulled the chained astrolabe back around her neck from where it had worked behind her in the night and, standing, looked at the sunlight coming sideways through the trees.

On the ground, her blanket companion turned on his back.

Beyond dead ashes, the blond head was completely hidden, but a foot stuck out the bottom.

Pryn rubbed at her waist where lying on her knife had made her side sore. At her feet, brown eyes blinked above pitted, hairy cheeks. (In firelight that face, with its deep, irregular shadows, often looked quite marvelous. Mornings, however, puffy with sleep and occasionally with beer, it reminded her of broken cheese.) Tousled hair raised an inch. "Where're you going ... ?"

She whispered: "... some water, from the brook we passed before we made camp last night ... ?" Then she went and got the clay jar from the provisions end of the cart. For the hundredth time she repressed the urge to look under the strapped-down canvas at the other end that hid whatever it was they were taking to wherever it was they were taking it. Once she *had* looked—only to find another canvas. But, as the elder one had explained, since it could get them in serious trouble if they encountered one of the Empress's inspectors, the less she knew about it, the less likely she was to have problems should something go wrong.

Pryn hooked the jug handle on two fingers and started along the

road, repeating: *nivu, nivu, nivu* ... which, among the things she'd thought last night, she'd decided did not have to mean either food *or* sex.

After walking for three minutes, she set the empty jug on a stump she passed. An hour later, she came out on a kind of road and turned along it. When a horse-drawn wagon came up, driven by an old man with two old women in the back, she asked for a ride and got one.

The old people didn't talk much, but one of the women gave Pryn some hard bread and an apple out of a tightly knotted bag that took fifteen minutes to untie and retie. About two hours along the road, the man remarked that the astrolabe around Pryn's neck looked like work of the area to which they were headed. He knew, because he'd seen designs like the one at the disk's edge on work like that before.

In brief, the story we might have written had things been only a little different would have told of bravery, wonder, fun, laughter, love, anger, fear, tears, reconciliation, a certain wisdom, a turn of chance, and a certain resignation—the stuff of many fine tales over the ages. But in those weeks Pryn did not once think of dragons.

Thus, we review them briefly.

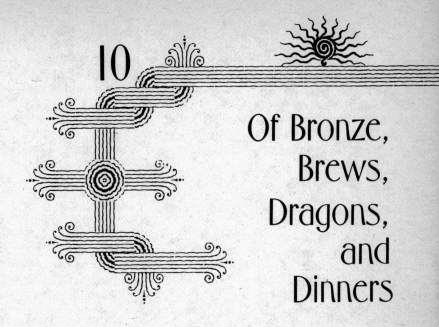

10

Of Bronze, Brews, Dragons, and Dinners

... the French people hated aristocrats about to lose their power more than it had ever hated them before, precisely because their rapid decline in power was not accompanied by any considerable decline in their fortunes.... When noblemen lost their privileges, among others the privilege to exploit and oppress, the people felt them to be parasites, without any real function in the rule of the country. In other words, neither oppression nor exploitation is ever the main cause of resentment; wealth without visible function is much more intolerable because nobody can understand why it should be tolerated.
—Hannah Arendt/*The Origins of Totalitarianism*

The dragon reared, lopsided, at the crossroads' southeast corner.

Pryn looked at it, scrambled behind it, came out, walked away from it several times in several directions—now on all four rutted paths, now off in the bushes—and came back. Eventually she decided that what was currently the junction's southeast corner had once been the center of a large, circular enclosure. Here and there the undergrowth paused at the edge of flat, uptilting stones that once, how long ago, had paved it all. Several stones were still set precisely together. And there were large cut ones off to the side that, with interruptions, defined a kind of rim. The traffic circle must once have been almost twenty meters in diameter. And on either side of the four rutted paths that joined here, hewn rocks off in the bushes suggested that all four had once been at least three times the width they were now.

It took Pryn a good forty minutes, scrambling around in the underbrush, to ascertain all this. She was looking at the dragon— half off its pedestal and leaning to the side—trying to envision it, free of vines and lichen, as the center monument in the crossing of two great highways, when she heard hoofbeats along the western route.

Automatically, she stepped back behind the pedestal's half-buried corner.

235

A minute later, the first six-horse wagon, shaking gilded fringe, swayed and thundered around the turn. Next came an open cart full of soldiers. The half-dozen closed wagons behind it were large as the mummers' portable stage and prop conveyances. The horses went at a light canter—though not faster than a person might sprint. For now Pryn saw a lithe runner leap from the draped portals of a rear wagon and overtake one, another, and a third wagon, to swing up on the running board and disappear within—while from another wagon at the front another runner dropped, to let the caravan overtake him, wagon after wagon passing, till he swung up into a rear one—delivering what messages, among what personages, Pryn could not imagine.

The caravan clattered around the turn and rumbled away north—the road down which, not an hour before, Pryn had come strolling.

Certainly, Pryn decided in the returning silence, those loud wheels were the ones the time-obliterated highways had been built for. Once, no doubt, caravan runners could sprint on smooth pavement instead of beating through the bush along the road's shoulder.

Pryn came out and sat on the pedestal's ivied corner, wondering where the caravan was coming from and what might be its business. Taking the north road like that, it could only have one destination: Kolhari—perhaps even the High Court of Eagles itself.

She pulled a leaf from a vine that clutched the rocky base beside her.

Through the settling dust, Tetya was coming down the road. He was the nephew of the local brewer, Old Rorkar, whose hotsheds and cooling caves were perhaps a mile up, where Pryn had been working now almost a week.

"Did you see them?" Pryn called.

Tetya nodded, ambling.

"Who do you think it could be?"

"Lots of people." Tetya crossed the juncture. "The Usurper of Strethi, perhaps—only his wagon colors are blue and orange, I think. And it could have been the Princess Elyne—though she hasn't made a trip to these parts during my lifetime; uncle says she used to come here quite frequently. Or it could have been Lord Krodar and his entourage, which is sometimes rumored to include the Child Empress Ynelgo herself—though we're never sure exactly when *she* comes. It's always very secretive. The only way to be sure who it is, of course, is if they stop at uncle's office and order a shipment of beer. They frequently do. But also they ride in wagons purposely painted with colors associated with great houses other than their own—to confuse the likes of you and me." Tetya dug a

forefinger in his ear. "So unless they stop to order a few barrels from uncle, there's *no* way to be certain."

Tetya was a gangling, good-natured boy. Pryn had found herself completely able to relax with his rural openness. But he also had his bothersome side. He seemed terribly young to Pryn—all elbows and ears and knees, like one of the gangling puppies lolloping about behind the brewery's equipment shed. His beard lay in little curls over his face, with great gaps of baby-smooth cheek between. Pryn had laughed at the changing voices of the twelve-, thirteen-, and fourteen-year-old boys of her own mountain town. But Tetya's voice seemed to have snagged permanently on those awkward intervals, still cracking and creaking, at an age when most boys she'd known at home had made at least the physical part of the passage to manhood. If only from the things she'd been through since her flight above the Falthas (for, after all, she had traveled and murdered and talked with the Liberator, been shown the memory of water by Madame Keyne and had made love with a smuggler), Pryn felt she had a right to consider herself a mature woman. But once, she and Tetya had actually sat down and worked it out (with Yrnik's help): Tetya was nineteen days older than Pryn.

"What do you think they were here for, Tetya?"

Tetya turned to sit on the pedestal beside her. "To visit the Earl Jue-Grutn."

Pryn frowned. Like most wanderers in that time, whenever Pryn stopped it was because she'd been suddenly overcome with the notion that if she followed the road further, it would soon give out entirely and she would have to confront the ultimate wildness, the unrectored chaos, the unthinkable space in which the very distinctions between earth, air, and water would soon break down. But here, a few hundred yards or so beyond what she had, once again, assumed to be the end of the world, was a major crossroads—or at least the traces of one. And a great caravan had just rolled by it. "Where are we, here, Tetya?" Pryn asked. "What's down all these . . . highways?"

Tetya *mmmm*ed and looked about. "Well, if you walk along there for half an hour, you'll get to the castle of Lord Aldamir— though no one has lived in it for more years than you and I've got, put together. Straight on, and you come to the ruins of the Vygernangx Monastery, after perhaps a mile, though the last feyer—that's the old barbarian word around here for priest—gave up trying to live in it half a dozen years back." Tetya pointed down the road from which the wagons had come. "And along there is where the Earl Jue-Grutn lives. He's pretty much the most powerful noble left in all the Garth." Suddenly Tetya twisted about, grasped some vines on the pedestal behind them, and yanked.

Tendrils popped and chattered; vines tore from the stone.

Surprised, Pryn stood up.

"Do you know what that says?" Tetya asked.

Pryn looked at the chiseled markings that had been hidden under the leaves. She reached out to trace one with a finger. Her other hand rose to her astrolabe.

"I thought you might know, since you're supposed to be teaching me to read—" That was one of the jobs Tetya's uncle, Rorkar, had assigned Pryn during her first days at the brewery. "Those signs look the same as the ones on that disk around your neck."

Pryn looked more closely. "They do look similar . . . sort of."

Bracing one hand against the rock, Tetya pulled away more vines.

As leaves came loose, Pryn asked, "You think they're writing . . .?"

"How should I know?" Tetya threw down the foliage and wiped his hand on his leg. "*You're* suppose to be teaching *me!*"

"If it *is* writing—" Pryn lifted the astrolabe from her chest to examine the marks about its rim—"it isn't any that I know how to read. Maybe you should get Yrnik up here, and he could tell you." The brewery foreman, Yrnik, could read and write too: he was also the brewery accountant. For some time now, apparently, he'd been asking Old Rorkar for a literate assistant, but none had shown up—until Pryn had wandered by, seeking a laboring job.

Old Rorkar himself was illiterate, and Yrnik had apparently come by much like Pryn, some years back; he had only slowly convinced the old peasant brewer of the advantages of written records. Still, the notion had seemed logical; and the logic had proved profitable. Illiterate though he was, Rorkar was still a clever man. With only one person around possessing the skill, it had not occurred to anyone to pass that skill on; but when it turned out that someone Pryn's age might, indeed, have the knowledge as completely as Yrnik himself, Rorkar had come up with the notion that Pryn tutor nephew Tetya, as well as assist Yrnik with the records. Pryn asked: "Has Yrnik *seen* these marks?"

"He ought to have. He's been around here long enough. They're on lots of old pieces of stone and old carvings and things."

"And he's never said he could read them?"

"He told me he couldn't."

"Then why did you ask me?"

"You're not Yrnik." Tetya turned to look back up the road. "Just because he couldn't didn't mean you wouldn't."

"Did Yrnik think it was writing?"

 238

"He didn't know either," Tetya said. "*I* think it is."

"It looks very old." Pryn turned and sat again on the pedestal's edge. "There're lots of old things around here. Did you know that this place here, maybe hundreds of years ago, maybe even thousands, used to be the crossroads of two great highways—oh, ten times as wide as they are now!"

"Fifty years," Tetya said.

Pryn had expected either to be praised for her discovery if he'd already known it, or challenged if he did not. She glanced at him suspiciously. *Fifty* years? But then, there was Belham's Bridge and Venn's Rock back in Enoch . . .

"Fifty. That's what uncle says."

"What was fifty years ago?" Pryn asked, mocking obtuseness. "*What* does your uncle say?"

"Fifty years ago these were wide, well-paved highroads; and the dragon stood at the crossing's center, with wagons and mules and goats and oxen passing about it on all sides."

"How old *is* your uncle?" Pryn frowned.

"Almost sixty—almost sixty-*five*, I guess!"

"And he remembers it from when he was a little boy?"

"He says so." Tetya shrugged. "I don't know if it's true or not, but that's what lots of the old people around here say." He stood up. "We'd better get back to the brewery—if you want to keep your job."

"What do you mean?" Pryn declared. "I finished all the work Yrnik set me!"

"My uncle," Tetya said, "expects you, when you're finished, to ask Yrnik for more—and not to go wandering off on your own. He says if you do it three more times, he's going to throw you out, whether you can read and write or not."

"Oh—" Pryn said, a bit more off-handedly than she felt. "Everybody *else* was almost finished, anyway. I just didn't think that—" She sighed. Pryn liked the brewery, with its sheds and barracks and caves; she liked the men and women who worked there. And even if it wasn't the end of the world—or hadn't always been—she wasn't ready to go on just yet. "Let's get back, then."

"*I* don't want you kicked out," Tetya said as they started back up the road, "because I'll *never* learn to read. Yrnik's too busy—and stubborn—to teach me."

"Then you'll have to work—and think—harder during our session tomorrow morning!"

"Maybe if I learn enough from you," Tetya said, "I can figure out what those marks mean by myself," which struck Pryn first as a silly idea, then as an interesting one.

 239

*　*　*

Across the road from the brewery was a tavern—if you could call it that. What it most resembled was the barrack-like eating hall in which Pryn had hauled grain and yams for an evening back in Kolhari. The markings on the ceiling beams, the painted ornamentations over the doors and windows, the shaggy bark on the undersides of the benches were so like the place she had worked (back then without really noticing any of them), she realized the city place must have been modeled on the country establishment—probably to make its barbarian clientele feel more at home in the impersonal city. Many of the barbarians who worked in the fields or in the brewery itself ate there, as most of them, Pryn had soon learned, were itinerant workers on their way north. Certainly, here the food was better than Pryn remembered from her night's scraps in Kolhari. And unlike the city laborers, a good third of the field workers and half the brewery staff were women. Field workers of both sexes frequently had a child or three in tow. The atmosphere was convivial. And though Rorkar owned the place, as he did the brewery itself; and though Yrnik came striding through it from time to time, with loud jokes and cuffings of the shoulders of the men and women passing with bowls and boards; and though Tetya sat at the long corner table with the noisy local boys blowing the foam from the tops of their mugs at one another and slapping at one another's heads in retaliation and generally indulging a constant hilarity that defeated female intrusion—still Pryn found the hall a place where she could get away from work, if not from the tangle of eating, sleeping, and playing in which work in that part of the land was bound up. She was even getting used to the strange spice, which she'd found out from the kitchen girl, Juni, who worked behind the counter, was called cinnamon.

Pryn had been presented with the inequities of city life so flamboyantly that she rather romanticized them in memory. The inequities of the rural life around her, of which the urban disparities seemed an intensified version, she could view with a kind of detachment. It only took her the time of one slowly sipped mug of red beer (what Old Rorkar brewed were strong berry ciders and low-proof grain fermentations that were often mixed in a variety of proportions for a variety of flavors—the range, in those days, going by the single term: beer) to see that for all the conviviality, there was only civil intercourse between itinerant barbarians and locals. Barbarian mothers cuffed any of their children who went to gawk at local workers. Local women with bowls held high edged by clusters of barbarian men who, instead of laughing and joking and even

240

assisting them to their seats as they did with their own, ignored them. The two-dozen-odd slaves Rorkar owned, who worked back and forth between the brewery and Rorkar's own home, came in to deliver messages or baskets of produce. Sometimes a worker would hail one of the iron-collared men or women to stay for a mug or a bowl. After all, they worked side by side in the same fields and orchards and fermentaries, no? But the invitation was always silently ignored, sometimes to the inviter's laughter, sometime to his anger. The slaves upset the barbarians particularly—because the slaves were all so clearly barbarian-born themselves. Once a man who Pryn thought was only teasing a slave suddenly attacked him; they had to be separated by onlookers.

"Why *don't* they let the slaves eat here?" Pryn asked Juni, who did many of the jobs in the eating hall Pryn had done back in the hall's city sister. "They could set up a table for them, or let them have a mug of beer after they made their deliveries."

"Slaves can't drink." Behind the serving counter, Juni wiped her hands on her apron. "They get whipped if they're caught at it. They'd be beaten if they ever ate here, too." She turned to pull a large crock, empty now, back across the scarred wooden counter. "Besides, the slaves have their own place. They eat on the slave benches out back."

It was raining lightly when Pryn, still with half a mug of beer in her fist, pushed out the hide-hung doorway and ambled down by the hall, over wood chips and cinders and pine needles, now looking off at the trees, now gazing down at the rim of her unglazed mug, darkening here and there with raindrops. Inside, the muffled noise of the eaters gave way to the noise of the kitchen workers. Pryn rounded the back corner.

Somehow, the fact that the benches were of stone surprised her. Twenty, thirty, maybe forty rows of them stretched toward the woods. Many were chipped or broken. Between some of the distant ones, brush had grown up.

Pryn walked over the wet gravel beside the near ones. Every half-meter along the bench tops, an iron staple had been driven in. Some had broken off. Old tar, used to retard rust, still clotted the iron half-circles.

On the bench nearest the hall, in the drizzle, hunched over clay bowls, five slaves were eating. Their collars were not chained to the staples. Still, they sobered Pryn. She knew there were no more than two dozen, all told, in the brewery. But how long ago, she wondered, had two hundred, or four hundred, or five hundred, sat, chained, eating in the same posture as the five there, rain salting their backs.

A gust; and a branch above her added to the sprinkle. Pryn walked on and sipped. A thousand years ago? she thought. A hundred? Fifty . . . ?

The man who walked from behind the far edge of the hall wore a wonderful cloak. It was a blue almost dark enough to be black, yet even at this distance, through the drizzly evening, it *was* blue, stunning and eye-absorbing. Here and there metallic embroideries glittered in it. The edges were myriad colors. The man was squat, with bushy white hair.

He carried a beer mug, a large one; it was glazed and decorated with ornate reliefs.

One slave looked up.

The cloaked man smiled and raised his hand in a greeting.

The slave nodded, grinned.

The cloaked gentleman walked out between the files of benches and stood a moment, sipped from his elegant mug (*Was* it beer he drank?), and turned. Pryn thought two things as his look swept her. (He had a short white beard that made the puffy hair clouding above his ears look almost comic.) First, his smile was inhumanly, unnaturally, preternaturally radiant. Second, though his eyes had, indeed, swept by her, Pryn was sure he had not seen her. As he completed his turn and began to walk back toward the hall, she wondered what, indeed, he *had* seen in the stony traces of such massive servitude.

He reached the benches where two of the slaves sat, pushed back his cloak, sat beside them, and began talking to the collared old woman hunched next to him; her head turned from time to time in its iron to glance at him or nod. Like all the slaves at the brewery, women or men, her hair was cut off short all over her head; and she was old enough to be somewhat balding anyway. The cloaked man sat very straight in the rain, while the slave hunched to protect her food.

Pryn chose a path that would take her through the benches and near enough to them to catch a word or two. If she paused to take a sip from her mug as she passed, he might not even suspect she were trying to overhear. Pryn turned among the benches and wandered over the shaly ground. What she heard, however, when she neared, made her pause longer than she'd intended.

"Here," the man was saying, holding out his mug before the hunched slave woman, "take a drink, Bruka. You've worked through this day long and hard—you don't have to tell me. I know the worker you are. Who deserves a drink more than you?"

"Oh, no, my lord." Bruka gave the man a worried grin. Some of

the woman's teeth were gone. "We're not supposed to, and I might get in trouble. It's not worth the beating, my lord."

The man laughed. "Now I know—and you know I know—that you folks have your own ways of getting your drink, that Old Rorkar, if he doesn't know about for sure, at least suspects. He's just decided to look the other way. Don't tell me you've *never* tasted the work of your own hand before, Bruka . . . ? How can a drink with me hurt?"

"If it's true that we get our own—and I'm not saying it is, my lord—it's only another reason why I needn't drink from that!" The old woman jammed a wooden spoon full of vegetable stew into her mouth, laughing and chewing at once. (It was the same cinnamoned stew Pryn had eaten earlier for supper inside.) "Besides, that elegant mug of yours—it's beautiful work, for sure. Why would a man like you want my dirty mouth on that!" Bruka laughed again and turned back to her bowl.

"A man like me . . . ?" mused the white-haired gentleman. "The truth is, Bruka, there are very few men like me in this world, lord *or* slave."

"That's true, my lord."

"And if I were so weak that the touch of a slave's lips to my cup would topple me from my position, what sort of a position could it have been in the first place? You've worked hard, and I know the thirst that must be upon you. As a child, didn't I spend my share of days working in these fields? I know how thirst can crawl into the bones and dry the body out from within. Drink, Bruka."

"You speak the truth again, my lord." The slave shook her head. "But my father told me, my lord, when I was a child: 'Never drink from the master's or mistress's cup. For the slave, such a cup holds only the dregs of disgrace, pain, and death.' "

"Did he, now, Bruka? And let me tell *you:* when *I* was a child—before you were born—I saw my father, with this very mug, go to the slave-barracks where your father lay, sick with the fever that killed off a third of both your family and mine, and give him a drink. Your father took a long, cooling draught from my father's hands out of this same cup I hold now. *Your* father drank from it. And *you* refuse?"

"Did he now?" The slave woman frowned. "I didn't know my father very long, my lord. He died the same week your late mother sold me and the rest of the orchard gang to Old Rorkar, here. Rorkar's a good master, my lord. But he's not your father."

"I know, Bruka. Murjus, there, was one of that same gang, weren't you, my man?" The gentleman gestured to another slave hunched on the bench ahead, who glanced back now and said:

"Yes, my lord. That's the truth, my lord."

Bruka was still looking at the mug. "My father, you say?" Suddenly she put her bowl down on the stone beside her. "I think I *will* take that drink!" She seized the green-and-red ceramic in both hands. (Two of her nails were deformed from some injury, and another was split to the quick.) Bruka put the mug to her mouth and raised it, while her adam's apple rose and fell, rose and fell in her red, wrinkled neck.

Pryn watched—she had stopped only two meters away. All that had really surprised her from the exchange was the realization that the man in the cloak was older than the woman in the iron— though both had almost equal bald spots.

The adam's apple *still* rose and fell. The slave-woman was draining the mug—the gentleman realized it, too. His bushy eyebrows rose. Consternation worked into the lines around his lips and eyes before amusement blurred it.

"That was good, my lord!" Bruka wiped her mouth with her wrist.

Shaking his head, the gentleman took the mug back. "Well, you certainly *were* thirsty, old woman!" That was when he saw Pryn— who suddenly wanted to move off in several directions or bury her face in her own mug, all at once.

But she stood and looked.

"And hello, young woman!" The gentleman put his mug on one knee and his large, clean hand on the other, regarding Pryn with a friendly enough look. "Now *you* certainly can't be from around here. Let me see. I'd say ..." Still smiling, he narrowed his eyes. "Mountains ... yes, a young woman of the mountains. From somewhere near ... Ellamon? Go on, tell me I'm right!"

Surprised, Pryn nodded.

His smile broadened. "Ever ride a dragon?"

Mouth open, Pryn nodded again.

"So did I!" Spreading his elbows, the gentleman leaned forward, so that the wonderful cloak fell down around them. " 'Now look at that!' my father cried, on our way down from the high slope where we'd gone to watch the little girls and their trainers put on their fabled performance. 'They've got one here the *kids* can ride!' " Smiling, the white-haired gentleman dropped his head to the side, as though inviting Pryn into his memories. " 'Well, *he's* not going to ride it,' declared my mother. But then, you know, nothing would do my father but that I try—I couldn't have been more than half your age. But I remember it all, just as clearly! Oh, yes, at Ellamon—my father took me up to the bark fence, with mother looking stern, and father reassuring her that it was bound to be perfectly safe, and when would we be back at Ellamon any time

soon, and just how often *did* a boy get a chance to ride through the
air on a dragon. It was a very old dragon." The gentleman chuckled. "The little corral, all decked out with perfectly useless prods
and flails and dragon-manacles to look like a real one, was out on
a stony ledge. The very bored young woman managing it explained
to my father that the dragon took off and flew over that gorge
there, landed on the ledge over *there* (where we could see another
young woman sitting), at which point it would turn around, take off
again, and fly back *here*; and, yes, it was a *very* well-trained dragon
and had been doing it for years—all this in a peremptory tone that
rather put my father off, I think. He wasn't used to being spoken to
like that, though it pleased my mother, who assumed it was what
he deserved for condescending to such foolishness in the first
place. Finally my father said, yes, go ahead, and the young woman
put a wide belt around me and buckled it—not very tightly, either. It
had four metal rings on it. She lifted me on to the dragon's hard
back. The beast wore a leather body-harness, with several straps
hanging from it down to the ground. She picked up one and
another, and put them through the rings, lashing me on. Then she
handed me the reins to hold—I'd already noticed they didn't go to
the dragon's head, like the reins on the dragons we'd just seen
performing; they were tied to the harness's shoulder strap, so that
no matter how hard or in what direction I might pull, they wouldn't
have guided it anywhere. But that, I suppose, was in case I got it
into my head, midflight, to take my dragon off somewhere I wasn't
supposed to. 'Don't you think there should be a rope or a chain to
the creature from the corral here?' my mother asked in a loud
voice. 'When it's flying, I mean. Just as a precaution . . .?' No one
answered her, which only confirmed her notion that the concession
was evil, silly, and dangerous. The young woman dashed around to
the other side to tie the other straps to the other rings. As she was
lashing the last one to the belt, the scaly old thing waddled forward,
lifted wide wings—When it went off the edge, I was quite terrified! I
mean, it just walked to the cliff and . . . fell. But then those laboring
sails beat, and beat, and beat again; and we began to rise through
the late morning, while I tried to lean forward and hug its cool,
windy neck. I remember glancing behind me. There was my mother,
holding on to her chin, and my father, looking like he might
leap after me, and the bored young woman, who'd sat down on an
upturned barrel, all growing smaller with the swaying mountain. I
tried to sit up—and was brave enough to *half* do it. But we'd
already reached our glide's height. Wings banked for descent to
the far ledge . . . I remember hearing claws scrape rock. My
dragon scrambled a few steps over stones. The young woman

waiting there wasn't as bored as the other. I looked down at her as she seized the dragon harness to walk the creature about on the ledge. To this day I can recall how dirty her nails were. Her short hair was wrapped through with some decorative cord. As she came around with us, she tugged one of my straps to make sure it was tight—I guess it usually was. Then she gave me a big grin. I think I fell in love with her. The beast completed its turn. She slapped its haunch—

"And we fell off the cliff again." The old gentleman's eyes blinked above wet cheeks. (Was it raining harder?) "No, my parents agreed, this time in accord, I could *not* do it again. My father paid with both gold and iron, so it must have been rather expensive, even for those days. And I played at dragons and dragon riders all the way to the aunt's brother-in-law's niece's where we were being hosted for lunch; and where I charmed some of the guests—and bored some others, I'm sure—with my loud version of dragon riding, till one of the servants took me with five or six other children down to the lake by the fountain. After we paddled about a bit, a slave brought *our* lunch out in several ceramic bowls, one of which had a dragon painted on it—I'm afraid it only got me going again." He sighed, smiling. "And *that's* practically all I remember of the entire Ellamon trip!"

After moments Pryn said: "My dragon was a wild one. I caught her myself."

"Of course you're much older than I was," the gentleman said.

Pryn said: "I don't think they have the dragon ride anymore. For children." She looked at her mug. "The dragon corrals still put on exhibitions for people who come up to see. But some of the corrals have been closed down—they tore down the biggest when I was nine. My cousin was on the work crew . . . but the rest still put on shows." She blinked because of a drop of water on her eyelash. "There're not so many dragons anymore."

"Never a hearty breed," the gentleman said. "They'll probably be extinct in a hundred years. That's why they were put under Imperial Protection."

"My aunt said something once about there being a children's dragon ride, a long time ago. But they . . . closed it down. Before I was born."

"This was *certainly* before you were born!" The gentleman turned to pick up his mug. "Forty years ago, at least—fifty years ago. *More* than fifty years ago!" He shook his head. "I *am* getting on. We are getting on, aren't we, Bruka?"

Just then the rain doubled, then—in the next breath—tripled.

On the bench ahead Murjus looked at the sky with a whiny grunt.

The gentleman stood, pulling his cloak first over one shoulder, then over the other, "We'd better be going inside."

Pryn walked with him between stapled benches, gone dark and shiny with rain, back toward the building. The slaves hunched further over their bowls, spooning faster at their stew. The rim of the gentleman's empty mug appeared and disappeared from under his cloak's edge. The roof stuck out enough to give them some protection. He moved in front. She followed on the strip of drier ground, her inner shoulder bumping the wall, watching drops stand on the deep nap of his outer.

"That slave drank all your beer," Pryn said. "She was a greedy creature."

"I *was* looking forward to a last mouthful before I went in, yes." He glanced back, smiling (so Pryn stepped up beside him). "But slaves grow thirsty too."

"Would you like some of mine?"

A bushy eyebrow rose. He looked at Pryn, at his own mug, at hers again, at his own. "Eh ... no. Thank you, no." He stepped ahead at the door, and pushed back wet hide,

Pryn stepped in behind him.

She watched him walk through the hall, water dripping and gleaming from the dark embroideries. Making her own way to the counter, she climbed to the stool.

The gentleman had stopped to speak to three barbarian workers—and in their own language, too, just as clearly as he had been speaking with Pryn in hers. Yrnik knew a few barbarian phrases that he could shout to get the workers to move faster. And Tetya had told her some words you were *not* supposed to say—which barbarians said all the time. But now, with both that man's hands on his blue-black shoulders, now with his own hand on the shoulder of that one, the gentleman seemed a kind of magnificent little barbarian himself. Pryn sipped her beer (was it watery from the rain?) and watched two women nervously wait behind some men—to present their five children to him, Pryn realized. Days ago, indeed, one of those little girls had been made to return a peach Pryn had given her, which had bothered Pryn a while, before she had realized the kinds of separations that existed about her. She put her elbow behind her and leaned back on the counter. "Juni ... ?"

With the hem of her apron around her forefinger, Juni was rubbing at a spot of spilled food which had escaped the general wiping and dried to the wood.

"... who is that?"

Juni looked up and opened her mouth. "Why, it's the earl!" She

leaned closer to touch Pryn's arm. "Didn't you see the caravan that went by here a while ago?"

"That was *his?*"

"No," explained Juni. "That was his visitors! But now he's finished entertaining his friends from the north, he can come along here and pay us a visit." She laughed. "Look at him there! You know, he's a great magician. So *if* you look at him, don't look at him wrong!"

Pryn frowned.

"Oh, it's true!" Juni went again to picking at the food spot, this time with a fingernail. "Now I've never *seen* any of his magic, but I've heard tell! And I'm telling you what I've heard. Ah—" and she tapped Pryn's arm again. "Look there!"

Pryn turned.

Hide swung back from the door again. Old Rorkar came through, some new laborers behind him, toward the serving area.

The morning he'd hired her, Old Rorkar's broad, knobby feet had been bound in broad leather sandals. Since then, however, Pryn had not seen the peasant brewer in any kind of shoe. Behind the counter the cook, Cyka, saw them coming, jammed her flat wooden spoon into the stew crock, turned to the counter, and planted both hands on brown, wide-splayed fingers. It was her most frequent gesture, and whenever she did it, Pryn thought of some farm woman snatching two root clusters from the earth and flopping them down on a rock for view. Cyka grinned over teeth ice-gray and perfect.

"... not find it like those city jobs you're heading to, where you can wander in at any hour of the morning or afternoon. Lateness won't be tolerated." Old Rorkar slapped his own small, hard hand on the wood. "Cyka, these are some new men. This is Kadyuk." With a patriarchal arm around towering Kadyuk's shoulder, Rorkar moved him forward.

"Kadyuk," Cyka repeated with a nod, turned to take a dish from a pile of dishes, and ladled into it a flat of stew. She placed it in the hands of the tall, hairy-armed barbarian.

"And this is Zaiky." Another arm around the shoulder.

"Zaiky." Another nod; another stew bowl.

Juni came up beside Cyka to deal out wooden eating spoons, which the laborers picked up.

"This is har'Leluk." Another shouldered arm.

"Leluk ... har' Leluk." A nod; a bowl.

Leluk was a woman—and *har,* Pryn had just learned, was a barbarian term meaning 'radiant' when it preceded a woman's name; otherwise it was a general intensifier, like 'very' or 'terribly'

248

or, indeed, 'radiantly,' when it sounded, as it frequently did, in general converse.

"This is Donix."

"Donix." More stew.

A week back, Pryn had been presented to Cyka in the same way, with the same arm, the same nod and bowl. Once you were presented as a worker at the brewery by the owner, Cyka would give you a bowl and a mug every evening thereafter—though the mug came only after the first full day's work. Rorkar, they said, remembered each worker's name long enough to get from the hiring table to Cyka; and Cyka remembered it through all eternity. At least three times Pryn had seen her refuse food to a man who'd been fired a few weeks before but who had tried to come back and sneak a free meal.

"And this is Jarced."

"Jarced," who got his arm from Rorkar, his bowl from Cyka, and his spoon from Juni.

Finished serving, Cyka put her hands on the counter and nodded beyond Rorkar's shoulder.

"Eh . . . yes, Cyka? What is it?"

Cyka gestured with her bristly chin.

"Eh . . . what?"

Rorkar looked back, turned.

At that moment the earl left the group with which he'd been speaking and started up between the tables, much the way he had walked among the benches, with that luminous smile.

Old Rorkar took on a look of repressed excitement that made Pryn see a little of his nephew across that wide forehead, under those bushy brows, and in the prominent jaw and unevenly bearded cheek. "My lord!" Rorkar raised the back of his right fist to his forehead.

On either side of the approaching earl, men and women were rising. "Rorkar, my man!" Reaching the peasant brewer, the earl gently pulled the wrinkled wrist away from the high forehead, bald as his own. "Now, now, I've told you many times: such gestures are unseemly within the walls of your own place of business, Rorkar. Save them for those public occasions when both of us are equally bound by the constraints of ritual."

"And I have told you equally many times, my lord: I do not forget that this was not always *my* business, but belongs to me only by the generosity of your late and noble father—all Nevèrÿon is the poorer for his passing."

"Yes, yes, you've been saying that for twenty years! And I notice another year has gone by where you have not taken my advice—a

lusty peasant like you should find himself a young wife to get him a son as an heir to take over in his old age."

"And I have told you, my lord: wives are not for me. I am married to the brewery here."

"And *I* have told *you:* if it's your waning powers that worry you, my man, I have ways ..." The earl raised a finger and lowered a brow, which made some onlookers laugh and others draw in breath.

"My lord, my hopes are—still—all in my nephew, Tetya. Tetya?" Rorkar looked about the hall. "Tetya, are you here? Come, pay your respects to his Lordship!"

Grinning, Tetya pushed up, all elbows and ears.

"Why, Tetya, you've grown a head since I saw you last!" the earl cried. "It lets me know how long it's been since I last visited!"

"My lord!" Tetya blurted, smacking his fist's back to his forehead. "It's only been three or four months since you were here!"

"And I *didn't* see you that time because you were away at your cousin's—or did I see you just when you got back? Anyway, you've shot up like a sapling!"

"My lord," Rorkar said, "we've made some changes since you last came. I've hired someone to teach Tetya to write. A young woman from the north ...?" Rorkar looked about. Catching sight of Pryn, he beckoned her over.

Pryn got down from her stool.

"This is Pryn." Rorkar's arm fell about Pryn's shoulder.

Imitating Tetya and Rorkar, she raised the back of her fist to her forehead. "Your Lordship ..."

"Ah, yes. I've already met this remarkable young woman." The earl folded his hands, the mug still hanging on his forefinger. "Well! Not only do you ride dragons, you can write! And read, I presume?"

Arm still about her, Old Rorkar called to some general audience that seemed to be just beyond the actual onlookers, "You see! You see! He's already met her! Nothing escapes his Lordship!"

"What system do you read and write by?"

Pryn was not sure what he meant. "The one they use from Kolhari to Ellamon—so that you can speak the words written. It uses larger characters to begin people's names ...?" She wondered if she were differentiating it enough; and, if so, from what.

"Ah, yes. The syllabics that came from the Ulvayn Islands about fifteen years back. I gather they're now the most popular system throughout Nevèrÿon. Would you believe, among the six or seven systems I've mastered from time to time, it's not among them!" He laughed. "Well, you *are* an exceptional young woman! I should like to invite you to my home. My wife and I would be happy to receive

 250

you for dinner. Perhaps tomorrow evening ... about five o'clock?"
The earl lowered his chin; his glance took in Rorkar, who made
some gesture that seemed to say both "of course" and "it's nothing." Only seconds later Pryn realized the invitation meant she
must miss the last hour's work. "Good, then. I shall send a carriage
for you at four-thirty—No!" The earl's free hand rose from his
cloak. "Don't protest!" (Pryn had not thought of protesting.) "Come
as you are. It will be an informal evening. Wear one piece of jewelry,
one bit of gold or jade more than that bronze pendant you have on
now, and we shall consider you frightfully overdressed. I shall be
wearing exactly what I wear now. I shall expect you to do the
same."

Pryn, who had no jade or gold to wear, became aware in one
instant of three things: relief from an anxiety she had not even
realized she felt until it vanished. Also, everyone around her, including Tetya and Rorkar, had been holding their breaths; she knew,
when they all started to breathe. Finally, the astrolabe, which she
had never thought of as jewelry, suddenly seemed a notable weight,
worthy of mention, if only because the earl had mentioned it. "Yes,
my lord." Her aunt would have wanted her to add, and so she
added, "Thank you, my lord." Then, as an afterthought, she clapped
the back of her fist to her forehead again.

The earl pulled his cape about him and looked at Tetya. "My
respects to your family." He turned to Rorkar. "My best wishes for
your nephew's continued progress." Without waiting for a response
from either, he turned and walked toward the door.

"Well!" Old Rorkar dropped his arm from Pryn's shoulder. "Well
... you ... er ... really, I think it's very fine of the earl to invite
you. It's fine with me. Really, it's fine. And why don't you come up
to *my* place this evening. I mean later. Not for dinner. You've
already *had* dinner, haven't you? Here?"

"Yes, she has," was Cyka's oblique interjection.

"Good. Come by the house for ... for a late mug of beer, then.
Tetya will be there. Yes, do come by. As informally as you would go
... to his Lordship's. Yes!" Rorkar let out a laugh that seemed as
perceptively unsure as the earl's smile had seemed obliviously
confident. "In an hour: you and Tetya. Of course you will, won't
you?"

Having first taken Rorkar's words as an order, Pryn now began to
hear their entreaty. As she said, "Yes, sir," she wondered if the
proper thing to do were again to touch her fist against her forehead.

The earl reached the hide.

The hide swung back.

The earl stepped back.

Yrnik stepped in—and punched himself in the head! (That's how it looked to Pryn.) He started to move aside, then remembered and grabbed the hide back for his Lordship. The marvelous cloak sailed up and after its colored hem and was gone. The hide fell. Yrnik's fist opened and his fingers turned on his forehead to scratch his nappy head. Blinking in the doorway, Yrnik looked about the hall.

"Yes?" Rorkar's horny hand again touched Pryn's shoulder, but lightly. "You'll come? You and Tetya. And Yrnik. Yrnik too."

"Of course." Then, because she felt uncomfortable, Pryn walked off down the hall, glanced back, and called again, "Yes, sir!" She passed the craggy-faced foreman and pushed outside.

Damp air wrapped her round with cool evening light.

The eaves dripped. Beyond the brush, a wagon trundled away on the wet road. Rain from the eaves hit her shoulder.

A hiss made her look left.

"My lady . . . ?" Hand to the wall, face wet, body crouching; the eyes blinked.

"Bruka . . . ?" Staring at the iron collar, Pryn was not sure it *was* Bruka.

"My lady, have you come here to spy?"

"Spy . . . ?" Pryn raised her hand to where the chain hit her thumb. It was Bruka; and Murjus emerged from behind the far corner of the hall, waiting. "Why do you ask me if I—?"

Bruka walked up to Pryn, bent as though it still rained and she still protected her meal. (Was it her spine?) The slave-woman grasped the astrolabe. "Where did you get this, girl! Tell me, what northern lord sent you here?" The chain jerked against Pryn's neck. "Which one? If you love life, tell me! *He* has seen it: there's nothing to be gained by hiding!"

"But I'm *not* hiding anything!" Pryn said. "Someone just . . . gave it to me! The Liberator. In Kolhari. I only wore it because . . ." and realized, as she searched for reason, there was none she could mark down.

Bruka glanced back at Murjus, then turned to lift the astrolabe on its chain. "Once again Mad Olin's circle has returned to the Garth, unbidden, by chance, simply because someone *gave* it to you?"

"—and *he* has seen it?" Murjus rasped from the building's corner. "It has come back to destroy us!" He walked up by the wall. "To bring that back into the Garth is to unleash on us the madness of Olin herself—*you* must be mad to bring it! You should have never set foot in the Garth Peninsula. When the Vygernanx Monastery thrust even the tip of one tower over the tree tops within the circle of your vision, you should have turned yourself around to

ride, run, crawl away as fast as you could go, till you were away from any and all lands ever part of Lord Aldamir's domain! Your heedlessness will loose ruin and destruction on all Nevèrÿon!"

"But he *has* seen it!" Bruka exclaimed. "I saw him look. He knows it's here as well as we. It's too late—"

"Does he *want* it?" Pryn demanded. The agitation broke through to her in a way she experienced as both annoyance and anger, though later she would realize it had been even more than fear. "*I* don't want it! Let him take it—"

"But he *can't* take it," declared Murjus, from behind Bruka. "The earl could no more take it from you than one of us could—unless you gave it of your own free will!"

"And perhaps not even then!" Bruka whispered. "Its power is too strong!"

"But I don't *want* it!" Pryn suddenly pulled the chain from around her neck and over her head. "You take it! Throw it away if you want—"

Bruka's hands, both of them, jerked behind her. She stepped back, and back, and back again. Murjus pulled behind the house till just a blue eye and some wet hair showed.

"I didn't bring it here for any reason!" Pryn shook the chain at the two retreating slaves. "I'm *not* a spy! I told that to ... to the man who gave it to me! And I tell you, I don't—"

The sound behind her made her whirl.

It was the hide squeaking on its wooden pegs.

Rorkar stepped out, his arm about Tetya. Yrnik came after them. Rorkar glanced at Pryn. His faint frown took in the astrolabe swinging from her fists.

Had the metal disk with its angular markings burst into sparks, Pryn would not have been surprised. At a tickling on her shoulder she looked sharply behind her. But it was only drops from an overhead branch.

The slaves were gone.

She turned back.

Rorkar still looked. "You *will* come?" he asked. "In about an hour?"

"Yes, sir." Pryn lifted the chain back over her head. The astrolabe fell against her breasts. It didn't burn; or freeze; or hum; or ring; or quiver.

Rorkar walked on with Tetya and Yrnik.

The feel of the chain on her neck returned her to more normal conjecture. Certainly Rorkar had seen nothing peculiar in ... Olin's circle. The circle of different stars? ... Was that what the tale-teller had called it so long ago? For the first time in a while,

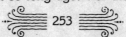

Pryn remembered the young queen who had murdered all those people. All Rorkar had just seen, certainly, was a foreign girl adjusting a local-made pendant. But then, she thought as she started across the wet grass, his Lordship the earl had not made any special gesture of recognition at the sight of the astrolabe either—unless his exhortation to come tomorrow wearing *exactly* what she wore now . . .

The overhead branch, sighing, splattered her again, which sent chills down about her shoulders as she reached up to rub the drops away.

It wasn't really *a* house.

Several thatched cottages had been reinforced, expanded, joined together, here by the addition of a wooden wall, there by the erection of a stone one. The grove around it still sprinkled the tufted eaves. It had rained and stopped and rained and stopped again since Pryn had left the hall. The western hills were snarled over with clouds, slashed through by long wounds from the sun. The high brush near her broke up some of that coppery light and laid it in swatches over the daubed wall. Down the eastern slope the orchards, the brewing sheds, the laborers' barracks where she slept were sinking into a shadow-like pool that had slipped in as if from the sea she knew was somewhere beyond those crags and shaggy pines.

Pryn knocked. The door, this one of plank, swung in an inch, not locked. But no one came to answer it.

Pryn knocked again.

A breeze in the branches gathered the leaf chatter into a roar, then shushed it. Perhaps this house, which had been pointed out to her and into which she'd several times seen Rorkar go, was *not* the house . . . .

Pryn knocked a third time—this time caught the leather-covered boards on her palms and pushed them back on their rope hinge . . .

Sunset through the west window fell over the floor mats whose damp odor momentarily threw Pryn miles and years away to the mountain hut of a married cousin on a winter morning when it had actually snowed in the night and the white powder had begun to melt . . .

A young woman came into the room, drying her head with a print cloth that flopped about her hips. The towel fell from short, curly hair. "Excuse me . . . ?" Naked save the collar at her neck, she was not much older—or younger—than Pryn.

"I was . . . supposed to come here."

"Oh," the slave said. "*You're* Tetya's tutor?"

Pryn nodded.

"The master's mentioned you on and off this whole week now." She balled up the cloth. "Somehow I just thought you were a boy. And an older boy at that. Come in." She put the cloth down on a bench at the wall and started off through a doorway.

Pryn followed down a passage, one wall of which was stone.

As they stepped out of the hallway, Tetya turned at the wooden table where he was sitting and smiled; and Rorkar did not.

At the porch's edge, Yrnik leaned on a supporting pole, gazing out over slopes, valleys, hills—the view here was astonishing—while the roof edge dripped.

The house slave said: "Can I get you anything?"

Rorkar grunted.

The house slave, apparently understanding, went off to get it.

Under the wooden table legs, Pryn saw the old peasant wore sandals.

Pryn stood for the length of half a dozen breaths, till Tetya said: "Come here and sit down. Uncle doesn't mind."

As Pryn started to the bench beside Tetya, Old Rorkar grumbled, "Who are you to say what I mind or don't mind?" so that Pryn stopped again. Rorkar glanced up at her, apparently surprised at her surprise. "Well, go on! *Sit* down—if you want. Why should I object?"

Feeling as uncomfortable as, moments ago with the familiar dampness of the mats, she had felt at home, Pryn slipped onto the bench beside Tetya.

"I mean," Rorkar went on, "this is not a house like his Lordship's, mind you, with 'Come in,' and 'Do sit down,' and 'Won't you have some of this or that?' Even if I *have* a slave or two, it's because I need them. You do what you want here. It's just an ordinary house. You can do the ordinary things that anyone wants to."

The house slave returned with a wide tray of woven slats on which were a pitcher and some mugs. She set the tray on the table.

Rorkar said: "Have some beer . . . if you want some."

But as Pryn reached for the pitcher, he waved his hand. "No, let the slave pour. What do you think we have her here for?" As Pryn pulled her hand back to her lap, he added, "No, no; go on—go on, take it yourself, if that's how you want to do it. You just do what you're most comfortable doing. Go on."

Pryn glanced about, about as uncomfortable as it was possible to be.

"Just because she can write—" Rorkar chuckled—"I think she feels she's too good for our ordinary ways here, eh?"

Mild confusion became mild anger. Pryn thought (and as she

thought it, she thought of the characters it would take to write it): *I've* never had a slave pour for me in my life! At the same moment she pictured the Liberator. She picked up the pitcher and poured copper liquid into a mug till yellow foam crested the rim.

Then she set the pitcher down.

Foam still rose, brimmed the mug's red lip, and rolled over.

The slave filled the others.

When Pryn lifted hers, foam dripped into her lap. In a distant part of the country, she thought, setting the mug back on the table, perhaps you must *expect* to feel uncomfortable. Written symbols still flickered among the words. And the Liberator had worn an iron collar too. "Why did you want me here?"

"Well, his Lordship invited you to his house. I just wanted to see why he ... well, I thought it would be nice to invite you here. As well. We're very ordinary people, here, you know. Not like his Lordship at all. If you didn't want to come ... ?"

Pryn shrugged. "Thank you for inviting me. It was very nice of you." Great-aunt would have approved.

"I had the feeling, you know, that you didn't want to come. I said to myself, why should she want to visit me just because she's been invited to visit his Lordship. There'd be no reason."

Yrnik sucked his teeth and turned from the post.

"Well, it's true! I would understand if she didn't. Who wants to make someone do something they don't want to? Perhaps she thinks she deserves to be invited?" Rorkar leaned toward Tetya. "Hey, do you think that's what she thinks?"

Pryn turned toward Tetya, vaguely curious as to what, precisely, he *did* think. Tetya handed Yrnik up a mug. Then he took one for himself—and blew foam, splattering, onto the table.

Pryn exploded with laughter—while Rorkar batted at his nephew's head:

"Weasel! Badger! Dirty shoat! You think you're in some barbarian shambles? This is a decent home, with decent people living in it! I suppose you'd do that if his Lordship invited *you* to his home too!"

"His Lordship," Pryn said, recovering, "seems to be a very fine man." Her aunt's endless sullenness and interminable suspicions came back among all the reasons she'd yearned to leave home. Here, looking directly at this mummer's skit of it, she felt oddly free of them. It had occurred to her that these insults and wheedlings were far less shattering than murder or sex, so that she could suffer them with the provisional interest of one who had ridden in the sky—and could write about it.

"Hey. . . ?" Rorkar turned to her.

"I said, 'His Lordship seems a man comfortable with all peoples, a fine and good person.'" Pryn realized, as one who could write, that this was not what she had said at all.

"Oh. Well ... I suppose his Lordship *is* comfortable enough. He's certainly rich enough to be comfortable. Not as rich as he once was, though—and you can be sure it galls him. But he's comfortable. Well, so am I. Comfortable. Here in my house. Here. I'm comfortable enough with what I have—here—with what I've made for myself, out of it all. Though not with people. It's true. You're right." Rorkar took a long drink from his mug. "I'm not comfortable with people. New people. Just like you say." He laughed again. "Always wondering what they think of me, you know? I'm just an ordinary man. I've been a little luckier than some—worked a little harder than some others."

"I never thought you were uncomfortable." Pryn *had* thought the old peasant was barbarically rude; the notion, however, that this rudeness might be a manifestation of an equally barbaric discomfort intrigued her enough for her to stay seated. "With people."

"You didn't?" Rorkar inquired. "Well, believe me, I *am*! I'm a very ordinary man—have all the feelings any ordinary man has—or, I dare say, an ordinary woman. Even an ordinary girl. Like you." He smiled, actually looking at Pryn directly for the first time since she'd come in; which was when Pryn decided both that she did not like him, and that he was probably not a bad human being. She smiled back—and felt somewhat sorry at her judgment.

"I like you," Rorkar continued. "I liked you from the first I met you, out at the hiring table. In the field. When you came up, looking for a job—looking like a fat little chipmunk. That's why I hired you in the first place. I don't hire somebody that I don't take to—certainly not as a tutor for my nephew. But of course that wasn't decided on till later. When Yrnik found out you could write. I asked you up here, you know, to see what his Lordship might possibly see in you to invite you to his home! It can't *only* be that you can write. Yrnik there can write, and *he's* never been invited to his Lordship's. But now I think I see it. It's simply because you're a nice, ordinary person. Like me. Like any of us. And you're honest about it. The way I am. His Lordship looked at you and saw that. Me, I'm too uncomfortable with people to look at them and see that right off—to look at strangers and see that. Before I get to know them."

"Yrnik never got invited to his Lordship's because Yrnik's not a pretty girl." Tetya scooped more foam from his mug with a forefinger and sucked it off. "That's all. Uncle doesn't trust his Lordship."

"Well, now I never said ..." Rorkar frowned at Tetya, at Yrnik (who had taken his mug back to the pole and was again gazing moodily on the darkening landscape), at Pryn.

"If all your land and your slaves once belonged to his Lordship, you probably *shouldn't* trust him." Pryn smiled to hear her aunt's inflections in her own voice and found them, so far from home, both warming and annoying. "*I* wouldn't."

"Well ..." A corner of Rorkar's mouth pulled into a half-frown. "Oh, it certanly wasn't *all* his. Some of it was, I admit. Most of the parts you see, I suppose: the barracks we converted into the eating hall and the land around it. And the orchards that front the road, of course—but I had the road built. The road's mine ... but *all* this land belonged to one lord or another. What land in the Garth didn't? And it wasn't *all* the earl's, by any means—though he's very anxious, the Earl Jue-Grutn, whenever we meet, that it be clearly stated whose land it *once* was. In twenty years I've never met him where it wasn't clearly stated. You will never meet him where he doesn't state it, I'll bet you. And if, somehow, he's tricked out of stating it, or distracted from stating it, he'll be a very unhappy earl!" Rorkar laughed. "Won't he? No—" Rorkar's mug came down on the table—"I *don't* trust him! Why *should* I? Do you?" That to Yrnik—"You grow up, boy, and take over this brewery—" and that to Tetya—"believe me: You'll *be* a fool to trust him! You say he gets along with all kinds of people? Well, why doesn't he get along with *me,* I ask you? No, *I'm* very much the one who has to get along with him! You heard him, this evening? All of you did—you too, girl. 'Why don't you get married, old peasant?' 'If you're *too* old, *I've* powers to restore you.'" The elderly man puckered his lips in a disgust so strong Pryn thought he might spit on his own floor. "Why should a man's marriage be *any*one's affair but his own—it's not as if I were some witless fool—like your father, Tetya—or my own father, for that matter, who needed a master to tell him in which wench he'd do best to look for offspring. I tell my own workers today—when they ask me—which strapping fellow or strong wench will give them a child with a good back and fine character. I can judge differences in men—and women. And he would tell *me*? Ha! I never wanted to marry, and I have my reasons—though certainly he would never understand that. When last I was at the earl's home—" Rorkar suddenly frowned at Pryn—"for certain you didn't think he only invited *you* to his house and never invited *me,* did you?"

Pryn shook her head.

Rorkar shook his too, more slowly, ponderingly. "Imagine, thinking something like that! The last time I was at the earl's house to dine with him and his wife—that's not the wife he has now, I'm talking about. The earlier one—I've met the new one too, of course. Anyway. The *other* wife. It was after dinner. The earl and I were walking in one of the gardens, and his Lordship put his hand on my arm and said, 'Really, Rorkar. I'm always joking with you about marriage, but you've become a man of property and prestige. You *should* take yourself a woman, a practical and industrious woman, to help you run your business and to keep up appearances. A man in your position—or mine—we *look* better to our underlings when we have wives.' His last wife left him, you know. Just like that—so for 'appearances' he divorced her and took another. He's got a third, now, the youngest of the lot." Rorkar humphed. "When *I* tell a worker what suitor she should choose to give us good sons and daughters, the woman and her mate *stay* together. A mate for appearances! Can you imagine it?" Rorkar bent toward Pryn and laid his hard, small hand on her arm. "Who would mate like that? That's certainly not what *I'm* about! No, that's not what we're about at all in this house—no, this is not a great house at all. It's the ordinary house of an ordinary man. Perhaps an earl worries and frets about appearances. But not an ordinary man like me! Why should I?"

While he'd leaned toward her, under the table, Pryn noticed, he'd taken the opportunity to work his sandals off. They lay, one rightside up, one upside down, by the table leg. Pryn rubbed the edges of her bare feet together.

"What uncle really gets mad at," Tetya said, "is the way his Lordship calls everyone 'my man'—just as though we were still his slaves."

"Who are you to say what I get mad at and what I don't!" snapped the peasant. "And I was *never* his slave! Nor was my father a slave of *his* father's . . . *one* of my grandmothers, it's true, was owned by Lord Aldamir. But she escaped and only came back after ten years; she took over a piece of land to farm and was never bothered by his Lordship. At all. That's the truth. It *is* true: the earl addresses everyone as '*my* man.' One day when he comes by, I *should* simply say, 'Well, hello there, my man'—even before he opens his mouth to speak to me at all. Now *that* would be a joke. Don't you think?" Rorkar took another swallow, and elbowed Tetya. "A fine joke!" He settled back and drew bare feet beneath him.

Yrnik turned against his post to gaze at the table with the same moody expression with which he'd been gazing out at the evening.

The naked house slave, whom Pryn had not noticed depart, returned through the hall door. The girl looked about, rubbing at one ear, then stepped in and squatted by the jamb as if awaiting instruction.

"Of course I shall never do it." Rorkar looked into his mug. "I'm not a joking man. Never had time for jokes—not with the brewery, here. But it would *be* a joke, now. If I did it. Nothing serious—he'd pee all over himself, like a drunken slave caught dipping in the barrel!"

Pryn smiled.

No one else did.

Rorkar looked up. "Where do you know his Lordship from?"

Pryn smile dissolved in puzzlement.

"Come on. He said he'd already met you. When did you meet him? And where?"

"I ... I only met him outside the hall," Pryn said. "Minutes before you came in. In the rain." Part of her confusion was that she did not want to mention her exploration of the old slave benches. "We only spoke a few words."

"Only a few words?" His frown deepened. "In the rain?" Rorkar held his mug against his tunic belly. Small, knobby fingers meshed around it. "Now, I didn't know that. *I* thought he meant he'd met you at some great house or other, when he was visiting some other important lord. That's what I *thought* he meant—back when I asked you up here. Though, of course, you didn't strike me as *that* kind of person—you seemed like an ordinary enough girl. Even if you can read and write a little. Yrnik there can read and write, and he's an ordinary enough man. Aren't you—Yrnik, my man!" Rorkar laughed. "But that's why I want Tetya to learn. There's nothing that says ordinary folk can't know a thing or two. *I* can't read or write. And you heard his Lordship: even *he* doesn't know how to read and write by the system you do ... that's probably because it's a commercial system. His Lordship knows nothing of commerce. And I *still* don't trust him ..."

Pryn had a sudden premonition Tetya was about to say something like: *Uncle only invited you up here because he thought you were somebody the earl thought was important*—and interrupted this Tetya-of-the-mind with: "Does this—" She lifted her astrolabe— "have anything special about it?"

"Hey?" Rorkar squinted. "Is *what* special?"

"This." Pryn had already decided that there was no secret in the astrolabe that she might want to preserve or exploit, even such a treasure as the tale-teller had spoken of. (That was for non-existent masked warriors with double-bladed swords!) As she lifted it, she saw how much the evening had dimmed. "Do you know anything about it? Any of you?" The sky was as deep a blue as some dahlia at Madame Keyne's. "Tetya already said he didn't—only that the marks around the edge might be writing. A kind of writing ..."

"Let me see." Yrnik stepped forward. "That thing you wear around your neck?" He put his mug on the table and laid thick, dark fingers on the wood, leaning. "I've seen such marks on old stones around here. But the thing itself is not something I know—a sailor once showed me something like it for finding where you were on the open sea, he said—something to do with different stars. Here, I can hardly make it out . . ."

"Let *me* have a look." Rorkar lifted the bolted disks and turned them, squinting. "It's good work. Local work. Old work, too—like something that could well have been made around here, from the marks on it. Like Yrnik said. It's the kind of thing we might turn up as boys, exploring some old abandoned great house."

"Somebody gave it to me in an all but abandoned great house in Neveryóna."

"Neveryóna?" Rorkar frowned. "What would a girl like you know of Neveryóna—an ordinary, northern girl?"

Pryn looked at him, puzzled.

"Well," Rorkar went on, "I suspect you just happened to *be* there, that's all! Before you were here. And you met somebody else who happened to be there who gave it to you. There's nothing out of the ordinary in *that*!" He let the astrolabe fall. (Pryn sat back.) "There's your explanation!"

"Sir . . . ?"

"It's a piece of local work. You were in Neveryóna. You met somebody there who gave it to you. Just like you said. When *I* was a boy, sometimes when I'd go exploring, *I* used to find things. Old things. Like that. Sometimes I gave them to people. If I didn't want them myself. That's nothing extraordinary."

Although Pryn didn't want to protect *or* exploit the astrolabe, she was wary of mentioning the slaves' responses. Those responses were now clearly in her mind. "And you?" She leaned forward to look across the table at the girl squatting at the door. "Do *you* know anything about this?"

"Ah, you see!" Rorkar cried. "She asks the master *and* the slave, both—now *that's* his Lordship's style! I think she wants to be a little *like* his Lordship. Well, everyone does. It's a fine style too, as far as it goes—at any rate, it makes a fine appearance. Though I *still* don't trust him—however it looks! I'm not saying you should or you shouldn't. He's invited you for dinner. It's up to you. What *could* be special about it, anyway?"

Pryn blinked. The old peasant could switch subjects as abruptly as he could ride one beyond bearing. "I really don't know," Pryn said. "I just thought you might know something more about it than I did."

"Oh." Rorkar grunted. "Well, I don't. And it's getting dark." He drained his mug, set it down. "No more," he said to the squatting slave, who was not about to move toward refilling. "This isn't one of those places like his Lordship's, where cookfires and nightlamps battle with darkness halfway to sunrise. No, I'm an ordinary man who must toil like all ordinary men." He put his palms on his knees.

"And I'd best get back to the dormitory before all the light's gone." Pryn stood up from the table. She added, just to try switching the subject on her own: "I'd heard talk that his Lordship was some kind of magician." She stepped around the table's corner. "But it was only chatter from some workers."

"A magician?" Rorkar grunted again. "Oh, yes, the barbarians will chatter on about such things—and so will he, from time to time, with his 'ways to assist the waning powers.' But *I've* never seen him do any magic. Not that one reserves belief *only* for what one can see—like some ordinary worker who won't even believe there's a town over the hill unless you carry him there in a cart. Still . . . I wouldn't trust him."

Pryn walked toward the door. "Well, good night."

"Good night," Rorkar said. "Yes, good night. It was good of you to come. Good night."

The slave stood.

"Yes," Rorkar said loudly. "I forgot. I didn't *mean* anything by forgetting." He waved his small, knobby hand at the slave. "Show her to the door."

Because the master's answers had revealed so little, Pryn found herself staring at the back of the slave preceding her along the dark passage. But the slave had answered nothing either. In the dark, all the anxiety of Bruka's outburst and the earl's—yes—unmotivated invitation swelled. Walking behind this girl, this slave, this faceless sign of the human, this collared node of labor and instruction, Pryn felt a moment of disorientation which imagination answered with an image, not of the Liberator, but of Pryn herself wearing the iron collar. She was astonished to feel before that image a relief as intense as the previous anxiety, an intensity as strong as any desire, sexual or other, she'd ever known.

Outside, it was lighter than she'd expected.

Leaving the house to walk down the hill, she began a silent dialogue, mostly with Old Rorkar, about what an exasperating, embarrassing, and rude man he was; how all his prattle about lack of appearances and doing the ordinary thing had made her, an ordinary girl, as uncomfortable as it was possible to be—what must his nephew have felt! That she didn't have to ask. She had an aunt, no different from him at all! *That* terrified pettiness was what she

had left! That was what she had abandoned. A good man? Yes—
even perhaps a Tratsin when he was twenty or twenty-five. But
today, he was Rorkar. And that was *not* what she had come to the
end of the world to find! Throughout this little mummer's skit she
kept protesting: 'Sitting there, at your table, you made me feel like a
slave!' Or: 'Bound in the ordinary restraints of good manners, I
might as well have *been* your slave!' Sometimes playing through, at
this point she would march over and take the collar off the squatting girl by the door and clap it around her own neck. Sometimes
she would arrive for the encounter already wearing the shocking
iron—that she would get a smith to forge for her from the growing
collection of small coins under her straw pallet with which Rorkar
was paying her. Well, she didn't have quite enough just yet ...
During the ninth or thirteenth time through this playlet which gave
her such satisfaction—and which she'd all but resolved she *would*
write down sometime tomorrow—it occurred to Pryn: She hadn't
felt all *that* much embarrassment or discomfort, at least not with
the intensity that, in her little drama, she'd been declaring. But she
had ridden a dragon; she *was* extraordinary. That was what freed
her to protest—or to take on the collar. After all, she realized, she
really wanted to wear it because the slave was the one person in
the room whose feelings she had *no* notion of whatsoever (was she
really ignorant? Or did she, like Bruka, know, perhaps, everything?),
so that finally it had seemed that within the iron ring was a space of
mystery, excitement, and adventure where *only* an extraordinary
person might go without terror (perhaps a *little* fear, yes), like
herself—or the Liberator. Who else would dare? Certainly not his
Lordship—not somebody who had ridden a dragon under such
tamed conditions it practically didn't count.

Or did it?

She reached the workers' barracks, with its slatted door, its
vermin-infested roof beams. (Had *these* once been slave quarters?)
She went to the women's end of the dormitory and found her
blanket on its fresh straw, between two barbarian women, one of
whom slept with her eight-year-old son who had something wrong
up his nose and snored wetly. Well, Old Rorkar had managed to
give her one piece of information, however clumsily, that she was
glad of. She shouldn't trust the earl. She shifted the astrolabe on its
chain from under her shoulder to a more comfortable position, felt
the knife secreted with her sparse moneys beneath Madame Keyne's
washed and folded shift on which her head lay. But of course, she
reflected, what *was* there to trust or not to trust him with, even if the
astrolabe *were* the object of his interest? She envisioned herself
removing the chain from her neck and tossing it to him—or

presenting it graciously to him as a gift—in either case, the same sort of amusingly arrogant gesture as taking on the collar. And probably as unnecessary.

Pryn slept.

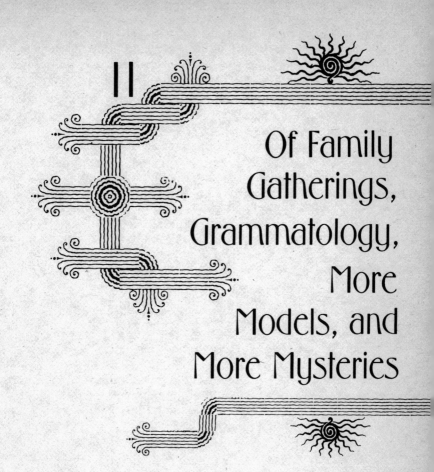

II

Of Family Gatherings, Grammatology, More Models, and More Mysteries

The birth of political power, which seems to be related to the last great technological revolution (cast iron), at the threshold of a period which would not experience profound shocks until the appearance of industry, also marks the moment when blood ties began to dissolve. From then on, the succession of generations leaves the sphere of pure cyclic nature and becomes oriented to events, to the succession of powers. Irreversible time is now the time of those who rule, and dynasties are its first measure. Writing is its weapon. In writing, language attains its full independent reality of mediating between consciousnesses. But this independence is identical to the general independence of separate power as the mediation which forms society. With writing there appears a consciousness which is no longer carried and transmitted directly among the living: an *impersonal memory,* the memory of the administration of society. "Writings are the thoughts of the State; archives are its memory," (Novalis).

—Guy Debord/*Society of the Spectacle*

After the noon eating break came an hour when the auxiliary cooling cave produced huge amounts of noise. The chains and pulleys, by which empty barrels were hauled down from the barrel pile, knocked against the stacked containers; the swinging barrels rasped and banged the hauling links.

There was not, however, much work done.

Pryn had discovered the shirkers on her third day at the brewery. She'd wandered around the half-opened wooden gate of the main cavern into the much smaller cave. This is what she'd seen:

One workman lowered a barrel by a chain and pulley, taking as long as ten minutes to do it, while another knocked it back and forth with a guide pole—to make more noise.

On the rocky floor, a dozen workers just . . . stood.

Then the more industrious ones, usually women, took down the long wooden paddles to skim the fluffy scum off the troughs over

267

the chamber floor, knocking the mess into the barrel. The paddle handles clacking the barrel rim made more moise still—while another barrel got lowered from the barrel stack, and sometimes raised again, then lowered once more. The scum-filled barrel was finally rolled out through the main cooling cave and put with the barrels of scum skimmed from the main cave's troughs. Set out in a clearing by an oak grove, they stood till local farmers, driving up, carted them off for fertilizer.

During the same hour, the main cooling cavern was a fury of after-lunch activity, with mule carts and paddle cleaners and troops of skimmers and barrel-stackers and barrel-rollers. But anyone passing the half-closed gate of the auxiliary cave heard such a racket knocking and banging within, that they'd surely think twice as much work was taking place inside as in the bustle out here.

It was all acoustics.

On Pryn's fourth day, Yrnik had assigned her, among her accounting duties, to keep count on the comparative number of scum barrels that came out of the auxiliary cave and out of the main cave. Once stacked outside, the barrels' origins were indistinguishable; and the farmers were always coming up to pick up a barrel or two of free fertilizer anyway, so that even markings would not have been truly efficient.

Pryn kept count.

Each day the main cave produced between forty and fifty barrels of yellow-green gunk.

The auxiliary cave, Pryn realized as she stood among the men and women along the cave wall, listening to barrels bang, could easily have filled twelve or thirteen, given the number of wide, wooden, first-fermentation settling troughs foaming over the floor.

That afternoon it produced three.

Pryn passed hours watching the whole infinitely delayed operation. When she went off to the equipment store (the converted barracks that included Yrnik's office), she stood for a long while before the wax-covered board Yrnik had hung on the wall for temporary notes. On a ledge under it was a seashell in which Yrnik kept the pointed sticks he'd carved for styluses. An oil lamp with a broad wick sat beside the shell. You used it to melt the wax when notes had to be erased over a large area. Pryn picked up a stylus and looked at the board's translucent yellow.

Once she said out loud: "But I'm *not* a spy . . . !"

The main cave had put out forty-seven barrels of fertilizer that day.

Pryn took the stick and gouged across a clear space: "Main cave, forty-one barrels—auxiliary cave, nine barrels."

She looked at that a while, rereading it silently, mouthing the words, running them through her mind as she had run her dialogue on the way back to the dormitory last night: 'Forty-seven'? 'Three'? she said to herself in several tones of voice. 'Who am I to commit myself to a truth so far from what is expected?' Over the next few days she could push what she might write closer to what she'd seen. But that would do for now. 'To write for others,' she thought, 'it seems one *must* be a spy—or a teller of tales.' She put the stick back in its shell.

The wax was covered almost equally with her own and Yrnik's markings. (In the bottom corner were some of Tetya's practicings, in signs notably larger.) Bushels of barley, barrels of beer; names of fields, numbers of workers; names of workers, numbers of barrels; names of customers, numbers of orders; comments on qualities of rope, quantities of carrots, amounts of crockery for the eating hall, numbers of pruning hooks for the orchards. Notes Yrnik decided to keep more than a few days, Pryn would transcribe on clay tablets that it was also her job to flatten, carry out to dry, and bring in to stack against the barracks wall. Sometimes she remembered har'Jade, with new sympathy for a secretary's job—for "Yrnik's secretary/Tetya's tutor" was Pryn's official, double title. When the wax on the board was melted with the lamp and pressed flat, now with the thumb, now with the hand's heel, frequently it retained ghosts of old characters within its translucence. Still on the board were the half-legible memories of more than a year's production. Surface and ghosts together waited for new inscriptions.

For the next three days Pryn watched the men and women loitering in the auxiliary cave. For the next three days she adjusted her figures.

This afternoon, however, standing around with the other loiterers, she noticed something—or rather, began to think articulately about something she'd noticed in the days before. Most of the workers gathered here in the auxiliary cave were old. Five were definitely sick—she could imagine Madame Keyne sending them home. A few, like herself, were new or inexperienced. Nobody laughed or joked; it was too loud. The workers stood or leaned on the wall, watching. The first day she'd come, their faces had been strange; but now this aging woman, the other old man, that hare-lipped boy were familiar. For them all she could construct solid reasons why they used this hour's sham work—a sham that seemed to have grown without conspiracy. Watching, she tried to remember if she had known all this on the first day she'd stumbled on them here, so that she'd altered her figures out of inarticulate knowledge of the

greater situation. But no. It *had* been more the anxiety at writing down something too far from the wanted.

Finally she went back out into the main cave: fifty-one barrels.

The auxiliary cave had filled two.

Returning to the storehouse office, Pryn was wondering whether to adjust that 'two' up to a 'six,' a 'seven,' or an 'eight,' when Tetya passed the office door: "I saw the earl's cart drive up—!"

Pryn grabbed a stylus from the seashell, scratched "fifty-one" and "two," then dashed out.

Would it be a great wagon with six horses like the ones that had rumbled past her the afternoon at the crossroads, when she had first heard the earl's name? No. She repeated it to herself three times, five times, two more times. No. No. She should expect nothing grander than the canopied cart that had conveyed her to Madame Keyne's (Might the earl drive himself . . .?) and must not be disappointed if it were an open workcart of the sort she had ridden away from Kolhari in, or even the flat wooden-railed kind that rolled up to the oak grove to take off the fertilizer. She came out the storehouse door. His Lordship was the sort of man to *value* the utility of a common workcart . . .

Pryn stopped.

Standing on the road—well, it *was* a cart, because it had three horses at one end. A woman drove it—a slave with a white damasked collar-cover. The object itself, however, made Pryn want to laugh, not from derision, but from inability to take in its opulence! Her first writable thought: it was an oversized reproduction of something yanked from the earth, a rootish knot with all sorts of excrescences, off-shoots, and out-juttings.

She walked toward it. Was it symmetrical? The far side, which she couldn't see directly, still exhibited the same overall form as the near.

She walked around it.

The slave made a point of not watching.

The back was more ornate than the front. Its sides were intricately carved. Certainly the designs looked regular—though the reason she would have written 'certainly' in their description was because, when she was three steps closer, it became clear that they were not; both the 'certainty' of their similarity and the 'clarity' of their differences were lost in the decorative profusion. Well . . .

It had wheels. There was a place to climb into it.

Pryn climbed.

The bench was covered with material beneath which was something soft as fresh straw but without straw's pokes and prickles. Bits

270

of torn fabric? The finest moss? What, she wondered, was under
that dark purple? The soft, sloughed scales of baby dragons?

While she wondered, the driver bent forward; the cart started
south.

Relinquishing the mystery of the cushion stuffing, she looked
over the far side of the cart's carved wall—the carvings there were
completely different from those on the side she'd first seen. Those
on the side she had climbed up suggested animals, rocks, and
clouds. She immediately slid back over that side to make sure;
those on the far side (while she looked at animals, rocks, and
clouds she *was* sure) had suggested plants, birds, and fish. She slid
over the wondrously comfortable cushion to make sure: yes (while
she looked at plants, birds, and fish), they were clouds, rocks, and
animals . . .

Catching her breath, she threw back her head, because suddenly
the cart *was* the whole world—or an image of it. Blinking, she saw
the whole world around her—oh, only a part of it, with any certainty, any clarity. But the trees she passed, the rocks she passed, the
clouds she passed under, the animals and birds they might contain
very much suggested the whole, in its greater indivisibility.

She went back to examining carvings, this time on the cart's
inner rail, so that she hardly noticed the slave swing right at the
crossroads. She only glimpsed the lopsided dragon when she
happened to glance back at some bird call.

The carved beast disappeared around a bend.

The road ahead was all wonders: rocky streams, shaggy trees,
flowering copses—each, a moment later, followed by some artfully
made thing, a wooden bridge, some group of winged stone leop-
ards, a marble bench. Culture informed nature with a host of
human ghosts, or nature surrounded culture with a field of breath-
stopping beauty and unknown history. In concert, astonishment
and agnosis abolished their own distinctions. (Was that magic?)
The cart slowed.

A woman ran up. "You're here!"

Pryn had never seen her before, but her smile was familiar,
though Pryn was too a-quake from the ride to remember from
where. The woman wore a shift of a brilliant red Pryn had never yet
seen in fabric. The dress was finished at sleeves and hem and
scooped neck with bits of something shiny that may have been
gold or may have been red. The way they flashed and flickered,
Pryn couldn't tell. The woman's toes pushed and poked from the
glittering hem. Were her nails the wrong color? As she came, they
glimmered and teased the eye on the polished terrace flags. Yes,
for some reason her toenails were also red!

"I'm so glad you could come. The earl's account has left me mad to meet you!" She reached up, taking Pryn's hand and, by subtle motions to the left and right, helped Pryn down so that descent did not feel like climbing but floating. "I'm the earl's wife—Lady Nyergrinkuga—but *do* call me Tritty. Everyone does. His Lordship is waiting for you inside. Did you have a nice ride up from Rorkar's?"

"Yes!" Pryn said. "It was wonderful!"

The nameless slave—though she could, just then, have been the nameless god of all travel—drove the cart off among trees.

Tritty took Pryn's arm. Her sleeve against Pryn's forearm was shockingly soft.

Noting it, Pryn searched among wonders to compare it to. Tritty smiled, and Pryn told her of the jade-backed flies that had deviled one of the horse's haunches, the angle of two great trees that had crowded by one bend of the road, the profusion of tiny yellow flowers that had lain out all along the bank at another—things Pryn would not have ordinarily chosen to speak of, but things that would have come back to her had she been writing, say, later; and because she could write, when pressed for talk, such things had become, more and more, what she talked of; for years that would make her, to some listeners, at any rate, an interesting conversationalist. She talked . . .

At one of Pryn's silences, Tritty said: "You *are* enthusiastic! That's charming."

What had silenced the girl was two stone beasts with raised wings and grasping claws. Eagles? Dragons? They walked between them into a foyer a-flicker with burning bowls of oil set on high tripods.

Tritty spoke now: "The earl only told me you were coming this morning, so I didn't have time to plan." They passed hanging cloths with colors as astonishing as, if more delicate than, Tritty's red. The far wall had defeated the stone dresser. It was as rough as a cooling cave. Firelight flickered over banks of weapons: racks of spears, lapped shields, an overhead beam hung with thirty or forty swords. "You're catching us, I'm afraid, at our most 'at home.' A confession: when he invited you, his Lordship hadn't realized *all* the children would be descending at once—which they have! Ardra, my boy—he's not far from your age, I'm sure. He's fourteen . . . ?"

"I'm fifteen."

"Are you? You seem quite a mature young woman—though I was only a year older when I married my first husband. Fortunately, he liked to travel. Otherwise, I'd have seen as little of this wild and wondrous land as any village girl. My first husband was Ardra's

father. The rest of the children are the earl's by his former wife—
now they're a *little* older than you. The earl said you were very well
traveled." They passed through another arch. "Where are some of
the places you've been recently?"

"Before I came here I was—" Pryn looked about the hall. Distantly, she heard free water rushing beyond the ornate rail that crossed
the hall's center. This space was even larger than the Spur's
ancient cellar—"in Kolhari. And I was in Enoch too." But before
such domestic grandeur, Enoch didn't seem worth mentioning.

They walked out across the dim cavern; here and there in it rose
a sculpted pillar. Tritty returned Pryn's open-mouthed and upward
stare to ground level with a press on the arm. "We'll be using one
of the informal receiving chambers this evening. I know the Large
Hall is more impressive, but really—anything less than a hundred
guests and you feel simply lost." She turned Pryn toward a side
door, over which a stone beast arched. "Last week the Usurper of
Strethi was with us, along with a retinue of thirty-seven. We never
even went *near* it—didn't even use the Small Hall here!" Tritty
gestured at the cavern as they left it for a corridor. "I thought we'd
use one of the receiving chambers this evening." She bent nearer.
"Tell me of Kolhari. I've only been there a few times—for six weeks,
once, when I was a year younger than you, at the High Court of
Eagles—but I never got outside the palace! Though everyone I
talked to was filled with tales of the city itself, the Old Market,
Potters' Lane, the Bridge of Lost Desire ..." She sighed. "To me,
that *was* Kolhari—the Kolhari I never saw."

"I *did* see those!" Pryn said. "Some of them."

"And that's why I like my husband's visitors! The Usurper of
Strethi comes to pay his respects to *me,* you understand—while his
Lordship drives out in a common cart on the highway and comes
back with adventurers, warriors, even—sometimes—merchants.
Though, really, traveling merchants tend to talk only about money.
It makes for a dull evening. But we love interesting people, my
husband and I; and when the choice is yours and you gain a bit of
experience as his Lordship has, it's not too difficult to avoid the
bores."

They turned through a smaller door.

A young man wearing a short leather skirt stood up from a hide
hassock.

The same moment, someone shrieked from the corner stairs. A
boy with pale, nappy hair leaped down the last six of them. Laughing hard, a young woman chased him. Both stopped at the steps'
foot.

Standing by a dark fireplace filled with things that could have

273

been for torture as easily as for cooking (though they looked too shiny and polished to have been used much for either), the white-haired earl opened his marvelous blue cloak back from his white robe. "Well, you've arrived, Pryn! You've met her Ladyship, I see. And these, I'm afraid, are my obstreperous children. This is my stepson, Ardra." He gestured toward the boy at the stairs' bottom. The boy wore rough cloth shorts and a sleeveless shirt of the same material that did not come all the way down his thin, heaving belly. Seeing him standing there returned Pryn to a moment in child-hood: She was bringing the cloth-covered food bowl to her mother's kid brother, who had run away from the army to hide for weeks in the tool hut of a neighbor. Ten-year-old Pryn had pulled open the hut door. Her young uncle, waking, had leapt up in sudden sunlight, his armor—some rusted, some gleaming—in the straw about his feet: Ardra wore the traditional undergarments for a light-armed soldier. "Hello," Pryn said.

"Ardra, this is our guest for the evening, Pryn."

Breathing heavily, Ardra just blinked.

Had Pryn not been filled with the ride's beauty and the house's size, she might have found the silence rude. But all she could see now was wonder.

"And this is my daughter, Lavik."

Lavik was short, no taller than Pryn—and plumper. Her black hair was handsomely braided over one shoulder. Her brown shift looked as though she had picked it up in the brewery commissary where, a week before, Yrnik had issued Pryn the one she now wore. "Hello." She came down the steps and paused with her hand on her stepbrother's shoulder. She looked about twenty. "Ardra, speak to father's guest now."

"You work at the brewery," Ardra said. "Father won't let me. He doesn't think it's right."

The earl raised a bushy white eyebrow, then laughed. "I think it'll be right—when you're at least as old as this young woman here." He looked at Pryn. "You're sixteen now, aren't you?"

"Fifteen," Pryn said.

"Oh," said the earl. "Well. I see nothing wrong with my children working in some local field or orchard. I did it. Lavik did it. So did Jenta. But I simply require that you be of the age of reason."

Tritty moved to her son. "I thought you *didn't* want to work in the brewery, dear ... ?"

"I don't."

"What do you want to do?" Pryn asked.

"I want to be a general in the Imperial Army and go about putting down rebellions in outlying provinces."

"Only I'm afraid," said the young man who'd first stood before the hassock, "Ardra hasn't quite resigned himself to the fact that he's now a lord of just such an outlying province—one that's been, in its time, as rebellious as anyone could wish." Everyone laughed, except Ardra, who sat down on the bottom step, elbows on his knees, chin on meshed fingers, watching with bright, rather dazed eyes.

"Pryn, this is my son, Inige." The earl gestured toward the young man standing. "He just arrived from the Arganini. We *weren't* expecting him—"

"We *were* expecting his brother, Jenta," the earl's wife said, "actually. Only Jenta sent a message *yesterday* that he would be arriving today, sometime this evening. You see, we are in a state. Darling—" this to Lavik—"where's the baby?"

"Upstairs," Lavik said. "Asleep."

"Is she all right?"

"She's sleeping," Lavik said. "Hasn't shit in four hours."

Tritty took in a relieved breath. "Lavik came home three days ago, with Petal—they'd been off somewhere together in the *very* deep south. The baby picked up a case of dysentery—it's just been constant diarrhea! When she came, she looked like a sun-shriveled apricot. I thought we were going to lose her. But she's seemed to rally. And she's been *so* good through it all!"

"How old is she?" Pryn asked.

"Three months," Lavik said. "She's a wonderful baby. But she's been *so* sick—that's why I brought her back. I know she would have died if I stayed down in that horrid swamp where I was."

"Did your husband come, too?" Pryn asked.

"Don't have a husband," Lavik said with a great grin. "Don't want one, either. I've been trying to get dad used to the idea that *this* one's father is actually quite a well respected warrior in a famous hunting clan. Dad would like him—if he'd consent to meet him. The way I figure it, he's about the equivalent of a captain in the Imperial Army. That's the rank Ardra will start at if he ever gets a commission. He's the youngest son of a warrior who was once the leader of his whole tribe. This particular clan changes leaders every six years, by vote. It's very different from here."

"And I've been trying to explain to Lavik—" the earl's white eyebrows lowered—"that youngest sons count for very little, even if their fathers are, or have been, noble lords."

Tritty looked at her stepdaughter. "You're going to upset your father—"

"No," Lavik said. "He isn't going to be upset." She stepped around seated Ardra, smiling at Pryn. "Did you ever have a baby?"

275

Pryn shook her head. "No."

"It's scary," Lavik said. "Though I'm awfully glad I did it. I mean, now that she's going to live; though I cried all yesterday morning when I thought she wouldn't ... Really, *except* for the dysentery, the south's wonderful! You're a traveler—you must go there some-day. It's beyond Nevèrÿon, and there are times I think life doesn't even *begin* until you get outside the very muzzy borders of this tiny and terrified land. Believe me, it's better than being cooped up in court—oh, dear!" Lavik put her hand over her mouth. "I was about to tell a story! But I can't. Dad's always liked it, because it insults the north. But mother—" Lavik glanced at her stepmother—"hates it, because it insults the court."

"Well, yes, I think it's a funny story," the earl said. "But I never really *liked* it that much."

"I don't *hate* it," Tritty said. "It's something that happened, so there's no reason not to tell it. Do tell it, dear, if you want. I just don't think it's ... well, as representative as you do. I'm certainly not denying it happened. Go on. I don't mind."

"Well ..." Lavik paused in quizzical concern. Then she asked: "Does the idiocy that goes on at the High Court of Eagles interest you at *all*? I mean, if it doesn't—"

"Oh, yes!" Pryn declared. "Please tell me! You've been there too?"

"All right." Plump, braided Lavik smiled (while Pryn suddenly wondered if Lavik assumed the 'too' referred to Pryn rather than to Tritty, as Pryn had intended). "You know it's customary for the daughters and the sons of outlying nobility, when they reach age seventeen or eighteen—"

"When I was a girl, it was fourteen or fifteen," Tritty said. "But they expected more of children back then."

"—to go to court and spend six weeks, or even three months, meeting people, getting to know other nobles of the realm, learning about power across the nation from people with first-hand experience—"

"When I was a girl, a talented youth with real ability might stay at court as long as three years, or even five, working as an attaché to the ambassadorial wing or as a secretary to an older official." Tritty sighed. "I don't know why they've discontinued that."

Pryn glanced at Tritty.

Lavik did not. "The court, you know, is huge. It's more a small city-within-a-city than it is a single castle—"

"And we didn't *compare* court to things," Tritty said, "when I was a girl. That, I suppose, is what distresses me most. There were formal ways to speak about things in my day, and, believe me, you could say anything you wanted within those formal protocols. But you didn't say court was *like* anything. Court was court, origin and end, of all benevolence and all power; and the reign of the Emperor—I was at court before Her present majesty, the Child Empress, you see—was always fine and felicitous. Lord knows, people will say *any*thing of this reign now!"

"My dear," the earl said, "if you *don't* want Lavik to tell her story, we can always talk about something else—"

"Oh, no! No!" Tritty said. "I *want* her to tell it!"

"Please don't worry," Pryn said, wondering whether it was the stepdaughter's tale or the husband's rebuke that brought the distress to Tritty's mahogany features. "I'll laugh and smile at the right places—but I won't *judge* any of what Lavik says until I go to court myself—which is not likely to happen for a *long* time!" It didn't seem to relieve Tritty. Watching her and wondering if they'd caught her oblique confession that, indeed, she *hadn't* been to court, Pryn lost the beginning of Lavik's next sentence.

"... hundreds of people living there! You could take ten of this house here, pile them together, and you still wouldn't fill a third of it. There must be twenty-five kitchens. They feed the various suites— so of course when you go, you must go under the patronage of someone aleady permanently connected, who has a kitchen and staff. Well, Father had arranged for me to go under the patronage of his cousin, the Countess Esulla—so there I was, all of seventeen, creaking and joggling up the north road to Kolhari, alongside a wagon full of clothes and furniture and ... well, once upon a time you had to bring your own servants, but that never worked very well. Now they ask you to bring only one attendant and a driver, for general dressing and carrying. The countess was *very* sweet, but she was also very forgetful. And she had six young women and three young men under her patronage that season. Over the first few days, we were presented at various private lunches and suppers, where we reclined on cushions and drank wine—no beer at the High Court of Eagles!—and met all sorts of fascinating people, heard all sorts of fascinating talk. Indeed, I suppose if I'd been listening harder, I might have avoided what happened. But the fourth night, after we'd made just dozens of informal acquaintances, we were presented at a marvelous supper-ball. The Empress sent Lord Krodar himself to make a welcoming statement. We danced, we ate, we met dozens more lords and ladies, some who'd been there a while, and others, like ourselves, who'd just arrived. I've no idea what time I got to bed! But the next morning I woke up in my very small, very stony room—the furniture hadn't been brought up yet, because there were no porters in the countess's

277

retinue who were free to carry it in through the stades and stades of corridors and up all those narrow little stairs ..." Lavik looked about with wide eyes. "Anyway. When I woke up, there wasn't a sound! Everything was silent! Nothing moved ... Now if you've ever lived in a castle with a complement of over a hundred, you *know* how unusual that is! By four o'clock in the morning there're always servants about in the halls to get things ready so that you may rise comfortably by five. And because I had been up so late, I knew it was at least six-thirty. Finally, I wrapped a day-robe about me and went out into the corridor—no one! I went to the rooms of the other young women recently come under the countess's patronage. Their beds were made, their clothes were hung up, and their rooms—empty! The countess's own rooms were locked. So was the kitchen! You might imagine, I was terrified! Over the course of the day, as I wandered up and down the hall, a thousand dreadful thoughts came to me: there'd been some political coup during the night and everyone had been taken out and executed, while I had been accidentally overlooked; or some sorcerer had put the whole castle under a spell, but thanks to one of dad's counter-spells I'd been spared—"

"Now, Lavik—"

"That's what I thought!" said wide-eyed Lavik. "I went through the whole day with nothing to eat, and when it got dark, I went back to my room and lay down—and woke up the next day, still alone. No food—for another whole day. Do you know, I spent *six* days in that empty wing without eating, or talking to a soul!"

"Why didn't you just leave?" Pryn asked, quite wide-eyed now herself. "Six days! You could have starved to death!"

"Well," Lavik said, "you don't know how big that castle is! I mean, you don't go 'in' and 'out' of it just like that—at least not when you've been there less than a week! At any one time, half of it's deserted anyway; there was a whole hive of unlighted and unoccupied rooms between the countess's suite and the next inhabited chambers. I was afraid that once I plunged into those without a guide, I should be lost forever! As far as starving to death, I suppose I wasn't really afraid of that. Dad goes on fifteen-day fasts periodically, and I had made up my mind not to get upset over *that* part until at least the tenth day. Still it was terribly bizarre—there I was, with a family name as old as a god's ... really, our family name is a good deal *older* than the nameless craft-gods they pray to in the north today! I might as well have been a slave from thirty years ago walled up in one of Old Rorkar's abandoned brewing caves for a week of solitary confinement!"

"How did you get out?" Pryn asked.

"They came back." Lavik laughed. "Apparently the countess had decided to take the entire suite with her on a mission to consult about taxes in the west. She thought it would be very educational for the new youngsters to see just how such debates are carried on. Only somehow, nobody had mentioned it to me—or somebody had and I hadn't heard. When I didn't join them at five in the morning, it was just assumed I had been spirited off by some other lord or lady for the duration." Lavik laughed again. "But really, that—to me—*is* life at court: three months of hopelessly complicated intrigues in which, at any moment, you may be toasted at an imperial ball one moment, then turn around and starve for a week! This is the part that mother hates, but it's true! There isn't an aristocrat in the land over fifty who hasn't been clapped into prison for six weeks or six years at *one* time or another in their lives! Considering what's happened to some people I know with names a lot less notable than ours, I feel I got off rather light!"

"Now that's what I mean," Tritty said. "I *was* in prison once, yes. But I was released after less than a year, with full apologies and reparations. They said it was all a mistake—"

"The countess said it was a mistake what happened to me, too!"

"—but when I was at Court," Tritty said, raising her chin a bit, "please believe it, dear, nothing like that happened to me! *Your* problem, Lavik, is that you *haven't* been in prison. The two aren't comparable."

"But Mother, *you've* even said court has gone downhill since you were there."

"I certainly have."

Inige said: "We all know you're not anxious for Ardra to go."

"I'm not. But that's because I don't think Ardra's ready. It's the same reason your father doesn't want him to take a local job. Certainly when I was at court, there were lots of young hot-heads with no business there. But that's not what your father and I want for Ardra."

"To go to court," Ardra said, still sitting, "would be the fastest way to get an officer's commission. Anyone can get a commission at court."

"*I* couldn't," Lavik said.

"That's because you're a *girl*!" Ardra put his hands between his knees and looked up. "I mean anyone who *wanted* one." But he frowned.

"You know," Lavik said, "I don't think what happened to me *could* have happened to a boy."

"Now this—" Inige smiled at Pryn—"is not a traditional part of the story. The rest we've all heard a hundred times before. But

that's the problem with serious discussions." He folded his arms and looked at his sister. "All right, Lavik. *Why* couldn't it have happened to a man?"

"I *said* boy. And you know the answer as well as I do—you were at court three years before I was and told me all about it!"

"Oh, Lavik ..." Apparently it *had* been said to Tritty.

"It wouldn't happen to a boy because the dozen-odd old men who finally rule *every*thing at court are all as mad about talented, sensitive, lonely boys as Old Rorkar, down at the brewery, is—with the exception of Lord Krodar, who was once as mad about the Child Empress apparently ... or so I gather from twenty-year-old gossip."

"Dear me." Inige smiled at Pryn again. "I think this *is* where it becomes dull for anyone who hasn't been to court herself—or himself."

"Really," Lavik said. "You know, you achieve a kind of inner sensitivity when you become a mother—even of a dying, or an almost dying, daughter." She grinned at Pryn. "Are you bored with this discussion?"

"Well," Pryn said, "I'm learning things from it, but not about court."

"What *do* you think of Old Rorkar?" Tritty stepped in front of Pryn, shielding her from the rest and shifting the subject with a directness Pryn found awesome. "To me, I admit, he's always seemed an unhappy man. His Lordship and I, we have an annual harvest party for all the local businessmen in the area. I've stood in this very room with him, right where we're standing now—for five autumns in a row—and felt myself *overwhelmed* with the dissatisfaction from that man! And yet I must say, I think he's the most *complete* man I've met in this area. But perhaps to be complete, here, *means* to be dissatisfied. Perhaps it's a necessity. For example, I think Lavik is the most complete of all my children—though I don't think I could put my finger exactly on why."

"That—" Lavik stepped up to put her arm in its rough sleeve around her stepmother's thin, gleaming red shoulder—"is because Tritty really *wants* people to feel good, and she'll say anything to make that happen. It's a sign of real caring; and I think it's just marvelous!"

"I'm not a hypocrite," Tritty said. "But I *do* care how people feel."

Lavik smiled with faint amusement, nodding. "I know it." She gave her stepmother's shoulder a squeeze.

Pryn had, indeed, located the spot of true boredom for all discussions and digressions about court and such places and peoples of which she knew nothing and was halfway through a strategy that would result, ten or fifteen seconds from now, in her saying something about it, when there were loud footsteps in the corridor and a resounding:

"Hello . . . !"

They turned.

Striding in through another arch came a bearded man with furs over his shoulders and a scarred and ragged leather kilt. Certainly he was of the earl's family. He seemed, if anything, a bigger, rougher Inige. His beard and hair were rumpled enough to make Pryn realize how carefully the slim Inige's had been cut. He came up and gave Tritty a great squeeze and a kiss, loped off to his father, threw his arms around the earl, and gave him an equally bearlike hug. The gentleman grinned. "Hello, Jenta—Jenta, this is our guest for the evening, Pryn."

Passing the steps, Jenta reached down to rough his stepbrother's hair. Ardra answered with a complaining grunt. One of Jenta's hands went to his brother Inige's shoulder and fell away, while another fell on his sister Lavik's.

"This is his Lordship's oldest son," Tritty said. "Jenta."

An affable smile and slightly wrinkled eyes gleamed above the reddish beard; yes, it *was* the earl's smile—and Tritty's; but it sat firmly among those rough, young features, while on the faces of the older couple it floated with unsettling freedom. Both Jenta's hands came together to clasp one of Pryn's. They were as rough and hard as, if cleaner than, the hands of the benchmaker at Enoch, or the young, pockmarked smuggler, or even Yrnik. His large gestures and great grin seemed too big for the big room—though it struck Pryn that he was really no taller than his father or brother. Indeed, the seated Ardra was probably the tallest person there by a head.

Tritty said: "*Why* didn't you bring Feyatt with you? You know we were all looking forward to seeing her!"

"Oh, you know Feyatt—she's scared of Father. She thinks he'll turn her into a fieldmouse!"

"Feyatt looks like a fieldmouse already," Ardra said from the steps. "At least *I* think she does."

"You must tell her we want to see her! We really do!" Turning, Tritty laid a hand on Pryn's shoulder. "Jenta and his young woman, you see, live very simply. It's their own decision. They've moved to a little farm, where they've built *every*thing themselves! It's very simple, very impressive. His Lordship and I have visited them. They eat only the food they can grow with their own hands in their own garden; they wear only the clothes they can make from animals

281

they catch themselves or from cloth they weave on their own loom—Jenta, here, is quite a weaver! Really, to visit them—I mean to live with them for a time and assume their ways, it's practically a religious experience." Tritty looked at the earl. "You said that, dear."

Pulling his cloak around him, the earl stepped up. "Yes." He smiled. "I did say it."

Did he gaze at the astrolabe?

"But here we are," Tritty said, "showering our guest with our entire lives, when we should be asking about hers." (Actually Tritty said 'ours' by mistake; the intention was clear, however, and no one else seemed to notice; finally it was too small an accident to record without giving it undue attention—which made Pryn feel unduly uncomfortable for the next three minutes.)

"But I don't know what to tell you," Pryn said. "You all seem to have done everything I have, and done it better." (They smiled—all except Ardra; it suggested they agreed.) "I mean ... I *know* all about myself already anyway. What I want to do is ask you questions. I mean—" She turned to furry-shouldered Jenta—"your mother says you're a good weaver. And I wondered if you used the spinning stone my aunt invented ... oh, thirty years before I was born—because that makes thread-making go so much faster. And the cloth *you're* wearing—" She turned to Tritty—"doesn't look as if it *could* have been woven!"

The earl laughed. "Weaving, you know, if one of those practices that's invented and forgotten and invented again. When I was your age and everything around here was still bark fiber or furs or tooled leather, we knew a man who talked about the possibility of the loom—said, even then, it was an idea that had been floating around in his head for years. He simply hadn't run into anyone, back then, interested enough to develop the notion and work until the bugs were out of it. He had too many other things he wanted to pursue himself, he said. Perhaps you've heard of him: a genius just from south of here, named Belham. Marvelous man; spewed out brilliant gadgets right, left, and center."

"... *no one found a place to sit*

"*and Belham's key no longer fit* ..." Inige recited. "You must have heard the children's playing rhyme."

"He invented the fountain," Lavik said.

"And the corridor," Tritty added. "And the coin-press, I believe."

"Yes," Pryn said. "He was a friend of my great-aunt."

There was a moment's silence.

"Your aunt knew Belham?" Inige asked, with a kind of welcoming warmth that made her suddenly find him much less brittle.

"She said he was a southern ... man—" she almost said barbarian, but somehow it didn't seem appropriate—"who drank too much and was half-crazy, by the time she knew him, anyway. But he was supposed to be very smart and have invented lots of things. Like the loom—my aunt helped him with it. And it was her idea to spin the fibers into thread before weaving them."

"Now I would have thought the idea of spinning thread came *before* weaving," Tritty said. "But then, what would be the reason for making any thread at all until one had *some* cloth already woven, at least to repair, if not to weave afresh."

"Feyatt twists thread for me," Jenta admitted. "But I couldn't tell you what peasant woman first told us we had to if we wanted the weaving to be strong and hold well."

"Well, she must have spoken to someone who had spoken to someone who had spoken to someone who knew my aunt." Pryn felt the reckless freedom of assertion. Presenting such facts to strangers who would not contest them, rather than avoiding mention of them in a neighborhood that had snickered over them and distrusted them and doubted them since before Pryn had been born, was elating. "My great-aunt said Belham was a brilliant man—he lived in our shack while he was in Ellamon, the same one I live in at home. He must have thought a great deal of my aunt, too. She said they talked and talked and talked about everything—about all the places he'd been, the things he'd done. He told her she was one of the few people he'd ever met who really took the time to understand him." At first Pryn read the silence as appreciative; but as it extended, she felt anxiety revoice it. "And I wanted to ask you—" she said suddenly to overwrite the anxiety—"if you knew anything about this." She picked up the astrolabe from from her chest. "I thought perhaps these markings were a kind of writing that maybe you knew how to read." The ghost of anxiety remained within the silence's translucence.

From the steps, Ardra laughed.

"Now that—" The clean-limbed Inige glanced at his father—"is an interesting question."

"I think what we all want to know," the earl said, shrugging under brilliant blue, "is whether *you* can read it."

"Why do we all want to know that?" Ardra asked from his seat on the steps. "*I* don't."

Momentarily Pryn considered lying. "No," she said. "I can't."

"Then I'm afraid there isn't a simple answer to your question," the earl said. "It isn't quite writing in the sense of the commercial script you have mastered. Indeed, in the same way that weaving

283

has been invented many times and in several ways, so that it can weave both canvases and silks, so has writing."

"Would you like to see some of those ways?" Inige asked. "Father has a fine collection of different kinds. I'm sure he'd like to show them to you. It's one of his hobbies."

"It's what the locals think of as my 'magic'—but I'm sure you are too experienced to be dazzled simply by different kinds of writing."

"I *would* like to!" Pryn declared. She tried to envision what "different kinds" of writing might be; as her mind went from the writing she knew to the marks on her astrolabe that might be a "different" writing, she felt something which she might have written as "my concept of writing was revised" though she could not have written (without the actual writing of it to clarify, if not create, her thoughts) exactly what it had been revised to become. "Yes, if you could show me . . . ?"

"We'll begin dinner, dear, when you come down," Tritty said. "That'll be all right, won't it?" Beside the stair hung an ornate ribbon. Tritty took it and pulled sharply three times.

"Certainly." The earl motioned Pryn toward the steps.

"Can we come too?" Lavik asked.

"Of course you may," her father said.

Jenta laughed. "I haven't been up there in years!" He stepped after them.

"I'll stay down here and help Mother," Inige said, surprising Pryn a little, since it had been his suggestion. But she was glad the others were coming.

As they crowded to the steps, Pryn had to step around the seated boy—

"Ardra, move!" the earl said, loudly.

And the boy was up and off somewhere out an arched door while Pryn, with broad Lavik before, strapping Jenta behind, and the earl beside her, trooped up.

At sounds behind, Pryn looked back—

Tritty's ribbon had apparently summoned four, five, over half a dozen slaves! They moved about the room below, in their white collar-covers, shifting hassocks, carrying bowls, trays, bringing in new tables.

Where in the house, Pryn wondered turning back, had they come from? Not that the house wasn't large enough to hide a hundred. She was struck with a vision of dozens upon dozens lurking, just out of sight, lingering behind doorframes, beyond windows, in adjoining rooms—and all the while writing down everything they heard! The earl interrupted with a distressing congruence of subject that made Pryn recall Tritty's *hers/ours,* to question the whole

notion of the arbitrary. "Two things slaves are never allowed to do: learn to write—and drink. Both inflame the imagination. With slaves, that's to be avoided."

The stairs rose by several more arched doors into several rough-walled (and two tapestry-covered) rooms.

"I wonder if I should go check on Petal," Lavik said. "But I'm sure they're keeping an eye on her." They climbed on.

Ahead, light lapped down the rough wall over bowed steps. Pryn looked up, expecting a window. As they reached the next turn, however, the whole outer wall fell away. Only a waist-high rail of piled stones ran by the continuing steps. She looked out at shaggy hills. Glimmering water lay between them, strewn with rags of algae, and here and there a small island or a great branch caught on a submerged bar, before the inlet joined the darker glimmer of the sea. Pryn caught her breath.

Lavik said: "It *is* a fine view, isn't it?"

Jenta said: "Did you ever get the steps at the turning there re-carved?"

"About a year ago," the earl said.

Indeed, the steps that carried them around a turn in the runneled wall were not shallow and bowed like the ones they had been climbing, but high and cleanly angled. "It had gotten too danger-ous to let the children come up here," the earl explained. They passed a rectangular cell cut into the stone beside them, perhaps six feet high and sunk another six feet into the rock face. "That—" (Inside, Pryn saw some benches, a table, and a pile of armor in the far corner, from which stuck five or six different length spears, their rusted heads against the wall.) "—used to be my 'observatory.' For about three weeks, as I remember, when I was Ardra's age—though, as my father was fond of pointing out, there was singularly little to observe from it other than the fog rolling down from the hills at sunset to cover the water. But I saw it as a place to get above his unreasonable sulks and slave-beatings and angry outbursts at what, I can look back from this distance and recognize, were finally just his understandable distress at his ever-dwindling properties. He made me give it up in less than a month when I sprained my ankle, falling on those steps right there—" he pointed behind them with a flourish of blue and a happy snort—"that I only fixed last year!"

"Shows how long it's been since I've been back!" Jenta gazed out to sea.

Pryn looked up.

On the rocky overhang above them, small bushes grew, and moss put its moist green over the undersides of the jutting stone. "Where *are* we . . . ?"

Jenta laughed. "It's still the house. Many of the original rooms were cut into the side of the palisades here. Five or six—the Great Hall, the Small Hall, the Red Chamber, one or two others—were natural caverns. That's why they chose to build out from them. There're inner passages where, if you wander down them far enough, you suddenly come to a carved-out suite of rooms, complete with old, dusty furniture, that great-grandfather, or great-great-great, thought there was reason to construct—rooms even we've forgotten about!"

"It plays havoc with the local folklore," Lavik said. "Some years ago a bunch of *very* serious people came down from the north to look for remnants of some ancient general who, according to a tale they had traced to this region, had been walled up in some underground pit 'at the back of a deep cave.' Now, down in the back of our basement are an *awful* lot of walled-up chambers, holes, cells and what-have-you—really, it's creepy down there! Obviously they were looking for somebody some great-great or other had fallen out with back at the dawn of history. After all, our dungeons *were* caves for an awfully long time. But no, the tale-teller hadn't said 'a castle dungeon'—he had said 'at the back of a deep cave.' They had their version and they were going to stick to it. So they went poking about down in the cooling caves Old Rorkar uses at the brewery—as if they'd find anything there except the bones of slaves that had spoken out of turn to some overseer!"

"And you don't think Old Rorkar enlightened them, now do you?" Jenta laughed again. "He was tickled silly by the notion that Lord Babàra's bones might be under one of *his* beer troughs—that's who they were looking for, Lord Babàra. He named this whole region after himself once, when he first came down from the north. Though I'm afraid it never stuck—*except* in the north. In fact, I think by now it's even died out there. Rorkar must have kept those poor people picking and poking a whole month or more with his own 'suddenly remembered' versions of this or that old tale."

Ahead, the steps ran out—or rather turned, Pryn saw as they neared, into a narrow crevice in the rock. The stone rail ended. Pryn looked down at craggy boulders, grass mortaring them here and there.

The steps leading up into the fissure were much steeper. The opening itself was hardly a foot wide.

The earl stepped aside for Pryn to mount.

At the edge of sunlight, Pryn suddenly frowned. "Lord Babàra . . ." Pryn looked at the Earl. "You say he named this whole region after himself? Is that why we call you people 'barbarians'?"

"I believe that *is* the origin of the word," his Lordship said.

Pryn laughed. "I always assumed it was because you people spoke such a strange sounding langauge—I mean, of course, strange sounding to *us*. You know: ba-ba-ba-ba-ba!" She imitated a child's version of barbarian chatter.

"Now *that's* silly." Jenta put a hard, friendly hand on Pryn's shoulder. "We don't even *have* that 'ba' sound in our own language. 'Ba-ba-ba'—that's how you people up north sound to us down here!" and with a movement of only the slightest impatience, he started Pryn edging up the crevice steps.

"I told you I have mastered some several systems of writing over the years. With a number of others I have teased out the rudiments of their methods, if I have not really gained fluency in their practice. I keep them in this chamber here, have for a number of years. As I am sure you'll see, though, the question soon becomes what is writing and what is not. The distinction itself, as examples proliferate, becomes more and more problematic." The chamber they entered was fairly sizable. On the counters and shelves were seashells in which leaned brushes, styli, and chisels—like the shelf under the wax tablet in the brewery office. The walls were hung with parchments and diagrams. To one side, between a row of thick columns above a waist-high wall, you could look out over hills and water toward the ocean. The sun was low enough so that at one place it put an unnaturally straight line of bright gold over the wide, shallow inlet. "Here, for example." The earl stepped up to a shelf on the wall. Pryn turned away from the carved balustrade to see what he indicated. "I have no idea how old this is, and yet it demonstrates for me the problem with all writing systems. You see these painted statuettes: three cows, followed by two women bent over three pots, followed by those pyramids stippled all over; I have it on authority they represent heaps of grain—"

"And those are trees there!" Pryn pointed. "Five, six . . . seven of them."

"The same authority informed me that each tree should be read as an entire orchard. The barrels at the end are most likely lined with resinated wax and filled with beer, much like the brews you help Old Rorkar produce."

"It looks like an account from a brewery."

"An informed reading," said the earl. "At least that's what my authority informed *me*."

"But what about those two pictures beside it?" Pryn asked. Standing in a frame on either side the row of statuettes was some sort of picture. "Is the one there drawn on fabric?"

"Actually the one you're looking at, there to the right, is inked on a vegetable fiber unrolled from a species of swamp reed."

Pryn looked more closely: simple strokes portrayed three four-legged animals. From the curves at their heads, clearly they were intended to be cattle—no doubt the same cows that the statuettes represented; for next to them were more marks most certainly indicating three schematic, sexless figures bending over three triangular blotches—the pots. Pryn recalled the ceramic buckets from the New Market and wondered, as she had not when looking at the sculpture, whether the original buckets had contained fresh water or excreta. Beside them were more marks picturing trees, grain, barrels ... "And this other picture?" Left of the sculptures, in the other frame some dry, brownish stuff was stretched. On it were blackened marks, edged with a nimbus that suggested burning. "What's this?" Asking, she recognized the even clumsier markings as even more schematic animals, people, pots, trees, barrels, grain ...

"The same authority assured me it was flesh once flayed from his own horridly scarred body—he was a successful traveling merchant when I knew him, which leant its own dubiously commercial reading to the three pieces he sold me. Myself, I'm more inclined to suppose it is the branded skin of some slave's thigh, stripped from the living leg; all too often—five times? six times? seven?—I saw my father oversee the commission of such atrocities on the bodies of the criminals among our own blond, nappy-headed, blue-eyed chattels. From even further north than you, that scarred black man had, no doubt, as many reasons for speaking truth as he had for lying. But consider all three—"

Pryn did; and frowned.

"All instinct tells us: one of them must be art, the one that demonstrates a clear concern for the detail of what it represents that is finally one with its concern for the detail of its own material construction, so that either concern, whether for representation or just skill in the maneuvering of its own material, might replace the other as justification for our contemplation without the object's abnegating its claim to a realism including and transcending either accuracy or craft. The same instinct tells us with equal insistence that one must be what we have come to think of uncritically as writing, if only because of its smooth, dispassionate surface that proclaims an enterprise which, even if it were contained in some larger, committed reality—commercial, explorative, vengeful—still, as it *is* contained, is separate from the container. That instinct also tells us, shrieks at us, rather, that one must be pure ideological imposition, both undeniable accusation and irrevocable sentence

carried out with the same terroristic strokes, the trace of an act that is both violation and revelation of the worst that can pass between two persons blinded by the illusion, ensnared in the reality, of what we slight with the word 'power' and only observe accurately when we imagine gods beyond language. That you and I, from the north and south, would probably agree on which of the three models corresponds to which of my three descriptions is only, itself, a sign of the unity of our cultures despite the illusory distance between them. But because we have both traveled those distances, you once, and I many times, no doubt we can both conceive of cultures that could read any of the three differently from the way we happen to—which conception itself is merely an ornamentation, a flourish, a personal nuance of handwriting on the common sign of our political commonality, only meaningful in terms of the political difference it might—someday—engender. The problem, however, about which my authority was simply mute, despite his other lies and truths, is: Which of the three came first? For even market mummers could easily construct three different skits, depending. To restate (and so, thoroughly to distort) the question: Which one of the three inspired, which one of the three contaminated, which one of the three first valorized the subsequent two in our cutural market of common conceptions? Suppose the brutal, unitary accusation-and-punishment was the initial construction ... and later two unconnected scribes tried to create their later models, one purely beautiful, one purely factual? Certainly, the terroristic origin would haunt both their efforts for the knowledgeable reader, destroy-ing any claim to either responsible beauty or responsible disinter-est. But then, suppose it was the disinterested scribe who first realized, in the material under hand, that pure description of fields and fruit and workers, from which, at a later time, some brutal creature, blinded by justice or pride or profit or the subtle interplay between, realized, while contemplating that disinterested account, that a slave had lied, that a crime had been committed, that report and reality between them displayed some incriminating incongru-ity, and who responded by a brutal reproduction of the disinter-ested report to convict the slave bodily, a report which, in one of those models, we now—for our awed, if not cringing instruction—possess. Suppose, at the same time, another scribe was dazzled by the coolness of the disinterest enough to realize how beauty burns over and around that rigid, frigid abstraction and so created a scorching rendition of it to tease and terrify us with its ever-proliferating suggestions for further readings? Doesn't the originary disinterest, however polluted by these later visions, somehow redeem them? As we pursue our readings, aren't they clearly revealed *as*

misreadings, misreadings that might be judiciously, if not judicially, forbidden as an intolerable abuse at a later, happier hour? Only *now* suppose the aesthetic construction came first: the beauty of some purely natural process, involving real cows, real pots, real orchards, real grain, and that other reality—of real clay, real papyrus, real ink, real flesh, real fire—came together in a moment uncalled-for by any connivance save its own evanescent intensity; and suppose, later, two scribes made their own copies, one a pure description, a purely memorial schema, a purely critical reduction, the other an angry recognition of some cruel replication in life of what art had suggested, repressed, portrayed, distorted. Again, the initial apprehension of beauty, in an entirely different way from the initial apprehension of disinterest, redeems both modes of later inhumanity it engenders on the grounds that they are, still, misreadings—one an underreading, one an overreading certainly, but nevertheless both misguided, because impoverished, because unappreciative of the mystical, beautiful, originary apprehension which a more generous reader can always reinscribe over what the misguided two chose to inflict in terms of pain or boredom. Observe the three, girl. One of these is at the beginning of writing—the archetrace: but we will never know which. The unanswered and unanswerable question—that undismissable ignorance—signs my authority's failure. And I foresee the trialogue, now with one voice silenced, now with another overweeningly shrill, now with the three in harmony, now with all in cacophony, continuing as long as people cease to speak—and all speech is, after all, about what is absent *in* the world, if not *to* the senses—before the wonder, the mystery, the confusing, enciphered presence of a written text. But certainly you have seen these ...?" The earl stepped along the shelf.

Pryn followed, glancing for a moment out between the hills. Lavik had taken a seat at one end of the railing; Jenta sat at the other. Both looked at the inlet. The glimmering gold line had lengthened on the surface with the falling sun; another glimmering line now crossed it, as if some irregularity beneath the water were creating a difference in the surface ripples that was, over that distant area, brilliantly distinguished by the lowering light.

"These ceramic tokens here—" The earl pointed; and Pryn turned to look—"are an old method of account-keeping employed both north and south of Nevèrÿon. This has been used time out of mind and will probably go on long after the wonders of our nation are forgotten. Each clay token represents a different product, just as the more ornate statuettes do, and the amounts are represented by the number of tokens or, sometimes, by special tokens used in conjunction. A non-Nevèrÿon merchant might seal a number of them in a soft clay jar, which then becomes the contract, the order, the invoice. But notice the jar, here." The earl lifted an ovoid bulla, definitely dry. He shook it, clinking the tokens within. His hand carried the dull clay from shadow into light. "The marks on the surface are where whoever sealed the message inside first pressed the tokens into the surface of the jar while it was still wet, so that we might have a visible list of the contents—as though representation itself were a containable product that might, itself, be represented, ordered, organized as to type and quantity. The list allows us to see some picture of what is within, which picture can always be checked—in a moment of contention—by breaking the jar before witnesses. But again, we are left with the problematics all sculptural writing, whether monumental or amphoral, invoke. What should be called original and what should be called copy? Does the visible list merely confirm the accuracy of the representation within? Or do the tokens, when revealed, prove the accuracy of the list? Is it the visible writing or the invisible writing which merits the privileged status of 'originary truth'? Those so necessary instincts tell us that the copy, whichever it might be, is of the same order of reality as the tools with which it is made—merely an instrument in some representational enterprise. Still, it is only the most unsophisticated and uncritical notion of commercial or judicial time that supports the instinctive, social, uncritical answer." The earl stepped on.

Pryn stepped after him. Beyond the columns, the glimmering lines had spread more than halfway across the inlet.

"Here, a stylus; here the waxed board—the same one I brought down, five years ago, to show Yrnik so that he could make one for the office wall at the brewery. Do you recognize the marks that have been pressed so carefully into the surface? They are from the stylus, but they mimic the impressions from the tokens we just saw on the clay jar. With a sharp stick one can do a passable imitation— as well as mark the Ulvayn syllabics that allow one to sculpt, to portray, to represent actual words. But one has still not evaded the endlessly deferred question of origin and copy that inheres in all sculptural representations. I see, however, that your gaze has already moved on to the parchment against the wall here; yes, it contains the same class of markings that your astrolabe bears around its edge and that so many of our local monuments carry here and there, like signatures, at their base. Would it surprise you to know that they are an early invention of that Belham who, you tell us, spent some of his later days in your aunt's cabin in the north? This marking system, which, so the tale goes, he devised when he was no older than you, is the first invention that brought

him to our attention—that is, to the attention of the rich and powerful who saw, in Belham's explanation of the system's potential, the control of a certain nuance to power that we coveted. Let me translate the basic signs and their meaning for you. This sign here, for example, stands for the number 'one.' This sign stands for the number 'two.' The sign following them stands for the number 'four.' To create the missing number, *three,* between them, you merely put the sign for 'one' and the sign for 'two' together. The next sign, here, is 'eight.' By devious combinations of the signs that come before it you can again supply all the missing numbers—five, six, and seven—between it and its predecessor. The next sign is 'sixteen,' and the next, 'thirty-two.' But let me continue on—" the earl pointed to sign after sign—" 'sixty-four,' 'one hundred twenty-eight,' 'two hundred fifty-six,' 'five hundred twelve' . . ."

Pryn was about to mention that she recognized the sequence. Was it a part of some ancient tale? She started to say, like a memory, *I see how fast it goes up* . . . ! But at that moment a play of light caught her eye and she looked out between the stone columns again. The sun, lowering still further, had expanded the pattern of glimmerings, which now ran here and there, crossing and recrossing almost the entire inlet. As well, there were squares of gold in which were darker circles, the pattern having extended now across most of the water. Suddenly Pryn caught her breath.

". . . 'one thousand twenty-four,' 'two thousand forty-eight,' 'four thousand ninety-six' . . ."

What Pryn saw was a city.

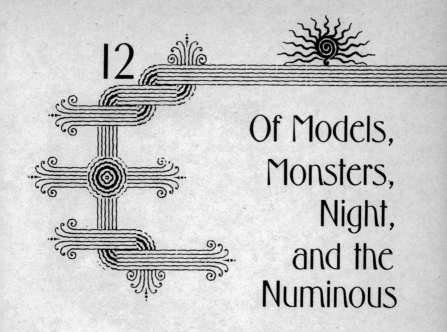

12

Of Models, Monsters, Night, and the Numinous

The city: grime, glamor, geometries of glass, steel, and concrete. Intractable, it rises from nature, like proud Babel, only to lie athwart our will, astride our being. Or so it often seems. Yet immanent in that gritty structure is another: invisible, imaginary, made of dreams and desire, agent of all our transformations. It is that other city I want here to invoke.... Immaterial, that city in-formed history from the start, molding human space and time ever since time and space molded themselves to the wagging tongue.

—Ihab Hassan/*Cities of Mind, Urban Words*

Pryn blinked.

More accurately, what she saw was a map of a city, a map on which one might measure, in rippling gold, gray, and silver, distance and direction. There ran one golden avenue; there another crossed it. There lay a glimmering yard, in the midst of which was a dark circle, the cistern at its center, where, no doubt, long-vanished children had run up to bounce their balls against salt-stained stones. There was the dark rectangle of a large building. That stretch, there, might have been a market square. Several smaller rectangles abutted it, suggesting an irregularly set line of smaller houses. Around and between them all ran glittering alleys, some broad and gently curving, some narrow and straight, some thin and tangled. On one island, green brush continued the line of some bright walkway till, on the differentiated waters, gold ripples took it up again. On another, half covered with shrubs, now Pryn saw two mostly fallen, but real, stone walls that joined: the remains of a building corner among a group of buildings, the rest of which were only scried by angular darknesses in the glimmering ripples around.

She started to speak.

Then Pryn saw something else.

"... 'eight thousand one hundred ninety-two,' " the earl's voice droned on.

On the column nearest Lavik, clamped in iron top and bottom to

295

the stone, was a sword. Indeed, on each of the dozen columns that rose to the chamber's roof swords were clamped. The one on the column directly before Pryn, however, like a double bar across the vision, had *two* blades rising from its hilt. They were joined for the first three inches but after that were separate, like a blade and its after-image an inch to the side, or a blade and its strangely diffracted shadow—though which was which (because both were real metal) was impossible to tell. Pryn looked at the next column. The blade there was single. There was also a single blade on the next. But on the next—and, indeed, on the one after that—there were double blades. On the next, indeed on the rest, were single blades.

But three of the swords displayed on the chamber's columns were clearly twinned weapons.

Beyond them, the sun touched a hill. One side of the golden city, a spot of blackness formed, a simple shadow intensified by the surrounding glimmer. It spread the water, lightening as it moved. In the shifting angle of the sun, avenues, alleys, big and little buildings lost definition.

A breeze—and half the city was wiped away by copper fire!

Pryn blinked at the ripples, trying to recall their previous form. The earl's voice continued: "... 'two hundred sixty-two thousand one hundred forty-four' ..."

The city disappeared ...

More accurately, the evening's darknesses and glitterings spread their more flamboyant, less distinctive illumination over it toward the sea.

"... 'one million forty-eight thousand five hundred seventy-six,' " the earl intoned. "Tell me." He turned from the parchment to regard Pryn. "Do you notice anything about these signs?"

Pryn had been both dazzled and confused by the pattern the sun had struck so briefly on the water. The swords, however, were clear and real.

"I'm sorry," the earl said. "But I asked you: Do you notice anything about these signs?"

With silence ringing over everything she saw, Pryn looked at the parchment. *What was that city?* was the question in her mind. She said: "Well, I ... the numbers get very big. But the signs for each of them are ... all very small, a single mark for each."

"Yes!" The earl's smile threatened to tear loose from his face and go careening about the chamber. "You have noted the profound economy Belham was able to impose on these huge, unwieldy concepts. And in the same manner that one can represent the numbers missing between 'four' and 'eight' by a unique combination of the signs up to and including 'four,' so one can supply the numbers between any sign and any other by a similar recombination."

Pryn was still wondering at the warning swords clamped to the column.

"But an even greater economy suggested itself to Belham," the earl went on. "He found he could master fractional numbers as well by the use of pairs of numbers from his new system. A 'half' was simply *one* divided into *two* equal parts—represented by the sign for 'one' with the sign for 'two' below it. One-and-a-third was four divided into three equal parts: the sign for 'four' subscribed by the signs for 'three.'" As the earl spoke, his finger moved to other configurations of marks on the parchment that, as Pryn looked at them, more and more clearly were the same as she had seen on the dragon's pedestal or that rimmed the disk she wore at her neck. "Three-and-a-seventh, for example, was twenty-two divided into seven equal parts: 'twenty-two' above 'seven.' The young Belham felt he had mastered the entire range of number, from the greatest to the smallest, covering all fractional gradations. With his economical system of signs, he thought, he could express any number, whole or partial, any man or woman might conceive. Now as I said, Belham invented this system when he was not much more than a boy; by the time he could rightly be called a man, he was easily the most famous man in all Nevèrÿon—certainly the most famous from our part of it. So you see, that 'writing,' which you have seen here, on our local monuments, represents number, or what can be expressed by number: dates of origin, specific moments of the day or year, costs, measurements, angles of degree—words that mean something in our old language, but little in yours, mainly because Belham happened to be ... a barbarian. They are like your commercial script without the pollution of greed and profit that motivate commerce—not that greed and profit are absent from such writing. They are merely elided between its signs, as my little divagation on the nature of all writing should suggest. So." The earl's hands went back beneath his cloak. "Now you know the secret of our local writing that graces our monuments—and the rim of your astrolabe." He smiled. "Is there anything else you want to ask? Tell me what you think of it all?"

Pryn pressed her lips together. She wanted to speak as carefully as she might write with only a limited area of waxed board on which to create her thought. "I was thinking of—I was *remembering* a morning, not so long ago, when I stood on a hill, *in* the morning, just north of Kolhari, looking down through the dawn fogs at the city. If I'd never stood there, if I'd never thought the thoughts I thought then, I doubt—I don't *think* I would ever have seen what I . . . what I just saw. Yes, there's something I very much want to ask." Pryn looked again out between the sword-bearing columns at the inlet. The sky's blue had visibly deepened over half its vault. "What city was that out in the water?"

From his seat on the end of the railing, Jenta laughed. "What city? There's no city there."

"I don't mean," said Pryn, "there's a city there *now*. There *was* a city. Once. It foundations, its empty cisterns, the broken paving of its streets and the overturned flags of its alleys are under the water now. I want to know: What was the city that *used* to be there?"

"But there's *only* water there." Lavik turned at her end of the rail. "Perhaps there's a paving stone or two on some of the sand bars. Yes, there are some old foundations along the edge of the inlet, where the children go out looking for old trinkets. But a few ruined huts and stones aren't a city!"

Pryn said: "I've stood on the hill north of Kolhari at dawn and gazed down through the fog and *seen* the city, erased and faded till it is only a shape, a plan, a dream. I know a city when I see one! There is—there *was* a city there!"

"Well," Lavik retorted sharply, "when *I* went to court at Kolhari, I was never let out of the wagon when we stopped on the dawn-fogged hills above it. So I've never seen *your* city! There's *no* city there!"

"Do you think she's a spy from the north?" Jenta leaned forward, his elbows on his knees. His smile took on a mocking play. "You wouldn't believe the number of spies they *do* send down here, to ferret out with great stealth what any field girl or dye-house boy would tell them if they only asked."

"I'm not a spy!" Pryn turned abruptly. "I'm not! I told the rough-necks on the road, I told the Liberator, and I told the Wild Ini! And I tell you!" Looking down at herself, she picked up the astrolabe. "I didn't even *know* this was Olin's 'circle of different stars' until that slave, Bruka, told me. I only wore it because Gorgik gave it to me when I snuck into Neveryóna—"

Jenta's elbows left his knees and the smile vanished. Lavik got up from the rail, to stand beside it. The earl's expression underwent some baffling transformation that, Pryn realized, was simply that its animation—a part of that luminous smile—had stilled. "*Bruka* told you . . . ?" Silence spilled down like the hill fog spilling across the burning bay.

"Come here," Lavik said, suddenly, nervously. "Yes, over here. Look there—no, not *there*. Over there. At the hills to our left. Do

you see that low stone building, in the mist, now, with the four, stubby stone towers at its corners? That's the Vygernangx Monastery, once the home of the most powerful priests in Nevèrÿon, when the conflict between the north and south was an open military dispute. For years the north sent spies here—and *still* sends them!—to learn if there is any power left at the Vygernangx. Let me tell you! Ten years ago there were perhaps ten doddering feyers within its crumbling walls. Today, there are none! The last left or died or simply moved on to another location where priests are more respected. The monastery is deserted. Any local youngster will take you to explore for yourself, let you wander the leaf-strewn chapels where you can kick aside fallen birds' nests, scare up snakes and beetles from the rubbish on its stone floors. But power, there, is absent. And now you know what the lords of the High Court at Kolhari are *still* plotting and planning and scheming to learn. There is nothing there—as any barbarian boy who climbs through its ruined windows of an autumn evening can tell you."

"Here," Jenta said from the other end of the rail. "Come here. Look out . . . there."

Confused, Pryn moved from Lavik.

With one foot on the floor now, Jenta leaned a furred hip against the stone rail. "No, not down at the inlet—to the right. You can just glimpse the castle, through the trees, sitting on the plain. It's like a smaller version of the High Court of Eagles itself, isn't it? It's the castle of the Dragon Lord Aldamir. If there have been no priests in the Vygernangx for ten years, there has been no lord in the Dragon Castle for twenty. Yet yearly the High Court at Kolhari sends down its spies to check on the extent of the deception by which the power of the lord is maintained. There *is* no Lord Aldamir! For all the power he ever wielded, there might as well never have been one. There is only an empty castle, where groups of barbarian girls go to lose one another in the roofless halls, leap out at one another from behind crumbling corners and shout 'Boo!', then fall to giggling. At the castle of the Dragon Lord, power also is absent. And now you know what the High Court throws away handful after handful of gold to learn and relearn and learn again—a fact that any tavern maid grown up in these parts could tell them!"

The sound was sharp, astonishing, unsettling, a single syllable of laughter, for which Pryn realized there was no written sign. She looked at the earl, who'd uttered it. Such a laugh was clearly the extension of that distressing smile. "We are, I'm afraid, all of us, very nervously proceeding in a way that tries to allow the possibility that you are, indeed, a spy, while we take you at your word that,

299

indeed, you are not. Let me confess it: such duplicity even informed my initial invitation."

"It did?" Pryn asked. "Oh, it did ... I mean, you *did* invite me here because you saw the astrolabe?" She let it drop back against the cloth.

"A simple 'yes' or a simple 'no' would insult my motivations and your intelligence. You have asked a question. Let me—simply— answer it. Out there where the waters lie between the hills was once a great city, the greatest in all Nevèrÿon. Its name was Neveryóna."

Pryn frowned. "But Neveryóna *isn't* a city. It's a neighborhood, where the noblemen used to live on the edge of Kolhari ..."

"And where do you think those noblemen came from when they moved north to the new and thriving village that, even in those days, as it claimed itself capital and High Court, was about to *become* a city? Oh, the actual streets and avenues of Neveryóna sank below the waters well before the nobles took their wagons out on the once fine highroads that had served it, to leave for the north. But they took with them the memory of a city that had once named the nation. No doubt you know that when they took power at the High Court they even tried to rename Kolhari herself. But place names are tenacious; and they could not affix their displaced dream to that northern town any more than Babàra could affix his to the fields and forests of the Garth."

At the railing, Lavik laughed. "Oh—you meant the city that *once* was there. I mean ... that *isn't* there now. That's Neveryóna!"

"You meant Neveryóna?" Jenta cried. "But it's only a *memory* of a city—you said 'ruin', and it's not even a ruin, most of it. It's just a pattern in the water that shows up under the proper light. If I'd known *that's* what you'd meant—" He laughed—"I would have told you!"

Looking between them, Pryn again saw the swords clamped to their columns. Swords of heroes, she wondered, men and women come on some task they had failed ... ? Were they true warnings or was her reading only tale-teller's stuff? "The circle of different stars," she said, "the sunken city—it was a story I heard, made up by a tale-teller from the islands. She told it to me even before I left from my—"

"The island woman who made up *that* tale," the earl said, "would be a *very* old woman today. Though I will credit your aunt with an ancient acquaintance with Belham—for rumor is, yes, he died somewhere in the northern Falthas—I rather doubt you ever met *this* woman, unless you are both older and more traveled than I thought!" He laughed. "I know because she was a friend of mine. Her name was Venn—a brilliant woman from the Ulvayn Islands."

(Pryn frowned, hearing the name of this unknown woman a third time in her travels.) "She had a truly astonishing mind. I met her in this very room for the first time when I was younger than you. And I last saw her at her home in the Greater Ulvayns, when she took me around with her to see the tribes that lived in the island's center, discoursing on their manners and economy, introducing me to a son she had left among them—only a few years before news of her death reached me from across the water. But she had many friends who respected her to the point of adulation for her marvelous powers of intellect. She never had the fame of a Belham—but Belham sought fame, and Venn fled it. And she may well have been the greater thinker. Belham was a flamboyant lecher, a drinker, a carouser, a wit when he wanted to be, and a tyrant to his patrons when his patrons displeased him. Venn was sharp-tongued, yes. But riches and notoriety never interested her. Still, she very much interested me. But all that was many years back."

"The island woman who told the tale to *me*," Pryn said, "was older than I am, yes—but not as old as you. And she was very much alive." Once more she glanced at the swords.

"No doubt," the earl said, "you've heard people here speak of me as a magician?" He grew solemn. "Venn taught me what I know of real magic, right here, in this very room. I was just a boy. My father had invited her here—to join with Belham, as a matter of fact. Venn had come from the Ulvayns to Neverÿon, and my father had immediately taken an interest in the reports he heard of her, for back then when the world was younger we had a respect for pure mind that seems to be missing from our modern enterprises. Belham, you see, had a problem. Whenever he met a bright youngster—as Venn must have seemed to him back then—he would explain his problem and ask for a solution. When he was younger, when he first realized he *had* a problem, it was very shortly after he'd invented the number system I outlined to you. At first he used to give the problem out in hopes of an answer. As he grew older, however, and the problem remained unsolved, he began to toss it to the young geniuses of Neverÿon he was called on to confer with as a challenge and, by the time my father summoned him, as a foregone insult to put the youngsters in their place—as it seemed to him the nameless gods, by allowing the problem to exist, had put Belham in his." The earl moved to another parchment on the wall. Drawn on it was a large circle with a vertical line down its middle. "Almost as soon as his numbering system had been invented, many lords—at Belham's insistent urging—asked him to build buildings for them, using the great

accuracy his system allowed, demanded he landscape one or two of their prize gardens for them, wanted him to build bridges, lay out roads. From time to time someone asked him to construct a circular building. So this problem, as you will soon see, was a real one. Belham wanted to know what two numbers, one of which might divide the other, expressed the number of times the diameter—" The earl ran his finger down the vertical line halving the circle— "would divide the circumference—" His finger traced about the circle itself— "of its own circle. Let me ask *you*: how many lengths of cord this long—"He indicated the diameter again—"must be laid end to end around the edge of this circle to surround it?" Again his wide forenail outlined the circle itself.

Pryn tried to take an imaginary strip of vine the length of the diameter and lay it around the edge. "Two and a half lengths . . . ?" she hazarded. "Three? It looks to me it would go about *three* times."

The earl nodded. "Belham's *first* estimate, when he was only a year or so older than you. Within days of making it, however, if not hours—because he was that kind of young man—he took a real piece of vine, anchored one end down, drew a real circle, measured out the diameter on a strip of vine, then laid it out around the edge in order to see." The earl's finger went to the top of the circle, moved along the circumference till it reached a small red mark, somewhat below the first quarter. "*One* diameter's length around the circle, as Belham laid it out." The finger moved along the circle, down under the bottom, and started up the other side till it reached a second red mark. "*Two* diameters' lengths around the circle." The finger continued up the far side until it reached a third red mark a hand's span from the circle's top where it had begun. "This is three diameters' length around the circle . . . which still leaves this much left over." Here he switched fingers to outline the remaining arc.

The circle on the parchment was perhaps twice as big as the earl's head, like a full moon low on the horizon—with its palm's-width anomaly exceeding the three diameters laid about it. "Is it three-and-a-third, then . . . ?" Pryn suggested. As she said it, though, she immediately saw that the remaining arc was much less than a third the diameter drawn down the center. "Three and . . . a *half* of a third?"

"Belham's *next* estimate, which, in this northern tongue we southern aristocrats teach our children and our slaves to speak in deference to the High Court, till it has become the language even of our peasants, can only be talked of—clumsily—as three and a half of a third. In Belham's own notation, that becomes nineteen divided into six equal parts: one could say three-and-one-sixth. To a northerner, I suppose, where all fractions are expressed as thirds, halves, quarters, or tenths, though you'd be able to figure out what it meant, it still must sound clumsy."

It did.

"I will not reproduce the thinking which led Belham, after much speculation, to revise that estimate to three-and-one-seventh, or, indeed, the later reasoning that led him to the inescapable conclusion that even three-and-one-seventh, while it was *closer* than three-and-one-sixth, was still not *absolutely* accurate. Three-and-a-seventh, in Belham's system, is 'twenty-two divided into seven.' When Belham returned from a trip to the western desert where he had been called on to supervise the construction of such a circular monument for some reigning desert potentate, my father told me he'd actually taken the time off to experiment. He told my father: 'Three-and-a-seventh is certainly close enough for any practical use one might want to put it to in building any real building on the good, solid ground. But just suppose one *wanted* to build a circular fortress an entire fifteen stades in diameter! If one laid out the diameter across the land and used the figure three-and-one-seventh to calculate, say, a length of a rope to wrap precisely once around the outside wall, one would have—using such a figure—too much rope by the height of a good-sized man.'" The earl laughed. "He'd apparently found this out, he told my father, by laying out the outline for such a fortress on the western earth and measuring it with real vine. Such experiments, of course, can only be carried out in a locale with slaves—as well as potentates obsessed by the desire for such knowledge, or at least potentates who can be convinced to finance the experiments. But then, they've always been particularly harsh on slaves in the west." The earl laughed again. "At any rate, this ultimate accuracy became Belham's problem, Belham's challenge, Belham's obsession. One of Belham's other early inventions, as you no doubt recall, was the lock and key—till then, slaves' collars had been permanently welded closed. But frequently he used to say that the existence of this problem was as if his key no longer fit his lock, and he was now its slave forever. This was the problem he presented to anyone for whom a claim of mind was made: find two numbers such that one divided by the other will express exactly the number of times the diameter of the circle wraps its circumference. This was the challenge Belham presented young Venn, when my father introduced them. I must tell you, Belham explained his system of numbers to Venn in this

room, just as I explained it to you, but just as I would not be surprised if you had heard it before—"

Pryn hadn't.

"—I would not be surprised if Venn knew of it already. For it was, as was the problem by then, famous in the circles that concerned themselves with such things. That explanation took place in this very room. My father stood where you stand now. Belham stood where I stand; Venn stood near the balcony where Jenta is sitting. And I stood—" He looked about—"just at the door, hoping not to be sent from the room for coughing too loud or asking an importunate question." The earl took an inking stick from a seashell on the shelf below the diagram. "With this inking stick Belham drew this very diagram I have just shown you. Using this stick as a pointer, he explained his problem. When he finished his explanation, he took the diagram—" The earl reached for the circled parchment and slipped it from the several metal clips by which it was held to the yellowed backing board—"and gave them to young Venn—you must remember that parchment in those days was regarded as even more valuable, since there was more need for it. 'Use the back of this for your solution. You may come here at this same hour tomorrow morning to show us what you've found.' Venn seized them both, parchment and stick, I remember, and practically fled the room. That evening, at about this hour, she sent a slave to call my father and Belham to come here to the chamber at the seven o'clock bell—she had found her answer! My father was taking an early evening nap at the time; yawning and complaining about these mad commoners who ordered titled lords about like slaves, he arrived here five minutes late. In a fury lest he be presented with another hopelessly garbled non-solution, Belham arrived five minutes early. Because I was a child and could lurk more or less unobserved, I watched Venn wait nervously in a lower hallway just until she saw the slave go to ring the hour bell; then she dashed up the steps with the parchment and the marking stick in her hands so that—as I dashed after her—she walked through the door, there, just as the bell rang. When my father arrived, Venn looked nervously about, then laid the parchment on the floor—" Rather imperiously (for a nervous young woman from the islands, Pryn thought), the earl tossed the parchment before him, face down. Across its back were inked evenly spaced parallel lines, forming a grid across the whole of it. "Clutching the marking stick—" The earl held the stick up—"Venn explained in an intense, soft voice: 'I have measured out the lines across the parchment so that they are the same distance apart as the length of the writing

implement, with which I inked them. They run edge to edge across the whole piece. Now, if I toss the stick down onto the parchment, giving it a little spin, you can see that it will fall—on the parchment—in one of two ways: either it will fall touching—or even crossing—one of the lines; or it will fall so that it lies wholly between the lines, not touching or crossing any line either side of it. Belham,' she said, 'you will never find two numbers that express *exactly* the number you are seeking. But if you throw down the stick repeatedly, and if you keep count of the times it falls touching or crossing a line, and if you keep count as well of the times it lands between lines, touching or crossing none of them, and if you then divide the number of times it touches or crosses a line by the number of times it lies free, the successive numbers that you express, as you make more and more tosses, will move nearer and nearer the number you seek. Sometimes the number you express will be more, sometimes it will be less, but it will always, eventually, return; and when it returns, it will return to an even closer approximation than before. Thus you are limited in the accuracy of your estimate only by the number of times you toss.' Then Venn thrust the stick at my father, blinked at Belham, and, stepping across the parchment, fled past me down the stairs—and went walking in one of the gardens with my mother, where they talked deeply and intently with each other for several hours of matters I never heard for myself." The earl looked thoughtful a moment. "Venn always got along better with my mother than my father ... At any rate: My father, surprised, dropped the inking stick, I recall—people did not usually thrust things into his hand that way. Belham snatched it up off the floor, paced back and forth, tossed the stick onto the grid, some ten, fifteen, twenty-five times. He frowned a while. Then he ordered me and my father to go away—he was perhaps the only man who *could* give my father such orders. Belham stayed here for most of the night, calling for lamps when the sun got too low." The earl spun the stick and tossed. It landed on the lined parchment, its upper end a-slant a line. "One," announced the earl, "to be divided up into what number of equal parts we do not know ... ?" He laughed and let his cloak fall over his hand. "Quite late, Belham called my father back up here—I came along too, because I was a curious boy. 'She's right, you know,' Belham said. 'What's worse, I don't know how I *know* she's right! But I've already been able to determine that with only five hundred tosses, I'm now at an approximation more accurate than my twenty-two divided by seven! Another five hundred and I shall be a good deal *more* accurate! Now, the ends of the stick describe a circle as they fall, turning—two circles,

actually, one for each end—two interlocked helices, that may be interrupted at any arbitrary point. But then, there're always two lines on either side they might fall on to compensate ... and the lines are the same distance apart as the length of the stick. The sum of all possible angles at which the stick can land so that it *crosses* a line, divided by the sum of all possible angles it can land so that it *doesn't* cross—but what sort of sum is *that?*" The earl laughed again. "Of course they called Venn up to talk to them about it in the morning. And she did talk with them, quietly and intently, late into the afternoon. One thing I remember she said before I grew too bored and went down to my suite: 'The problem you have put me will remain a problem till the globe of the world and the globe of the sun meet in their common center and the one consumes the other. This answer I have proposed, however, humanity will know and forget, know and forget, know and forget again. And that knowing and forgetting will approximate the peaks and depths of civilization as closely as the quotient of your tosses approximates that number which, rationally, we know is not there.' And as I turned from the door to go, I thought: 'What can be known ... What can be forgotten ...' And I became a magician—though no doubt I have left out all sorts of details that might elucidate what certainly will strike you as an enigma—"

"Daddy—" Lavik got down from the railing—"what you've left *out*—forgotten, I suppose—is the reason grandfather called Belham and Venn together in the first place!"

Jenta walked from the rail, picked up the lined parchment, the inking stick, and returned them to the counter.

The earl said: "But I didn't think our guest was really *interested* in that ..."

"Of course she is!" Lavik said.

Jenta looked back out between the columns. "She probably wants to know ..."

"Well." The earl shrugged beneath his cloak; the edges swung before his robe. "What my father had called them *both* here for, you see ... He wanted them to build an engine. He wanted them to build him an engine that would raise a city from beneath the waters where it had sunk."

"Now," Lavik said, "you *know* he doesn't think you're a spy—anymore. At least he's decided to treat you as though he doesn't."

"Really, Lavik," the earl said, "why should I think she was a spy? She's only a girl, even younger than you are." He looked at Pryn. "Building the engine, of course, was a job they never completed. Belham gave up on it in a week, after driving my father almost to

distraction by doing lots of things that required lots of money and lots of time and had as little to do with his assigned task as laying out miles of vine in the desert when you're called on to build a three-story circular fortress. 'It can't be done,' he said at last; and besides, he was more interested in other things. But Venn finally did invent a sort of engine—another approximating engine. It's been working, now, for quite a while. It included a story, and a magic astrolabe ..."

Pryn looked out at the waters where the late sun no longer revealed a city. "The engine," she said, "was this astrolabe, and the tale-teller's story, and the old tales of Olin's wealth and madness, the rumors among the slaves, all the signs around Nevèrÿon that bring heroes to this spot in the Garth ..."

"Heroes and spies, heroes and spies—though it's sometimes hard to tell the difference." The earl's smile returned to its radiant absolute. "One might revise your details. But you have outlined, approximately, Venn's solution to my father's problem; although for all its efficacy it was as far from successful as were Belham's attempts—at least he abandoned his. We should be going down to supper shortly. I've told you the history of this chamber—but Venn's 'engine' was put together downstairs where we shall be eating. Perhaps we should discuss it there?"

"Your father wanted the city raised in order to get the money," Pryn said.

"One assumes." The earl took the edge of his cloak which had drifted open and pulled the brilliant blue closed.

"And heroes come with swords, don't they," Pryn said, "all kinds of swords, seeking the same treasure?"

"All kinds of heroes," the earl said. "All kinds of spies—"

Jenta said: "The spies usually carry small knives—"

"—which they leave at home tucked under the straw of their sleeping pallets when they're invited for dinner." Lavik laughed.

Pryn looked at the earl again. Was he gazing at the double sword more than the single?

"I suppose my father felt, like so many of his breed, that the discovery of the treasure would restore a certain glory to the south that had already begun, even then, to drift north. For once, in the days of Neveryóna, this was a very different land."

"And this astrolabe ... ?" Pryn looked down. "Mad Olin's magic circle of different stars—it was to guide people here to ... the treasure?"

The earl nodded.

Suddenly Pryn bent her head to loose the links from under her hair. "Here ..." She lifted the chain from her neck. "I'm *not* a spy.

And I'm certainly not a hero. *You* take it!" Surprised she'd actually said it, she'd wondered, rehearsing it in mind, how much her hesitation had been idealism and how much, indeed, simple fear. "I think when I want to find a fortune, I'll go back to Kolhari and see what I can win in the markets there. I have the key to Belham's lock, I've been shown the memory of water, and I've flown a dragon—there ought to be *some*thing I can do. Go on. You take it."

The earl raised an eyebrow. "You would just . . . give it to me?"

Pryn extended her two fists. "It was just . . . *given* to me." On its chain, the bronze disk turned and turned back in the late sunlight. "I have no use for it, need of it, nor, really, knowledge about it—at least that I knew, when I got it, would turn out to *be* knowledge."

"Oh . . ." The earl pondered. "Well, the truth is . . . *I* have no need of it either!" He smiled again; the stocky little man's cloak drifted open. "I don't, believe me! Take it with you back to Kolhari— if you go. Pass it on to someone else. You see . . . how shall I put it?" He coughed. "It's as if my voice deserts me when I most need—" He turned first left, then right, looking among the unknown writings on the various parchments for some prompt to articulation. "The astrolabe is a tool to *bring* people here. But once it, itself, *is* here, it has finished its job—until it is recirculated abroad. Once it reaches the origin, the center, the heart of the system, however, it is, so to speak, excluded from the the system, and the system itself threatens to come to a halt without that vital part."

"But perhaps *you* want the money . . . ?" Pryn said, tactfully, she hoped—though it just sounded suspicious. "Take it. Certainly it would be an easier job if you had it to help you than if it were off, sliding and slipping all over Nevèrÿon."

"Jobs, work, tools, engines, hearts—the engines that drive the workers to use their tools and function on their jobs! Production! Ah!" the earl cried. "I have been associating with Old Rorkar and his like so long now I only know how to speak of the world as if it were all a huge brewery! Your astrolabe is a sign in a system of signs. It has a meaning, yes, but that meaning is supplied by the rest of the system, which includes not only the tales of history, madness, and invention, but the similar instruments sailors use to orient themselves at sea, the play of power in the land, and the language by which they can all of them be—systematically— described."

Again Pryn frowned—though whether it was her inherited suspicion or real confusion, there was no one to say. "What is this astrolabe's power?" she asked suddenly. "Why are the stars different?"

"Good! Good!" the earl exclaimed. Momentarily, his expression passed near something Pryn could recognize—before it retreated into beatific certainty. "For a moment, I thought I had misjudged you, both in your ignorance and your knowledge. Some of your actions, words, statements seemed to mark you as a creature from another world, another system entirely!" He breathed relief. "You want to know how—as Old Rorkar and the other peasants around here who know no other language than the language of labor would put it, the language our fathers who owned them first taught them—it works?"

"I'll show her!"

Pryn looked at the door.

Panting from his run up in his millitary underwear, Ardra blinked about the stone chamber. "I can show her!" He held the jambs.

Behind him on the rocky landing stood a tall man, his head shaved, a white collar-cover around his neck. He waited with his arms folded as Ardra came in.

"I can show her—like I saw you show the last one who came!"

Lavik laughed. "That was years ago. You couldn't remember—"

"Let him try!" Janta stepped back back to the rail and sat. "Let's see if he remembers ..."

The slave in the doorway was barefoot. One toe looked as though it had started out to be two, then gotten stepped on for its ambition. He scrunched them—the normal nine and the deformed one—relaxed them, scrunched them again.

"Give it to me!" Ardra took the chain from Pryn and turned to the counter. With his forearm he started to clear the wood of models, statuettes, rocks, shells—

"*I'll* move those!" The earl lifted some of the tiny objects and put them to the side, lifted some others.

Ardra blinked at his stepfather. Then he took the astrolabe and turned it on its back. The bolt that joined its several disks was held by a twist of wire. "Here, you bend this to take it apart—" Ardra grimaced, twisted. The wire slid from its hole to tinkle the counter. "This back disk, when you take it off, is a map, just like on the astrolabes sailors use. Do you know how the sailors' work?"

"I've heard it has to do with finding where you are by the stars ... But I don't really know how it—"

"Neither do I." Ardra handed Pryn the bottom disk. Etched on bronze was the twisted suggestion of an involuted coast. Measurement lines gridded it. Contour lines wound on it. Pryn glanced between the columns again. Certainly the scribed lines *might* indicate such an inlet. "It's a map of the area here ... ?"

"Can you tell which side of the coastline is water and which side is land?" Working the other disks apart, Ardra glanced over. "I can't."

Pryn looked again at the greenish metal and watched what she'd assumed inlets become peninsulas—and peninsulas become inlets!

In the doorway, the slave unfolded one arm, reached up, and rubbed his earlobe vigorously between thumb and forefinger, then folded his arm again.

"The rhet here—that's what this disk is called," which wasn't really a true disk but a spidery filigree cleanly cut from one, with a center hole for the bolt, and many little points, juttings, and curvings, in each of which was itself a small hole, "—is the 'stars' part." Ardra held it up. "The holes—they're the stars that hang in the sky over the map." The sun put the rhet's involuted shadow half on the rock wall and half on some parchment hanging there. "You hold it."

Pryn took it, while Ardra went scrambling through things his stepfather had moved away.

The curlicued shadow, a bright dot in the tip of each curl, moved on the stone as Pryn looked at what the boy pawed through.

Ardra picked up a gray block, spat on it, took the marking stick from the shell, and rubbed its point on the wet spot. "Ink ..." He spat again, rubbed the point some more. Gray turned black. "Now hold the rhet up—no, over here." He moved Pryn's wrist so that the shadow was entirely on the parchment, then turned to the earl. "Is it all right if I use the corner of this piece ...?"

"I would *rather* you wouldn't ..." The earl looked up at the inscription in still another unknown script that filled most of the parchment's top half. "But then, I suppose it's all right, really. Go on."

Ardra turned back to Pryn. "Hold it very still." With the inking stick clumsily in his fist, he leaned across the counter and placed a black dot on the parchment at one of the luminous pinpoints, then at another—he moved his own curly head aside from where its frizzy shadow obscured the rhet's—and at another. "These are the stars. Do you know the patterns stars make at night and the names the sailors give to them?"

There had been times, during her journey south, when Pryn had gone a little ways apart from her campfire to look up at the night, when she had thought, as do all such travelers, that between her changing days the stars' array was her one permanence. She'd even thought to spend more time looking at them, to familiarize herself with them, to try and write down what she saw in them and

310

the patterns they made; but, as so frequently happens with such travelers, what was illuminated in the immediate sphere of her own fire had finally reclaimed her interest. "No ..." Pryn blinked.

"Don't jiggle!"

"... No, I don't know them. Not really."

"Me neither." Ardra finished placing his last black 'star' within its tiny halo. "There ... You can put it down."

Curlicues of light and shadow slid down the parchment. Black 'stars' remained.

Pryn lay the rhet among the loose disks.

"Can you see the pictures such stars as these might make on the sky?" Ardra leaned over the counter again and drew a line between two dots; and two more. "Is that right ... ?" He glanced back over his shoulder.

The earl nodded.

"That's the part *I* thought he wouldn't remember," Jenta said.

With out unfolding his arms, the slave turned to rub his chin back and forth on his shoulder—for the tickling of the gnats swarming just outside the door in the damp crevice.

Pryn looked at the parchment again.

Ardra had connected one set of stars all to a single star above them; he was making a similar pattern beside it. More black stars on the tan 'sky' speckled down between the two spined wing shapes. The trajectories of the rhet's curlicues and filigrees had obscured the pattern Ardra now traced. The boy marked an angular line down from a kind of beak, to a neck, to a body that joined both flared wings.

"It's a dragon ... !" Pryn said.

"Yep!" Ardra connected the 'stars' that formed the beast's curving tail. "It's the constellation Gauine, the Great Sea Dragon, that rears aloft in the night, guarding Mad Olin's treasure at Neveryóna. Have you ever looked up at the unchanging stars and seen her among them?"

"I'm not ... sure. My aunt, when I was a little girl, sometimes took me outside at night and pointed out some constellations. But she said people saw different ones in different parts of the country. And I never could remember their names, anyway, so I don't know if—"

"I haven't seen her," Ardra said. "You haven't seen her either. Because there aren't any such stars, at least none in this pattern. The holes are set to suggest any number of southern constellations, so that a northerner who's seen the sky maps southern sailors make might think this one is from our region. But there's no constellation—north or south—it actually and accurately represents."

Lavik said: "*I* didn't think he would remember that!"

"You could look for it all night long, at any time of the year, in any part of ..." Once more Ardra glanced at his stepfather—who nodded him on (and Pryn realized she was listening to a recitation). "... part of the world, as the unchanging heavens circle and tilt through the night and the year, and still you'd never find it. It doesn't exist. That's why these stars are 'different.' And I ..." Ardra faltered again. He put down the stick. His shoulders drooped; his gaze, then his smudged fingers, fell among the disassembled astrolabe. "... I *don't* remember about this next part."

It had formed the top layer, a disk from which two opposing semi-circles had been cut, so that what remained was just a flat ring with a band left across its center, in the middle of which was the hole for the bolt. About the rim were inscribed the signs that had identified it with this odd local writing which, Pryn reflected, must have no need of capitals.

The earl took it from his stepson's hand, held it up, turned it. A ring of shadow collapsed and opened over the angular dragon. "But I'm sure our guest can see for herself ..." He handed it to Pryn.

Taking it, Pryn looked at the markings on the metal that had formed the astrolabe's rim. "They're Belham's signs for numbers, but *what* numbers I don't—?"

"That's precisely what they are," the earl said. "More to the point, they are no more." With his forefinger he reached over to indicate a sign on the bronze. "'One—'" His finger moved on—"'Two—'" and on—"'Four—'" and on—"'Eight—'" and on—"'Sixteen—'" and on—"'Thirty-two—'" and on—"'Sixty-four; and so on, about the circle. A circle of numbers counting nothing. That's all."

"I'll put it back together now!" Ardra pushed between them, taking the circle from Pryn, reaching to pull the other disks together across the counter.

"Ardra—!" the earl said.

"I'm sorry. I'm going to put it back together now." He blinked at Pryn. "Is that all right?"

Pryn nodded.

"So you see—" the earl stepped from the counter—"your astrolabe, as a sign in a system of signs—"

Behind Pryn, Ardra said: "It's a map of a non-existent coast under an imaginary constellation on an impossible sky in—" he grunted, twisting something—"the middle of a ring of meaningless numbers. That's why it's powerful. That's why it's magic."

"Now I hope you see," the earl said, "what your astrolabe is *not*:

It is not a tool to perform a job; it is not a key to open a lock; it is not a map to guide you to the treasure; it is not a coded message to be deciphered; it is not a container of secret meanings that can be opened and revealed by some other, different tool, different key, different code, different map. It's an artfully constructed part of an artfully constructed engine which, by the maneuvering of meanings, holds open a space from which certain meanings are forever excluded, are always absent. That alone is what allows it to function—to work, if you insist on the language of the brewery—in the greater system."

"Like a great castle with no lord in it," Lavik said.

"Or a monastery from which the powerful priests have all gone," said Jenta.

"Or the Liberator's headquarters—" Pryn looked about the chamber—"in Neveryóna."

The earl frowned.

Just then Ardra stepped around Pryn. "Here you are." Reassembled, the astrolabe hung from its chain.

"That's really very good, Ardra," Jenta said. "That's very good."

"Your astrolabe functions in the system in its particular way," the earl went on, "because that is the way, finally, all signs function."

Ardra put the chain over Pryn's head—which surprised her, because she'd intended to take it back herself. "I never understood that part, either." The boy stepped back.

With some frustration, the earl turned to the parchment on which Belham's numbers were written in that strange script. "Take Belham's sign 'one.' Excluded from what it can mean are 'two,' 'three,' 'four,' 'five' 'six,' or 'twenty-two-divided-by-seven' . . ."

"Whereas it *can* mean an apple, a pear, a kumquat, a great castle, a lord, or even one other number," Lavik said. "They're *not* excluded."

"What *is* excluded from it—" the earl lowered his hand—"what it is empty *of,* alone, is what makes it meanin*gful.* Ardra, why are you up here anyway?"

"Oh." The boy blinked. "Well, I . . . I brought a message. From mother." He looked at the doorway.

The slave waited.

The earl, Jenta, and Lavik looked too—and Pryn had a suspicion they hadn't even seen the man till now.

"Oh, you brought a message. Well." The earl said. "What does the Lady Nyergrinkuga say?"

"My lord," the slave answered (Pryn was surprised at the voice, which was somehow shriller than she'd expected), "the lady says that dinner is ready."

"Dinner is ready," the earl repeated. "Oh. Thank you, Ardra. You may go—" this to the slave, who unfolded his arms, touched the back of his fist to his forehead, turned from the doorway, and hurried down. "Why don't we all go down, then? Shall we?"

Jenta walked up to Pryn and put his arm around her shoulder in a way that, for a moment felt comfortable and made her smile with the memory of the way the earl or Madame Keyne had been with the workers, but, a moment later, as they followed Ardra out through the door into the crevice steps, became, through its uncertainty of lightness and pressure, a man touching a woman—which, Pryn thought, had it been Inige rather than this hairy, affable, eldest son, would have been acceptable. Then, because of the narrowness of the crevice, his hand fell away; Jenta fell behind. Pryn glanced back to see the earl's cloak open as the little man descended after Lavik. Pryn hurried down, away from the tickling of the almost invisible gnats to the sunlight below.

"Myself, I suspect it's a kind of madness: the madness that makes one repeat whatever one is trained to repeat. Do you agree?" Inige asked from his couch beneath the brace of lamps. "Common sense says all the workers would need to do is demand ownership, and Rorkar certainly couldn't oppose them. Nevertheless, Yrnik comes in every morning and opens the brewery—whether Rorkar sleeps on the hill or no. Of course, the truth is that father's soldiers used to be called in, when, occasionally, the workers *did* try to take over. That ill-remembered association is the real bond between father and the peasant businessmen around here. Somehow, though, as father's soldiers drifted away, the rebellions ceased. The workers who *do* remember them have somehow got it confused, so that, when they talk about them today, it's the lack of soldiers—today—that makes rebellion unnecessary. And I'm sure no one talks to Yrnik about the men and women who held his job previously that father and Rorkar together ruined or removed or obliterated as thanks for their desire to better the lot of those around them. But that's the sort of thing Belham's language can't write of; and no one has yet cared to write them in the new script."

"Nor does anyone care to talk about it," said the earl.

"Is that what they teach you in the north is proper dinner conversation?" Tritty asked. "Really. You know," she turned back to Pryn, "Queen Olin, whom you were discussing with my husband, was often a guest here—at least in his Lordship's father's day." On her couch, she turned to the earl. "Or was it your father's father's?"

"You know, I was never really sure." The earl reached from his

couch to a tray, passing in the hands of a slave, piled with sliced and peeled kiwis, a fruit of which Pryn had never even heard before that evening. "It *is* hard to keep the past organized. And when the past is disorganized, the present is ... well, as you see it: all barbaric splendor—and misery. But as long as I can keep clear the principles by which the present orders itself, I suppose that's why I stay one of the most powerful of the remaining, real barbarian princes—'Earl' is the title the northern aristocracy has granted us. But the fine points of such terminology have never troubled me."

Lying on her back, Petal reached for unseen heights with, alternately, toes and fingers.

"My father is prince of one of the Seven Clans." Sitting on the floor by her own couch, Lavik gently shook the baby's foot. "The Dragon Clan, actually."

Suddenly Petal, with a great rock, *almost* turned over.

"—which hasn't existed *as* a clan," Inige added from his own couch, "for more than a hundred years ... which, I suspect, is what they've been saying in these parts for at least *five* hundred." He dropped a handful of tiny bird bones he'd collected in his palm into a dish on the carpet with all the other bird bones. "But that's the way in a world without history. And that, as the lawyers in the north with whom I shall go back to study in the fall all tell me, is what makes us, here *in* the south, barbarians!" He laughed.

So did the others.

Pryn wondered how one got to study with a lawyer—and wiped her fingers, which she could not bring herself to suck as they did of all the various food juices, on the brocade over the edge of the couch she had been given. For the third time she caught Ardra staring with a gaze that could as easily have masked astonishment as desire or loathing. Certainly she could see nothing wrong with her wipings, but within the blank look from the adopted son (a look that the others might simply have been too polite for), it was too easy to inscribe, along with desire in its positive or negative form, starkest disapproval. Her hand went back to her stomach, then behind her neck to scratch at the chain, then to her hip, then to the couch edge again—as if to work loose from the compass of his wide, wet eyes.

Her other elbow, propped on the embroidered bolster, was getting sore. Pryn shifted her position and wondered what she might eat now.

"But we're at it again." From her couch, Tritty ladled dark gravy over an impressive roast on a tray held by a young, white-collared woman with very wide shoulders, who took the meat off to a side table where an older man, with the same white collar, waited, carving knives poised. "*I* want to know where our guest has been, what *she's* seen, what's fascinated her most on *her* travels!"

"Yes," Jenta said. "Where have you been? What have you done?"

"What has fascinated you about it?" Lavik pulled the infant into her lap; the little creature curled up, closed her eyes, and began an infantile snore.

Pryn pushed herself further up, suffused again with pride at being the focus of such a gathering. "What I have been fascinated most by, in all my travels—indeed, what I began my travels with, caught up between its beating wings and flung out under the sun by it, to land wherever I might and make my way from there with only its chance trajectory for guide—indeed, what I love to observe, to gaze down into and explore its subterranean workings, is ... power!"

The earl's family listened, smiling—approving, Pryn decided.

"It's been an education," she went on, "finding the various places where it ... *writes*—" She could think of no other word—"its passage, its process, its however fleeting presence."

"And where," Jenta asked from his side of the room, "have you been observing all this power?"

"All over!" Pryn declared. "It's inscribed as clearly in the stone carvings above your mantel there—where some person must have hammered and pounded and chipped the stone to chisel it to shape—as it is in Old Rorkar's oldest—" she started to say 'slave bench,' but because a slave passed between them, said, "beer barrel, whose staves someone must have shaved down and whose edges someone must have pitched together and whose rope bindings someone must have tied on with wet rope so that it would shrink dry!" She looked about again, wondering if, indeed, the barrel makers here were the same women who made rope-bound barrels in fabled Ellamon. "Where I got a chance to observe it most closely, I think, was in the city." (The expectant smiles of her country listeners did not change.) "In Kolhari. There I fought along with the Liberator against the intrigues and conspiracies that wove about his efforts to free all the slaves of Nevèrÿon." There, she'd said it!

"Free the slaves?" Tritty asked. "Well, all of us have had our problems with the institution. Between the time I was at court and the time Lavik went, they've forbidden slaves there. And I thoroughly approve—there's just no need for them in the city." Tritty nodded to one of the white-collared servers who passed among the couches again with another platter of fruit, on whose red and purple rinds the lamplight slid and slipped. "But you say *all* the slaves of Nevèrÿon? Someone is actually lobbying for their freedom? Of course it's *not* the same situation in the country. Still, it sounds like an advance."

"Tritty—" Pryn laughed—"someone is fighting for it tooth and nail! He himself wears an iron slave collar and has sworn not to remove it till slavery in Nevèrÿon is gone forever. I've seen plots of unbelievable insidiousness launched against him! I've seen more blood spilled in his cause in a day than, indeed, I've ever seen spilled in my life!"

"He sounds like a powerful man." Inige smiled in a way that, for a moment, made Pryn sure that in his northern law study he'd learned more of the Liberator than she could ever know.

"He's called Gorgik, and his name makes people pause in the poorest alleys and the wealthiest homes throughout Kolhari."

"I'm only surprised," the earl said, "that we've never heard of him here. We had guests from Kolhari only days ago; he wasn't mentioned."

"Oh, he *is* a powerful man," Pryn said. "When I left, he'd at last secured an audience with one of the Empress's own ministers to plead his cause!"

It was Inige's chuckle that broke the silence. "You know, the Empress has over a dozen ministers, advisers, viziers, and vizerines. All day every day, groups and individuals meet and confer with all of them, pleading, begging, demanding, cajoling, sometimes trying to bribe, sometimes trying to reason. Most such petitions, as you must know, are of necessity refused. To receive such an audience does not necessarily mark your man as powerful—if anything, the fact that he has only just received such an audience suggests he is among the *least* powerful of that city's numerous players in the game of magic and power."

"Oh, I don't think—" Pryn paused. "But that was not all. I met an important merchant woman with a great home in the suburb of Sallese. She was helping finance the construction of Kolhari's New Market, as well as building a whole set of warehouses for—"

Lavik's laughter was louder than Inige's chuckle. "But nobody who's anybody lives in—" Lavik stopped, looking around to catch her parents' reproving gaze. She cuddled her sleeping child a little closer, still smiling.

"I think—" Inige said—"what my sister was trying, in her way, to say is that it's a little surprising for us to hear of a truly powerful personage living in such a neighborhood. That's not the usual sign by which power can be read from an account of a person's—"

"Neighborhoods *do* change—" Tritty suggested.

"What," Inige said over his stepmother, "is this powerful ... merchant, you say? What is this merchant's name? Most of the real power in Kolhari resides either at court or in the homes of royalty in the suburb of Neveryóna."

"She lives right at the *edge* of Neveryóna," Pryn said.

"No," Tritty muttered, "that isn't the best part of the neighborhood ..."

"—and she really *is* rich. Her name is Madame Keyne."

"Ah, a Madame Keyne?" Tritty said. Then: "Really, that kind of snideness from my stepdaughter is most unseemly. And yet it's no secret to us, so while you are a guest in our house it shouldn't be kept from you. We who move in court circles have always tended to consider Sallese a neighborhood of pretentious tradesmen and vulgar commercial interests, people who would ape and mimic the accoutrements of power, mystifying and declaring magic those elements that were beyond them or that they simply did not understand."

"Belham made her fountains ..." Pryn said, hesitantly.

"He also lived in your aunt's shack," the earl said. "Is there a way to put this delicately? Belham was a brilliant man. But the careers of the brilliant are not always rising flights."

"Myself," Jenta said, "I always thought that from the way we went on about the vulgarities of Sallese—at least back when I was at court, or visiting Neveryóna—meant there was *some*thing going on there."

"Now," the earl said, "my eldest son speaks the truth." He gave a wise nod (the exact nature of whose wisdom Pryn did not quite follow, as she had decided on a mango and had found that a bite taken from one direction was deliciously juicy, while a bite from another made it all string and pith). "I told you, we had guests here just recently from Kolhari, and there, so said our guests, the talk is indeed of many great, far-reaching projects. And there was, from time to time, even in these halls, mention that some of the better-connected Sallese residents have joined their moneys with some of our truly powerful friends in Neveryóna—"

"Our friends," Ardra said from where he'd moved again to the bottom of the steps, "don't like it, either."

"There was talk, I believe—" the earl pondered a moment—"of a project that will take some ten years to complete, which would involve doubling the length of the Kolhari waterfront, rebuilding it dock by dock. Was your Madame Keyne one of the tradesmen who'd agreed to lend some support to this great undertaking?"

 318

"Oh, no—" Pryn began. "At least I don't *know* if she was. She never mentioned it."

"There was also some talk, as I recall, about another project to repave the entire southern road that runs from Kolhari to the Garth and beyond." Inige spooned up some spiced mush from a glimmering tureen, which Pryn had first declined but was now having second thoughts about—though the slave carrying it did not seem inclined to give her a second chance. (How *did* one ask?) "They want to expand it along its whole length to something like three times its present width till it's as wide in the north as it used to be at this end in the heyday of Neveryóna—our Neveryóna, that is. Then Rorkar and the rest can export their goods to Kolhari with ease. The smugglers who run their tiny amounts up and down would be driven out of operation, and both import and export for the whole south could be reorganized along real profit lines. There *were* some Sallese people involved in this project, too—although we're talking about an undertaking whose completion time is estimated at twenty years. Was one of them perhaps your Madame Keyne?"

"I don't . . ." Pryn was uneasy. "I don't *think* so. She never spoke of it."

Lavik made a cooing grimace over the baby, now asleep in the crook of her knee. She looked up. "Of course there are some truly powerful merchants, or what have you, in Sallese. And as much as it irks us, we're forced to hear their names too. But they are the people who are involved in enterprises that will change the shape of Kolhari, and thus the future of Nevèrÿon. They are the ones who are engaged in projects that might well *make* it reasonable to build one, or ten, or twenty-five new markets. And no doubt one, or ten, or twenty-five new markets will be built by one or ten or twenty-five canny, money-grubbing pot vendors run amok. But you mustn't confuse that with power—with *real* power—any more than you let yourself confuse the notoriety of some radical upstart, wrangling a hearing from a court minister while friends and enemies both mumble that at any moment he may become the next emperor, with the power of court itself. Come." She hoisted the baby under a plump arm and pushed to one knee. "Take a walk with me outside. We'll be having cheeses and wines in a few minutes. I always like a turn about the nearer gardens after I've eaten. And no matter what that old iron-bound harridan upstairs says, the evening air *is* good for the baby!" Lavik pushed the edge of her couch with her free hand to stand.

"Oh, can I carry her!" Pryn cried, impelled as much by anxiety over the haphazard way Lavik lugged her drooping daughter as by

319

a childhood conviction that babies were the warmest, sweetest, most wonderful things in the world—a conviction that had vanished, she'd noted, when she'd thought she might be having one but that, now she knew she wasn't, had apparently returned.

"Sure!" Lavik extended the child, even more awkwardly.

From Tritty: "Dear, don't stay out with her *too* long. Of course, I don't mean that I object . . ."

The baby didn't fall; but Pryn was there to take the warm, wheezing thing as though she might.

From the steps came an adolescent grunt.

Cuddling the snoring baby in its loose swaddling, Pryn glanced at Ardra.

He sat with a fist on each knee. "You know, *I* usually take Petal for her evening walk around the grounds!"

"Oh, darling . . . !" his mother said from her couch.

"I only let you do that last night because you asked," Lavik said. "It isn't a ritual. Besides, when you play with her, you always pretend she's going to grow up to be a little general. I don't know whether I like that."

"Well it's only fair that I get a chance to play with her before she grows and becomes a *girl*—don't you think?" Ardra stood. "I'm going for a walk around the near gardens anyway. Just as though we didn't *have* a guest." He strode across the room, in stiff-legged mocking of a military strut.

"If he really wants to—" began Pryn, while the earl and Tritty and Jenta all thrust out consoling hands and uttered stabilizing protests. The last voice over all was Tritty's: ". . . to learn that he can't always have his own way!"

But Ardra was out the door.

"Come on," Lavik said. "I think it's important that lots of people hold her, so that she gets a sense of the range of society. Don't you think?"

The sleeping Petal probably had little sense of anything right now. Shoulder to shoulder with Lavik, Pryn carried the baby between the dining couches. Behind them Tritty clapped her hands; the room filled about them with white-collared men and women, some younger than Pryn, others quite old, some of whom Pryn had already seen serving, many of whom she hadn't. Lavik led her through a smaller arch. "If you get tired, just let me know."

Pryn had expected to pass through at least as many corridors and halls as she had on her journey in with Tritty. But they walked through a low, stone passage with blackness at its end, and stepped out into it . . . Pryn thought they'd entered some cavernous hall, a

roofless one with dozens of lamps set at unfathomable distances, making myriad small lights . . .

But they were outdoors.

What she'd thought lamps were flares about an expanse of garden that, it was clear, even in the dark, would have dwarfed Madame Keyne's walled enclosure. Pryn remembered the plural that had always accompanied their references to the grounds. *One* of the gardens? They walked along a path, paved—they passed a flare and Pryn glanced down—with brick. Yellow? Red? Some other color? She couldn't tell. In the distance, holding aloft more brands, each with its raddled smoke ribboning up into the darkness over its own pale halo, moving along other paths, pausing here and there to light another pathside flare, moved innumerable slaves!

Some dozen steps ahead walked resolute Ardra—though Pryn only realized who it was when he passed one of the brands.

Lavik said: "He thinks he's protecting us."

Pryn glanced at her. "From what?"

"Was *your* home ever occupied by soldiers?"

Pryn shook her head.

"Ours was, once. Right after dad and Tritty first married. I was ten. Ardra was only three, so you wouldn't think he'd remember. But *he* became the occupying soldiers' mascot. Tritty'd been through things like that before—so had dad, I suppose. But for me and Inige—and Jenta too, I guess—it was awful." She sighed. "Ardra, however, hasn't thought about anything but growing up to be a soldier ever since. I *say* he's protecting us. Sometimes, though, I think he dreams of slaughtering us all in our beds. The soldiers who were here—when I was ten—did some of *that* too! Jenta is dad's oldest *living* son. But we used to have two more half-sisters and a half-brother, by his first wife—only she was related to all the wrong people; they wouldn't let her—so we heard later—*or* her children live." Lavik hunched her shoulders. "It wasn't pleasant. Believe me, that's the only reason dad tolerates my running off to have babies with jungle savages or Jenta's going off to live like a hermit with a girl goatherd, nice as she is, from the next town over. I mean it's a way of survival, of putting us outside the normal political considerations of bloodlines and alliances and the like— the sort of things that get you clapped into dungeons or murdered, when you're really interested in other things entirely. What real power can buy, of course, is anonymity, and dad *doesn't* have enough for that. So we use other means. Now with Ardra, of course, it's different." Lavik nodded ahead at the would-be captain, stalking the garden night. "Thanks to the people *he's* related to,

321

both through Tritty and his real father, he doesn't have our options. Oh, he's safer here than he would be in the north—and don't think Tritty isn't grateful to father, either. The odd thing is, though, he's turning out exactly the way he should. Inige and I have spent *hours* discussing it! Oh, I don't mean the way dad would want him to be, or even his mother. But he's exactly the sort they're going to want to do all the jobs that are waiting for him as soon as he comes of age. You'd think there was some sort of power guiding it all." She took a large breath and gave a small sigh. "Really, it's uncanny. I wish there were something I could do to make him a little ... I don't know—looser, I suppose. But maybe it's just as well. I'm glad you're here," she said suddenly. "I mean it's nice to have ordinary visitors who aren't always plotting to do someone in—especially when it's you. Honestly, we *all* think so!"

"I'm ... glad I'm here too!" Pryn looked at the young man walking ahead, whom, she felt now, she'd deprived of the warm, marvelous responsibility she held.

The warmth shifted; the breathing changed.

Pryn looked down. "She'll be all right, don't you think?"

"Sure," Lavik said. "She's been on the mend for two, really three, days now. Though, if you listen to the old slaves upstairs, who, for some reason, everyone thinks *know* about such things—and that's all Tritty ever listens to—they'll scare you to death!" She glanced at Petal over Pryn's arm to check her own pronouncement of recuperation. "She'll be fine. You know—" Lavik's tone grew thoughtful— "I was thinking about something you said—to father, when we were up on the hill. When you travel to Kolhari from the south, the road really goes around the marsh below the city, joins the northern road, and enters over the same hills you come over from the mountains. But you've seen it on maps ... ?"

"Yes?" Pryn said, listening to the dark around them, which sounded the same tone on which Lavik spoke.

"Do you remember," Lavik asked, "when I said I'd never seen Kolhari at dawn from the hills?"

"Yes?"

"Well, when I went to court, it wasn't just *my* furniture in the provision wagon. In fact I went with nearly a dozen nobles' children, boys and girls—more girls than boys, actually. When we reached the hills above the city, they stopped our sleeping carriage—it was dawn. We all woke up, the few of us who'd managed to sleep. The drivers and chaperones called the boys out to see. *Every*one started out, I remember, but they told the girls that we had to stay inside, because it wasn't seemly for young ladies go pell-melling out on

the highroad in their night shifts, even if it was dawn and nobody was about. So *we* stayed in, all excited at what the two—yes, there were *only* two—boys might be doing. And you know something? As soon as he came back from court, Jenta *immediately* saw the city in the water—Neveryóna. Just the way you did. But *I* couldn't! We'd both always heard about it, of course. But it had to be explained to me, and the streets and alleys and buildings had to be pointed out and outlined before, at sunset, I could even be sure it was really there! And it was only because I *had* seen some city maps of Kolhari, finally, that I was able to be sure what the rest were talking about." They walked through the dark gardens, whose extent and plan Pryn kept silently trying to assess. "Do you *know* what a map is? I mean a real map?"

"Yes . . ." Responding to Lavik's deep seriousness, Pryn spoke a little lower. "Of course. Of course I do."

"You've *seen* one?" Lavik asked. "I don't just mean the silly scratches on the astrolabe this evening that don't mean anything at all."

"Well, I've certainly heard of them," Pryn said. "Heard people speak of them and describe what they do. Sailors use them for navigating coastlines—my aunt explained to me about that. And I've seen *one* of them, anyway."

"What did it look like?" Lavik asked.

"Well, it was . . . made of clay and stuff. It was of a garden. It was covered with something that had the same texture as grass. And little molded trees were set about on it. And a toy house. Water ran through the space where the stream went, down the falls, and over bits of ceramic molded like rocks and statues—"

Lavik laughed, quietly and shyly. "*That's* a garden maquette! We've got over a dozen, scattered among the maintenance sheds all over the grounds. They make it easier for the gardeners to keep the plants in order if you've really got extensive landscaped property— another one of Belham's notions. Most gardeners, you know, don't read—maps or anything else. But *you've* never seen a map . . . !" In the dark she looked at Pryn. They passed a flare, and her serious, southern face brightened—flickering—and faded.

Pryn looked away in the dark and saw nothing.

"You *haven't* seen a map! A map is just marks on a piece of parchment. Oh, you can read distances and directions on it—but not much else." Lavik paused. "I *knew* you'd never seen one. Somehow, from things you said, I just knew you hadn't really seen one. *I've* never seen a city—I mean a real one, from outside it, all at once! And *you've* never seen a map!"

Pryn looked back at Lavik, who now looked away—and who sounded as alone as Pryn had ever felt. Pryn watched her, and felt as close to her as she had ever felt to anyone. After a few moments, Pryn looked away, so that she could not see if Lavik looked back at her.

Petal coughed.

The two plump young women, one a mother and one all but motherless, walked through the dark garden, shoulder brushing shoulder, bare feet now loud and now soft on the leaf-strewn brick, and were alone together.

Ahead, Ardra's back, in the rough cloth, became visible as he passed another torch.

"Something in the way you talked about it just made me sure you'd never seen one," Lavik repeated. "Though I swear, I couldn't tell you what. I don't know, but once you have a baby, you feel a lot of things—but you don't do too much analytical thinking."

"I know," Pryn said, who, in fabled Ellamon, had baby-sat for many of her cousins' children and had been, for days at a time, the sole care of her baker cousin's two-year-old son. "When I take care of one for more than three hours at a stretch, *I* can't think at all! That's why I don't want to have any myself." She hugged Petal, sweet and sick as she was, who felt wonderful.

"Oh, that's not *true!*" Lavik protested. "I mean, well ... after a week or so, you begin to think again. A little bit, at least. You really do. That is, *if* you take care of it all by yourself. Of course once the slaves begin taking over, *then* what you spend all your time thinking about is how to get them to take over *more.* But you really do get back to some ... thinking. Eventually—I think."

"*I* think," Pryn said, "that babies are wonderful and beautiful and comforting and rewarding, the solace of the present and the hope—the real hope—of the future." She sighed. "And I *don't* want one. At least not now."

"Mmm," Lavik said.

Pryn glanced at the young woman beside her and saw her looking ahead at her step-brother.

"Well," Lavik said, "I *feel* the same way; and I *am* glad I have mine. Now. And ..." She looked down at the brick—"I'll die a thousand deaths if she *does* die. But still, I don't see how anyone who *has* taken care of one couldn't understand what you say." When she looked up in the passing flare, her face bore her family's absolute smile.

Pryn looked at the stiff-kneed boy marching ahead of them and wished he *would* come and carry little Petal, who, small as she was,

had begun to seem heavy—for now Pryn also felt that, without the baby between them, she might be able to talk about more with Lavik. At the same time, she resolved not to offer Petal back to her mother until they were again inside the house.

Lavik said: "It *is* nice of you to carry her for me. I appreciate it."

Pryn wondered if her great-aunt had felt the same way when she'd been presented with Pryn's own, wiggling, wheezing self by Pryn's mother, fifteen—well, a month shy of sixteen, now—years ago.

"We're almost at the door." Lavik touched Pryn's arm. The path had taken them in a circle through the near night.

Ahead, Ardra walked up to a vast, mottled nothingness and disappeared into it: the door.

Then Pryn, Lavik, and Petal went through it too.

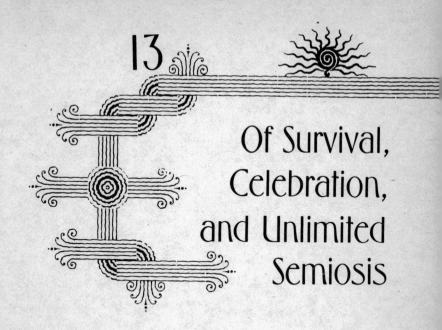

13

Of Survival, Celebration, and Unlimited Semiosis

> ... *those who fail to reread are obliged to read the same*
> *story everywhere* ... [Barthes]
What does this paradoxical statement imply? First, it implies
that a single reading is composed of the already-read, that
what we can see in a text the first time is already in us, not in it;
in us insofar as we ourselves are a stereotype, an already-read
text; and in the text only to the extent that the already-read is
that aspect of a text that it must have in common with its
reader in order for it to be readable at all. When we read a text
once, in other words, we can see in it only what we have
already learned to see before.
> —Barbara Johnson/*The Critical Difference*

"There." Tritty pointed to the goblets on the tray the elderly
slavewoman carried: their sides were joined slabs of vitric red and
blue, framed in cast metal, hugely heavy.

"And here ..." The earl lifted a thin pitcher from a tray of
pitchers the red-headed slaveboy brought up. "This one's yours."
He tilted it—and Pryn quickly brought her goblet, in both hands,
beneath the lip. Water-clear and tossing back firelight from the
lamps' flaming and the goblet's own glistening sides, liquid filled it.

Because it was so heavy, she lifted it quickly to taste: the coldest
water, with a fruity ghost—sharpness interrupted, which made her
take a larger swallow in memory of initial cool.

Greater sharpness made her head reel.

The earl set the pitcher down, picked up another, and poured
dark liquid into the goblet Lavik held.

"Now you *must* tell us your own story." Inige came over with his
own goblet, which his father filled from still another pitcher with
something opaque and green. "Tritty's right. It always happens
when you invite guests that you expect to entertain. All you end up
doing is trying to impress them. You must tell a story of your own,
because we really want to hear it!"

"Ardra," Tritty said, "come here and have your drink. It's tradition, darling."

"I don't *like* the blue," Ardra said. "I think the red tastes better." He stood up from the stone steps, strode forward, picked up a goblet from the proffered tray, a pitcher from the other, and poured himself a goblet of blue liquid, set the pitcher back on the tray, went to the steps, and, taking a noisy sip, sat.

"*Ardra* . . . !" Tritty said.

"The trouble with stories—" Pryn laughed—"is that when I write them in my head, they're fun because I can write them slowly, make changes, correct them if they're wrong, make sure all the names have the right initial signs. But if I *tell* them, then they come out any-old-how or however. I don't think I'll ever be a tale-teller. I suppose I could tell about my trip from Ellamon to Kolhari, the men who captured me, or the women, or what happened to me later in the city—only . . ." She blinked about the room and, in momentary embarrassment, took a long, throat-burning draught. The strange sharpness struck. She coughed. "Only . . . I don't really understand all that happened, myself. And besides—" She coughed again—"you're not very interested in the people I met, which is all I could talk about anyway . . ."

Pryn thought she saw their hand-waving protests, but heat blurred her eyes and made her unsteady. Somebody put a hand on her shoulder—she fell, or sat (she'd *thought* she was going to fall . . .) on the couch behind her.

She still held the goblet.

"Are they going to bring the baby back down again . . . ? I suppose it's too late. I could tell about when I came south from Kolhari. This man I came with; and his friend. Smugglers—only I'd be embarrassed to; besides, *I'm* not interested in those people anymore . . . though they taught me enough. A story?" She took another long sip from the metal rim, because the drink's effect seemed the less the more of it she swallowed—this one didn't burn so. Was her mouth numbing? "A story. Well. There was an ordinary, fifteen-year-old girl who looked like a beautiful young queen . . . or was there a queen who looked like an ordinary, bushy-headed girl?"

"This sounds like a *real* story!" she heard Inige say.

Pryn smiled.

Her goblet was vast as the torchlit sea, its clear wines sloshing pink and blue slopes.

". . . only I can't remember what version I'm supposed to . . . I could tell them all. Now . . . after the girl had done all sorts of terrible things and learned all sorts of magical things, in their

330

proper sequence, her maternal father ..." Pryn frowned into the drink, which seemed to have cloudy streaks through it, perhaps from her own spittle. "In one version, it's her dead father, I think. In another its her maternal ... uncle—he took her up into a stone chamber, on a hill, or in a tower, just like yours I guess, where she saw a ... city!" Pryn looked up and narrowed her eyes in the lamplight's dazzle. Tears banked her lower lids, obscuring the backlit listeners reclining about the chamber. "At a great dinner for her—really, this has been a *wonderful* dinner! I've never eaten food like this before in my life or drunk such ... at a great dinner, her absent father, or her maternal uncle did *some*thing terrible ..."

The silence broke in lingering waves; after lots of it, Ardra said, swinging his fists between his knees: "It's a good story. We all know it. And that's a good place to pause. But it doesn't end there. You have to go on."

Pryn took another drink that was so cold yet made her so warm. She blinked. "... He did something *terrible*. Only I don't remember ... his family name. There's good reason to remember it, only I don't know if I ever knew what it was." One of them had moved ...

Pryn looked up on red. Her eyes moved up over red. It was Tritty's dress, because Tritty's face was at the top, smiling down.

Tritty touched her shoulder. "That's a marvelous story—one I've loved for years. We all have. Old stories are the best, I think. That's one of the most beautifully crafted parts of the engine to raise Neveryóna. But you *can't* sit here and tell me you've forgotten the family name of the queen's maternal uncle! That's the whole point—at least it is if you're telling it to us!"

"I'm *not* a good tale-teller," Pryn apologized. "I'd much rather write it down, where I could think about what I'm supposed to be saying." She felt unsteady, unhappy, and out of place. "If there weren't the pressure of having to *tell* it, I could find out the real story, all of it. I could write why it means something special to me, too, as well as you—"

"Jue-Grutn," Tritty prompted. "Go on, now. We all know it, so it doesn't *matter* how well you tell it. Jue-Grutn was the family name of the queen's maternal uncle. The name of my husband—and his father; and his father's father. With *very* old stories, such distinctions cease to matter. But that's the part we love to hear most—here. Whenever we can, we get a guest to ... But it's part of the engine—my husband said he was explaining it upstairs? We have a vested interest, of course. I'm sure you can understand ..."

Pryn's gaze lost itself in her shimmering drink. "The Earl Jue-Grutn gave her ..."

Then, at once, what shimmered was terror. Whether it was inside her or outside her, she didn't know. She didn't move.

Under flamelight, liquid flashed.

Did she hurl the heavy goblet?

Did she scream?

Did she throw out an arm, upsetting some small table?

Did she overturn her couch as she stood, so that the bolsters flopped on the carpet?

Did she lurch across the floor, shoving aside first Inige and then Lavik, who moved to stop her?

Later she was able to reason that she had done at least three and had definitely not done one. But which three and which one, though she would list them and list them on wax, clay, and parchment in every conceivable order, she was never sure. Was it the Wild Ini's blade she waved above her head? Was it a carving knife snatched from the side-table that made Jenta spread his arms and fall back, while the earl came up behind him, then turn to grab Ardra, who'd rushed forward. She remembered the earl's cloak, flung up and out, tenacious of its blues in lamplight. Did he try to stop her? Did she run into it? Or through it? Someone yelled, "Stop her!" Certainly it was the earl and not she who bellowed, "The astrolabe, no—!" Certainly someone yelled, "No, don't let her—!" But she was out one arch or another.

And nothing, really, was certain.

Did she run through myriad halls, searching through corridors and chambers for an exit? Did slaves in white collar-covers run out and, confused at her career, step back? Did she plunge through the low stone passage to burst into the black garden, starred with lamps—

She pushed through hangings, half-opened doors, bushes, branches, into dark. She remembered grasping a branch to come to an unsteady halt—torchbearing men passed below the rock she swayed on, Inige at their head, iron and white cloth about the other necks, talking: "This way ... gone in this direction ... you said you heard ..." mixed with the barbarian tongue. Later she hesitated on a muddy stretch before a stubbly field, out on which she could see a leafless tree—so there must have been moonlight ... ? She had no memory of a moon. Were there voices? She dashed across the stubble, hearing her feet slap in the ground below the grass, wetter than she'd thought. She plunged into dappled dark that cut her and tickled her and beat her hips and shoulders, catching in the chain about her neck as if the twigs were trying to snatch away the clinking astrolabe, which she would have gladly torn off her neck and given up. She'd *said* she didn't want it ...

 332

. . . blinking, trying to push herself up, with pebbles under her hands. She blinked again, at something huge and pale. She tried to turn her face away from it before she realized it *was* the moon, bigger than she had ever seen a moon in the mountains, just above the horizon—which rippled.

Pryn pushed back, pebbles under her hip, dragging her feet beneath her. Pebbles rolled down the slope. She looked up at a tall rock, with trees beyond it. She looked behind her. Another rocky finger prodded crookedly at the night, but shorter.

Both rocks were chalky white.

Pryn pushed to sitting, dragging her heels back, and locked her arms about her knees, resting her chin on them, in a lucidity that seemed near sickness, though if she didn't move, she might be all right. She bit her inner lip and looked across rippling fog.

At the moon . . .

Cawing, and she looked up—to see leaves fall and what seemed a flurry of leaves; only it was the bird itself, momentarily at the proper angle for her to catch the wing's green before ivory light leached all color. In a chatter of little stones and leaves, Pryn suddenly pushed to her feet. She stepped to the ledge.

Below rolled fog; below that, water. Pryn blinked. Wave rolled over wave. Taking a great breath, which made her stomach ill and her balance shaky, she shouted as loud as she could: "I am Pryn, and I have come to warn the Worm of the Sea of the Blue Heron's . . . !" She did not know where the words came from, nor their proper conclusion. But a sudden gout, breaking silver above the mist, made her push the heel of her hand up hard against her mouth and step back.

Through the ripplings at the slope's foot something else . . . rippled. Now catching light and glimmering, it looked like water. Dark and heaving, it seemed a solider fog.

Out there . . . ?

Something splashed and she looked off at it.

Somewhere else, a splash—Pryn looked over there. There was another, below her. She looked down: water broke like a metallic flower, falling open and dropping shattered petals into mist, beautiful and burning in the chill.

The ground's shaking was almost too slight to feel. Then a whisper only as loud as the slightest breeze by her ear grew to a tremble, a roar.

She thought to sit again, lest she be thrown. But she saw, at three places, fog break from something solid and dark as power.

Not fog.

Stone.

Dripping and streaming, stone poured water into fog. The towers rose, two taller, one smaller, a bridge between the three, spurting out windows, spilling through newels.

Sea foamed. Buildings shrugged water into it. There and there were other roofs, a broken wall, more walls standing, two buildings: one nearly whole supported one nearly collapsed.

Driven from the sea, fog hung above her, before her, about her. She stood in an emptiness she knew was permeated with mist she could not see. Frothing, the water mixed jade and ivory. Enough buildings had risen to see streets. Where two crossed, water whirled, swirled, rushed out by the walls.

A wall fell . . . ?

No, a mud bank broke from stone, to slosh off between the ruins.

Pryn saw them first as a row of regular eruptions in the rush.

Six, seven, eight, nine carvings cleared the flood, which, as the water lowered, were the capitals of nine columns, one of the line—the sixth or seventh—missing.

The columns rose. Weeds strung away. Water lowered more. Weeds dropped on algae-filmed stone. The column fallen across its base rose above the ripples. Some of the muddy streets were paved with patterned blue flags. Other buildings had broken columns before them . . .

That was when she saw it, glittering.

The earth rumbled; the water raged. Muddied and weed-streaked, it still gleamed, so much of it as had washed free of mud and refuse. Whatever desires she'd pushed away to give it up surged back, like foam, like wind. She *didn't* want to take any—only to see it from closer . . . only perhaps a *few* coins.

There was so *much* of it!

It filled alleys. Glimmering, it spilled into wider avenues. There, that must have been a whole house, or even several small houses, piled over with it.

Half running, half falling down the embankment, Pryn only managed to get her feet under her when they plunged shin-deep in mud. She staggered on, arms wheeling, till she reached the first pavement. Weeds in windows hung on wet stone. Mud clung to the wall beside her. Fallen masonry, broken shells, and soaked branches made her progress by the dripping pillars as slow as it had been in the silt. Dirty-footed, wet-handed, scratches on her shoulders and legs, Pryn edged between cold rocks, pushed away a cool branch of driftwood, moved close along a broken wall, its carvings veiled in moss.

She could *see* gold at that alley's end!

334

But the tiny street was too blocked and clotted with some half-fallen building to get through. Did it move ...? In the heaps of nuggets, trinkets, coins, did some tremor in the risen seafloor cause that momentary cascade of wet metal?

That's when she remembered the dragon.

Pryn looked up. Beyond the broken cornice, yellow fogs drifted, luminous before a moon she could no longer see. But I *only* want to see it ... Pryn took hold of her astrolabe, as cold as if it, too, had lain in the waters. She moved to the building corner, looked around it ...

Six wagon-loads ...? *Only* six? More like six *hundred* ...! Heaping the far side of the yard, most of it was yellow, but a lot was iron-dark with tarnish or silver-green with algae. What part of the ruins were under that sloping glimmer?

The heaped treasure was mountainous!

Pryn looked the other way at the half-crumbled cistern, beyond which were more free-standing columns—and started! But the gleaming head, demonic, half on its side, was also gold ...

Then the mountains moved!

A ripple passed over the glimmering slope—not the shimmer from high to low of tumbling coins, but sideways, over the whole of it; then another ripple, bottom to top. Gold unfolded over gold.

The building corner struck Pryn, buttock and shoulder blade. (She hadn't realized she'd been backing away.) Rising, gold articulated along some glittering numismatic pleat, then along another fanning from it, then yet along another. Between, the loose and flashing folds billowed and rose, a wing scaled with coins, taut, spined, darkening a fifth the sky, dragging its shadow over the yard, opaque to all moonlight with its auric load, yet still glittering within its black, become beast, become Gauine herself.

Beyond the columns, the golden head rolled upright and—looked at her!

Mouth open, Pryn crouched, back against uneven stone. Somewhere, distant in the ruins, another gold wing rose above roofs.

The head slid. Some half-standing wall fell before the huge muzzle rose. Black puddles in pits of crumpled foil, the eyes, now one, now the other, lowered slow, brazen lids and lifted them. Hovering above the columns, above the smashed cistern, above Pryn, the long, ragged lip, clotted with gems, lifted from teeth not gold but stained bone, some whole, some split, all hilted in coral gum.

Pryn pushed back, slipped, almost went sprawling, but got her feet under her. Standing she looked up. The great wings, first one, then the other, moved.

She heard wind.

She heard water.

She took another breath and called, loud enough to hurt her throat: "Oh great Gauine, I have come to give my treasure ..." She stopped.

Because the golden head, staring down, that rose and rose above her, now descended!

Fear? Terror? What she felt was not terror, because the beast above her *was* terror itself, and to gaze up at it—all jaws and eyes—was to watch, as jaws opened and eyes blinked, terror's articulations entirely from without. She felt herself in some reckless state where ecstasy and obliviousness, daring and distraction, were one.

The gesture came from the same place as the words, though—then—she could not have said where that was. She grasped the chain at her neck and pulled it over her head. First it caught under her ear, then in her hair, but she yanked it loose.

Pryn hurled the astrolabe as high and hard as she could.

Gauine roared.

Gauine beat her wings.

The sea and the winds leaped to answer.

And Pryn ran.

Gauine's roaring didn't stop.

Pryn's feet splashed on streaming flags. She pushed from a slim pillar swaying on its pediment, dodged shaking driftwood. Water rilled at her ankles, rushing. Pryn went off paving—into mud!

Mud shook.

Mud quivered.

Beating at her, splashing about her, the water wet her knees. She slogged, flailing. Water was at her waist. Pryn fell, grasping foam, but came up spluttering and this time grabbed the root sticking from the embankment, managed to pull herself up, now going crabwise on the slope, coughing and trying to spit the salt from her throat. (Her aunt had never told her the sea was salt!) She didn't remember gaining the ledge. But she remembered backing through low bushes, her shift dripping down the backs of her thighs.

Water spilled together over the unbearable city.

She remembered coming out from trees again, and again, and then again to the edge of the rocks, with the inlet spread before her, a few sand bars interrupting the glitter that the night breeze unraveled over the whole of it.

The moon was high and small.

She remembered walking in the moon-speckled forest.

She remembered sitting wide awake with her eyes closed.

 336

She remembered walking a *lot* more.

She remembered blinking, with leaves blocking deep blue.

Leaning against tree bark, she realized that it was dew-wet, that the leaves against her shins were wet too, and that perhaps it had just rained in the faint dawn-light.

She squatted by some bare ground, where the sick feeling passed long enough for her to pick up a twig and scratch her name in the wet dirt. Something was wrong with it—it lacked both capital and diacritic! Again the nausea welled, but it was not as strong as it had been for hours now. She stood, temples throbbing, a stinging along the backs of her legs from squatting so long.

Pryn moved among trees.

She first realized she was on brewery grounds when, at the hillcrest, she saw Old Rorkar's house. Up the nearer slope was the workers' barracks, where she slept. Down there was the office shed. She remembered taking a momentary account: her name *was* Pryn—she *did* know how to write it. In the pockets of her dress were . . . no iron coins? Her blade—Ini's blade . . . ? But Tratsin's carving tool—no, the earl's carving knife; or some memory that doubled them both . . . at any rate, it had gone even before the city had risen. Pryn blinked, frowned, and remembered what had occurred. Almost like relief, the nausea welled again, driving it from her mind. She opened her mouth, taking shallow breaths. Her few coins and the Ini's blade were under her straw in the barracks.

Pryn felt at her neck.

The chain and astrolabe were, yes, gone.

Her hand went to her hair, found a leaf, and pulled it away. I must look like someone who's slept in the woods! she thought. The nausea passed again, leaving her still unsteady. Her mouth was very dry.

Standing with a hand on the tree beside her, Pryn felt two conflicting urges. One was to go to her barracks, take her knife, her coins, and strike out on the north road without a word. The other was to go down past the cooling caves, cross the road to the eating hall, take her morning bowl of soup—Rorkar always said, though Pryn had only heard it quoted, 'A heavy meal in the morning slows the worker till noon'—and fall into her usual routine, again without a word.

". . . a kind of madness," she whispered. Someone had said that recently. But she was not sure who or why.

There was another urge, of course: to go into the barracks, lie down on her straw, and sleep; but because she was fifteen, and because this was a salaried job, and because the job carried

a double title that separated her somehow from the others, she dismissed that one as childish—though in five or ten years it might well have been the one she would follow. As it was, while she decided between the first two, the hide-covered planks of the barracks door were set aside and one, then three, then five women came out. (The women usually managed to leave before the men.) A few more came—one waited for a friend who joined her.

Pryn stepped behind the tree.

Two barbarian men came out.

They were all headed for the eating hall.

Three more women left, two with their children behind and before them. One barbarian shooed the snoring eight-year-old out ahead of her with gestures for which Pryn could hear Tritty saying, "Now Ardra ...!" Would Petal snore when she was older? Would Lavik make such gestures? But Tritty and Ardra, Pryn remembered, weren't barbarians anyway, were from further north, or east, or west ... What Pryn decided, because she was that kind of young woman, was to follow both her first two urges.

More women came out of the barracks—which meant her end of the dim sleeping hall would be almost deserted.

She walked forward.

One man, leaving, looked at her—which made her decide to pick over her hair for more leaves and make sure to wash in the stream behind the building where, each morning, one half or the other of the workers kneeled to splash their faces and arms.

She went and washed.

The money was still under the straw. She took it out. And the knife. She put on the green dress Madame Keyne had given her, because it had two sizable internal pockets, whereas the work-dress she'd gotten here had none. She put her money in one. She stuck the knife into the sash on her other hip, then bloused the green shift over it so that the knife was more or less covered, though no one would be surprised at her carrying a blade. Still ...

She went outside—*should* she go back in and sleep?

Twice she'd thought she might throw up. She'd decided to forego breakfast.

Pryn walked down to the office.

Pushing inside, passing piled barrel staves and nested pots, she realized what she didn't remember—*couldn't* remember—was waking. She had no memory of opening her eyes in the forest, of going from a nothing to a now that would let her locate discontinuity with some previous thought or feeling, a discontinuity that could be read as containing sleep—a sleep that contained a dream. Equally lacking was any memory of the dream of the golden dragon

ending . . . *Had* it ended? Could that giant bejeweled fact suddenly peer at her from behind some shack or tree or keg?

When she stepped into the office cubicle, Yrnik turned from the waxed board with the little erasing lamp flickering in his hand. "Pryn . . . ?" Did he look at her strangely? She wanted to feel her hair for more leaves. "Pryn, I think you've made a . . ." His forehead wrinkled above ivory eyes whose irises looked like circles cut from dead leaves. "I'm sure you've made a mistake in these figures. The last ones here—only two barrels of fertilizer out of the auxiliary cooling cave for *all* of yesterday? You must have made an error. It just doesn't tally with the numbers you've written down for the rest of the week." He read: " 'Nine,' 'eight,' 'twelve,' 'ten' . . . Now '*two*'? I mean you can't just go writing down things like that about those people. That's why I sent you to watch them. Carefully. And to write down—carefully—what you saw. *Two*? If I tell that to Rorkar, he'd turn all of the workers in there out on the road. And you must know, they're the ones that can least afford it."

"Perhaps you shouldn't tell him," Pryn said.

Yrnik frowned. He turned back to melt more figures to ghosts. "What . . . ?"

Pryn took a breath. "I must have made a mistake. Yes. I meant to write 'twelve.' Only the earl's cart came for me just then and—"

"Oh," Yrnik said. "Twelve. That sounds better, certainly. 'Twelve' —and while we're at it, 'forty-nine' is a little high for the main cave. We'll make that 'forty' and start over again, all right? And no more mistakes."

"Yes," Pryn said.

Yrnik pursed his lips, setting the lamp on the shelf below the cleared board. "They were looking for you earlier, you know. When you weren't in the barracks."

Pryn's eyes widened. She tried to relax her whole face. She opened her hands.

"His Lordship and Old Rorkar, this morning. You must have had quite an evening at his Lordship's. I said you'd probably gotten up early and gone walking."

Pryn moved dry lip on dry lip. "Yes . . . I went walking—earlier." Had the dream, she wondered, begun at the earl's? Suddenly she said: "I'm going to the eating hall to catch Tetya on his way up. For his writing session."

"Oh, I don't think—"

But Pryn turned and sprinted away among staves, pots, leaning tools, hanging baskets and out flapping hide.

* * *

 339

More workers stood in front of the eating hall than usual. Many were climbing into a large, open wagon. Ahead on the road, another wagon full of men and women was just rolling off north. Everybody was in a good mood. Half a dozen men stood at the road side, bending and hooting with laughter at a story from a heavy woman at the wagon's edge. She gestured and grimaced, making strange growls and grunts—in the narrative, Pryn caught the passing *nivu*, the casual *har'*, but understood none of the barbaric comedy.

She crossed the cool, yellow dirt and turned from the door when a bunch of jabbering men came out followed by several silent women.

"*There* you are!" Juni ducked from the door hanging, drying her hands on the work apron. She wore a dress that was *very* blue.

Juni hurried over to her. "What in the world happened to *you* last night?" (Pryn thought it might be reassuring to take out her knife. But wouldn't it look odd to Juni ...?) "His Lordship drove down here this morning, woke up Old Rorkar, and the two of them were in the hall soon as we opened, asking if anyone had seen you." Juni's dress had none of the metallic glitter of the earl's cloak, but it was definitely the same color.

Pryn put her palm against the knife and felt it through the doubled cloth.

"The earl said you'd decided to come home by yourself ...? He said he'd offered to have you driven back, but there was some misunderstanding ...?"

Pryn blinked. "Yes." She thought: I'll just say 'yes' to everything anyone asks until a dragon plucks me up and away and I'm gone ...

"It's an awfully long walk back from his Lordship's estate," Juni said. "But then, the moon was full last night. It was still out when I got up to come here this morning. I just wish it hadn't rained, though ... Well, when they went to the barracks, you weren't there!"

Pryn nodded.

Juni took a large breath. "Finally they went and got Bruka *any*way. And took her out back! It was awful! Afterwards, when his Lordship had driven off, Rorkar came in and sat in the empty hall and kept on saying this *wasn't* the way he wanted to begin the Labor Festival. I felt so *sorry* for him ...!"

"Bruka?" Pryn frowned.

"They should have waited to find you," Juni said. "That's what Rorkar told his Lordship. I mean, even a slave has *some* rights— and there's *supposed* to be a witness. But his Lordship got very

angry and said I'm sorry, my man, but for all he knew the silly girl—which was you—wouldn't *be* back! He said they'd looked for you several hours before they decided you must have made your own way home. And besides, he said, when Bruka was confronted with it, she'd confess." Juni tossed her apron hem down. "They went and got her and took her out in the back ..." Her dark eyes widened. "They *used* to do it here in front, you know, for everybody to see. Two big logs, sticking out of the ground right there by the road, with manacles hanging on them! I remember, because when I was six or seven, my cousin drove me by and we saw them doing it. It bothered me for days, weeks—oh, it *still* bothers me ... Where are you going?"

Pryn walked away along the wall.

She heard Juni come up behind her, stopped when Juni put her hand on her shoulder. "*Don't* go back there ..."

Pryn glanced over her shoulder.

"There's nothing you can do. I mean there was nothing you *could* have done, even if they'd found you—since they didn't wait. They'll cut her loose when everyone comes back this evening—"

Pryn walked again.

"Well, don't stay there too long, then!" Juni called. "I'm going to get in the wagon ... I wish you'd come, too; and tell me all the wonderful things that happened last night at his Lordship's ..."

Pryn turned the back corner of the hall.

There were some barrels on the eating-hall's back porch. That's all. It didn't feel particularly like morning. She looked across the stone benches stretching to the forest.

She'd expected a stake driven into the ground somewhere and the old woman dangling, chained to it.

She saw nothing.

Out in front she heard another wagon pull up. Someone was shouting for someone else to hurry, hurry up! Someone else was laughing very hard about it—or something else entirely.

Pryn walked out between the benches.

Reaching the aisle, she crossed over dandelions and sedge. Weeds tufted gravel and fallen leaves. She walked between the next seats. The tarred staples left rusted halos on the stone. In various chipped indentations, water had gathered. A third of the staples had broken off. Many were only nubs.

At the bench's end, Pryn walked around the weedy dirt piled against it.

Five, or six, or seven benches away, a rope was tied round one of the staples. It went over the stone's edge and down.

It was moving.

 341

Pryn frowned.

She climbed up to stand on the bench nearest. With a long step and a jump, she got to the next; and the next; and the next—

The woman lay on her side, face against the rock. The vine rope was lashed half a dozen times around her bony forearms, from her wrists halfway up to her elbows, which were pressed together. The skin above the rope was red. Her dress had been stripped to her waist. She was breathing very quietly.

As Pryn stood looking down, Bruka opened her eyes. She didn't look particularly surprised. But after a few moments, she closed her eyes again and shifted her bound arms. The vine rope slid an inch along the stone.

The first thing Pryn thought was that it wasn't as horrible as she'd expected.

It was only rope, not chain; and only along two of the dozen welts on her back had the skin broken enough to bleed—though as Pryn climbed down, she saw a splatter of red on the weeds. And there was a brown smear on the bench's side.

Pryn squatted, looking about. There was no one—though later she told herself it wouldn't have mattered if there were. She would have done the same. She took the knife from her sash under the fold, grabbed one of the lengths of vine rope tied to the staple, and began to saw at it. Getting through it took about two minutes—it was much better rope than she'd been able to make for her dragon bridle.

She was halfway through the second when Bruka opened her eyes again and said, "What are you doing?"

"Cutting you free."

"Did he send you? Is the sun down?"

Pryn shook her head and kept sawing.

"You're freeing me . . . !" Bruka struggled to sit up.

Pryn grunted; the rope was jerked from her hand. She pulled it back and kept sawing.

"The indignity . . . !" Bruka whispered. "They wouldn't do it out front, where people could see. No. They hid me away here in the back—pretending it wasn't happening! Why do it, then? But they know, now: people won't tolerate it—not the free ones! Then why *do* it, I said. Who's it to be an example to, I asked. Not an old woman like me, an old slave . . . there won't be anymore slaves, soon. They won't put up with it . . . You're freeing me? You're mad!" The old woman narrowed her eyes. "You're mad, you know. You know what they'll do to you—a lot worse than this! It's a crime what *you're* doing—"

Pryn stopped sawing. "Do you want me to leave you here?"

With her fingers on the bench edge, Bruka dragged herself up. "No ...!"

Pryn grasped the rope and sawed at it some more.

"But you're mad—!"

"Me and Queen Olin," Pryn said. "Since I got you into this mess with that useless astrolabe—it's gone now, by the way, so don't worry—this seems the *least* I can do." On *least* the rope parted. "Let me see your arms."

Bruka thrust them forward.

Pryn pulled at the rope, but it was knotted at both ends of the lashing. Bruka's fingers and hands were puffy.

"Here ..." Pryn moved around beside her, so that she could get the bound arms under one of hers to steady them. "Hold still, or I might cut you ..." It was hard sawing; and Pryn still didn't feel all that well. In the middle of picking and cutting at the knot, her forehead broke out in beaded water, and her sawing arm began to slip against her side. "What are you going to do when you get free?" She cut more.

"Oh, they think I don't know, because I'm an old woman. But I do! There are ways for a slave to get north to Kolhari and not *once* step on the main road. There're the little trails and paths the smugglers use. There're the little roads. *I* know ..."

"You're going to Kolhari?" Pryn glanced back at her. "Me too. Perhaps I'll see you there." She went back to her cutting.

"They don't have slaves in Kolhari," Bruka said. "Only free men and women."

"Mmm," Pryn said. She pushed away the image of an old woman alone in those crowded streets.

"There's a Court of Eagles," Bruka said. "Where everything is decided fairly. With real eagles, too. I talked to a man who went to Kolhari once, and *he* said he saw no eagles. But I said there must a real eagle there, someplace. Don't you think?"

"Oh, there is," Pryn said. "It's huge. Its wingspan would block the sunlight away from this whole brewery. Its feathers are gold and iron. Its beak and claws are clotted with gems. And it guards the city and keeps its markets and businesses running quite smoothly, thank you. But they keep it hidden. You'll be in Kolhari quite a while before you ever get a look at its glittering face. They're vicious birds, you know—eagles. Mountain birds; and I come from the mountains. Dirty, too. Really, they're just a kind of vulture—"

"You're mad," Bruka said.

The rope came free. "There ..."

Pryn put the knife up on the stone and unwrapped Bruka's bound arms. The grain of the vine had printed itself on the yellow

flesh—and of course there was another place, Pryn saw as she unwrapped more lashing, where the rope was *again* knotted about her forearm. But that only took a half minute to untie.

"It happened to my father, too," Bruka said. "The same way. I wish I'd known him, at least long enough for him to tell me—but it wouldn't have done any good. They always said I was a headstrong girl." The last of the rope came away, and Bruka suddenly grinned. "Like you, eh?"

Pryn waited for the old woman to flex her swollen hands. But she only stretched her arms out; sitting up tall, she looked over the bench tops.

Pryn looked too.

There was still no one.

"You're sure you can get north to Kolhari . . . ?" Pryn asked.

The swollen hands on the marked and raddled forearms came back to Bruka's neck. The old slave grimaced, slipping two fingers of each hand under the iron collar at each side. She pulled.

The lock separated, and the collar came open on its hinge. Pryn had an impression of incredible strength, a strength that, if it could tear open such a collar, could easily have broken the ropes!

Bruka looked at her, then frowned at what was certainly an odd expression on Pryn's face. "But I *never* wear it locked," she explained. "In the day it's all right, I guess. But at night it chokes me . . . someone got a key here, years ago. Old Rorkar never knew. But I think the lock's broken by now, anyway. The hinge is tight, so it holds . . ." She took the collar from her neck and put it on the bench. Once more she frowned at Pryn. "I'm not too old, you know. I've always wanted to go. I can. I know how. I've always known. Thank you for freeing me." Bruka reached forward, touched Pryn's knee. "Thank you, my Lady . . ." Then she scrambled awkwardly to her wide feet, pulled her dress up over her dark-aureoled breasts, stuck her yellow arms through the ragged holes, turned and hurried toward the trees. Bent nearly double, she was among them; was within them; was gone.

Pryn stood.

She wiped her forehead with her fingers and shook them. Drops darkened the stone. She picked up the knife, lifted the blousing, stuck it in her sash, and let green cloth fall.

She picked up the collar, holding an iron semi-circle in each fist. The metal loop to attach the neck-chain separated the second and third fingers of her right hand. She brought its double tenon into the groove: a click.

She pulled.

Another click—it came open again, though the hinge was indeed firm enough to hold it at whatever position, opened or closed.

Pryn raised it to her neck.

The iron was a neutral temperature against her skin. Holding it with both fists, though, she couldn't close it all the way; so she took it off again and stuck it around her sash, closed there, pulling enough cloth through to cover it.

Pryn walked back among the benches toward the building corner. She felt as though she'd been here an hour—though, really, it was probably no more than ten minutes. When she came around the hall, they were only just starting the wagon. Horses clomped forward. Then, at the wagon's edge, Juni hollered at the driver to stop, stop, please, stop, just once more, and everybody groaned or laughed as though this had happened two or three times already.

"Come on, come on!" Juni waved at Pryn.

Because the wagon was going north on the road, Pryn went over to it. Juni and someone else helped her climb up over the side. (One of the things they'd apparently had to stop for already was for Juni to take off her apron and bring it back into the hall. She wasn't wearing it now.) "All right, all right!" Juni called to the driver when Pryn was still half over the rail. "We can go!"

The wagon started.

Everyone cheered.

As Pryn settled on the straw, Juni leaned close to her. "I hope you're satisfied! I *told* you not to go back there—oh, don't look so sullen and suspicious!" She slapped Pryn's knee playfully. "Try to remember that it's a holiday. *I* want to hear all about what it's like to dine at his Lordship's. What did you eat? Was it marvelous ...? I know it was, because I've heard rumors among the slaves—"

"Juni," Pryn said, "why would they do that to that poor woman? She's all tied up back there. She's been whipped. She's just lying there, like she's half dead. I mean, just because she read my—well, she *didn't* read it. She only recognized it."

Juni made a disgusted face as though she were *not* going to discuss it. Then her hands flopped together in her lap and she sat back. "It *is* sad. But slaves are not supposed to drink. Bruka knows that. And from the earl's own mug ...? It was just spiteful breaking of the rules. Even Rorkar agreed it was the kind of thing that *couldn't* just be let pass ... And Bruka's half-mad anyway. It's the kind of thing she'd do!"

Pryn was frowning again.

"Well, they *said* you saw it!" Juni declared. "The earl was in the back, talking to you that day. He put his mug down on a bench—you know, the fancy one he carries whenever he comes to visit here? Bruka just picked it up and drained it. He said you were right there."

"Yes, but—" Astonishment worked its way through the numbness that had enclosed the morning. "But her *father* had—"

"—drunk out of the same mug?" Juni closed her eyes and raised her chin. "That's what she was shouting and screaming when they dragged her in the back." She looked at Pryn again. "Then his little Lordship boomed out—he's got quite a voice when he's riled—yes, her father *had* put his foul lips to that mug, and he too had been strung up and whipped for it. Then Bruka screamed she didn't *know* about that part. Nobody had ever told her *that* part before—which I have to admit I didn't believe, because slaves, you know, remember everything. But by then, of course, they'd got her tied up in the back. And Tetya had returned with the whip—"

"Juni—" Bewilderment joined astonishment— "that *can't* be the reason . . . I heard him *tell* her to—" But she did not want to draw more of Juni's thoughts to her real reasons for outrage. "I mean, why didn't his Lordship say something about it yesterday—*two* days ago, when it happened?"

"Cyka said it to me." Juni looked dour. "Rorkar said it to his Lordship. It's what anyone would have thought. But his Lordship said that when it happened *he'd* thought to let it pass, because, after all, she was just a crazy old slavewoman who had belonged to his father and who still had a malicious streak. But he had forgotten about the Labor Festival. And in his father's day, this was the holiday when good slaves were rewarded for their obediences and bad slaves punished for their defiances. Precisely because it *was* the morning of *this* particular day, he'd felt obliged to come by and say *some*thing. After all, rules are rules. And even Old Rorkar said, yes, that was true." She blinked at Pryn. The wagon jounced. The workers on the other side had started a song. "She didn't deny it, you know. Still, after two days, and with a crazy old woman . . ." Juni shook her head. "You know, it's just like his Lordship to do something like that. Nobody around here trusts him." She gave a small *humph*. "Not know it was the Labor Festival, indeed! It happens every year, and always on the same day. Myself, *I* don't believe it any more than I believe Bruka." She glanced up. "I hope it doesn't rain again."

Of course Pryn had not known it was the Labor Festival either. The why was simple. The area's most important holiday of the summer and held on the longest day of the year, it was an occasion every local knew about and assumed everyone else knew, too. No one had thought to mention it directly to Pryn any more than anyone had thought to mention, "There's sky overhead," or, "There's earth underfoot." What references she'd overheard were all oblique enough so that, without knowing what they referred to, she'd had no way to interpret them and so hadn't really heard them at all.

Pryn tried to reassess the morning in terms of what she'd seen and heard last night, what she'd seen behind the eating hall, what she'd just heard from Juni. No doubt you have put together a more or less coherent explanation for what occurred at the inlet under the moon. Because it was a long time ago, and because the fashions in such explanations change, Pryn had put together a possibly very different one—though no less coherent to her. No matter how different the explanations, however, she had reached some conclusions from it that should be understandable to you and me. Either the greater explanation she was seeking was too complex for what was merely simple and ugly; or that greater explanation which would encompass all these jumbled details was of a complexity beyond any she could presently conceive. In either case, she did not like it here. She was glad she'd freed the old woman, and hoped she got to Kolhari—though to think it was to doubt it.

She was glad to be leaving herself.

Which is when the wagon turned from the north highway onto a narrow road. Trees lowered over.

Pryn seized the wagon's side.

"What's the matter with you?" Juni said. "You look like you're about to jump out!"

"Where are we going—?"

"To the Labor Festival. Down at the beach . . . ?"

"Will Rorkar and Tetya be there? And Yrnik?" But she had seen Yrnik that morning; nothing had happened. "Will his Lordship and his family come?"

"Oh, Tetya and Yrnik will wander by about two or three. Rorkar will arrive at four—though I wouldn't be surprised if Tetya *didn't* show up this year. When he left the hall this morning, he didn't look like a young man ready for a party. I don't think he has much of a stomach for slave whipping."

"*Tetya* did the actual whipping?" Broken welts, smeared stone, splattered weeds . . .

"Oh, his Lordship was *very* insistent about that! The younger generation and all." Juni put on a pompous voice and a practically death's-head leer. " 'If *your* nephew isn't up to it, my man, I can always call in *my* son. Inige is waiting for me in the carriage . . . ?' " She brushed straw from her lap. "Drinking. It's so stupid—for Bruka, I mean. Today she could have drunk herself silly if she'd wanted—on Festival day, *everyone's* allowed. Oh, even some of these good people around us now will behave quite disgracefully before the day's over. That's why I go home early. I mean when everybody's sick and falling all over the beach, I can tell you *I'm* ready to leave! I'll stay for the first *three* fights. After that, I'm gone—though I'm always back an hour later!" She giggled. "You asked when the earl will come? His Lordship and his lady will drive by for a bit, just at sunset—to gloat over the remains and watch the torches reflected in the water. That's pretty, as long as it's too dark to see what a mess everyone's made on the sand. The earl's children may come earlier—they like this sort of thing. Did you meet them last night?"

Pryn nodded.

"I think Jenta's as handsome as they make a man—though I hear he's *quite* strange." Juni raised an eyebrow. "The daughter's supposed to be a bit of a character, too. I heard something about her having a baby ...?" Sighing, she reached over to pat Pryn's knee. "But don't worry. It'll be fine this morning. Oh! Stop the horses!" And she was half up, waving at the driver. "Come on, stop! Stop, up there! Just once more? Please!" Steadying herself first on this man's shoulder, then on that woman's, Juni made her way across to the other side of the wagon.

Pryn turned.

Trees fell back from the wagon's far side.

Grinning over his shoulder and shaking his head, the driver pulled up before a thatched shack.

In the yard, beside some pots and baskets, an old woman had set up her loom. She pulled back on the tamper, thrust her shuttle through the strings, tamped again, then leaned forward in her threadbare shift and twisted the intricately ridged and ribbed stick that reversed the height of the alternates. The shuttle shot through shaking strings.

"All right, Auntie!" Juni called. "Will you come with us? I told you I'd stop by for you again. Here we are!"

"Go on," the old woman said. "The Festival's for young people. Not for me—nobody wants me there. Besides, I have too much to do." She bent down to turn over a handful of coarse yarn in one of the pots.

"But it's a holiday, Auntie," Juni said. "You're not supposed to work today."

"I'll work if I want to. It's the Labor Festival. I want to labor. *You* young people don't know what work is. Go on, now. You don't want me around. I don't know *how* to have a good time—I hear you say it. And you're right."

"Well you might learn if you'd come!"

"I don't like jouncing in wagons. My bones are too brittle." She

348

tamped, sent the shuttle back, leaned forward, and gave a sharp twist to the separator. "*You* won't stay past three o'clock yourself—I know you. You'll be back early; you always are. Who wants to watch a bunch of drunken men, impertinent slaves, and crude forest folk all pretend they like each other till they can't keep it up any longer and fall to fighting—when they're not getting sick all over themselves! There's bound to be an accident. You know, there was a drowning down there three years ago. People get careless at these things, go drown themselves, if not each other."

A man leaning on one knee said: "I was there three years ago. Nobody got drowned!"

"It was seven years ago," a woman near him whispered. "No, eight—*nine* years now, I think! But she always says three. She doesn't really remember. She says it every year."

"There was a drowning three years ago. I haven't gone since, and I'm not going now. Thank you for your trouble. Now get on your way!"

"Are you *sure*, Auntie?"

"I *said* I wasn't going." She leaned; she twisted. "How sure does a woman have to be ...?"

Juni sighed loudly and sat back from the rail.

The driver had watched it all. Laughing, he turned to the horses and started the wagon.

The shuttle shot.

Juni turned from the rail on her knees. "Well, I tried." She crawled back between grinning workers across the straw to Pryn's side. "Everybody saw me. She just won't come."

From the yard the old woman called: "You can tell me about it when you come back this afternoon!"

Juni closed her eyes. "Yes, Auntie! Goodbye, Auntie!" She opened them and sat back. "Well, I *did* try. But there's no changing her."

With some assurance that she was not being pursued by omnipotent powers, Pryn let herself smile.

"She's not really my aunt, you know," Juni said. "She's my older cousin—but *I* didn't know that till two years ago! She's really a good sort. You wouldn't believe it, but she used to have a reputation as the girl who always danced till moondown. But that was a long time ago, and such things change. I hope *I* don't—though I suppose I will. It's bound to be a family thing, don't you think? But then, she's only a cousin—even if I didn't know."

Pryn thought: I'll stay a few hours at the beach, then head back for the north road. Maybe I'll only stop a day or two at Kolhari, before I make my way further north ...? No, Kolhari deserved at least a week. A few weeks, even; or months ... She didn't want to

return to Ellamon. Somehow, though, it was easier now both to be here—and to leave.

Trees dropped back from Pryn's side of the wagon. Beyond dense brambles, she saw the thatched roofs of several distant buildings.

Juni leaned toward her. "The dyeing houses . . ." She nodded at the far structures. "I worked there for a summer, before I came to the brewery. It's *harder* work—I suppose you make more money. But Nallet, who owns them, is much more of a stickler than Rorkar. I guess that's because he's younger and feels he has to show he won't take any nonsense. Nallet's workers will be at the Festival too, of course. But I didn't really like it there. I'm glad I've got the job I have now. Still—" She held up the hem of her dress for Pryn to see. Sun through the trees played over the night-dark blue. "They do nice stuffs, don't you think?"

Pryn nodded.

Trees closed around; trees opened. The sun had burned off the overcast. They came in sight of the crowded wagon ahead. Soon they almost overtook it. Someone there started another song. Some people in Pryn's wagon joined. Juni got into a conversation with some other women.

Pryn looked over the rail at passing pines.

Again trees fell back. On a rocky field where she thought there might easily be the same kind of caves as on Rorkar's property, Pryn saw a number of long buildings. Beside one stood a dozen plows. Some were small and single-handled; others were large enough to need an animal or a person to haul through the ground.

"Now that," Juni said, "used to be the site of our weapons manufactory. Armor, swords, helmets—everything for the soldier and the fighting lord. This whole area used to be known for it. But that was years back, when auntie was a girl."

"Has it become a farm?" Pryn asked.

Juni laughed. "No, silly! They make stone hammers and farm equipment now!"

The wagon rolled.

Someone told her this beach was called Neveryóna. Yes, there were a few old ruins off in the woods, and some ancient foundations out on the islands she could see from here, but nothing to speak of. Was there ever a city? she asked. No. No—true, some folks said as much. But it couldn't have been more than a village. No, not a city. But the Festivals had always been held here. Pryn was told this out on the sand by a hefty, sunburned man of about twenty-one, who had a barbarian accent so thick she could barely

understand him. He worked in the dyeing houses and showed her his hands to prove it, if she didn't believe him! Yes, this was where they'd had the Festivals in his parents' time; and in his parents' parents'.

Was it sacred to some god, perhaps, Pryn wanted to know.

No.

Well, had it *ever* been sacred to some god—perhaps a great dragon god, guardian of the ruins, who lived among the stars?

No. He knew of no such gods around here.

After that she stayed pretty much to herself, sitting at the edge of the grass with her feet on the sand, looking out across the inlet to the gray hills or off at the glittering sea. It wasn't too hard to be alone. There were a lot more people than just the brewery folk—enough, indeed, to populate a small city!

She said that to herself several times.

The friendliness local people can extend to strangers is always, beyond a point, problematic, as Pryn's stay at Enoch had reminded her. From time to time there had been strangers in Ellamon. From time to time Pryn had made friends with them. But you just couldn't draw a friend of a week into the alliances, aversions, shared concerns, mutual suspicions, committed bonds and vague acquaintances of a lifetime—not at an affair like this, where any one of those relationships might change in an instant.

She said that to herself several times, too. (Off with this group, off with that, Juni had not spoken to her for forty minutes.) Pryn felt lonely and thought, really, she ought to go now. She wondered why she stayed.

Sitting on a rock beside some bushes out of sight of the road where the wagons pulled up, she listened to the neighing horses and pictured them nosing one another. She could hear them beyond the ridge. She also thought about her father, whom she had never seen—who, indeed, had been absent from her speculations almost as long as her aunt.

What would he have her do?

Then she thought: Really, her aunt, her mother, Old Rorkar, Yrnik, even Cyka in the eating hall, any real father she might have had, Madame Keyne, the Liberator—even the earl, however vindictive, however despicable. (Was it *only* power that allowed him to reinterpret reality like that? Pryn suddenly knew: if she'd known what Juni had later told her in the wagon, lost in an attempt to find the nature of the slave's true guilt or the lord's true reason, she would never have cut the old woman free.) Yes, *all* of them were authorities for her. She did what they seemed to ask when they confronted her. When they were not there, she found herself still doing what they might want, as though all of them only stood for that obsessive, absent father who was with her always. Oh, he listened to them and modified his concerns in the light of their demands, to be sure. But he was the real enforcer of any submission, overt or intuited. For what, she wondered, did *he* stand—

Among the youngsters playing in the shallows, in retaliation to a splashing, one skimmed her forearm over the water, sending up white gold into the sun. On her rock, Pryn started with a momentary image of a gold wing rising from the waters—till it shattered about the girl's shrieking pursuers; and perspective, with the fixing of attention, returned.

It still set Pryn's heart pounding.

She had a momentary intuition of all the conflicts between the north and south of all Nevèrÿon contoured by such jeweled eagles, such gilded dragons. But then, what could such fanciful beasts actually *do*, save finance a few of the real strokes wielded by a Rorkar, a Madame Keyne, even a Gorgik, or a provincial earl more powerful than them all. Such strokes seemed rather paltry before her father not there . . .

A kind of madness . . . ?

Pryn stood up from her rock, determined to leave that moment—and saw several real and solid reasons to stay.

Over a rock-walled furnace out on the sand, a man turned a triple spit, each tine set with several trussed fowl. In dull dresses too long for the heat, which had already grown notable, women carried shovels full of smoking coals to a shallow pit a few feet off, over which, on a crusted, blackened grill, two split kids barbecued. At the trees, people rolled out dripping barrels, from where they'd been stored the night in some stream, and set them on rough tables in the shade. A dozen people stood about with mugs, sampling what was clearly Rorkar's contribution to the Festival. With a long journey ahead and little money, it might be wise to eat first and take a bag of food with her—if she could put one together unobtrusively.

At another fire lay several sacks of yams. Some children gingerly placed the red, rooty nodules about the flames.

A grizzled man came down the beach, a net sack over his shoulder filled with what looked like flat, gray stones. A youngster ran from the water to accompany him to a fire, where a large eathern pot had been set to boil. (Save her single afternoon at the Old Market, Pryn, who was after all a mountain girl, had never seen a clam. And despite all auxiliary roastings and grillings, the Labor Festival was essentially a clambake.) The net was dumped into the

steaming pot; two women pushed a circular board cover over the top.

People applauded.

The net was thrown down on the sand. Pryn thought: Maybe I can get one of those, when they're finished boiling their rocks . . .

Someone was lugging another off toward another pot.

As the morning went on, the beach became all cooking, all eating, all noise. People with instruments covered with leather heads pounded them. People plucked drawn strings over hollow gourds and shells, yodeling accompaniments.

Men drank beer, gossiped, and boasted about themselves.

Women drank beer, gossiped, and boasted about men and women not there.

Pryn drank beer, ate some roast chicken . . . and *a* clam. "If you don't *like* it," Juni said, having turned up at the same fireplace, "you don't *have* to eat them! Oh, what a face! Here, I'll take your bucket! There's lots of other things to try. Weka?" who was about eleven, all black eyes and freckles. "Weka, take Pryn and make sure she gets some baked sweet potato! And don't forget to let her dip it in the honey!" So Pryn went with Weka and peeled back the flaking skin from a hot potato and dipped it in a large, messy honey pot with a few leaves and some sand in it, and ate a piece of barbecued goat . . . and three *more* steamed clams, which she decided were not that bad. Just . . . different. Besides, who knew *what* the fashion in foods might be when she got back to Kolhari.

The sun burned the fog from the hills. (Was that thing that seemed part of the mountain on the other side of the water his Lordship's home? Yes, someone said.) It also burned away some of her fatigue.

She managed to find a discarded cloth sack, in which were some bread crumbs, which she carried about wadded up under her arm. For a while, she despaired of getting anything into it, without being obvious. Finally she managed to get in two roasted potatoes; then several cuts from a roasted goat's leg; and three separate quarters from three roast ducks, from three different fires. It was too full to carry under her arm now; she just dangled it from one hand.

Ambling round a bend, Pryn now saw the beach was longer than she'd thought. There was as much activity down this stretch as there'd been on the former hundred or so yards. The ground here, she saw as she walked along the muddy sand by the water, split into an upper and lower level. A six-meter earthen slope widened between, its black dirt stuck abouts with roots, rocks, and small brush. She walked along the lower strip, swinging her sack and looking at the people strolling at the edge of the upper. There was music above, whose source she couldn't see.

What stopped her were the tops of two rocks over the upper ledge. Both were chalky white. One was substantially taller than the other. They looked like two giant, aged fingers prodding at blue air ...

Three little girls came barrelling down the slope, shrieking. Pryn began to scramble up. She grasped at roots with her free hand—now she climbed over a weedy tide-line; for a while she went crabwise.

People were cooking at the rim, right where she came over. Someone offered her a hand at the top, and Pryn thanked her, while the others stood laughing, and did she want a bucket of clams?

"No, no thank you. No. Not right now ..."

Between the two rocks a colorfully painted wagon had parked. One side had been let down into a platform. Drummers and musicians sat at either edge of a stage decorated with fantastic props. A very fat man was just finishing an energetic dance with a tall, supple woman. Breathing heavily, feathers shaking on his shoulders and gold paint in wings about his eyes, he walked to the front of the platform and bowed. "Thank you! Thank you, ladies and gentlemen!" Then he said something in the barbarian language, which may have meant the same thing—but it made one group in the audience standing about laugh loudly. "This will be our last show for the day," the fat man went on. "Afterward, we'll pack up to head off north. But you'll see us again next summer, at your wonderful, joyous, generous Labor Festival! But we're not finished! There's more to come—so you *can* be generous with your gifts as our musicians pass among you. *Please* be generous! And now our show continues ...!" He turned sharply, clapped his hands over his head, and skipped ponderously from the stage.

People laughed.

Some of the musicians sitting on the stage's edge jumped from the platform to move among the audience, collecting small iron coins, either in their cloaks or in the bodies of their actual instruments. Other musicians came out on the platform, already playing a rhythmic melody. A moment later, with her scarfs and bells, diminutive Vatry dashed to the platform's center and began frenetically to shake her red hair and leap and smile and wink into the audience, now and again turning one of her astonishing flips!

People *were* generous!

Three times Pryn saw gold held up, to be thrust a moment later

over the shoulder of another watcher and tossed into some musician's basket or outstretched cloak.

To one side of the audience in a loose group stood a dozen or so slaves. Most wore their collars on naked shoulders. None was from the brewery. Pryn saw a few white collar-covers, but not many. Given her coming journey, she did not want to give the mummers any of her coins. But everyone else seemed to be, in laughing, clinking handfuls. The musicians were *not* asking from the slaves . . .

Pryn stood near a grove of pecan trees. Vatry did another flip, and all attention, including the musicians', went forward. Pryn put down her sack, reached under her bloused-out shift, pulled the iron collar from her sash, and raised it to her neck. She pushed the iron semi-circles closed—a small click.

Dropping her hands, Pryn looked about.

She felt a tingling over her entire body. No one *seemed* to be watching. It struck her for the first time, as she dropped her chin almost to hide it now she wore it, that the collar was not particularly comfortable. She picked up her sack and stepped out from the other side of the trees. She walked, leisurely (she hoped), toward the slaves at the clearing's side.

A musician passed her with several different kinds of flutes tied top and bottom with thongs and strung about her shoulder. Her spread cloak sagged with iron coins—and at least as much gold as Pryn had once seen Madame Keyne thrust into the hands of a would-be assassin. With her oddly angled, wide-spaced eyes, the musician only glanced at Pryn. Pryn felt her body heat from ankles to ears. But the musician did not pause for any contribution.

The slaves she moved next to did not look at her either. While Vatry continued her dance, Pryn looked at them a lot, though—mostly for differences between herself and them which might betray her to some more-practiced eye. Were their hands, as they clapped at Vatry's next flip, held differently from hers? Was there something special in the way this one beside her carried his sloping shoulders? Or in the way that heavy woman toward the front there kept rubbing her hand back and forth on the print skirt at her thigh? Or the way that one enfolded his cracked mug in both hands with the fingers interlocked at the front? What about the way the one with the collar-cover stood, one sharp hip thrust out? Certainly there must be *something* that marked them as different, marked them as belonging to the collar—which, now that she had become part of its meaning, was, after all, only a sign.

For a while Pryn found herself trying to imitate the gesture of one, the stance of another, seeking whatever might give her impos-

ture more authority, till her attention was caught up by the skit that had replaced Vatry on the platform.

There was a beautiful princess, played by the leading lady, who somehow looked much younger than Pryn knew her to be from the time she'd eaten with the mummers back in the Kolhari Market. There was the great and glittering monster, operated from offstage, who wanted to eat the princess. There were several dashing young men, some of whom had mothers and some of whom had girlfriends, and all of whom seemed to be in furious, comic competition; there was also a slave, who seemed, as far as Pryn could tell, to belong to everyone, since everyone gave him orders. He received many comic kicks and beatings, but nevertheless was always getting away with something—now a glass of wine from a fine supper that had erupted into a comic argument, now with a piece of gold from a stupidly mismanaged bargain. Both the slaves on one side and the workers on the other laughed. Indeed, two slaveboys, no older than she and both with brimming mugs, poked each other in the sides and made such loud comments, and seemed so generally tickled at seeing themselves represented on stage at all, it looked to Pryn as if it might grow into a real disturbance. Some of the workers were clearly annoyed; but none of the slaves seemed inclined to stop it. A few musicians still moved about, taking some last coins. In the excited state the collar produced, Pryn grew sweatingly uncomfortable at the rowdiness beside her. Finally she lifted her sack and moved toward the back. At the ledge, she just glanced down at the lower beach—

Along at the water's edge, kicking bare feet at the wet sand, were Yrnik and big-eared, gawky-elbowed Tetya! They were laughing about something. Indeed, Tetya did not look like a boy who only that morning had beaten an old woman into insensibility. But then, Pryn thought as she stepped away, she probably did not look like a girl who'd just freed one.

Certainly they hadn't seen her. Nor did they look as if they were headed up here.

The idea had been with her. But at a glimpse of someone from the brewery, idea became movement. Vatry was not in the skit. Two other mummers' wagons—for props, scenery, and sleeping space— sat either side of the rocks. Pryn took her sack off beyond the wagon she'd recognized as the prop cart in which, when she'd last seen them in the city, Vatry had been housed.

The side wagons were angled back to the tree. Some musicians not in this skit stood at the wagon's end near the horses. The musician who'd passed Pryn with her cloak of coins now cuddled the feedbag around one red muzzle. She stroked the bony forehead while the creature ate. Pryn felt something of the tingle again; she went further along beside the trees. She planned to work her way through the brush into the backstage area. But the further away she was when she started in, the less chance there'd be of someone shooing her off. Sack over one shoulder, she pushed in among saplings and undergrowth. If she'd gotten through here last night, certainly she could get through it today. When she reached the shadow of the larger trees, the undergrowth lessened. She worked her way to where the wagons must be, then started out.

She saw the rocks; she saw the wagon tops.

The center one had painted houses hanging on its back. Behind the wagon to the right, five mummers in their costumes hauled away a third of the monster, who'd apparently devoured the slave and just met defeat for it at the hands of the most sympathetic of the young men, who'd been played by a very tall, very beautiful, very black actor. On stage, the young man and some fishermen and the princess were singing about it now—

There was Vatry!

The little dancer stood in the door of the nearest wagon, talking to a man with a sun-browned, muscular back. He wore a dark loin-rag wrapped around his hips and between his legs; a shaggy sheath hung at his belt.

Vatry's hair was wild and unkempt.

The man's was black and tied with a rag. He was handing Vatry a sack, not much larger than Pryn's.

Vatry took it and thrust it inside behind the wagon's door jamb.

The man turned to walk away—and became a woman!

Pryn caught her breath.

Of course it had been a woman all along—she'd only thought it was a man! The black rag that held in the thick hair did not go across her forehead, but across her eyes. In it were two eyeholes, though Pryn could not have been more surprised if there'd been three, or five, or seven!

She walked toward Pryn. Her breasts were not large, but they were definitely a woman's, not just muscular pectorals, for all Pryn tried to read them as such.

She strode right into the undergrowth, pushing back leaves. As she passed, she looked at Pryn with only mild surprise.

It was the first anyone had looked directly at her since she'd moved off with the slaves.

Between frayed slits, the eyes were intensely blue.

Pryn thought for an awkward moment: *Her hair's blue, too!* But it was only sun-dappling slipping across one of the blue beads she wore chained in her hair. Sun flaked over terra-cotta shoulders.

And she was off among trees; was only a shadow; was a sound in leaves; was—like Bruka—gone.

Pryn stood, astounded.

Beyond the leaves, Vatry lingered in the wagon door, still in her bells and scarfs. Slowly, she stepped back inside.

Pryn swallowed. Then, sack bouncing, she pushed from the undergrowth, crossed the clearing, was up the wagon's single step, and through the colorful hanging. "Vatry . . . !"

Inside the wagon was a smell of incense and old varnish. Paintings of castles, of waves, of forests, of houses, of mountains leaned against the walls. Ornate armor hung from the ceiling. A trap in the roof let in sunlight. Sitting on a shelf-bed against the back, Vatry pushed away a hanging blanket and peered through dusty sun. "Yes? What do you—?"

"Vatry, *who* was . . ." Pryn lost her question to the strangeness of the wonder-cramped wagon.

Vatry frowned. Her eyes were winged with paint. "What do you . . . ? You? Oh, that girl . . . from the city!" She stood up, pushing the blanket further back on the rope over which it was strung. "It's Pryn . . . ?"

Excited, Pryn nodded. She'd really thought Vatry might not remember her at all.

"*What* are you doing here at this . . . ?" Suddenly the little redhead's hand went back against her breasts. "But you've been captured!" she cried in her odd accent. "Oh, you've been taken! That's awful! Is there anything anyone can do?" She leaned forward in complete sincerity.

Which bewildered Pryn—till she remembered the collar. "Oh, this . . . ? No, it's just a . . . it's not real. I mean, it's broken!" She dropped her sack to the floor, raised her chin, slipped a finger into each side of the iron band, and tugged—of course this would be the moment when the broken lock held . . .

But the hinge gave.

Pryn took the iron from her neck. "I was only pretending—using it, as a disguise." Then she said: "It's for you!"

Vatry frowned. "What?"

"I mean for the skits. You do skits with slaves in them. I thought they might use it . . . for the show."

Suspicion found its way into Vatry's voice. "Oh . . ."

"Vatry, I have to get away from here! I want to get back to Kolhari!"

"Don't we all!"

"When you pull out this evening, could I ride along—?"

"This evening? *Oh,* no!" Vatry shook her head. "We don't hang

358

around these places till evening! These local shindigs get a little rough by sundown. Everyone's gambled away all their money, or gotten too drunk to follow a skit anyway. Every local hooligan thinks the holiday isn't complete unless he's stolen something or other from our props as a souvenir. And any little tramp diddled behind the rocks, who decides she doesn't like it, always finds it easier to blame it on one of *our* boys instead of the leering local lout who actually got to her. It makes less trouble for them later. Well, I did it myself once—but I've been paid back many times over! No, we don't hang around these kinds of places. We should be packed up and rolling inside an hour."

"That's even better!" Pryn said. "Oh, please, *can't* I come? You see, there're some people looking for me—at any rate, they *may* be looking for me. I did something that they won't like. Of course, I don't know if they realize it was me, yet—"

"What did you do? Steal some old geezer's hard-won hoard?" Vatry pointed toward Pryn's sack.

"Oh, that's just food I got for the trip." Pryn took a breath. "What I did was free one of the old geezer's slaves!"

"*That* was noble," Vatry said, "I suppose—if foolhardy!"

The sack the masked woman had brought lay on rumpled cloth at the foot of Vatry's bed. "What's in that?"

"What's in what?" Vatry said.

"That bag the woman gave you?"

Vatry pulled in her small shoulders. Her forehead wrinkled. "What woman?"

"Well, she *looked* like a man, but I'm sure—I *know* it was a woman. In that sack there."

Vatry considered a moment. "There wasn't any woman here—or man."

"Of course there was. With a black rag mask." Pryn was trying to remember the tale-teller's tale. *Blue Heron* . . . ? But that had been *her* name. "She passed right by me when—"

Vatry leaned over, reached into into the sack, and pulled out something small and black. "What's this?" She held out her hand.

Pryn looked. "I don't . . . know."

Vatry closed her fingers, turned her hand over, threw the black pellet down on the wagon floor—*thack!* It bounced back into her hand. She turned her palm up to show Pryn.

"It's a ball . . . ?"

"Yes. A child's playing ball, that you see the children tossing about on the streets all through Kolhari. It's nothing special—absolutely not worth a mention." Her odd accent gave her a measured tone. "It's not worth any kind of mention at all, is it, now?"

"Oh, no." Pryn shook her head. "Of course it's not!"

Vatry rolled the ball between thumb and forefinger. "These come from further south of here. I'll bring this bag of them with me up to Kolhari. I'll sell them for a few iron coins to some vendor in the market, who'll sell them to the passing children for their end-of-summer games. It may keep me from having to break my back carrying sacks of onions for noisy barbarians in the eating halls for a day or two, when the troupe here lets me go. Certainly there's nothing wrong with that, is there?"

Pryn shook her head again. "Of course not."

"Certainly it's not worth *any* sort of a mention—to anyone. Do you understand?"

Pryn remembered the smugglers she'd come south with, and their cartload of contraband, against which this minuscule enterprise seemed laughable. "Vatry, there may be *other* people after me too. What ancient custom I violated or bit of intrigue I might have tripped over, I don't begin to understand and don't want to. But they tried to *poison* me last night! At least I *think* they did. They may try again—and maybe they won't. But they're bad people. They order slaves to be whipped for nothing. And I don't want to stay to find out why—and no, I saw *no* woman here. Did she give you a sack? *I* certainly didn't see it! What was *in* it? I wouldn't have a clue!"

Vatry looked serious. She pulled the sack into her lap, put the ball back in it, then pushed it behind some bedding at the bed's other end. "You say they tried to *poison* you because you freed one of their slaves . . . ?"

It seemed hopelessly complicated to explain right then that it was the other way around. Pryn nodded.

"Well," Vatry said, "I've heard of stranger things in this strange and terrible land." She looked at Pryn a little sideways. "I tell you what. We'll go to the director. I'll ask—just once, mind you—if you can come along. I won't insist. I'm not going to make a nuisance of myself just for your sake. If he says yes, fine. But if he says no, you've got to promise me you'll go on about your business as best you can and not make any fuss."

"If he'll just let me ride along with you for fifty stades—"

"We'll *ask*," Vatry said. "He may say yes; he may say no. Now come on." She stood and stepped around Pryn.

On the rumpled bedding, where the sack had lain, was a very long knife. It wasn't a full sword; but two inches beyond the hilt, the blade became . . . two blades! Both bore the file marks of sharpening on inner and outer edges.

"Vatry—Oh, please . . . *one* more question?"

"What?"

"That *is* the kind of blade they use in the west—in the Western Crevasse?"

Vatry looked put out. "How would *I* know such things?"

"I just thought maybe, with your accent—I mean it isn't southern, it *certainly* isn't northern. And it doesn't sound like island speech— you might be one of those women from ...?" Pryn suddenly wished she hadn't spoken. She was overcome with the conviction Vatry would turn on her and accuse her of spying from the bushes. She felt herself start to deny it before the accusation was made, and thought desperately: By all the nameless gods, let me be silent! Let me keep still!

And the real Vatry before her, who after all was as good-hearted and sentimental as it was possible to be in such primitive times and still survive, said: "It's just a prop. For the skits. Like this thing—!" and she pulled the collar from Pryn's hand, held it up, then tossed it back on the bed, where it clinked against the twinned sword. "Come on. And no more about this silliness or I'll send you on your way right now!"

Cheeks still rouged, eyelids still gilded, the fat man had doffed his feathers for a cloak of coarse canvas and was directing the loading of the scenery being hauled down from the middle wagon, now the skit was over.

Vatry said: "My friend here's in some trouble, it seems, and needs a ride north. She was wondering if you'd let her come along with us—at least for a while."

"I wouldn't *think* so!" the fat man said. "We can't just take up strangers like that. There's hardly enough room for us." He looked at Pryn through his fantastic make-up—then smiled! "Oh ... the little girl from the Kolhari market! How in the world did *you* end up in this forsaken backwater?"

The recognition made hope leap. "Well, I—"

But the fat man went on: "I'm sorry, my puffy little partridge, but we can't give a ride to every stray we run into—you understand."

"I'll work," Pryn said. "I'll do *any*thing!"

The fat man paused, tongue filling one rouged cheek. "Well, as I remember, you *don't* play the drum very well. You're obviously not a dancer. Can you sing?"

"I never—"

"Then you're not a singer." He turned to Vatry. "You know, we're in enough trouble as it is, what with Alyx taking off like that last week. I'm trying to keep all the accounts in my head, as well as work up dialogue for the new skit, that nobody seems to be able to—or *wants* to—remember lines for. Once I make them up, *I* can't remember them. I've got too many other things to think about if I want to keep this troupe together. Now if your friend here could write down words and keep accounts like Alyx—but she's only an ignorant mountain girl who's somehow gotten herself lost in the country. My heart goes out to her, but—"

"But I—!" Pryn interrupted.

"But you what?"

This is how, after her days among the changeable mysteries of the barbaric south, Pryn came to be riding with the mummers on the north road at evening. ("I think she'd better stay out of sight until we're actually under way," Vatry said. The fat man said: "Ah, it's one of those? Well, it's not the first time for us. I doubt it'll be the last." Besides her dictation, accounting, and dialogue coaching duties, at their next performance stop, the director told her, Pryn would take a few gold coins into the audience. During the collection she would wave one, then another over her head and make a show of tossing them into the passing cloaks or baskets. Pryn said: "Oh . . . !" And when they were actually rolling down the beach, staring out a chink in the wagon door she passed as close to Ardra's face as yours is to this book! He was turning to Lavik, who pulled him aside, laughing, and said, "Watch out for the *baby*—!" He carried screeching Petal.) They didn't put her in with Vatry. There were already too many other people sleeping in that wagon.

The bed she got was just above one of the musicians; yes, the one she'd passed with the coins—who turned out to be as well the third wagon's driver. When they were a goodly handful of stades along the north road, Pryn climbed up the ladder at the wagon's end and out the roof-trap. She perched in the corner, dangling her feet inside.

The driver sat forward at the edge, holding the reins and not quite humming.

A wagon joggled ahead, beneath tall trees, toward the hillcrest. Behind fields there was just a sight of sea. Clouds banked before them, silver and iron, walls and pillars, towers and terraces, shape behind shape.

"It looks like a city," Pryn said.

Topping the hill, they started down.

The driver glanced back. She had broad cheekbones under odd, foreign eyes. One of her flutes was strapped behind her shoulder. "We still have cities to go through before we reach Kolhari—little cities, to be sure. Towns, is more like it. Villages ..." The wagon joggled. She turned to the horses.

"*That's* the city you must learn to read," Pryn said. "That's the city you must write your name on—before you can make progress in a real one; at least *I* think so!"

The driver laughed without looking back. "You're a strange one."

Pryn watched the clouds.

"I hear that you can," the driver said. "Read and write, I mean."

"I do all sorts of thing: read, write, free slaves, ride dragons—kill, if I have to." Pryn guessed the driver was about twenty-five.

The foreign musician flipped her reins. "I wish someone would figure a way to write down music. *That'd* be something! Then I could be sure to remember my tunes."

"I don't see why it can't be done." Pryn thought: Now I've had all sorts of experiences that might be of use to the Liberator among his causes. (The astrolabe was gone, yes, but she had retrieved the iron collar from Vatry's bed. Perhaps she could fix the lock.) Perhaps when I get to Kolhari ... "If you can write down words," she said, suddenly, "I don't see why we can't find a way to write down ..." And hadn't some successful musician been pointed out to her in the Kolhari market? "I'll work on it!" At Kolhari, she might just stop by to see Madame Keyne—oh, if only for a while ...

The driver laughed.

Pryn sat a long time staring at the sky.

Now, old city of dragons and dreams, of doubts and terrors and all wondrous expectations, despite your rule by the absent fathers, it's between us two!

Montreal—New York
July 1980—November 1981

 363

APPENDIX A:

The Culhar'
Correspondence

[The *Nevèrÿon* tales, of which *Neveryóna* ("The Tale of Signs and Cities") is the most recent, are based on an ancient text of approximately 900 words known as the Culhar' Fragment or, sometimes, the Missolonghi Codex, which has been found translated into numerous ancient languages. Because of the Culhar's incomplete nature as well as its geographical dissemination among so many cultures, it has been difficult to assign an even reasonably indisputable origin to it, either as to date, land, or language of composition. In 1977, however, a comparative retranslation of the text from the various languages in which various versions have been found was presented by a young, black, American scholar, K. Leslie Steiner, along with an extensive commentary. Steiner's work is notable not only for its linguistic interest but also because of its mathematical side. The first collection of tales (*Tales of Nevèrÿon*, Samuel R. Delany, Bantam Books; New York, 1979) was clearly in dialogue with Steiner's findings. That volume concluded with an Appendix, written by archeologist S. L. Kermit, giving a general review of the Culhar's history as well as the thrusts of both Steiner's mathematical and interpretive work. Among the responses to both the tales and the appended monograph, one, addressed to Kermit, seems worth publishing *(en appendice)* along with the engendered correspondence, for the readers of the present (or indeed the absent) text.]

New Haven
February, 1981

To S. L. Kermit:

I have just read your comments on the Culhar', and Steiner's translation of same, and I feel that some remarks are in order.

I have checked the literature, and the Appendix to Delany's work seems to be your first foray into archeology or text redaction (unless you are the S. Kermit who wrote the annotations to the

367

most recent edition of Dee's *Necronomicon,* in which case my congratulations; it was a solid piece of work). I would suggest that before you make another attempt you learn something about the topics you discuss. Or rather, learn something more; you're obviously not ignorant, but your knowledge fails you at a number of points. Some examples follow (page numbers from the Bantam edition of *Tales of Nevèryon,* New York, 1979).

p. 249: "Proto-Latin." I haven't any idea what you are referring to, unless it be archaic Latin. The prefix 'proto' is used to refer to reconstructions of early stages of languages, 'early' here being some time before those languages were reduced to writing. Thus, you can't *have* a text of a proto-language. If you do, it is an attested language, and no longer a construct. The proto-language which is the postulated ancestor of Latin is referred to either as proto-Italic or proto-Italo-Celtic, depending on your theoretical bias.

p. 249: "... 4,500 B.C., or even 5,000 B.C., which would put it [the Culhar' Fragment] practically inside the muzzy boundaries of the neolithic revolution." The two scholars I asked agreed that the neolithic period was roughly 6500 B.C.—3000 B.C. Thus your dates are about as solidly neolithic as is possible.

P. 250: You mention that Blegan found a Greek version [of the Culhar'] in the fourth level down at Hissarlik, *i.e.*, at Troy VI. This is highly interesting, as it is the only evidence I know of that the Trojans spoke Greek. Given the location, an Anatolian language seems more likely. Nor is it possible that it was put there by the Greeks, since the numbering of the cities is done from the bottom up, and VI is older than VIIa, the historical Ilium. Any text in VI was in Troy before the Greeks got there.

p. 249: "The only ancient people who did not, apparently, know of the Culhar' fragment were, oddly, the Attic Greeks ..." This is indeed odd, since it implies that the Ionic and Doric Greeks did, and if this is so, it is about the only thing the groups didn't share. Greek culture of that period was a nearly seamless whole; we differentiate among them by the recorded dialect differences.

p. 253: "... the young engineer Michael Ventris ..." Ventris would probably be slightly wounded by this, as he was an architect.

p. 253: "The parchment itself ... most probably dates from the third century A.D., but it is also most probably a copy made from a much older source ..." You're damned right it is! Linear B ceased to be used around 1200 B.C., with the fall of Pylos! This makes it just about dead certain that whoever copied it didn't know the meaning of the characters. And by the way, Linear B didn't have 'letters.' Letters are those graphic symbols used in an alphabetic

system only. You can no more refer to syllabic characters as 'letters' than you could hieroglyphs.

p. 253: "... written in the same ink ..." How can you tell?

p. 253: "... transcriptions of block-letter Greek inscriptions, that sculptural language written on stone in upper-case letters ..." First, I have no idea what 'block-letter' is supposed to mean. Are you implying the Greeks also made cursive inscriptions on stone? And what is a "sculptural language"? I can give a good metaphorical reading for the phrase, but that doesn't seem to be what you intend. Do you mean that it was the script used on stone? One presumes that the same script was used on parchment; however, no parchment texts have survived, Greece's climate being wetter than Egypt's. And 'uppercase letters'? The Greeks had no lower case. No one did. Minuscule letters are a Byzantine development. The phrase 'upper-case' is thus empty of content.

p. 253: "Indeed, it is the only fragment of Linear B ever to be found outside of Crete." Garbage. Linear B is found on Pylos, not to mention at several sites on the mainland.

pp. 253–4: *Transpoté.* Is this a direct transliteration of the Linear B text? Are you *sure*? *Trans-* is Latin! If the ancient Greeks (or whoever) were calling something trans-anything, then we are witness to a considerable revolution in archeology. A Greek name with the meaning you want would be *Peripoté* or *Parapoté*. And *poté* does not mean 'never.' Never. To do so, it must take a negative particle. And 'across when' is not a possible Homeric meaning. Homer simply doesn't use it in that sense.

p. 254: "... Linear B was used only in the very early stages in the history of the neolithic palaces at Cnossos, Phaistos, and Malliá." Hold it right there. The phrase 'neolithic palace' is oxymoronic. A culture which can build a palace isn't neolithic. Further, Linear B is from the late period of the palaces.

pp. 261–2: Steiner retranslates 'The merchant trades four-legged pots for three-legged pots' as 'The merchant (female) ceases to deal in three-legged pots and now deals in four-legged pots." Something tickled just over my brow line when I read that reinterpretation. I went and dug out the Culhar' Fragment in *Inscriptiones Graecae,* where it is referred to as Kolharé. In the passage Steiner cites, the verb translated as 'trade' is αλλασσειν. This does indeed mean 'trade.' I can find, however, no evidence of its ever being used in Steiner's sense. She might be thinking of μεταλλασσειν. While it would suit Steiner's translation, however, it wouldn't suit the earlier one. In short, there is no Greek verb which carries the ambiguity which *trade* does in English. I am wondering if Steiner was simply looking at an English version, without bothering to cross-check.

 369

But I have gone on long enough. Your effort is praiseworthy, and with some revision can become a useful commentary.

Sincerely,
(signed:) Charles Hoequist, Jr.

New York
August 4, 1980

Dear Charles Hoequist, Jr.,

Back in February, when your letter arrived, I dutifully forwarded it to the address for S. L. Kermit that K. Leslie Steiner had left with me before going off to take a guest-teaching position at the University of Bologna.

Last week, when I got back from my vacation trip across the Canadian Rockies, I found—finally!—Professor Kermit's reply, sent in care of me. Professor Kermit's description of the state of your letter on its arrival in the desert (see below) does not even approach the state of his on its arrival here! Besides the indecipherable over-stampings, there was clearly a heel-print on it. At one point the letter had obviously been wetted, Lord knows with what. (Visions of incontinent camels are called up just by the smell!) As well, the whole had been ripped in half and the envelope badly taped together. The sheets inside were still in two pieces. Because of the wetting and the generally deteriorated state of the air-letter paper, I decided it might be best if I transcribed it for you. I just wouldn't trust it to another trip through the mails. Also, Kermit does not exaggerate about his handwriting. With diligence one can make it out, though the transcription took me a full three days and about 25 consultations with various friends over this or that squiggle, masking a j, y, or g; over that or the other near-contourless line, ghosting an m, n, or u. (I recall Hyder Rollins's labor over the hen-scratchings of the "Keats Circle" and gain new respect!) I hope you don't object. If you could see the state of the original, I'm sure you'd understand.

My best wishes,
(signed:) Samuel R. Delany

[*Transcription follows:*]

My dear Hoequist,

Your letter, dated February, reached me yesterday—and it is June! Though would you believe, not one of us here at the dig has been sure precisely *what* day of June it has been for two weeks now? Some time when the next provision caravan passes through and I can start my answer to you off on its circuitous way back to New Haven (I just assume you are at Yale, in the shadow of that great, transparent library where writing is at once displayed, displaced, and entombed, like a gleaming metaphor of its own historical position), perhaps we here will be able to orient ourselves again. But since Professor Wellman, hauling that architrave from the cinder basin, smashed up his Seiko LED, we have truly dwelt in a land without time. My own watch has only its sturdy little Donald Duck hands, semaphoring about the day—and no date window.

Really, we could be living in the middle ages, here at the site, rather than in the last quarter of the 20th Century. (It *is* the 20th Century, isn't it?) Unless you are familiar with the absurdly primitive techniques expediency makes traditional for the archeology of this region, I doubt you would believe the arrival of your letter: in the haversack of a pack camel, the envelope crumpled, soiled, opened at least three times (as is all the mail that reaches us here—a fraction of that which is sent, I'm sure), and re-sealed and over-stamped with the blurred colophons of Iraqi Government Security (why all our mail must go by way of Iraq, which does not even border on this country, to reach us here, is beyond me—unless it's because the wealthy Kuba family of that nation, still out of favor, has footed part of the expedition's costs), in runny blue and screech orange. In this half-excavated oasis, two hundred miles from any place with a pronounceable name, much less a post office, I feel I am sequestered in some parallel world of the sort Leslie used to make me smile over when we had our separate rooms in that shabby student house just outside Ann Arbor. (Field work delayed my doctorate until 1964, when I turned thirty-one, the same year that the then-nineteen-year-old Ms. Steiner took her first advanced degree in math.) How many hundreds of years ago *is* that now? Communicating with what I've nostalgically taken to thinking of as civilization could not feel more exotic here than if I were sending up smoke signals to be seen from Mars.

Indeed, in terms of communication your letter brings me information that you apparently assume I have been apprised of long since, but which, alas, I simply had not known. For example, yours is the first indication that the "article" I wrote at Leslie's somewhat

hysterical behest, two and a half years ago in a tent on the icy foothills of the Kapwani Mountains, has actually been published.

How bizarre. How unexpected.

There, as far away from anywhere as I am now, I drafted it in long-hand at a single marathon sitting over the back of some foolscap sheets, on the other side of which was a mimeographed proposal for a UNICEF grant to study water-tables in the suburbs outside Leah-Sohl, that had somehow ended up among the pale-ontology journals I'd stuffed in the book-carrier on the side of my canvas suitcase. Leslie stood outside the while, puffing and pacing in the snow, waiting a good four hours for me to finish it—that is, when she was not spatting with Yavus, who'd come skulking up the blustery slope behind her, all the way from Ephesus, where she'd apparently picked him up again, a continent or so away. Research assistant indeed! The only pay Yavus ever received back at the museum was for unloading boxes from the rickety army trucks that occasionally carted in crates of artifacts, that summer we were all together in 'Stamboul. That pay, incidentally, came directly out of *my* meagerly lined pocket! Oh, yes, he can be an entertaining, even an affectionate, companion from time to time, nor is he without a certain street-wise humor that, of an evening's stroll together down Istiqlal, can be quite charming. But Leslie is a rather heavy young woman—whereas I am a thin, even gaunt, middle-aged man. And Yavus, our handsome black-marketeer, simply made his choices along the lines to be expected of his class and race. But really, I am just assuming you know our—how shall I say?—broad-beamed Hypatia? Is a better term 'large-bottomed'? Perhaps 'a generous-breasted, round, brown Venus of Willendorf'? How she gets to the places she does leaves me awestruck! Once she simply "dropped in" to say hello at the bottom of an Afghani cave-complex I was excavating with old Pace and young Dr. Kargowsky. The circles in which her work or mine—not to mention the overlap—is likely to attract attention are notoriously small. Though in print we feign an impersonal formality, really—everybody knows everybody! I wouldn't be surprised if, at one time, I had actually met *you*, Hoequist, perhaps at some university conference or other (the arrival in blistering heat by commuter plane; Professor Rockeye's archaic '52 MG taking us to our limply chenilled guest rooms) held in the Indian Artifact Museum: two adjoining classrooms in the upper corridors of Fopping-Twee Hall, converted into a display area by the over-enthusiastic anthropology elective of 1938, its wall-hangings and glass cases dusted religiously, once a year, during Spring Intersession, ever since. What college would it have been ...? There was the obligatory under-ripe Brie on the cheese board and

sherry in plastic champagne glasses—with a stack of paper cups at the table corner, in case. If I recall rightly, Professor Widenose, in very dirty sneakers, kept apologizing for the failed air conditioning. Professor Parsnip yodeled out the conclusion of a story I'd heard her begin some years ago at another conference (with the same name, a different number, and the identical Brie and sherry) about her 1957 exploits among the Grungy-Grungy of the Lower Muddypigpuke. And sitting in the corner, working through her sixth champagne glass of Christian Brothers, bored out of her cornrowed natural, was Leslie, the tedium relieved by (for her, and just a whit less for me as only about one out of three was launched—dazzlingly!—my way) the smiles of that shy, white-blond, six-foot-seven Adonis of Polish-Ukrainian extraction, as at home on the gridiron as he was in the stone-quarries, where, since his fifteenth year, he had taken an annual summer job, but here, in this high and humid eyrie of abstraction, just the most engaging bit out of place. I found all this out by a gambit which began: "And what is your connection with our little group? Are you one of Leslie's star students?" Oh, no, he was just, well, hell, thinking of giving Professor Steiner a hand, if she really *did* decide to go off and dig in that Peruvian pot-hole next September. Above that bronzed cheek, with its faint, ephebic scars from a boyish brush with acne, between those gray-gold lashes, his blue eyes were challenged by nothing else in that room save his own (size thirteen and a half! Later I had an opportunity to check) adidas.

Leslie, at five-foot-one-and-one-quarter, has a mind like a steel trap and usually one to six stunning creatures in tow, from—should one put this more delicately?—the less intellectual strata of the societies she goes careening through. How she does it, with that bottom and those teeth, I'd give my own last wisdom tooth to know ... which was, incidentally, twinging again last night.

This desert is not the place for a toothache.

But we were talking of the Kapwanis, the snow. I remember Leslie said to me, "Kermi—" She *will* call me after that ingratiating green absurdity that hops through those hopeless children's puppet extravaganzas, while I, out of what in this day and age *must* be misguided chivalry, do *not* respond in kind—"Kermi, just say that Yavus was the research assistant who brought the Codex to my attention."

"Leslie," I said, "we were *all* sweating together down in that basement storage room. Yavus was going to use the damned thing to roll one of his super-dooper Turkish knock-out bombers, when you snatched it out of his hand!"

"Oh, Kermi, *please* ...!"

373

Anyway, I finished writing; and they made preparations to spirit it off down the mountainside, after leaving me a full ounce and a quarter of very fine hash, which she begged me not to consider payment for toning down any of the more risqué elements in the tale of her discoveries that I just might have been tempted to throw in for "human interest." They left then, the fur around her parka hood blowing in the snow-flurry, Yavus's hood thrown bravely and idiotically back from his hawk-profiled, dark-maned head (it was *cold* that evening!), the two of them chattering on about bus schedules in Ha'bini—as if *those* people had any better grasp of time than we do here at our desert site today.

But that is the article's genesis.

As to the informational points you raise in your letter, I feel a little foolish, Hoequist, claiming that I had no library or references at hand when I scrawled the piece for our brilliant but impetuous mathematician/cryptographer friend. But that is the case. Also, *some* of the errors you cite I'm sure are simply a matter of the decipherment of my none too limpid handwriting.

Transposté indeed!

I know I wrote *Telepoté,* regardless of what ended up in print!

Others, I suspect (and regret), were just those little slips of a mind cut off for months from all civil converse. Yes, of *course* Ventris was an architect, not an engineer. Of course Linear B was found outside Crete at Pylos and Mycenae—why else would they call it Mycenaean Greek? I know, *poté* means "never" in *modern* Greek, not Homeric (and usually, though *not* always, takes a negative particle). But that whole afternoon we had been speaking Demotike, in deference to Yavus, whose English, though brave, once it gets beyond "Change money!" grows too surreal for comprehension. Leslie, as I'm sure you know, speaks *every*thing, from Turkish to Aramaic to Ukrainian to conversational Coptic. Though I can read, somewhat haltingly, *at* it, I have no spoken Turkish to speak of. Where Yavus learned his very passable modern Greek, I don't know, unless it was among the older merchants of the Grand Bazaar, with whom Greek is as common as Yiddish used to be in the open-air markets of New York's Lower East Side, and among which, as a child, Yavus once carried tea and şalep.

Some of your other points, however, strike me as the potshots of a sniper emboldened by two or three direct hits who would now try to raze the entire town. Over the past twenty-five years the upper edge of the "neolithic revolution" has slid back and forth between 4,000 B.C. and 6,000 B.C. so frequently I've lost track. Such boundaries should be "muzzy" enough for anyone. "Attic Greek" is simply the school-boy term designating that period (*not* a geographical area) in the Greek language from which the best known (though, as we both know, not necessarily the best) Greek literature comes—Xenophon through Euripides. I simply used it to distinguish it from the earlier, dual- and digamma-plagued Homeric dialects and the later, impoverished patois of the New Testament. As far as "proto-Latin" vs. "archaic Latin," your exegesis is interesting, and I am not unfamiliar with it; still, for most of us it is simply a preference in terms. (You are no doubt familiar with the "very, very old" Latin pun: *Eva est mala,* which translates both as "Eve is evil," and "Eve eats apples"? Leslie likes apples too. Back in the snowy mountains, she brought a sack of them with her, along with the hash; I must have eaten three or four. And you know, that night, after they left, was the first time I ever had any trouble with this damned tooth!) Block-letter Greek? Well, that's what we called it back at the Archeological Institute in Athens—to distinguish it from precisely those Byzantine inscriptions you cite. A Greek text found at ancient Ilium VI doesn't seem too odd; certainly, there could have been interchanges between the Trojans and the Greeks in the centuries before Paris carted off Helen, especially since we have reason to believe that Greek was the trade language throughout Asia Minor for many, many hundreds of years before the poetic construct "Homer" began to recite, regardless of what Anatolian dialect was in fashion at Ilium proper. Also, there have been enough archeology texts, guide books, and the like referring to the edifices at Cnossos, Phaistos, and Malliá as "neolithic palaces" that I need not apologize for the term. As far as the similarity of the inks, which you question: well, Dr. Yoshikami (her single eyepiece, her cotton swabs, the Exacto knife with which she took her scrapings . . .) did extensive chemical tests.

So there.

But to defend myself too heatedly is, I fear, to suggest there may be reason for your attack. There isn't. And the truth is, we had sampled just a bit of the hash that afternoon over hard bread, apples, and yak butter—before I retired into my chilly tent to write the piece as we'd discussed it.

It was very good hash, too.

The only thought I ever really gave it, once it hurried off into the snow under the flap of Leslie's red student knapsack, was whether or not she might take offense at my faint chidings in the article of her feminist sympathies. She already considers me the most depraved of racist Orientalists. (Probably right, too. I've found that blacks such as Leslie have a sense of these things. Goes along with their natural ability to sing and dance.) She didn't have time to read it before she and her dark-eyed companion left. What we *had* discussed, of course, was how she would get the thing typed up, how she would *of course* get a copy of said typescript back to me for checking, to correct both the idiocies that invariably creep into any such transcription process as well as the inaccuracies I was bound to make under the twin pressures of Leslie's entreaty and Yavus's dope. ("Kermi, I need it *now*. This *evening*. I won't *be* here after six o'clock tomorrow morning!") Of course I never saw it again. As I said, your letter was the first I'd heard of it in over two years.

I tell you, *I* know Ventris was an architect.

Believe me, so does Leslie. She could have changed it.

But it would be just like her, on reading my gentle joke anent her politics, to leave in both the joke *and* my little slips of the pen, the latter as a kind of comeuppance for the former, and with, no doubt, the same self-satisfied smile I had when I wrote it. (If she had cut out the jokes, I *wouldn't* have minded, really ...) Well, perhaps my comments *were* over the mark. I know she takes such things seriously. More to the point, when she has talked seriously to me about them, she has been able from time to time to make me take them almost *as* seriously. Thus it is the one part of the whole enterprise I've actually been able to feel guilty about all this time. But such lingering guilt as mine, I know, suggests its origins were there well before Leslie, with Yavus trailing, came up that snowy slope.

All this, of course is in the realm of speculation—which is to say I know Leslie well enough to speculate on it. What absolutely baffles me, however: What is Nevèrÿon? What is Bantam Books? (Hopefully a more *recherché* line out of some small North English university press. But I doubt it.) And who is this Delany? Why must we angle our correspondence through him? Iraq is bad enough! Leslie used to be enamored of a bizarre species of anti-literature (more generously called "paraliterature" in the Pop. Cult. journals where some of her more eccentric offerings have appeared), published under gaudy paper covers—"scientifiction" or some such. She would sit around the top floor of our student house, in jeans with frayed knees, and a foul sweatshirt, reading the stuff for hours, even writing reviews of it for benighted mimeographed publications its readers seemed to put out all over what I first thought limited to the civilized world but which, after I had seen a bit more, I soon realized included many places fairly uncivilized as well. It sounds like she's gotten me involved, somehow, in this "SF," as she used to call it. (She actually would try to get me to *read* the stuff!) If that's what she *has* gotten me involved with, I shall never be able to set boot in the mahogany-panelled halls of the Spade and Brush Club again. (Professor Loaffer will guffaw and bang me

on the shoulder, and invite me for a pint, and ask rude questions about flying saucers until I have to say something rude in retort. Professor Cordovan, on the other hand, will not say anything at *all!*) Well, she'll certainly have paid me back tenfold if that, indeed, is what she's done with it!

She said "general readership." I thought she at *least* meant something on the order of *The Atlantic, Harpers*—a sketch for a more extensive coverage in, say, *Scientific American*.

I *am* appalled . . . !

I add these last paragraphs while the scar-faced gentleman in the very dusty jelabba, who sits stoically by the dirty white canvas tent in a strip of shade that does not quite extend to his brown, cracked toes, drinks slowly and steadily from a half-gallon canteen of Instant Country Time Lemonade, waiting for the evening to grow cool enough to resume his journey, taking with him the excavation team's several letters (including this one, soon as I finish it), toward . . . is there *really* such a thing as civilization?

And, no, he's not sure of the date either.

One of the things he brought, however, was a note from Abdullah Obtwana. Did you ever meet him? A lanky, large-handed, ebony-lipped youth—yes, another of Leslie's acquisitions. His mother, who made a microfortune at some dubious profession in Nairobi, sent him to one or another of our insistently liberal universities on the Southern Rim to take a pre-med course. After three terms, his advisors asked him if he wouldn't be happier moving to the agricultural college—and why didn't he take remedial English on the side? Abdullah was amenable enough, but in the resultant student brouhaha, he came under Leslie's . . . tutelage? More Brie. More sherry. (Was *that* the reception where I met you? You would remember, because Abdullah wore the adidas then—and rasberry red pants!) More luminous smiles—from a broad-cheeked face dark as the tenebricose pit. At any rate, through the desert grapevine (despite its wrinkled, dessicated fruits, its pale, tepid wines), news of my presence has reached him, less than a hundred miles away. He says he is coming to see us, here at the excavation site. He says he remembers our three evenings together with "an infinitude of pleasure." Don't you find Africans delightfully formal? At the end of *two* of those evenings, neither one of us could stand! He's bringing along a friend—from the details, *not* Leslie. The friend is male and probably young, since "he looks rather very good riding a camel." Rather very good indeed, I say! There will be pleasantry forthcoming in a day or ten, when Abdullah and friend ride up through the scrub—someone with whom to talk about my most

377

recent discoveries and complain to of Leslie's possible treacheries. Unless, of course, this tooth ... but I dare not speculate!

All right, then, I'll speculate: one of the books I am never without is my thin, green, India-paper edition of Layard's *Memoirs*. Perhaps you, Hoequist, can say what character-masochism makes me return again and again to this account from 1840:

> I had slept little, as I was suffering greatly ... The sheikh declared that there was a skillful dentist in the encampment, and as the pain was almost unbearable, I made up my mind to put myself in his hands rather than endure it any longer. He was accordingly sent for. He was a tall, muscular Arab. His instruments consisted of a short knife or razor, and a kind of awl. He bade me sit on the ground, and then took my head firmly between his knees. After cutting away at the gums he applied the awl to the root of the tooth, and, striking the other end with all his might, expected to see the tooth fly into the air. The awl slipped and made a severe wound in my palate. He insisted upon a second trial, declaring that he could not but succeed. But the only result was that he broke off a large piece of tooth, and I had suffered sufficient agony to decline a third experiment. . .

Enough of these McTeaguean horrors! (Really, I must go borrow Wellman's *Doughty* to drive such daymares off.) I close now—indeed, I have to if I want this letter to go out this week, as the barefoot Berber gentleman has just up-ended his canteen over the ground and shaken loose not one drop of Country Time for the thirsting sands.

My best regards,
(signed:) S. L. Kermit

[Some physical description of Hoequist's following letter may be appropriate here. The first two pages are typed on Corrasable bond; page 3 is typed on the back of a xerox of pages 8/9 of *Winnie ille Pooh*—on which *some*one has marked the long vowels in red ballpoint. Page 4 is typed on the verso of a purple hectographed reading list, in over-sized Cyrillic characters. Thence to Corrasable for the closing page . . .]

New Haven
August 1981

Dear Kermit,

Your letter, despite several forwardings, still reached here before I did. And when I did see it, my first response was to put it into a box, where it might conceivably survive the moving that was going on.

Yes, I am at Yale, though not many are aware of it. I cultivate unobtrusiveness. That, and the ability to read upside-down print, will take you a considerable distance.

I find your description of my letter's condition quite believable. A friend of mine spent some time recently doing excavation in Turkey, and attempts to get communication established have convinced me that the best thing to do is stitch one's correspondence on some fairly tough animal hide.

Indeed, we may well have met somewhere, likely at one of the Ivy conferences—"The Hero in Classical Literature," something like that. Or one of those where salted peanuts substitutes for Brie, due to budget problems. That was CCNY, I think.

Pardon the hiatus. Due to the unsettled nature of things, I must periodically leap up to answer the phone, so that I can tell increasingly insistent callers that no, he's not here, and, what's more, I never heard of him. There are also occasional trips to the hallway to help bring in another piece of furniture. And someone is celebrating something on the floor below, and if I don't have some champagne, it will be a grave offense.

So it is now tomorrow. Or rather, up there is yesterday.

I have looked over my previous letter and noted your comments on the situation in which the Appendix was written, and I am inclined to think that my tone was a bit harsher than was warranted. (I think maybe I'd just gone through a set of oral exams—no, it was something to do with thesis topics.) I must have been in the mood for some innocent's flesh.

I retract my comment on the 'neolithic revolution'; I simply wanted to point out that you could make your own statement a stronger one.

I reaffirm, however, my stand on 'proto-' vs. 'archaic.' It is *not* simply a preference in terms—not when discussing philology, which you were. And speaking of old Latin puns, how about *mea mater mala sus est*? It translates: "My mother is an evil pig," and "Come, mother, the pig is eating the apple." Which reminds me: it *was* CUNY that had the awful hors d'oeuvres. I was wincing, both at the

379

taste and at their linguistic punblication (I assure you, that was an unintentional typo!) *CUNYforms*.

All right, so maybe there was interchange between Trojans and Greeks. Kate from the Classics department is even willing to argue that the Trojans spoke a Greek dialect. Then again, this would not be Kate's only peculiarity. If you could hear some of her off-the-cuff etymologies . . .

The fact that the phrase "neolithic palaces" does exist does not justify perpetuating the silliness. No way. In fact, old Threadneedle turned utterly apoplectic when he saw that. I didn't realize emeritus professors had that much steam. I wouldn't have shown it to him if I'd suspected what he'd do. The worst part is not his anger, which is sometimes almost comic in its Continental excesses; he has unfortunately seized on Leslie's name and is convinced that George Steiner has gone off and had an illegitimate daughter somewhere, and now wants to meet her.

Ms. Steiner has done nothing to deserve this.

Thinking back, I may well have met her, and at a science fiction convention, of all places. ("Scientifiction"? My *dear* colleague, one would think you'd been keeping company with C. S. Lewis; I am told he's the last one who used the term consistently. They just call it *ess-eff* now.) Regrettably, your description of her doesn't narrow the field enough. I met several very bright women of that physical type. In fact, I met several men of similar build and intellect, some of whom were named Leslie. Does she by any chance know Greek folk songs? In that case, I *do* remember her. She was the only other person who knew "O, Pnevmatikos." We were singing it while walking around Faneuil Hall, which would have made it Noreascon 1.

I'm sorry, I digress, and on a path which is probably opaque to you. I'm quite surprised that news of publication hadn't reached you. Granted, you've been well off the normal paths, but science fiction fans have a way of leaking in everywhere; it seems odd that Ms. Steiner herself didn't drop you a line. I'll keep an eye out for her, if for no other reason than to tell her so; as you point out, we're more likely to have met than not.

Hiatus again. Hope I didn't keep you waiting.

It is now considerably later, and I am considerably hungrier. A raid is being organized to find the most decadent food in the vicinity, and I intend to be in on it.

Until I hear from you again, I remain

Yours sincerely,
(signed:) Charles Hoequist, Jr.

APPENDIX B:

Acknowledgments

Young writers take that most communal object, language, and perform on it that most individual act, creation. Years pass; and, doing much the same as they did when younger, older writers take an object now known to be, if not exactly private, certainly more idiosyncratic, individual to individual, than an empiricist philosophical tradition is comfortable with and perform on it an action now known to involve so many communal facts, from generic conventions and ideological reductions to just plain help, that the Romantic notion of "individual artistic creation" becomes hugely shaky—if it has not, indeed, crumbled. The older writers have not necessarily learned "craft" any better than the younger; nor have they even—necessarily—learned more of the language itself. They simply have more interesting critical material in which to observe play.

For the communal aspects of both talent and tradition, then, I gratefully make these acknowledgements:

Frank Romeo's film *Bye Bye Love,* about two small-town adolescents who journey to New York City and return, suggested a structure for the entire novel. But our almost daily conversations for four years, which covered the making of his second film, *The Aunts* (in which a present eye looks on a past moment), often touched on the encounters, the textures, the psychology, and the intimate details of life in upper New York State *vis-à-vis* life in New York City. They have left their imprint from first chapter to last.

Joanna Russ's *Kittatinny: a tale of magic* (Daughters Publishing Co.; New York, 1978) supplied the image for Gauine. To anyone who sees any mystery or resonance in the closing image of that fabulous beast, I commend the tale from which—with permission—I stole it.

Ihab Hassan, preparing his paper "Cities of Mind, Urban Words," was generous enough to ask me a question. The ensuing correspondence helped me develop some of the conceits herein.

Walter Abish's paper "On the Familiar" (with its side glance at the unbearable) helped me contour much of the material in Chapter Nine.

Charles Hoequist, Jr., has entered into the spirit of Nevèrÿon scholarship so good-heartedly that his contribution must be gratefully acknowledged.

Teresa de Lauretis introduced me, among her many generosities, to Umberto Eco's work in semiotics; his essay "On the Possibility of Generating an Aesthetic Message in an Edenic Language" (in *The Role of the Reader,* Umberto Eco, Indiana University Press; Bloomington, 1979) was directly stimulating.

Camilla Decarnin read, reread, and criticized the text in a detail for which any writer must be grateful.

Loren McGregor added some mechanical corrections to Decarnin's list for which I am most thankful.

Bernard Kay took time in his convalescence from a (happily successful!) bout with lung cancer to make copious and useful marginal notes for which I thank him sincerely, and in light of which I have tried to make intelligent repairs.

Robert S. Bravard, of the Stevenson Library at Lock Haven State College, most graciously sent me two pages of cogent comments, which have been the occasion for much thought and—hopefully— some meaningful changes.

Marilyn Hacker read the manuscript and offered a number of useful suggestions. Once again, I am grateful.

My copy editor, David Harris, besides the usual haggling over commas and restrictive and non-restrictive modifiers, offered a number of suggestions for fine tuning to the content. I thank him for them.

Karen Haas, my Bantam editor, has been as supportive as an editor can be throughout the production of a long and often difficult book.

Thanks is also due to Frederic Reynolds, Pat Califia, Lavada June Roberts, Mischa Adams, Luise White, Sally Hassan, Gregory Renault, Catherine McClenahan, and, indeed, a number of others who escape memory this sitting, but all of whom, now and again, added a twist to the thread from which this text is woven.

Anne McCaffrey shares an April 1st birthday with me. For years I have wanted to write something touching on dragons that could serve as a kind of joint birthday present to us both. Happy birthday, Annie.

As the beautiful Hispanic pop song, *Eres tu,* borrows the opening notes of Mozart's *Zauberflöte,* Act II, this text may be read, by some readers, as borrowing not only from those sources directly acknowledged but also from Albee, Bédier, Kafka, Balzac, or Baudrillard. If such readings initiate dialogue, so much the better; if they close dialogue off, so much the worse. With that in mind, I must add that

any reader who normally skips footnotes may skip the headnotes with which the various chapters begin with—certainly—no greater loss. ("While we sit discussing the word," quoted Christine Brooke-Rose at an MLA meeting some years back, "power works in silence ...") They only attempt to begin, by assertion, what Diderot attempted to begin by denial when he entitled a story *Ceci n'est pas un conte,* or what Magritte attempted when he entitled a picture of an upright brier *Ceci n'est pas une pipe,* or—indeed—what Guilden attempted when he made a colored poster in which scarlet letters proclaimed across a rose field (after having made one in jade and kelly portraying the same text) *This is Not a Green Sign.*

ABOUT THE AUTHOR

Born in 1942, SAMUEL R. DELANY grew up in New York City. His science fiction novels include *The Jewels of Aptor* (1962), a trilogy generally known by its collective title *The Fall of the Towers* (1963–'64–'65), *Babel-17* (1966), *The Einstein Intersection* (1967), the last two of which won Nebula Awards as best novels of their respective years, and *Nova* (1968). His other books include the bestselling *Dhalgren* (1975), *Triton* (1976), the sword-and-sorcery book, *Tales of Nevèrÿon* (1978), and a beautifully illustrated edition of his SF and fantasy stories, *Distant Stars* (1981). His essays on SF are collected in two volumes, *The Jewel-Hinged Jaw* (1977) and *Starboard Wine* (1982). He has also written an extended essay on urban communes, *Heavenly Breakfast* (1978), and a book-length semiotic study of the SF short story "Angouleme" by Thomas Disch, *The American Shore* (1978). After some years living in Europe and San Francisco and teaching in the Midwest, he again lives in New York.